WIND RIDER

ALSO BY P. C. CAST

P. C. CAST

WIND RIDER

Tales of a New World

WEDNESDAY BOOKS
NEW YORK

WIND RIDER. Copyright © 2018 by P. C. Cast. All rights reserved. Printed in the United States of America. For information address St. Martin's Press, 175 Fifth Avenue, New York, N.Y. 10010.

www.stmartins.com
www.wednesdaybooks.com

The Library of Congress Cataloging-in-Publication Data is available upon request.

ISBN 978-1-250-10078-8 (hardcover)
ISBN 978-1-250-31354-6 (international, sold outside the U.S., subject to rights availability)
ISBN 978-1-250-21538-3 (Walmart edition)
ISBN 978-1-250-10080-1 (ebook)

Our books may be purchased in bulk for promotional, educational, or business use. Please contact your local bookseller or the Macmillan Corporate and Premium Sales Department at 1-800-221-7945, extension 5442, or by email at MacmillanSpecialMarkets@macmillan.com.

First U.S. Edition: October 2018
First International Edition: October 2018

10 9 8 7 6 5 4 3 2 1

This book is dedicated to my dad,
eternally my Mighty Mouse and my hero.
This one was especially fun!

ACKNOWLEDGMENTS

As always I thank my agent and friend, Meredith Bernstein. How many is this now?

Thank you to my Macmillan family, especially Monique Patterson, Jennifer Enderlin, Anne-Marie Tallberg, and Jessica Preeg.

I appreciate the beautiful art created by my friend Sabine Stangenberg.

Thank you to my awesome daughter, Kristin, who is always there to help me brainstorm and listen to me complain and rejoice. "Writing is hard!"

And an extra-special thank-you to my dad, Dick L. Cast, who worked with me to mutate and create the fantastic post-apocalyptic flora and fauna in Tales of a New World. He is directly responsible for the Mouths and the Monkeys!

WIND RIDER

CHAPTER 1

THREE YEARS IN THE PAST—PLAINS OF THE WIND
RIDERS—RENDEZVOUS SITE

Dawn was teasing the horizon and causing the sky to blush when River made her way silently from the crowded tent she shared with her mother, her two aunts, five cousins, three younger sisters, her mother's mare and the two geldings who had many years ago chosen her aunts as their Riders. As Rider of the Lead Mare of Herd Magenti, her mother's tent was situated close to the center of the spiral of stone monoliths that marked the Rendezvous Site as a place of layline power, but even had the stones not been there, positioned like ancient, mute guardians, the cavernous underground opening that lay in the center of them was evidence of the destructive power of the sun that was so great that centuries ago it had opened the earth and utterly changed the world. River glanced at the mouth of the cave, trying to get a glimpse of the herd of weanlings that waited within, but all she could see were shadows thrown by torches, though she could hear their restless nickers and nervous movements.

River resisted the draw of the weanlings. It was against Herd law for any Candidate to interact with the young horses after they'd arrived at the Rendezvous Site—one reason they remained hidden away in the cave that usually housed entire Herds within the safety of its depths.

Today is the Choosing. I only have a couple of hours left to wait for something I've been dreaming about since I was old enough to dream.

River felt light-headed with nervous excitement. Even this early in the glooming before sunrise the huge campsite was already beginning to hum with activity. She turned her back on the cave and continued to wind her way through camp quickly, keeping her head ducked down— hoping not to be recognized.

"A mare's luck to you today, River!" called a vaguely familiar voice.

River didn't pause, but she did wave briefly in acknowledgment as she picked up her pace. She wanted just a few moments to herself before the day began and she became the center of attention.

Don't be so dramatic. Not everyone will be watching you—just everyone from your Herd, River chided herself with silent sarcasm as she wove her way through the rest of the bright purple tents that spiraled from her mother's and marked the boundary of Herd Magenti. Her Herd. Her life. And, today, the source of her nervousness.

Purple tents gave way to the differing shades of blue that marked Herd Indigo. River smiled to herself. Unlike her Herd, who valued one true, deep shade of purple to represent them, the Indigo Riders took pride in how many different blues they could create. It annoyed her mother, but River thought the variety was refreshing and beautiful.

This early morning she didn't stop to admire the array of colors as she would normally, but instead skirted Herd Indigo. She turned to her left and kicked into a jog, passing the yellow and red tents of Herds Jonquil and Cinnabar until she came to a gentle rise in the land as prairie met the cross timber line that meant a creek was nearby.

Relieved that this section of the clear, swiftly moving Weanling Creek was currently empty of other visitors, River rushed down the grassy rise to the sandy bank. She used one of the long, purple strips of cloth she'd grabbed from the pile of specially dyed and decorated ribbons that would very shortly be woven into her hair, and used it to tie back her unruly mass of ebony curls. Then she knelt in the soft sand and dipped her hands in the creek, ladling the crystal water over her face. River sucked in her breath at how cold it was, as it was too early in the spring for the prairie to have heated up enough to take any of the chill off the mountain-fed creek. But River ignored the cold and washed her face carefully before pulling off her nightdress and, naked, wading into the creek, carefully choosing her steps over the smooth rocks, until she was waist deep. Without hesitation, she submerged herself to her neck and closed her eyes.

Wash away my nervousness and doubts. Help me to make Herd Magenti and my mother proud. Great Mother Mare and Father Stallion, please let me be found worthy and Chosen as a Rider today.

Chosen today . . .

Those two words filled River's mind as she remained submerged, ignoring the cold of the water.

It was finally *the day,* and if it happened—if she was Chosen—after today her life would irrevocably change.

And, of course, should she *not* be Chosen her life would change as well. Oh, there would be other Rendezvous. Every child of the Herd who had known sixteen winters was Presented at a Rendezvous three times—given three opportunities to be Chosen in consecutive years—and those who were never Chosen were still valuable members of their Herd. But they were not Wind Riders. Sure, they could ride—everyone born into the Herd could ride—but there was a vast difference between being seated on the back of a horse as a passenger and being bonded mind, body, and spirit to a horse who Chose *you* as his or her Rider, Companion, and life partner.

River had grown up observing the bond between her mother and her beautiful mare, Echo, and she craved that incredible, unbreakable, indescribable connection. Preparing herself for today had been her focus for as much of her sixteen years of life as she could remember, and for the last year it had been her obsession.

"I don't care if the weanling who Chooses me is a contender for Lead Mare or Herd Stallion. I'd be happy with any horse—a sweet gelding would be wonderful. Just please, *please* let me belong to one of them. Let me be a weanling's Choice today."

"You shouldn't be worried. You know you have your mother's seat, and Echo Chose her at the very first Rendezvous she was Presented."

Slowly, River turned to face the voice behind her that drifted across the creek. He was standing on the bank, holding her nightdress and smiling at her. His hair had gotten so long! And it was braided with scarlet ribbons that matched his vest, which left his wide, muscular chest mostly bare and made him look more than just two short years older than her. River felt a rush of happiness that surprised her—she hadn't realized she'd missed him that much.

"Clayton! When I didn't see you the past few days I thought you wouldn't make the Rendezvous. I'm glad you did—even if it means you eavesdropped on my prayers."

"I didn't eavesdrop. I just showed up and you were already praying—loudly."

"Riiiight. I'll try to remember next time to pray more quietly. What are you doing out here anyway?" She grinned mischievously at him. "Want to join me bathing?"

Clayton snorted. "No! I missed you and I was out here looking for you, but I choose to bathe like civilized people—in a tub heated by a hearthfire—or, better yet, in a steaming hot spring."

"Still a baby," River teased, her full lips turning up.

"Still a brat," Clayton countered. "You should come out of there before you turn blue and have to petition Herd Indigo to join them. Plus, I have a good luck gift for you—though you don't really need it."

"A gift?" With no sense of modesty or seduction, River stood and made her way to the bank and Clayton, who handed her the abandoned nightdress. She dried herself using the end of the skirt as she looked up at her friend. "You got tall."

"Taller," he corrected.

"And vainer as well?"

"Nah. I'm pretty sure I'm still as vain as I've always been," he teased.

She slid the nightdress on and studied him. "You look stronger, too. I think you have more muscles. Herd Cinnabar must have kept you and Bard busy this winter. Where is your colt?" River glanced behind Clayton, expecting the three-year-old to be waiting in the lightening shadows that clung stubbornly to the grassy area beneath the verdant post oaks and willows that lined Weanling Creek.

"My mother insisted on taking out the red ribbons from his mane and tail and is currently braiding them with what she calls *the proper color.*"

"Herd Magenti's purple, of course."

"None other."

"Um, did she not see that you're wearing these?" River reached up and tugged on one of the scarlet ribbons in his hair. "Or this?" And tapped a finger on the blood-colored vest. This close to him she could see that it was intricately decorated with rearing horses in a deep sorrel thread made from a horse's mane.

"She did. She told me to take them out and change into a decent vest and then she shooed me away when she began cooing to Bard about how much she missed him and how it was well past time his mane was braided properly."

"Hey, want to see *real* cooing? Watch how everyone treats Echo." She laughed softly as she rolled her eyes.

But instead of laughing with her, Clayton's expression sobered. "Well, sure, everyone coos over Echo. She's Lead Mare, the wisest, strongest, soundest, most beautiful equine in Herd Magenti—many say in all the Five Great Herds."

River's shoulders slumped. "You're right. I'm sorry. I really didn't mean to sound bitter about Echo. She is magnificent and I love her as much as I love Mother."

"Then who did you mean to sound bitter about?"

She answered his question with two of her own. "Clayton, would you say Echo is an extension of my mother? That Mother reflects Echo's qualities?"

He didn't hesitate with his answer. "Yes, I would. Everyone would—in our Herd and the others."

"I would, too. My fear is that I don't."

"You don't what?"

"Reflect her qualities." She met Clayton's gaze. "I don't want to disappoint Mother or our Herd."

"You won't. You couldn't. Unless you've changed drastically over the six months I was gone?" His raised brows challenged her.

"No. I'm still me."

"Then you're the most dedicated Rider I know. Hey, don't let all the people and the talk get inside your head. You know weanlings can sense your nerves. Focus on being yourself and on being open to accepting any horse that comes to you today—that's all you need to do."

"Oh, that's *all*?" River rolled her eyes.

"Well, almost all. If you're Chosen you'll have the weight of the Herd's expectations on your shoulders, especially if a filly chooses you. And if you don't get Chosen you'll have the weight of the Herd's expectations on your shoulders as they worry about who will be Rider to our next Lead Mare . . ." He grinned at her. "There. Did that help?"

"Absolutely not," she said.

Then the two friends grinned at each other and Clayton opened his arms. "Come here, worrier. I missed you a lot."

River stepped into his embrace, finding it strange and familiar at the same time. He hugged her tightly and she clung to him as well. Then, as was her right as a daughter of the Herd, River chose to break the embrace, stepping back to look up at Clayton.

"I hoped you missed me, too," he said.

"I did!" She could see in his eyes that he wanted to say more and she held her breath, hoping he wouldn't make their reunion awkward. And, thankfully, he didn't. Instead he reached into his pocket and took out something concealed in his fisted hand.

"For you."

She opened her hand and Clayton dropped the crystal into her palm. It fitted perfectly there—a long finger of glistening quartz. It was warm from his touch, but as it connected with her skin it heated even further, syncing with the Magenti Crystal Seer blood that ran strong through her veins. River could feel it—feel the sleeping power of the crystal— and though she wasn't even a Wind Rider yet, the stone began to wake and harmonize with her, calming the firefly-like thoughts that had nervously been flitting through her mind since she'd arrived at the Rendezvous Site two days before.

Instinctively, her breathing slowed and her shoulders relaxed, and for the first time in days they stopped burning with tension. River opened her mouth to thank Clayton for the amazing gift, and then her thanks turned into a shocked gasp as the soft light of dawn caught the crystal's faceted surface, revealing what was within.

"Clayton! It's a phantom!"

"Keep looking. It's not *just* a phantom."

River lifted the crystal, squinting to study it, and her eyes widened. "Oh, Mother Mare! It's an amethyst phantom! Clayton, I can't accept this. It's way too valuable."

Clayton gently closed her hand around the crystal. "Not to me it isn't. To me it's just beautiful. It takes a female Wind Rider of Herd Magenti to wake its secrets."

"You could trade this for so many things—a whole tent of your own. Seriously, Clayton, take it back."

"I believe it's too late for that. You look relaxed—or at least you did before you noticed it was a phantom. It woke for you, didn't it?"

River couldn't help herself. She opened her palm and stared at the glistening gift. She could feel the rhythm of her heartbeat echoing through the crystal.

"Well? It's awake, isn't it?" he prodded.

"Yes." She couldn't take her eyes from the stone. "It's definitely awake."

"I knew it! You have more than your mother's seat. You're also a Crystal Seer!"

Her gaze snapped up from the crystal. She glanced around them as she told him, "Ssh! We can't know that for sure unless I'm Chosen by a weanling. You know it would be looked at as pure arrogance if anyone heard either of us say something like that."

"But it's the truth—you're holding the proof in your hand."

"All I'm holding in my hand is an extremely unusual, powerful crystal that recognized and resonated with my blood."

"Blood that has a history of producing powerful Seers," Clayton added. "Do you know what property the amethyst phantom signifies? After I found it I didn't want to ask anyone. I didn't know exactly what it was, but I knew it was a phantom and that was enough to make me keep it hidden until I got it to you."

River's gaze went back to the crystal, warm and pulsing in her open palm. "The amethyst phantom allows Seers to see the beginnings of each life cycle."

"Wow. But, uh, what does that mean?"

"It means that this crystal can be used to see what life lessons a person was meant to learn each life cycle, and knowing that, the Seer can help the person understand what he or she was meant to accomplish." River looked from the crystal into Clayton's dark eyes. "For instance, if you were depressed—I mean *really* depressed, not just a little sad—a Seer could use this phantom to look at your lives and see what it is that you haven't accomplished in *this* life that your soul is aching for."

Clayton nodded. "There was a girl in Herd Cinnabar who was like that. So, so sad. She and her mare went over a cliff—*purposefully*. No one could stop them. No one could help her. Do you mean this crystal could've saved her?"

"In the hands of a Crystal Seer, yes, probably. But don't be too hard on yourself. You didn't have any way of knowing that."

"It happened before I found the crystal. But I'm glad I know now, and I'm glad I found the stone and put it in your hands." Clayton reached out and cupped one of those hands in both of his, rubbing his thumb in a slow, sensual caress across the skin of her wrist. "Use it to help others, Crystal Seer."

"I'm not a Seer," she said automatically, though she could feel the crystal echoing her heartbeat.

"Not yet you aren't. Let's see what happens later this morning, though. At least it has helped relax you a little."

"More than a little," River said. Impulsively she tiptoed, hugged him, and then kissed him softly on his cheek. "Thank you! This is a wonderful gift."

As she pulled away he caught her face in his hands gently. "River, I thought about you every day I was gone."

"Every day for six months is a lot of thinking," she said. "I'm pretty sure you're exaggerating."

"I'm not exaggerating and I'm also not kidding around. I'd show you how serious I am if you'd give me the chance."

Slowly, River stepped back so that Clayton had to stop cupping her face. "Clayton, all I'm thinking about right now is the Choosing."

"That's all you *ever* think about."

Her gaze remained steady on his. "You're right. Becoming a Wind Rider is now, and has been for as long as I have memories, the most important thing in my life."

"But when you're Chosen today–"

"*If*," she corrected. "No one can predict a Choosing."

"Fine. *If* you're Chosen today then will you have time for more in your life?"

"I don't know," she said honestly. "I haven't thought beyond the Choosing."

Clayton drew a deep breath and then said all in one big rush, "Would you please tell me if you're even attracted to me or would you rather mate with another guy, or even a woman?" There was no bitterness in Clayton's voice. The Herd considered sexuality fluid, so there was no stigma attached to women loving women, or men loving men—or even a woman deciding she would rather live as a man or a man desiring to live as a woman. Sexual exploration was normal and natural, and as long as it was consensual, all was accepted.

River answered him with the only truth she knew. "I think you're pleasing to look at. You're smart and funny, and we've been friends since we were children. But I don't have sexual feelings for you. I've told you that before—many times. I don't have sexual feelings for anyone. I just want to be Chosen and begin my life as a Wind Rider and, hopefully, a Crystal Seer. *That's* what is most important to me. Can you understand that?"

Clayton's body language completely changed. He crossed his arms and took a step back. His expression went from cajoling to flat and emotionless. Bitterness gave his otherwise charming voice a hard edge. "Can I understand you not having sexual feelings for anyone? No, not really. River, you're sixteen. I'm eighteen. Everyone else our age—everyone we've grown up with and everyone we meet who's about our age from the other Herds—they're falling in and out of love and are pretty obsessed with it. So, no, I do *not* understand what the hell is wrong with you. But that doesn't change the fact that I care about you—as more than just a friend. And I wish you would give us a chance." He sighed and ran his hand through his hair. "I'd wish you luck today, but you won't need it. Your weanling will find you, and maybe then you'll have time for the rest of your life—for love and a mate."

Then Clayton turned away from her and was gone.

River waited, holding the crystal tightly and allowing it to slow her heartbeat and soothe her roiling stomach. Then she retraced her steps up the small incline.

I won't let it hurt me. I won't let it make me feel like I don't belong. Not today.

River paused at the top of the incline and gazed out at the Herds that spread before her on the Tallgrass Prairie. The sun had lifted above the horizon. It was fat and the color of a ripe peach, shining a light that seemed suddenly golden upon the Rendezvous Site.

The huge granite monoliths, mined centuries before by their ancestors from the nearby Rock Mountains, had flecks of crystals in them, and the caress of the morning sun made them sparkle magickally. They'd been placed in a careful spiral surrounding the slash in the earth that had been formed during the earthquakes that had razed the prairie when the sun exploded uncounted generations ago. Mirroring the spiral placement of the stones, the Herds circled around the cave, turning the prairie into a patchwork of color.

River's eyes found Herd Magenti first. Its purple tents and the long, swallowtail pennant that waved lazily in the morning breeze with the Herd's insignia of a cluster of crystals shimmered and drew her gaze like fire draws moths. River loved her Herd, and was proud that the blood of Magenti Wind Riders was the only blood that produced Crystal Seers—those who awakened crystals and their sleeping properties within.

There is nothing wrong with me! The Herd accepts me. Mother has never once chastised me for not choosing a lover or going on and on about wishing someone would desire me. We haven't even spoken of it. And my friends don't say much about it, either. Well, at least not much anymore.

But did she really have friends? Or had they stopped teasing and questioning her because she'd withdrawn from them, especially over the past year?

River clutched the crystal, drawing on the grounding properties of quartz to soothe the tumultuous thoughts Clayton had brought to the surface. She slowed her breathing. A wild neigh of greeting pulled her attention from the cluster of purple to the emerald green tents of Herd Virides and their pennant, adorned with the outline of a running stallion, as was proper for the Herd that consistently produced the swiftest horses. She watched a stallion prance to a woman dressed all in green. The woman embraced her Companion and then he bowed slightly—not in a sign of subservience, but in a sign of love so that she was able to leap onto his wide, bare back. Once she was astride the stallion the magnificent horse tossed his head and pranced before leaping up and kicking out spectacularly. River was sure she heard the Rider's joyous laughter echoing around her before she lost sight of them among the tents and other waking horses and Riders.

It would be nice to be Chosen by a colt—one that would someday become a stallion. Nice, but not River's dream.

Her gaze went from the green tents to Herd Jonquil and their bright, sun yellow tents. Their pennant was the easiest to read from a distance as the dark outline of a magnificent bison labeled their Herd as supreme hunters.

Beside Jonquil was Herd Cinnabar, with their bloodred tents and their pennant that showed a single black spear. From as far north as the great, frozen lakes, as far south as the brackish entrance to the Southern Sea, as well as all the way east to the Mighty Miss, the river that served as boundary of the prairie, to the base of the Rock Mountains just west of where they were now, young men and women Wind Riders came from all corners of the enormous prairie to train with Herd Cinnabar's unparalleled warriors.

Did Clayton go to them because of me? Because I rejected him? She'd not had that thought before and she immediately pushed it away. *If I am why he left, then that is his issue, not mine. I promised him nothing. I've promised no one anything!*

River squeezed the crystal around her fisted hand, letting the warmth from it thaw the anger within her that made her feel cold and alone.

Calm again, River's gaze went to the beautiful blue tents that marked Herd Indigo. Each was a unique shade, and from this distance she thought they looked like water refracting the sun's rays. She saw that this time their pennant was a sweet, summer day blue that showed off nicely the intricately braided circular pattern that filled the center of it, symbolizing that Herd Indigo were experts in the complex art of healing.

Each of the Five Great Herds was a unique part of a whole. Though different, they depended upon one another—they traded together; they shared the bloodlines of their horses; they mated with one another—they were together, yet separate.

Why is that not okay for me? Why can't I be part of our Herd, but not intimately tied with any one person?

It had confused River since she and her female friends had begun to develop breasts and bleed with their moon time. That change had affected River physically, as it had the other girls, but unlike them it hadn't affected her mentally—or at least not much it hadn't.

River's focus had remained the same—she wanted to be Chosen. She wanted to be the kind of Rider her mother and her Herd could be proud of. The other girls? They still did their assigned duties caring for the Herd, but where they all used to pretend to be Wind Riders together and daydream about racing over the Tallgrass Prairie and leading Herd Magenti into prosperous season after season, her friends now wanted nothing more than to rush through their duties so they could preen for and flirt with boys who not so long before had been too silly and immature for them to even bother being friends with.

River thought they were ridiculous for letting lust command so much of their lives. She sighed. If she was going to be honest with herself she had to admit that her friends obviously thought River ridiculous for *not* lusting after anyone.

Sure, she'd done some experimenting. She'd let Clayton kiss her—several times, actually, before he'd left for warrior training with Herd Cinnabar. The kisses—they'd been okay. Not great. Not awful. Just okay. Certainly nothing to gush and giggle over.

River had also kissed Gretchen, one of her childhood friends who very openly liked girls and boys. She'd liked how soft Gretchen was, and appreciated her beauty, but again the kiss was just okay.

"I don't understand what all the fuss is about. No kiss has ever made me feel even close to the excitement that fills my mind, body, and spirit when I'm with the Herd's horses. And why is that so wrong—so hard for my friends and Clayton to understand?" River queried the warming air around her as her eyes continued to scan the Rendezvous Site in appreciation of the combined might of the five Wind Rider Herds.

With a jolt she realized how sun-filled the morning had become and how much activity was happening on the prairie below her and she hurried down the lip of the bank, sprinting toward the purple tents of Herd Magenti.

🐎🐎🐎

"Hold still—I'm almost done!" River's mother reprimanded her as she fidgeted.

"Mother, I look great. I have too many ribbons in my hair already. *We're going to be late!*"

"You can never have too many ribbons in your hair," said River's Aunt Heather as she ducked inside their tent. "But River is right. Those being Presented are circling. The rest of the Herd is already there waiting to cheer our arrival. Time for us to go."

"Take the girls and go ahead. River and I will follow shortly. They will wait for all the Riders of the Lead Mares to arrive, especially when one of those Riders has a daughter being Presented," said her mother, completely unfazed by the nervous excitement that filled the air.

"Mother, please. Let's go. Now. My friends are already there."

"The last thing on your mind this morning should be what others do or think." Then her mother smiled, softening the admonishment. "They *will* wait. Cinnabar has a daughter of their Lead Mare Rider to Present as well. You can bet she hasn't arrived yet either." Her mother stepped back, studying River. "You are almost perfect."

"Mother—*almost?*" River paused, trying not to whine or bolt out of the tent.

"Yes, *almost.* And I know how to make you entirely perfect." Her mother went to the worn wooden travel box that doubled as a table. She moved aside the purple cloth draped over it and opened the lid, easily finding what she sought in an inside drawer. Then she straightened and approached her impatient eldest child, holding the sparkling necklace out before her. "*This* makes you entirely perfect."

"Oh! That was Grandmother's necklace. I thought it was entombed with her."

"No." River's mother paused, touching the necklace reverently. "She asked specially that this piece not go with her to the Otherworld Plains. She wanted you to have it on your Choosing Day."

"But don't you think Grandmother meant for me to have it only *if* I'm Chosen?" River blinked away tears as she stared at the necklace she hadn't seen in the five years since her Grandmother's death. It was just as beautiful as she remembered. Silver beads that had been carved with tiny images of horses were interspersed with the most exquisite amethyst stones River had ever seen anyone wear. The purple was the shade of spring lilacs. Each stone was the size of an unshelled walnut, but flat and faceted to catch and play with light.

"No. Your grandmother told me exactly what she meant. She said, *Give this to River on the morning she is to be Presented, and give her my love in a kiss that morning as well.* Now turn and let me fasten this on you."

River wiped tears from her eyes as she obeyed her mother. The necklace hung heavy and reassuring around her neck. River reached up to touch the two largest amethyst stones that dangled from the main part of the necklace. They were smooth and cool at first, though after just a few moments she could feel them heating and syncing with her heartbeat.

Her mother turned her and studied River again, this time with tears pooling in her eyes. Then she lifted a polished piece of precious glass, holding it so that she and her daughter could gaze into it together.

River touched the center amethyst stone, thinking that her grandmother's necklace looked extraordinary against her smooth, dark skin. Her mother always had been exceptionally good at braiding the Herd's ribbons into her hair, and this special morning Dawn had done a spectacular job on River's mane of black curls, weaving ribbons throughout in an intricate braid pattern that hugged her scalp, but allowed her hair to cascade freely down her back to mingle with purple ribbons embroidered with silver horse hair from her mother's precious mare. Even River, who rarely gave much thought to how she looked, had to admit that the effect was striking against her burnished shoulders.

"Is that really me?"

Dawn wiped a tear from her eye and put her arm around her beloved eldest child. "It is, and you are magnificent." She kissed River on the forehead. "This is from your grandmother." Then she kissed her daughter softly on the lips. "And this is from me. Remember that I will always be proud of you. All I ask is that you behave with kindness and honesty, and that you always do your best."

"And if I'm not Ch–"

"No!" Her mother cut off her words. "We are not speaking of weanlings now. We are speaking of my daughter, of whom I am now, and always will be, proud. Today be calm. Be present. Be open. Be yourself. That is all I, or any weanling, can ask of you."

"I'm nervous."

"I am, too!" Dawn gently touched her daughter's cheek. "But not because I doubt the outcome of today. I do not. I am nervous because my eldest child becomes an adult today, and that makes Echo and me feel very old."

As if on cue, the Lead Mare's head pushed aside the curtained doorway and she blew through her nose impatiently.

"I know!" River laughed, wiping away the last of her tears. "Tell Mother. She took forever with my hair."

River's mother went to the mare and stroked her wide forehead. River thought the mare looked particularly beautiful today with the specially decorated purple ribbons braided into her silver mane, which fell in graceful drapes over the mare's spotless coat—a coat so perfectly white the Herd often described it as silver. Her muzzle, a velvet charcoal gray, lifted and lipped her Rider's shoulder. Finding the strap of her heavily decorated purple tunic, Echo tugged.

"Okay! We're ready!" Dawn laughed at her mare.

River followed her mother from their tent and her stomach fluttered as she glanced around at the empty tents.

"My precious daughter, do not look so nervous. Remember who you are and what you represent. Hold your head high. You carry within you the blood of a famous line of Lead Mare Riders—something no one can deny."

"I'll remember," River said solemnly, shaking off as much of her nerves as possible.

"Echo, my beauty, let us show the Herds how the daughter of Magenti's Lead Mare Rider is Presented." Echo went to her knee and Dawn turned to her daughter. "Go ahead—mount her." She gestured to the silver mare.

"But, um, aren't you . . ." River stared at the magickal mare. It was a rare thing for Echo to be ridden by anyone except her mother, and even rarer for her to be ridden in front of the other Herds by anyone except her mother.

"Oh, I'll be right beside you, but today is *your* day, and Echo and I wish to honor you."

"Thank you, Mother. Thank you, Echo. I—I just hope I don't let you down."

Echo snorted at River and swished her tail.

"I agree," her mother said. "Echo and I have no time for that kind of negativity. Daughter, you need to remember that you are enough—just as you are at this moment. Anything else is simply extra blessings from the Great Mother Mare. Now, hurry and mount. You're going to be late!" she finished with a teasing smile.

"That's what I've been saying," River grumbled as she approached Echo, fisted a handful of shining white mane entwined with purple ribbons, and easily mounted.

Echo stood and her mother moved up to the mare's head. When she began walking, Echo did too. Heads held high, the Lead Mare Rider and the Lead Mare for Herd Magenti radiated beauty and strength. Automatically, River straightened her spine even as she sat deep, lightly gripping the mare's sides with her thighs—her bare skin dark against Echo's silver-white coat—River knew she and the mare looked striking together. Even walking Echo had an undeniable grace and River's heart swelled with pride as they entered the path that led to the huge outdoor Choosing Theater and then paused at the opening as first River's aunt caught sight of them.

"It's River on Echo! Herd Magenti!"

"Herd Magenti!"

"River and our Echo! Herd Magenti!"

The cheers lifted around them and Echo arched her neck, prancing in place.

"Go ahead, my beauty—take River to her spot," Dawn said, stroking her mare's neck. She looked up at her daughter, pride shining in her eyes. "Hold tight. Echo likes to show off. Sit tall and proud so that all the Herds might see the pride she and I have in you. Echo and I wish you a mare's luck, Daughter."

River started to thank her mother, but Echo had decided she was finished with waiting. Tail lifted, the exquisite mare shot onto the flat, grassy field, galloping around the circle already formed by those being Presented as all of Herd Magenti, and several of the other Herds as well, cheered her on. River felt as if she were flying. She could see that the rows of stone seats that rose tier after tier up from the floor of the theater were completely filled with people, all dressed in their finest, draped in ribbons and beads and jewelry in their Herd's color. All around the rear circumference of the theater horses stood, ears pricked forward—waiting and watching with such joyful anticipation that River could swear she could taste its sweetness on the breeze.

Echo slid to a stop before the group of Candidates decorated in Magenti purple and River quickly dismounted, hugged the silver mare, and then took her place with the others from her Herd.

"Finally! We thought something had happened and you were going to miss it," said her Herdmate, Skye, as she moved to make room for River.

"Mother had to be sure everything was perfect. Is Herd Cinnebar's Lead Daughter here yet?"

"Yes. You're the last to arrive."

River nodded, but said nothing. Her mother had decided when she would arrive, but there was no point in explaining that to Skye. Instead, River looked around the huge circle of Candidates. They were grouped together—purple, blue, red, yellow, and green, and they were obviously trying, with little success, not to look nervous . . . or terrified.

River turned to Skye. "May a mare's luck be with you today."

"Um, thanks. You, too," Skye responded insincerely.

Unfazed, River turned to the boy on her left. She recognized him as Clayton's cousin, Rex. "May a mare's luck be with you today, Rex," she said.

"Oh, thank you, River." He wiped sweat from his brow. "I just wish we'd get this over with. The waiting is horrible. Have you heard the count?"

"No, I haven't."

"There are one hundred and twenty-nine Candidates and only *ninety-nine* weanlings. That means *thirty* of us are not going to be Riders," Rex said miserably, wiping more sweat from his face.

"Only ninety-nine weanlings? The last count I heard was about one hundred and five or so. What happened?" She spoke aloud, but the real person she wanted to ask about the number disparity was her mother. *Why didn't anyone tell me several weanlings were missing?*

"They're from Herd Jonquil. Seems the weanlings somehow got into a clump of arrowgrass on the way here."

"Arrowgrass? That's awful! Did they survive?"

"Yes, thank the Great Mother Mare, but they're too weak to be at the Choosing. In a few weeks Jonquil will have a special Rendezvous and any leftover Candidates may attend. I can't believe you didn't hear about this."

"I've been spending a lot of time by myself since we got here—you know, meditating and preparing. I suppose no one thought to—"

Her words broke off as an ancient mare trotted stiffly onto the Choosing Theater field. Her Rider was as old and as gray as her horse—and as recognizable. Morgana was the eldest member of the Mare Council. She was Rider to Ramoth—some say the oldest mare in all the Herds. No one knew the exact age of mare *or* Rider, but their combined wisdom was legendary.

Rider and mare wore ribbons from all five Herds, signifying they were part of the Mare Council. The Candidates bowed respectfully, then the old woman raised her hand and the crowd went silent.

"Candidates, spread out to at least an arm's length between you!" Morgana's voice was deep and strong, and immediately River and the other one hundred twenty-nine Candidates spread their arms out, shifting the circle so that it grew bigger, but less crowded. "Good. Now be seated!" The Candidates sat cross-legged. The old woman lifted her arms to the sky and spoke the blessing. "Great Mother Mare and Father Stallion, we ask that you guide the weanlings to their perfect Riders, and that you do so with joy and love and wisdom. It has been said!"

"It has been said!" echoed every voice in the combined Herds.

"And now it begins. Candidates, may a mare's luck be with you. *Release the weanlings!*"

River drew in a deep breath as her hand automatically reached up to rest on the amethyst crystal that hung from the center of her grandmother's necklace. *I am calm. I am composed. I am ready. My thoughts are clear and I am open to whatever will happen next.*

The familiar thunder of horses' hooves vibrated up through the

ground, joining the staccato beating of River's heart. All eyes were focused on the entrance of the Choosing Theater—and then the weanling
herd burst onto the field at a full gallop. The Candidates sat very still as
the young horses wove between them to come to a milling halt in the
center of their circle.

River stared at them, trying to contain her excitement. They were so
magnificent! They represented the best weanlings each Herd had to
offer. Born the previous spring, one year ago, each had been raised with
care and compassion. They remained with their dams for the entire year,
and had only been separated from their mothers two days before. Though
the weanlings understood what was happening, and that it was time for
them to leave their mothers' sides to begin the road to adulthood, they
were visibly anxious.

River understood. They were lonely—missing their mothers and missing the attention that had been lavished on them by a doting Herd for
an entire year. But the young horses also knew that when they left this
circle they would be permanently bonded to their Riders—and neither
horse nor human would ever be lonely again.

The elder and her ancient mare entered the circle as well, moving
amongst the weanlings and speaking soothingly to them—calming
them; readying them for the Choosing.

River's gaze searched the weanlings, looking for Herd Magenti's
youngsters. Magenti was one of the largest Herds—with five nomadic
branches of several hundred humans and about half as many horses per
branch, they had brought a combined offering of thirty weanlings to the
Rendezvous. Fifteen of those came from River's branch, the largest and
ruling branch, Herd Magenti-Central.

She knew which colt she was looking for, though she had never admitted her favoritism, nor had she shown it—at least not in public.

There he is! River finally caught sight of him—the gorgeous palomino
colt that so many of the Magenti were talking about. His coloring was
the first thing people tended to notice about him, as his coat was so brilliantly blond it looked gold, and his mane and tail were almost perfectly white. He was standing a little off by himself, pawing the ground

restlessly. He had no name—none of them did until their Rider spoke it upon Choosing—so to herself River called him Ghost, because of his speed and his ability to move almost silently. He was larger than the other colts, that was easy to see, but his size didn't make him awkward or gangly. Unlike most yearlings, this colt handled himself with confidence. In the past year that River had helped tend the herd, working with the colts and fillies on a daily basis, she had never seen Ghost so much as misstep.

As if he could sense her attention, the colt turned his head and met River's gaze. Within his dark eye she saw intelligence and something else—something that looked a lot like sadness. Before River could fully process that, the old woman was speaking again.

"Remember, Candidates, do not leave the circle until the last weanling has Chosen." Then she turned her horse to face the weanlings. The old mare arched her neck, tossed her head, and trumpeted a call that all of the watching horses echoed—signaling the beginning of the Choosing.

River's world narrowed to the spot directly in front of her. She breathed deeply, grounding herself as her hand went from the amethyst crystal necklace to her pocket and the finger-shaped quartz phantom that rested quietly there. Her heartbeat slowed. Her nerves washed from her, absorbing into the ground and dissipating.

There was a shout from her left. River looked in time to see a sorrel filly halt before a girl wearing the bloodred ribbons of Herd Cinnabar. The filly reached her muzzle to the girl, and without hesitation the girl rose to her knees, cupped the filly's delicate face, and then blew gently into her velvet muzzle—bonding the two of them for life. Herd Cinnabar erupted into cheers as the new Rider stood to wrap her arms around her Companion. Then, side by side, the girl and her filly left the circle to join their Herd. Cinnabar's cheers were followed swiftly by joyous shouts from Herd Indigo and Herd Virides as more and more weanlings Chose their Riders.

It seemed a long time passed, but later her mother told River that the entire Choosing took mere minutes. The weanling herd had thinned down to a couple dozen horses. Those youngsters were standing in the center of the circle, ears pricked as they studied the seated Candidates. They moved in a slow clockwise fashion so that they could look at each of the Presented humans. Then a weanling would snort, toss his or her head, and move toward a Candidate, and another cheer would lift from the anxiously watching crowd.

Suddenly the palomino colt River called Ghost reared and squealed, parting the group of weanlings. He broke from them, galloping full speed around the circle of Candidates, throwing grass and dirt up behind him. To her right, River saw her Herdmate, Skye, cringe back, then shriek and sputter as she wiped a hoof-sized clump of dirt and muck from her face. River had started to lean toward her to encourage her to stay strong when a dappled gray filly she easily recognized as one of Herd Magenti's weanlings trotted up to Skye, looking obviously upset. She offered her muzzle, and Skye hastily finished wiping the dirt and grass from her face before she leaned eagerly forward and gently blew into the filly's soft nose before throwing her arms around her neck.

"I'm okay! Don't worry, Scout. Nothing could be wrong now that I'm your Rider!" River heard Skye croon to her newly bonded weanling.

Then gasps from the crowd drew River's attention from Skye and Scout. The palomino colt was acting more and more distressed. He'd stopped galloping around the circle and was thundering from one side of the huge theater to the other, scattering the weanlings as he tore through them. The elder and her mare tried to stay with him—tried to calm his increasing agitation—but it wasn't working. The colt's eyes were showing white and he was neighing in loud, panicked bursts—as if he were looking for someone he couldn't find. And then the colt did something truly odd. He slowed and made one more pass around the circle. This time he wasn't galloping in panic. He trotted slowly, obviously looking at each Candidate carefully. When he reached River she looked up and met his dark, intelligent eye.

What she saw there made her heart ache.

The colt was weeping. Tears rolled down his golden face.

"Oh, Ghost. What is it? Why are you so sad?" River blurted.

He slowed slightly, and for a heart-stopping moment River thought he was going to offer her his muzzle. Instead, he tossed his head and snorted, continuing around the circle. When he'd traveled the entire circumference he froze again. This time he was directly across the circle from River, and the remaining weanlings were few enough that she could see him clearly. He reared, striking out at the air as if battling an unseen enemy. Then he shot off, galloping directly toward River!

Shock rooted River in place. From the crowd she was sure she heard her mother screaming her name, but River couldn't move. The colt was going to trample her.

At that last moment he leaped, easily clearing River's head, before sprinting for the exit and disappearing from the Choosing Theater.

There was a stunned silence as everyone—horses, Candidates, Riders, and Herdmates—stared after the colt. River had never heard of a weanling not Choosing a Rider, and she knew a colt had *never* run from the Presentation.

"He's mad."

"Must be something wrong with him."

"Colt looked good, but he's obviously damaged."

River could hear the talk already starting. The only weanlings who didn't Choose Riders were those who were somehow damaged, either emotionally or—and this was more likely—physically. Damaged horses didn't live the full, long life spans of healthy horses. They knew they were flawed and usually so did their dams. Those unfortunate youngsters were never offered at a Rendezvous. They were kept with their home Herd, and cared for by everyone—loved and lavished with attention until their untimely deaths. But Ghost was a sound, healthy colt.

What just happened makes no sense. It's like he was looking for his Rider, but couldn't find her.

River was worrying her lip between her teeth and wondering about the sadness she'd seen in Ghost's eyes when a shadow fell over her.

She looked up.

A beautiful filly had stopped before her. Her coat was light gray—almost white—and her mane was dark, with black and gray streaks. Her legs were dark as well, going from white-gray to black. She was tall for a weanling filly, and River didn't recognize her, but her wide forehead, the power in her young chest, and her straight, perfectly formed legs said clearly that her bloodlines had been crossed with Echo's.

And River could *feel* her. The filly was excited and nervous—happy and anxious.

"Oh, it's okay, pretty girl. All is well," River soothed automatically.

Then the most miraculous thing in River's life happened. The weanling—this absolutely perfect, magnificent, intelligent filly—offered her muzzle to River.

River went to her knees and reached out to put her hands gently on either side of the filly's head, and then she blew softly into her velvet muzzle.

As horse and Rider breathed in, their lives—their souls—their destinies became irrevocably joined. River was washed in a swell of giddy emotions while one word, a name, blasted through her mind like a magickal clarion call.

"Anjo! You're my Anjo!" River stood and wrapped her arms around her Companion's neck and buried her face in her warm, fragrant mane as the victory cheers of Herd Magenti lifted around them.

CHAPTER 2

CURRENT DAY—THE RIDGE OVERLOOKING
TRIBE OF THE TREES

The Reapers are ready, my Lord. They only await the setting of the sun and your command." Iron Fist bowed low to his leader—his God.

Death barely spared him a glance. "Excellent. Tell the men to remain hidden and await my signal. I will go ahead of them and observe."

The Death God strode away, not bothering to look behind Him to see if Iron Fist, His second in command and the Reaper He'd named his Blade, would do as He commanded. Death knew he would because as Iron Fist was all too aware, not following the God's commands would cost the Blade his life.

Death came to the lip of the ridge that overlooked the main area of the forest inhabited by the Tribe of the Trees. Unlike the men crouched yards behind Him, Death did not crawl. He did not hide. He simply stepped up to the edge of the ridge and looked down on what was left of the burned and blackened city.

"Destroyed," the God of Death muttered to Himself. "Foolishly destroyed." He shook His head in disgust, causing His massive horns to throw bizarre, misshapen shadows against the surrounding trees. "But, no matter. I will rebuild the City in the Trees to a state of majesty worthy to be the home of a God." Death hefted the huge triple-pointed trident He'd ripped from the body of the lifeless statue the People used to worship. "No more will the People worship empty metal," he pledged softly. "Now the People know what it is to follow a real God. They know *real* power. Soon, they shall know *real* victory."

Death looked behind Him, wishing the sun would hurry and sink below the horizon. He could see a darkening in the sky, which was now turning more the dusky color of a dove's wing than the brilliant blue of a jay's feathers.

"Dove . . ." Death growled the name as He followed the ridgeline to His left, keeping a watchful eye on the dark, ruined city below. "I must do something about Dove. She does not seem to fully understand the role she is destined to play in our future." In His mind's eye He could see her smooth, eyeless face and her flawless skin. Yes, her body was, indeed, a perfect vessel for the Goddess, especially as being inhabited by the Great Earth Mother, Goddess of Life, would grant her eyes. "But her attitude is unacceptable." Death moved His shoulders as if he were trying to displace biting insects. "I have been too lenient with her. She needs a lesson in obedience."

That decided, Death continued to walk slowly to His left, following the ridge and looking for signs of life from the Tribe below.

But all He saw was the ruins of a once great city. No sounds of a vibrant, thriving society lifted on the wind. All that rose to Death on the ridge were the scents of smoke and decay.

"Where are your lookouts?" Death asked the charred trees below. "Where are your great Warriors who once were so powerful, so terrible that they were able to keep my People trapped within the confines of a poisoned city?"

As if answering the God, there was a flash of light, so brilliant that it instantly made Him think of sunshine.

"Fire? Have the Others somehow managed to set the rest of the forest on fire?" Dread had the God's stomach feeling hollow. He'd counted on there being enough of the City in the Trees left that He could move the People from the poisoned city to the forest as soon as He and His Reapers defeated what was left of the Others. Death walked faster. "No, I must stop the remains of the city from burning."

It didn't take Him long to follow the ridge and come to a spot from which He glimpsed the blackened trees give way to greenery and life. "Ah, there you are, Tribe. And I see there *is* still some of your city in the sky left untouched." The God peered down, at first not understanding what He was witnessing.

The Others were grouped around an ancient tree beyond the edge of the burn line. *She* was standing in the middle of about fifty men who were angrily shouting. The rest of the Others seemed confused or weak, on pallets or simply lying on the ground with their canines beside them, but Death dismissed them instantly. It was the girl who caught and held His attention.

She was standing in the middle of a ball of flame, utterly untouched.

Beside her was a young man whose body showed the bloody sign of injuries, plus two large canines. None of them were being burned by the fire she was somehow wielding.

The warriors of the Others kept trying to press forward to reach her— to no avail. They even fired arrows at the girl, but none of them penetrated the ball of flame. Instead they burned to ash as they neared it.

"What is she?" Death whispered to Himself.

Then the girl began to move and the flame shield moved with her. Increasing her speed as she reached the ruins of the tree city, the girl and her companions jogged on as the agitated Others followed, though they had to remain well back because of the heat of the flames.

Unseen on the ridge above them, Death moved with the oblivious group, more and more mesmerized by the girl who wielded flame.

As Death passed the spot where Iron Fist waited, He whistled sharply, and His Blade rushed to join Him, eyes growing huge when he followed his God's gaze.

"What magick is that?" Iron Fist asked, his voice hushed.

Death smiled. "One I must possess. Watch with me, my Blade, and let us see what we might learn about her."

"*Her?* A woman has magick?"

Death pulled His gaze briefly from the fire girl to send his Blade an admonishing look. "Never underestimate a woman simply because she is a woman. The Goddess of Life is female, and She is the only thing in this world mightier than death."

"Y-yes, my Lord," Iron Fist said instantly. "I apologize. I was only surprised. Um, my Lord. The sun finally sets!" He pointed at the empty horizon.

"Wait." Death held up His hand, stilling Iron Fist. "We will not rush down to be burned by this mysterious fire that—" And then even the God of Death's words failed Him as He watched the ring of fire fizzle from around the girl.

Only it didn't go out. Instead the girl—this spectacular young Warrior woman—lifted her arms as if she would embrace the dying flames. And the flames came to her! They formed a column before her. With a mighty shout of *"IT WILL NEVER HAPPEN!"* the girl made a throwing motion, which the flames obeyed, landing in an exploding blaze that neatly cut off her pursuers.

Then the girl, the young, bloody man, and three canines sprinted for the channel. Death's sharp eyes saw what was happening. "She's escaping to join her people on the channel," the God realized. He also realized this was the perfect opportunity for Him to take the City in the Trees. Death turned to face the army of men hidden on the shadowy ridge. "Iron Fist, remain by my side."

"Yes, my Lord. Always, my Lord."

Then Death raised His trident over His head, shaking back His cloak so that His massive silhouette was fully visible.

"ATTACK!" he bellowed.

"Death! Hu! Hu! Death! Hu! Hu! Death! Hu! Hu!" His army beat their tridents against their shields as they repeated their war cry over and over while they poured over the edge of the ridge toward the unsuspecting Others below.

"Now, my Lord?" Iron Fist was trembling with anticipation beside Him.

"Follow me!" Death commanded. Iron Fist obeyed, following his God as Death strode along the ridge, staring down at the fire girl, who had now gotten in one of the many small boats that were spreading out along the channel and begun swiftly rowing into the distance.

You will not escape me! Death channeled power into the thought and the girl looked up, meeting the God's gaze. *Yes! Know me! See me! I am coming for you, fire girl!* The God raised the huge trident and bellowed the mighty call of a rutting stag into the darkening sky.

As her boat drifted from his view, Death turned to his Blade. "Follow her. Find out where she is going. Do not return to me until you know her destination, but you *must* return to me."

"Always, my Lord!"

"Then, go with Death's blessing." He rested His hand on Iron Fist's bowed head. "And know that what you do not only serves me, but also my consort, the Goddess of Life, who shall soon be your Lady."

"Yes, my Lord! Thank you, my Lord! I will not disappoint you."

"Of course you won't, for then I would have to kill you, and I would find that most inconvenient." Death felt His Blade tremble beneath His hand. "Now, go!"

Death watched long enough to see Iron Fist slip a small boat into the water and enter the channel, paddling after the disappearing line of boats. Then Death turned His attention to the scene of carnage below Him.

Death smiled.

Already many of the Warriors of the Others had fallen. Many more, though Death could not rightfully call them Warriors, were fleeing into the forest. *I shall round them up and deal with them next,* He decided. It was the small circle of Warriors who were still battling His army that He looked to.

They'd taken a stand on a wide wooden platform that had been built into an ancient pine. Though there weren't many of them, their arrows and spears were carving a deadly swath through His Reapers. Death sighed in irritation and made His way down the ridge, but as He drew closer to the main battle, His irritation turned to amusement when He recognized the Warrior who was obviously in charge of the group of fighters.

"Ah, Thaddeus, and so we will finally meet."

Death waded into the carnage, forcing His way toward Thaddeus and his small group of men. His Reapers, appearing more animal than man as they fought, roared a feral cheer when He joined, and redoubled their attack—easily overwhelming the Tribe's meager, but persistent resistance.

As Death cleaved through the weakened Tribe, He became fascinated with the canines. He could feel the bond they had with their Companions. It was much like the connection that drew Him to Thaddeus.

Much like—and not alike at all. Death tasted and touched the Companion bond as He ended life after life, and was intrigued by it—by its fierceness and its loyalty. Except for Thaddeus's small group, the only real resistance to His Reapers came from the canines—huge Shepherds that fought valiantly beside their humans, not faltering or retreating, even when their Companions were cut down. Death watched a ferocious Shepherd stand over the body of his fallen Companion, still battling with his last breath.

Perhaps I shall have a canine—the largest, fiercest of the Shepherds—a God of Canines for the God of Death! That thought had Him smiling as He came into full view of Thaddeus and his men.

Death stood still and observed. Arrows still rained from Thaddeus and the Warriors, but it was easy to see that they would soon run out of ammunition and be overwhelmed by His Reapers, who milled anxiously around the tree, taking turns drawing their fire.

Death reached out, following the connection that had already been established between Him and the anger-filled Thaddeus when he'd chosen power over love and sanctioned the death of his canine Companion. The God saw Thaddeus startle, as if he'd backed into a hot coal, and his arrow went wide, missing the Reaper he'd aimed at and harmlessly embedding into one of the tall pines nearby. Thaddeus looked around, obviously searching the crowd.

Death raised His mighty trident and stepped forward, shouting, *"ENOUGH!"*

Every living thing within hearing of the God's voice reacted by pausing as their bodies—be they human, canine, bird, or insect—all responded on a visceral level to Death's command.

With no hesitation, Death strode toward the tree. One of Thaddeus's men panicked and fired a crossbow at the God. It hit him in the middle of His massive chest and, chuckling, Death brushed it aside as if had been an annoying, but harmless insect.

Several of his Reapers snarled and lunged forward, obviously determined to take the tree.

"Reapers—hold!" Death commanded. His army, though still snarling and bellowing, lowered their bloody, triple-tipped spears, and the exhausted Tribe dropped to their knees or leaned against trees, gasping for air and trembling with fatigue. "Thaddeus! Command your Warriors to hold!" Death ordered as He continued to approach the tree.

Thaddeus stared at the God and shock flashed across his easily read face, followed closely by recognition and then fear.

"Stand down! All of you—stand down!" Thaddeus shouted.

"Very good," Death said, looking up at Thaddeus. "I like this beginning, Thaddeus, though this is not, of course, the first time we've met."

Death saw the way the Tribe looked at Thaddeus. His small group of Warriors kept glancing from Thaddeus to the God—back and forth. Not in fear or anger, but rather curiosity, as if waiting to hear the rest of the story.

The rest of the Tribe reacted much differently. Their voices began to lift in concern and confusion. Many stared at Thaddeus with more disgust than they appeared to have for the God and His Reapers. *Ah, so, he has not yet found a way to control them all. I shall aid him with that, and when I am done using him, he will go the way of his canine and be sacrificed for the greater good.*

"Thaddeus, your people are weak. Your city is destroyed. It is time to choose." As Death spoke the Tribe fell silent.

"You say we have met before, but you have changed, Dead Eye."

"Indeed I have," said Death. "Dead Eye is no more. He willingly sac-rificed himself to awaken me, the God of Death. Much like your beloved Odysseus sacrificed himself to awaken the true Warrior within you."

"Odysseus died because of a mutant Scratcher bitch," Thaddeus hurled the words through bared teeth, looking so much like Death's Reapers that it caused the Tribe to gasp.

"Ah, but you and I know the truth of that, don't we?" Thaddeus began to spew more words at Death, but the God lifted His hand, cutting him off. "No. Save your lies and excuses for others—if you survive. Now you must choose. Put down your weapons and ally yourself with Death—or be claimed by it."

Thaddeus's gaze was sly. "Allies do not surrender to one another."

"Yes, well, Thaddeus, if you were the God then you could make the rules. You are not. I am. And I demand my 'allies' drop their weapons," Death replied conversationally.

"Don't do it!" shouted someone from the crowd.

"The Tribe will not surrender to Skin Stealers!" called another.

Death ignored them and locked His gaze with Thaddeus, speaking calmly, as if they really were old allies. "You have had a taste of it—of real power. Only I can show you how to feast upon it. Or I can kill you. Yes, certainly, a few of you will escape, but to what end?" The smile that spread over the God's face was feral. "You can always retreat to our city. The People and I will not be there. We shall be here, building a new city in the sky. *Make your choice!*" Death commanded in a voice that shook the boughs of the pines surrounding them.

"Tribe of the Trees! Drop your weapons!" Thaddeus shouted.

All around Death came the sound of crossbows, arrows, knives, and swords falling to the ground as the Tribe reluctantly did as the new Leader of their Warriors commanded.

CHAPTER 3

The night sky filled with clouds and darkness came swiftly and completely to the Umbria River. Mari couldn't help but think it was a reflection of the dark, disturbing horrors they'd left behind.

From his seat on the left ballast of the little boat that held Mari, Nik, Rigel, and Laru, the big male Shepherd whined, pulling Mari's attention from the oppressive sky.

"Hey, it's okay, Laru. I know this will take some getting used to, but it's going to be a long journey so you might as well settle in," Mari told Nik's Companion.

But instead of settling, Laru whined more urgently, and Rigel added to the emotional tug Mari already felt from his sire by sending her an image of Nik looking exhausted and covered in blood.

Carefully, Mari put her paddle down and moved along the little boat until she reached Nik, whose bowed back was to her as he methodically stroked the water. She touched him gently, causing him to jerk in surprise and grunt in pain.

"Mari, you have to keep helping me paddle—at least until we've rounded the far side of Farm Island and officially entered the Umbria River." Nik spoke between heaving breaths.

Mari realized her hand was wet from touching him. She rubbed her fingers together and smelled them—and the truth hit her deep in the stomach.

"Nik, you're bleeding. Badly."

"Gotta get us out of here. There'll be time to fix me later."

"Nik! Look at me."

Reluctantly, he sat straighter, pausing in his paddling, to turn on the little benchlike seat and face Mari. She felt his forehead and cheeks, sucking in her breath at the amount of cold sweat covering him and the clamminess of his skin. Then her hands flowed over his body, swiftly and competently, with her healer's touch finding the seeping gashes in his shoulder, side, and thigh.

"Nik, you're wounded and you're losing a lot of blood."

"I know, Mari. But we've fallen behind the rest of the Pack. We must catch them."

Mari looked behind them. Nik was right. Davis and Jaxom's boat had been just a few yards behind them, but now there was only the complete blackness of empty water. Her eyes searched in front of them, and she could just make out the lightening of the water that the other boat's paddles briefly disrupted.

"No, Nik. This won't do. If you pass out I'll never be able to catch up with the rest of the Pack." Mari cupped her hands around her mouth. "Davis! Nik needs help!"

"Mari! I hear you. Coming back now!" Davis called to them.

"No, Mari. Don't let them do that. We don't know if the Tribe is following us."

"Jaxom chopped holes in the other boats. We have time," she said firmly. Her hand covered his. "Stop paddling. You're making the bleeding worse."

With a sigh Nik dropped the paddle into the wooden hull of the boat. Mari was sitting close enough to him to feel that the instant he was no longer using his waning energy to paddle, his body began trembling. Not long after they'd launched safely into the river, Mari had dug through her travel pack for her shirt, and put it on. Now she started tearing strips of cloth from it and tying them around the worst of Nik's wounds.

"Mari, Nik—what is it?" Davis's voice was filled with worry as their boat bumped against them and Jaxom reached out with a paddle, which Mari grabbed, pulling the two little wooden canoes together.

"Nik's hurt. He's bleeding. A lot." She worked quickly, bandaging Nik. "He can't go on until I heal him."

"I *can* go on, but I will admit not for much farther," Nik admitted.

"No problem," Davis said. "Here's what we do. Mari, you and Jaxom change places." When Nik started to protest, Davis cut him off. "It's only temporary, Nik. The Pack isn't far ahead of us. Jaxom can help you catch up to them, and I can do the same for Mari. Once we reach them, we'll change boats again."

"Good idea," Mari agreed. "I'm assuming Antreas is in the lead boat?"

"He is," Davis said.

"When we catch them we have to get word to Antreas that we have to stop—at least long enough for me to draw down the moon and heal Nik."

"And yourself," Nik added grimly. "You called sunfire to you—several times. You saved Laru and Rigel and me."

"And Fortina! Don't forget about this special girl," Jaxom added. The young Shepherd had somehow curled most of herself onto Jaxom's lap, though like her littermate, Rigel, she was far too big to fit comfortably. Mari noted that Jaxom didn't seem to care at all that the overgrown puppy was wet and heavy. His hands continuously stroked her soothingly, and Fortina's gaze rarely left her new Companion's face.

"We wouldn't forget about Fortina." Mari managed a smile for Jaxom and his newly bonded Companion. "Welcome to our pack, sweet girl. I'm so glad you're with us."

"So am I!" Jaxom looked at Mari with happy tears pooling in his eyes. "She loves me so much. I can feel it."

"I know. I'm happy for you, Jaxom," Mari said.

"There is nothing like being bonded to a Shepherd," Nik said, nodding. Then he grimaced as even that slight movement caused him pain. "And I am happy for you, too. But, that doesn't change the fact that Mari saved all of us, and she needs the power of the moon for herself."

"I'll keep some of it, don't worry, Nik. But I'm also not as exhausted as I was last time I used sunfire. I'm learning, and this time I was able to absorb some of the sun's power for myself."

"But just a little while ago you were so sick," he said.

"I was, but that had more to do with seeing that creature on the ridge than sunfire exhaustion. Jaxom, pass Fortina to me. I'll settle her, and then you and I can trade places."

Nik acquiesced as they balanced carefully—first passing the pup over, which Rigel and Laru watched carefully, tails thumping in encouragement. Then Mari touched Nik's damp cheek. "We will stay close by," she reassured him before she and Jaxom exchanged places.

Rigel whined from his ballast.

"It's okay, sweet boy," Mari said quickly. "I won't be far away." Davis's little blond Terrier, Cameron, huffed a greeting and licked Mari's face, which made her laugh. "And Cammy will keep an eye on me."

Mari ignored Rigel's snort and petted Cammy while the Terrier wriggled with happiness.

"Easy, Cammyman. Don't want this canoe to overturn," Davis said, and his Companion instantly quieted.

"Jaxom, did you get holes punched in all of the remaining boats?" Nik asked.

"All but one or two at the very end of the row—they were both single seats. I focused on the bigger crafts first. I—I hope that was the right thing to do," said Jaxom.

"It was," Nik said. "Well done. And now I'm less worried about being followed."

"The Tribe is too busy fighting the Skin Stealer army to bother with us," Jaxom said. "I watched as long as I could, and saw no one coming after us."

"I feel terrible for them." Mari shuddered.

"Them?" Jaxom said. "You mean the Tribe that tried to kill you and Nik?"

Mari met his gaze. "No, I don't mean Thaddeus and the twisted

Warriors he's creating. I mean the rest of the Tribe—Ralina and the others—the ones not filled with hate."

Jaxom grunted and said nothing as he picked up Mari's discarded paddle and took her place in the rear of the canoe.

Davis and Mari exchanged a look. "It's difficult to have empathy for a people you don't know," Davis said softly. He touched her hand as he handed her Jaxom's paddle. "Thank you. Thank you for knowing and for having empathy."

She nodded and smiled sadly at Davis, longing for a world where empathy wasn't such a sparse commodity. Then she took her place in the rear of the canoe. "I'm ready."

"Okay, let's lean into it and stroke hard. The faster we catch the others, the sooner Nik can be healed," said Davis.

Mari bent to the task of slicing her paddle into the deep, black water. She tried not to think about the darkness below her. She didn't have any particular fear of water, but as an Earth Walker raised in Clan Weaver, she hadn't spent much time on the water. She could, of course, swim. All Clanmembers learned when they were children. They did fish, but only in the streams and lazy creeks that traversed Earth Walker territory. Never in the Willum River—it was controlled by the Tribe in the west, and the Skin Stealers in the east. Mari had never even glimpsed the Umbria River, which she thought might very well prove to be a good thing. That night she couldn't see the shore—not on either side of her—so Mari pretended that it was much closer than she had a feeling it actually was.

When they'd made the decision to voyage up the river and through the mountains to the plains of the Wind Riders, Sheena, Davis, and O'Bryan—led by Antreas—had given the Earth Walkers quick lessons on how to paddle the canoe-like watercraft the Tribe used. So, Mari bent to her task and drew on the reservoir of strength she'd managed to retain from calling down sunfire, paddling as hard as she could. She ignored her burning shoulders and listened for Davis's direction, "That's good, Mari. Keep it steady. Stroke . . . stroke . . . stroke."

When she could, Mari glanced behind her—each time relieved to see the bow of Nik's boat still within view. She lost all track of time, and was shocked when Davis called out, "Hello, the Pack!"

"Davis!" O'Bryan's familiar voice responded before Mari could differentiate Nik's cousin from the floating blobs that were suddenly coming into view. "Do you have Nik and Mari?"

"Yes! We're here!" Mari called back. "But Nik's wounded. He can't go on much longer. We have to stop long enough for me to call down the moon and help him heal."

"Come closer!" Antreas's voice carried easily from the lead position back to them across the inky water. "Tie up with O'Bryan and the rest of us will circle back to you."

"Will do!" Mari said.

Nik called out. "Jaxom and I are right behind Mari and Davis. We'll tie up with them."

Mari wondered what Antreas was up to. They needed to get to shore so she could call the moon to her, but perhaps tying up was part of that plan. Regardless, she was incredibly relieved when she saw the rest of her Pack paddle into view.

"Great Goddess! I am so glad to see you!" Sora cried as her boat drifted to them. It was bigger than Mari's—large enough for Sora to share it with Sheena and her Shepherd, Captain, as well as Rose with her little mama Terrier, Fala, and Fala's litter. Mari could see Sora's pup, Chloe, and her bright little eyes peeking out from the sling Sora had rigged to carry the canine close to her heart. "Nik?" Sora looked around worriedly. "Where's Nik?"

"Here, just behind us." Mari gestured to him.

"How badly is he hurt?" Sora asked as she began searching through a woven basket by her feet.

"I'm not sure. Thaddeus and his goons were using him for archery practice. He has several lacerations that don't want to stop bleeding. I thought they were only superficial, but his weakness and the feel of his skin tell me they're more serious than that."

"Hey, Moon Women. I'm right here. And I'm going to be fine. Although, sadly, I think you might have to sew me up. Again. And this time without the help of that tea that knocked me out."

Antreas paddled up to them in his little boat, expertly gliding around them as he assessed the situation. Mari thought his Lynx Companion, Bast, would look like a statue perched before him on the front of the watercraft had her yellow eyes not been shining as she gave the wide body of water suspicious looks. Then Danita's head peeked around from her spot in the rear of the canoe and her teeth flashed white. "Mari! Thank the Great Goddess! We were all so worried about you."

"It's good to be back with our Pack, that's for sure," said Mari.

Antreas maneuvered their canoe beside Mari's. "So, you're absolutely certain you must call down the moon now?" he asked her.

"Yes. Nik has lost a lot of blood, and he's still bleeding. I need to call down the healing power of the moon and then see if I have to close the wounds, or just clean and pack them." Mari tried to see through the darkness to glimpse the shore. "Can't we go to shore for a little while?"

"No," Antreas spoke grimly. "We haven't even gotten around Farm Island yet. I know the Tribe is under attack, so we shouldn't have to worry about them following us, but we have no idea about the size of the Skin Stealer army or their intention beyond invading the Tribe. They definitely could think we're part of the Tribe that is attempting to escape. It would be very bad for us if we gave them an opportunity to catch us."

"But do Skin Stealers even have boats?" Davis asked.

"They can swim. Amazingly well," Nik said. "I've seen them."

"As have I," came a weak voice drifting over the water.

"Wilkes? Is that you?" Nik asked.

"It is. Claudia and I made it to the Pack." Then he had to stop speaking as his words were drowned in racking coughs.

"Mari, can you just bandage Nik and make do for a few hours?" Antreas asked. "If we all bend our backs to it, we should be able to get far enough upstream that we can rest and you can call moon power to you then. I planned our first stop to be about ten miles from here. If we're lucky we'll get there in a little over four hours."

Mari's ears caught the sound of Wilkes's coughs and of another person, whom she guessed was Claudia, retching into the river. "Antreas, it seems Nik isn't the only Pack member who needs healing. And if the Pack is weak, we won't make it to your stopping point."

"We're fine, Mari." Claudia's voice drifted to her, sounding sick and wet and absolutely not fine.

"Antreas, could we stop to draw down the moon if we knew that the Skin Stealers weren't after us?" Sora asked.

"Briefly, yes. But we'd need to get going again as soon as possible."

"Well, good. That's an easy fix," Sora said. "O'Bryan, could you paddle over here to us, please?"

"Sure! Coming!" O'Bryan's voice came from somewhere in the middle of the group of boats that were all tied together and filled with nervous Pack members and supplies.

Soon, O'Bryan's boat, another one of the larger, multi-oared crafts, came into view. Mari could see that Jenna and Sarah were paddling with him. Jenna grinned and waved quickly to her before continuing to dip her oar into the water. There were no canines on their boat and it had one of the refurbished bed frames attached to the rear of it, loaded with supplies. Lydia, Sarah's older sister, whose back had been burned in the forest fire, was one of the three passengers. There were two other women sitting in the middle of the boat, and as they drew closer Mari was surprised to realize she didn't recognize either of them.

Then her initial surprise was replaced by shock as one of the women turned her face toward Mari—*her eyeless face!*

"Who are these girls?" Mari asked.

"Skin Stealers," Sora replied nonchalantly. "We found them on the way to the channel. They were fleeing their people. That's Lily." The younger of the two women—the one with eyes—bowed her head respectfully to Mari. "The other girl is Dove. *Your* Dove, Mari. The one from your dream."

Mari felt a jolt of shock, instantly understanding that Sora was referring to the dream Mari had shared with her about a dove seeking safe haven with the Pack and Mari's mother's voice insisting she should be given sanctuary, but on one condition only. "Did you make her swear?" Mari asked Sora.

"She did, Moon Woman." The eyeless girl answered for herself. "It is good to meet the second leader of this Pack."

Mari had little time for pleasantries and no inclination for them. "What was that creature on the ridge? The one with the horns?"

"They are antlers, Moon Woman. He is the God of Death. It is from Him that Lily and I fled."

Mari felt a terrible foreboding shiver through her body. "What is the intention of His army?"

Dove didn't hesitate. "To defeat the Others you call the Tribe of the Trees and to move the People from the poisoned city to the City in the Trees."

"Do you think He'll follow us?" Sora asked.

Dove moved her smooth shoulders. "I cannot speak for Death. I was His captive, not His confidante, so I can only repeat what I have heard Him say. Occupying the City in the Trees has long been His dream. He has not spoken of a desire to capture your people, the earth dwellers, but I have sworn to only speak the truth so I must admit that if He knows that I am with you, I believe He may come after me."

"What are the chances this Death God knows she's with us?" Nik asked.

"He did not know Lily and I escaped," Dove said. "He will not discover our absence until He returns to the city to get me."

"Dove, there are many more questions I need to ask you," Mari said. "But they will wait. Antreas, it sounds like it's safe to stop here—if only for a short time."

Antreas's sigh drifted across the water. "Okay, call down the moon and heal Nik and Wilkes and Claudia, but you're going to have to do it from out here. We need to stay in the middle of the river. We get too close to Farm Island and we're going to get caught by its unpredictable currents—same thing with the far shore."

"Can you do that? Draw down the moon on the water?" Nik asked.

Mari shared a look with Sora. The other Moon Woman shrugged.

"I've never done it before, and I don't remember my mother ever mentioning calling the moon from any body of water, but I'll try," Mari said.

"I hope it works," Antreas added. "We're going to be spending many nights tied together and anchored in the river."

"Sounds like a skill we're going to have to learn," muttered Mari, more to herself than to anyone in particular, but Danita answered.

"Then you can do it, I know you can. The moon is the moon is the moon. She is everywhere, even out here on the water," said Danita.

"I think she's *especially* out here on the water," Jenna said. "When I was captured and imprisoned in the floating houses in the Channel I used to force myself to stay awake at night as long as I could so that I could stare at the reflection of the moon on the water. It was brilliant, and it turned the Channel from green and frightening to silver and familiar. It was the only thing that helped me remember home through that horrible depression."

Several of the other women who had been enslaved with Jenna murmured agreement, and Mari found herself filled with gratitude for her people.

"Thank you, Jenna and Danita. I needed to hear that." She turned to Jaxom and held out her hand. "Help me get back to Nik." Carefully, they exchanged places again, lifting Fortina back to Jaxom's boat with him.

"Hey, is that another canine?" Sora asked.

"It is!" Jaxom's happiness was like a torch of sunfire. It blazed so joyously that the entire Pack could see it as the pup leaned into his side, gazing up at him adoringly. "This is Fortina. She is my Companion."

"Bloody beetle balls! Fortina?" Sheena gawked at the pup. "But she's Maeve's Companion."

"Not anymore." Jaxom put his arm protectively around Fortina. "She ran away from the Tribe and Chose me. She told me her name, and she's with me now. Forever. Right, Mari? Right, Nik?"

"Of course," Mari said quickly, understanding the fear in Jaxom's voice. Just the thought of being separated from Rigel made her stomach sick.

"Fortina left Maeve," Nik said. "I've never seen anything like it—never even heard stories of it happening before—but the pup Chose a new Companion, and that Companion is Jaxom."

"I have heard of it. It's rare, but it can happen when a canine is being abused," Wilkes said before he coughed so hard he, too, retched into the river.

"I'd like to hear that story after I've healed you and after we're out of danger," Mari said. Then she paused another moment to say to Jaxom, "Don't worry. No one will ever try to take Fortina from you." She turned to Sora. "I'm going to call down the moon now."

Sora nodded. "What do you need me to do?"

"Concentrate with me. Think of the moon and her beauty, and how she is everywhere."

"I will. You can count on me, Mari."

"You can count on me, too," Danita said eagerly, followed by Isabel.

"I'll concentrate, too, Mari!"

"Me, too," said Jenna, grinning at her friend and Moon Woman. "I can't draw down the moon with you, but I'll try to help."

"As will I, Moon Woman!" called another member of the Pack.

"And I!"

"Me, too!"

Soon, Mari's eyes welled with grateful tears. The love and support of her people swelled around her—and it made her feel invincible.

"Thank you—all of you." Then she raised her voice. "I need the boat that's carrying Wilkes and Claudia brought over here, close enough for me to touch them."

"On our way!" Mari recognized the voice of Mason, Jaxom's younger brother. Soon, he and Spencer, a young female Earth Walker Mari was learning to appreciate as capable and filled with energy, paddled the boat up so they could take the place Antreas vacated on one side of Mari's canoe, with Sora's boat on the other. Balancing carefully, Mari moved to stand behind Nik. She looked at Sora. "Ready?"

"Always," said the other Moon Woman.

Mari closed her eyes and began sketching a picture in her mind. She drew a wide, placid river. On the river she then imagined a cluster of boats. In that cluster she was careful to draw the boat she was in with Nik, as well as Mason's and Sora's boats close beside them. She took three long, deep breaths, letting each out slowly as she imagined reaching down, down, through the dark water to find the muddy bottom of the river. Then she raised her arms, threw her head back, opened her eyes, and began the ancient invocation, altering it just enough to reflect the newness of calling the moon to her on water.

> *"Moon Woman I proclaim myself to be!*
> *Greatly gifted, I bare myself to thee.*
> *Though not on land, burrow, or gathered site*
> *Still I call and ask for your powerful light.*
> *Find me here, your Moon Woman who calls to you*
> *Your child I am—faithful, loving, and true.*
> *Earth Mother, aid me, show your magick might,*
> *Lend me silver strength on this river tonight.*
> *Come, precious light—fill me to overflow*
> *So those in my care your healing will know.*
> *By right of blood and birth channel through me*
> *The Goddess gift that is my destiny!"*

In her mind, Mari continued the picture she'd so carefully fashioned by filling a clear night's sky with a brilliant moon. From that moon she drew rays of light that rained down in thick, shining ropes from above onto Mari, drenching her in healing silver magick.

She felt the cold strength of it and quickly completed the picture by sketching the silver power being channeled through her body and cascading from her hands, which she placed lovingly on Nik's bowed head.

When she spoke her voice was amplified by the strength of the brilliant, but invisible moon.

"Nik, I Wash you free of weakness and wounds, and gift you with the love of our Great Earth Mother!"

Nik's head was bowed, but after just a few minutes he lifted it, smiling brilliantly up at Mari. Because she was aglow with moon power, Mari could clearly see that Nik's cheeks were once again pink with health. "Thank you, my beautiful Moon Woman," he said.

She bent and kissed him on his forehead, noting automatically that it no longer felt cold and clammy. Then she turned to her left, where Wilkes and Claudia huddled beside each other in the middle of their boat, coughing and gasping for breath. Mari offered her hand. Wilkes nodded to Claudia, and the young woman didn't hesitate: She took Mari's hand, gripping it tightly. Mari felt the heat in Claudia's flesh and knew the sickness had rooted deeply within her body.

Mari closed her eyes and concentrated. She imagined moon power flowing from her into Claudia—a huge tide of it—drowning the horrible Skin Stealer disease.

"Claudia, I Wash you free of all sickness and gift you with the love of our Great Earth Mother."

When she felt Claudia's hand cool and heard her draw a deep breath that was free of wheezing and coughing, she let loose her hand and briefly opened her eyes.

Claudia was staring up at her with an expression of utter astonishment. "Thank you, Moon Woman! I—I feel like myself again!" From the rear of the boat where Claudia's big Shepherd, Mariah, was crouched beside Wilkes's Odin, came excited, relieved barking while Odin whined fretfully, staring at Wilkes.

Mark held out her hand to the Warrior, who took it eagerly. She closed her eyes again and painted a tide of silver, flowing from herself into Wilkes. She felt his hot hand spasm against hers, but he didn't release his hold—he only gripped her more tightly.

"Wilkes, I Wash you free of all sickness and gift you with the love of our Great Earth Mother."

His grip loosened as his skin cooled, and Mari opened her eyes. He was smiling up at her, his eyes filled and overflowing with tears of gratitude.

"'Thank you' is not enough, but that and my oath to always stand beside you—always believe in you and our Pack—is all that I have to give. Thank you, Mari, our Moon Woman."

"The Great Earth Mother asks only for loyalty, honesty, and kindness from her people—and what is good enough for her is more than good enough for me. You are most welcome, Wilkes."

Mari started to lift her arms again and thank the moon as she let the silver power ebb from her, but she staggered, and Nik had to take her elbow to keep her from tipping their canoe.

"You must not let it go yet, Mari," Sora reminded her. "Keep some for yourself."

Mari nodded and closed her eyes once more. Slowly, she lifted her arms and tilted back her head. And then she sketched one last picture, showing a gentle fall of silver from above, raining down on her, absorbing through her flesh and blood to fill her body with cool, healing light.

It only took a moment for her dizziness and weakness to wash away. "Thank you, Moon," she spoke to the orb that was cloaked in cloud. "And thank you, Great Earth Mother."

Filled with strength and gratitude, Mari looked lovingly at the cluster of boats grouped around and before her and felt so much joy and excitement that her heart could not contain it. She threw her arms wide, as if to embrace them all.

Mari shimmered.

Mari glowed.

Mari *blazed*.

"Pack! This is truly our beginning! Together we have chosen to start our lives anew and to work to create a world where we all can be our truest selves—where we all are respected—where we all are valued as individuals as well as the whole we form."

"May the Goddess keep you strong, Moon Woman!" Davis's voice rang over the water, which had turned silver with Mari's radiated light.

"She will! She will be with all of us on our journey. And so will the Sun God. It will be a powerful thing, indeed, to have a Goddess *and* a God blessing our Pack." Mari saw the surprised pleasure reflected on the faces of the Pack members who used to be a Tribe as she included their God in her thanksgiving. Her voice amplified by happiness and the power of the moon, Mari concluded, "So may the Great Earth Mother and the Sun God bless us as we begin our journey to our new life and our new world on the free Plains of the Wind Riders!"

As the Pack cheered Mari gently released the moon magick and, laughing, fell into Nik's waiting arms.

Iron Fist had found a single small canoe that the fleeing woman and her friends had left undamaged. He'd launched it silently, thinking how much swifter and easier to handle it was than the rough rafts the People used to traverse the river that flowed through their city.

It would have been simple to catch the slowly moving group, especially the two boats that had launched not long before him. They were lagging behind the others, laboring to catch up. Iron Fist had to traverse the rough shallows as he hugged the far side of the Tribe's island so that he didn't overtake them or wasn't seen by them, and it was only his enhanced strength that kept the boat from capsizing in the unpredictable current.

When he heard the shouts drifting across the water and realized the group was tying up together, Iron Fist managed to anchor his boat beside a grounded root ball as he waited for them to get under way again.

But they did not simply tie up together and continue. Iron Fist strained to make the sounds that carried with the current into words. He'd almost despaired of it and was formulating an alternative plan that involved shadowing them only long enough to capture one of the laggers and take him to Death to be interrogated.

And then the woman amazed him by beginning an invocation—something mystical, magickal—something that caused her youthful voice to swell with power so that it was magnified and Iron Fist was able to easily hear what she was saying.

The woman was invoking the power of the moon!

Then Iron Fist's amazement grew and changed to shock as the cloud-filled sky was suddenly shattered by blazing spikes of moonlight that found the girl—for as he got a good look at her Iron Fist realized that she was, indeed, little more than a child. But a child with incredible power. She glowed silver with it, so brilliantly that looking at her directly hurt his eyes.

He listened to the invocation in awe, hearing that she was a magickal being called a Moon Woman, invested by the Great Earth Goddess with the ability to draw down power from the moon—and that she claimed to have the ability to heal.

Iron Fist watched and saw her lay hands on first one, then another, then a third of her group. He saw their joy-filled response to her touch and realized that this Moon Woman did, indeed, wield the power to heal.

Iron Fist's mind was whirring with possibilities. The God of Death would be so very pleased to receive news of this magnitude. *The girl who threw fire as simply as a dry stick catches when touched to a red-hot coal can also call power from the moon and heal people in the name of the Goddess!* He could hardly contain his excitement.

And then he refocused on the Moon Woman as she addressed her people, the ones she called "Pack," and spoke of their new beginning, their new world, *and their destination*!

Then, in the illuminating light of the moon Iron Fist discovered something else that his God would be eager to hear. There, in one of the boats, smiling and cheering with the rest of the Pack people, were Dove and Lily! Iron Fist had stared a long time, hardly believing his own eyes, but Dove's sightless face was unmistakable, and Lily sat beside her, hugging her mistress and looking happier than he'd ever seen her look in the temple *where both women belonged.* The fact that the two of them had somehow deserted Death and joined with the fleeing people was undeniable—as undeniable as the vengeance the God would mete out to them.

Iron Fist looked forward to that. Perhaps Death would allow the Reapers to enjoy the two women before He killed them. Just the thought sent a shiver of desire through his body.

Iron Fist did not wait to see them paddle slowly away. He did not follow them. He'd discovered the answer to the question his God had sent him to find, and more. He knew that Dove had betrayed her God. He knew where the Moon Woman who could throw fire was going—to the Plains of the Wind Riders! And even though Iron Fist's secluded, poisoned life had not taught him where those plains might be, he knew his Lord, his God, would know.

Death knew everything.

With renewed excitement Iron Fist loosed the canoe and headed downstream and back into the Channel, eager to give such good news to his master.

CHAPTER 4

River knew she and Anjo were being tracked before the Flyer sounded its death call. She'd felt Anjo's uneasiness through their bond, but had initially thought that the two-year-old was just nervous because today was the day they'd agreed on for River's first official ride—something she and her filly had been anticipating for an entire year. Today, after seventeen years of wishing and waiting, dreaming and desiring, River was going to become a Wind Rider.

So, instead of trusting her horse and pausing to search the sky and the prairie around them for signs of trouble, River sent soothing thoughts to Anjo, assuring her that all was well—that they were ready for their maiden ride—and then River picked up their pace, jogging quickly beside Anjo and putting more distance between them and the spring campsite for Herd Magenti. Her thinking had been half good. River had reasoned that Anjo's nerves would calm if there was no chance of anyone interrupting them, and if she was being completely honest she agreed with her Companion. Two-year-olds were usually ridden slowly, gently, and under the watchful eyes of mature horses and their Riders, but as usual, Anjo and River were in agreement.

They weren't just *any* two-year-old/Rider pair. Ever since that wonderful day a year ago when Anjo had chosen River, Herd Magenti had been abuzz with speculation about the next Lead Mare—and that speculation was almost unanimously aimed at Anjo and River. It was justified. Anjo was growing into an exquisite filly, and with Echo's decade of reign as Lead Mare coming to an end in another year, it was natural that the Herd was considering who would be the next Lead Mare/Rider team. And it was also natural for the Herd to look to the talented daughter of the Rider of the mare that had led them in a decade that had been prosperous and had seen unequaled births of strong, healthy foals as well as content Riders. It wasn't possible for River *not* to hear the gossip and the musings, and she usually didn't let the talk bother her. As her mother consistently told her: *River, just focus on being the best version of you— not the version of you others want you to be.* But that didn't mean River or Anjo wanted an audience for their first ride.

Which was why they'd set out at dawn, jogging determinedly *away* from the sprawling Herd and looking for privacy.

The shrill cry of a Flyer had Anjo tossing her head and snorting as she sent River waves of fear.

"Ssh, it's okay, Anjo. I don't see anything yet." River cupped her hand over her eyes against the glare of the bright spring morning as she studied the sky behind them. The Flyer's distant cry had seemed to come from in front of them, but the dangerous creatures had the ability to throw their voices. Unsuspecting prey trying to escape from the death cry of a Flyer ran right into the hunting path of the creature. But River was far from unsuspecting. "We have time. Look, the cross timber line is there." River pointed at the distant smudge of green that seemed impossibly far away. Flyers only attacked their prey on the open prairie. They were unable to dive and latch onto their victims under the cover of even scrubby trees. "We'll be safe in there. Come on—I'll hang on and keep up with you." River wound her hand into Anjo's long mane so that as the big filly increased her speed from a trot to a canter, she would practically pull River with her.

But Anjo wasn't having it. She slid to a stop, snorted at River, butted her gently with her head, and then—as if it was an everyday occurrence— bowed to her knees, ready to be mounted.

"You know we shouldn't. Your bones might not be ready to carry me while you run. We can't mess up our future—all the decades we have together—and chance an injury, or worse, a break. No, I'll keep up if I hold on to you. Like I said, we have time."

The Flyer's scream sounded again—this time closer. River searched the sky behind them. Her stomach roiled when she sighted the black silhouette circling in the distance, getting closer and closer with each wing stroke. From River's vantage point the creature looked deceptively like a harmless vulture. But River knew better. Flyers were able to appear like vultures from below—though instead of feathers they had leathery wings with scales and dark fur that covered their bulbous bodies. And instead of being harmless carrion eaters, they only ate fresh kills, preferring to consume prey slowly while it was alive after diving from the sky to attack. One small bite from a Flyer's razor-tipped beak flooded prey with poison that caused instant paralysis, so the creature could eat slowly as its living meal suffered silently—unable to move or even scream for help.

Anjo snorted again and tossed her head fretfully, but she remained kneeling, even when the Flyer screamed its hunting cry once more—this time much, much closer. Anjo's body trembled, and she filled River's mind with an intense need to flee.

"You're right. We won't have a future if a Flyer bites either of us." River moved to Anjo's head, looking into her Companion's beautiful brown eye. "We're going to be careful. We're only going to go fast enough to get to the cross timbers before the Flyer reaches us." She rested her hand on her filly's broad forehead. "This isn't how I thought our first ride would be."

Anjo's swishing tail said that she agreed.

Moving quickly but carefully, River went to Anjo's shoulder, grabbed a handful of mane, and then slid onto her filly's wide, smooth back.

Anjo stood easily, prancing a little to the side as she got used to River's weight. River had, of course, lain over her filly's back many, many times during the past year—readying Anjo to bear her weight slowly, gently. No horse in any of the Wind Rider Herds was ever rushed to carry a Rider, which was one of the reasons horse-and-Rider pairs remained sound and healthy for many decades. Anjo was already used to her slight weight, though River had never sat fully on her filly's back until that moment.

Even with a Flyer stalking them, River was filled with excitement and pride. She leaned forward and stroked Anjo's smooth neck. "You're doing great—actually you're perfect!"

The Flyer screamed again, shrill and loud—which seemed to come from directly ahead of them. River didn't waste time staring behind them; she knew what she would see—a dark silhouette closing on them from above and behind. She gripped Anjo's sides with her thighs. "Let's get out of here!"

Anjo leaped forward into a smooth, effortless canter. River leaned over her neck, sending her encouragement but also murmuring, "Easy, easy, Anjo. We have time. Keep it easy, perfect girl."

The filly's stride was strong and true, and though River had been riding since before she could walk, she felt a huge rush of joy at the smoothness of Anjo's canter.

And then it happened. The amazing, miraculous bond that had begun that day one year before when Anjo had Chosen River expanded, strengthened, and was finally complete. River gasped as new sensations flooded her. Suddenly her sense of smell heightened, though not as much as her sight, which became crystalline sharp and expanded far past her limited human ability. And River *knew* things a human couldn't. She could *feel* that they were being hunted—*sense* imminent danger coming from the sky. She also shared Anjo's barely controlled panic and automatically sent soothing thoughts to the filly. *We're going to make it to the trees. We're going to be fine.* Then the power washed through her. River could feel her filly's strength as her muscles warmed and flexed and her hooves pounded into the soft, verdant ground.

"Oh, Anjo! This is what Mother and the other Riders talk about—this sharing of senses that you only understand when you're a Wind Rider. It's incredible!" The filly's ears twitched back to catch her words, and

River laughed because her hearing, too, was bonded to Anjo's and had become clearer.

"*SKRAAW! SKRAAW!*"

The screech sent a skitter of fear through filly and Rider. This time River's heightened equine senses screamed *DANGER* and she swiveled at the waist to peer up at the sky behind them.

The Flyer was closing on them. In moments the predator would fold its scaly wings and dive at them.

River checked the distance to the approaching tree line and knew that unless they moved faster they simply would not make it. Her fingers twitched against Anjo's mane, aching to unwind the leather strap from around her waist, fit the short throwing spear into it, turn her filly, and attack the Flyer with the momentum of a thousand-pound, galloping horse behind her spear toss. But she and Anjo hadn't practiced spear throwing—not yet. None of the two-year-old horse/Rider pairs did until their bond was completed after their maiden ride. River was a decent shot, but she didn't want their lives to rest on her inexperience.

Silently, River berated herself for not bringing her lasso, the throwing rope she'd been practicing using since she was a child. The lasso came easy to her, and River had no doubt that she could snap a noose around a diving Flyer's neck. *I will never leave my rope behind again!*

No—she couldn't attack the Flyer, not as long as they were on the open prairie. So River made her decision quickly. She leaned low over Anjo's neck, gripped the filly tighter with her thighs, and spoke the words the young horse was poised to hear.

"Run, Anjo! Run!"

River felt her filly's relief as Anjo's stride lengthened, pounding the ground as she ran. The wind whistled past River's cheeks, making her eyes tear and taking her breath, but her grin was fierce. Anjo's speed was incredible. The grasses that surrounded them were knee high to the filly, and as she sped across the prairie it seemed to River that they were flying over an ocean of green.

The tree line grew closer, so close that with her equine-heightened senses River could smell that there was a creek close within the cross timber line, and she scented something else as well—something darker, feral—something dangerous. In the same moment, Anjo reacted. Her head lifted and her gait faltered.

"What is it?" River shouted as she scanned the cross timbers, trying to understand why Anjo's senses had alerted them to danger.

The stallion seemed to materialize from nowhere. Later, River realized that he had to have been hidden in the scrub brush that dotted the area before the timber line, but at that instant his appearance was as magickal as it was surprising. He bolted in front of Anjo, squealing and nipping at her, forcing her to turn to her left. The filly panicked and lunged to the side, almost unseating River, who could only cling to her neck and stare, wide-eyed, at the beautiful but utterly crazed stallion.

"Ghost!" She could hardly comprehend it, but she definitely recognized the young stallion. "Stop!" River shouted at him. "Get away!" She even tried to kick out at him, but the colt was too fast. He kept herding Anjo to the left so that they were galloping parallel to the tree line. Anjo's ears were pinned back against her head and the whites of her eyes showed as she squealed her anger at the young stallion.

Ghost suddenly changed direction and gave her rump one last nip—this time herding her toward the tree line before the stallion slid to a stop and whirled around to face the Flyer.

"Go! Go! Go!" River shouted to Anjo, who needed no more encouragement. At a flat run, they finally entered the sanctuary of the cross timber tree line.

River kneed Anjo so that she spun around, and they watched as the Flyer came at the stallion. Ghost reared and struck out with his hooves and teeth, and the Flyer broke off its dive to circle and begin another approach.

"Come on!" River shouted. "Get under the trees with us!"

But the young stallion ignored her. She could see the whites of his eyes and he was squealing and tossing his head—obviously filled with anger that needed to explode at the Flyer. The dark and dangerous creature screamed its death call again.

"SKRAAW! SKRAAW!"

Ghost trumpeted his own challenge, turning to keep the Flyer in sight.

"Shit!" River cursed under her breath. *He isn't going to retreat and I'm not going to sit here and watch him get killed.* Anjo danced to the side, snorting and tossing her head as she filled River with her need to help the stallion. Frantically River unwrapped the wide leather strap from around her waist with one hand as she reached behind her and into the travel pack strapped to Anjo to pull out a throwing spear. She quickly hooked the notched end of the short spear into the center of the long leather strap. Then she tightened her thighs around her filly again. "I'm with you, Anjo. We haven't practiced together, but we can do this. We have to. We can't let that creature get Ghost." As she spoke she also sent her filly images of them sprinting together toward the stallion while River threw the spear at the Flyer.

Anjo's muscles tensed as she readied herself.

"SKRAAW! SKRAAW!"

Ghost was luminous with strength and rage as he reared, striking out at the Flyer with his deadly front hooves as the creature dived at him, shrieking its death call. He almost caught the Flyer this time, but the creature twisted midair, barely escaping Ghost's powerful teeth.

"Now! Go, Anjo! Go!" River's words were all the encouragement the filly needed. She burst from the tree line, racing toward the battling stallion.

The creature was circling low over Ghost, preparing for another dive attack as it folded its leather wings against its thick body. Poison glistened from the tip of the creature's beak as River used Anjo's massive forward momentum and threw the spear. It was a decent shot—not fatal, but it did hit the Flyer, scraping a bloody furrow across the creature's back, knocking it off balance so that it tumbled to the ground, where Ghost, screaming in anger, stomped it over and over again with his hooves until it was a flattened puddle of blood and gore mixed with grass and dirt.

River quickly hung the leather throwing strap over her shoulder and unsheathed the knife she, like all Herdmembers, carried with them out onto the prairie, as Anjo galloped to the stallion. Living or dead, just one scratch from the poisonous beak of the Flyer would be enough to hurt Ghost, perhaps even permanently, so as Anjo slid to a stop before the stallion, River dropped from her back and rushed to Ghost.

"Whoa, boy. Easy!" she soothed as she hurried to the irate horse. River glanced at the bloody mess that had been a Flyer and felt a wave of relief. The lizard-like bird was not much more than a gory stain, and no longer any threat to Ghost or anyone else. She shifted her attention to the golden horse. "Easy, boy. You killed it. All is well—all is well."

The stallion stopped rearing and stomping the dead Flyer to turn to face River and Anjo. He fidgeted to the side, snorting, as his ears pricked at her. He looked ready to bolt, so River focused on her own emotions. Every member of the Herd knew that all horses are intuitive— all can sense the emotions of humans, even unbonded humans. River stood still and calmed herself and deepened her breathing, and as she relaxed so, too, did the stallion.

Beside her, Anjo nickered in gentle encouragement as Ghost began to calm.

"Good—good," River murmured. "What are you doing out here all by yourself, Ghost?" She moved a little closer to him and he snorted and took half a step away. River was too experienced an equestrian to chase after a shy horse, so instead she turned to Anjo, whose coat was wet and steaming, though her breathing was already beginning to slow. She ran her hands carefully up and down Anjo's sweaty legs, checking for bowing or tenderness as she murmured assurances to her. The filly was still a little shaky, but seemed completely sound.

"Sand and water is what we need. I smelled water within the cross timbers, so let's go see what we can find," River told Anjo. She draped her arm around her filly's neck, but before they turned to head back into the timber line, River met the stallion's curious gaze—which was definitely focused on her and Anjo. "Come on," she encouraged. "Come with us, handsome. I'll tend to you, too." Then she clucked at Anjo and the two of them began walking into the tree line.

River didn't look back at Ghost. She didn't have to. With her newly awakened senses she could feel that he followed them just as surely as Anjo would. Sure enough, within several yards River heard running water. The bank was a gentle slope from the post oaks and scrub down to a sandy, willow-lined stream.

Anjo waded in eagerly and River followed her after hastily kicking off her pants. She untied the travel pack from Anjo's sweaty back and took it to shore as the filly drank from the shallow, swiftly moving stream. From the travel pack River pulled out a square of tightly woven hemp fabric and began to wipe down her filly while she pawed playfully at the water.

"That's good. Keep standing out here in this cold stream. It'll help those young tendons." River crouched, feeling carefully up and down Anjo's legs again, and breathing sighs of relief, as she—again—found no evidence of injury or strain. Anjo was sending River waves of reassurance and nuzzling her gently when her ears pricked forward and she snorted.

Ghost joined them in the stream. First, he studied the filly and Rider, then he dipped his muzzle to the water. River kept wiping down Anjo as she snuck glances at the stallion.

He'd grown a lot in the past year, and she was pleased to see that he was in good flesh. Somehow he'd made it through a long, icy winter with no visible injury. Sure, his beautiful, silver-white mane and tail were a snarled mess, but other than that he looked sound. There had been a lot of gossip about Ghost after he'd fled the Rendezvous, with the consensus of the five Herds being that the young stallion must be severely flawed. No one—not even River—expected him to live long on his own. River's mother thought that though the colt had appeared healthy and strong, he must have an internal, not yet visible flaw that would prove fatal. After all, a normal yearling *always* chose a Rider. It was only those who were sick, deformed, or broken in some way that didn't bond with their human. River hadn't wanted to believe it, but she'd been there. Ghost had leaped right over her head to escape the Choosing, so there had to be something wrong with him.

And over the past year the stallion had not once been sighted—not by Herd Magenti, nor by any visitor from the other Herds—even though there had been a concerted effort to find the colt. Everyone had assumed the poor weanling had fled to die a lonely death. It was sad, but it was also simply a part of the great, unending spiral of life.

Now here he was, looking strong and healthy and being oddly protective of Anjo and River.

She was using her fingers to comb through Anjo's tangled tail when Ghost approached the filly. He moved slowly, his neck bowed, prancing a little to show off.

As Anjo watched him, River made her way slowly to the filly's head, where she stood quietly, working her fingers through Anjo's mane and ignoring Ghost. The stallion moved closer. He nickered softly, stretching his neck long as he reached his muzzle toward the filly.

"Ah, I see. You like my Anjo." The sound of her voice had him trotting back a few steps, but River simply turned again to Anjo and continued grooming the filly while she talked to Ghost. "I understand why you like her. She's perfect, isn't she?" River smiled as the stallion's ears flicked at her, listening.

An idea came to River. "Come on, Anjo, let's finish up on the bank." Neither filly nor Rider so much as glanced behind them at Ghost, but both heard him wading through the stream after them. While Anjo dropped her head to lip the sweet, young grass on the bank, River pulled on her pants and went to the travel pack, reaching into it for Anjo's favorite treat, sweet spring carrots. Grabbing a handful, she returned to Anjo, who eagerly broke off grazing to eat a carrot.

When the stallion left the stream and walked hesitantly closer to Anjo, River slowly raised another carrot. "Here, handsome. Want one? I brought plenty. They were supposed to be for our victory celebration after our maiden ride. We didn't expect to have to share them, but we also didn't expect our ride to be so dramatic." Making sure she didn't move too quickly, River offered the carrot to the stallion.

Ghost snorted and backed several steps. River smiled and shrugged. "Don't want it? No problem. Anjo loves them. Here you go, perfect girl."

She gave the carrot to Anjo, who took it into her already carrot-filled mouth immediately and kept crunching happily.

When River turned back to the stallion, Ghost had moved several strides closer again. She lifted another carrot. "Change your mind?" River offered it to him again. This time the stallion stretched his neck out as long as it would go until he could lip the carrot from her hand, which he did quickly and then backed up several feet to eat it.

River offered another carrot, thankful she'd packed plenty. "Want more? We don't mind if you eat them. There are plenty back at Herd Magenti. You should come with us. We could do something about combing out your tangled mane and tail." She spoke conversationally to him, as if it were every day that she and Anjo came upon a rogue stallion, and while she talked Ghost moved closer. And then closer. Until finally he was standing right in front of River and Anjo. "Here you go, handsome." She gave him another carrot. This time he didn't retreat to eat it, and River instantly went back to fish more from her pack—giving one to Anjo and then offering Ghost the second. The stallion didn't hesitate, but accepted it right away—and that's when River took the opportunity to stroke his wide forehead.

He snorted and startled, but Ghost didn't move away.

"Good boy—sweet boy. Why did you run away from the Rendezvous? Why are you out here all by yourself?" River murmured to him as he munched carrots and she moved slowly beside him, running her hands along his neck—stopping at his mane, where she untangled a few clumps of silver hair. Ghost tolerated her touch, but when she bent to feel the length of his leg, he sidestepped, signaling that they weren't that good of friends.

Yet.

"Hey, I get it. I wouldn't let a stranger mess with my legs either," River told him as she moved back to his neck and continued to try to rake her fingers through his snarled mane, wishing for the wide wooden mane comb she used on Anjo. He did allow her to wipe his sweaty coat down with the grooming cloth, and River murmured appreciatively at his excellent muscle development and his smooth, golden coat. "I just don't see anything wrong with you—anything at all. Actually, you're as magnificent as I thought you'd grow to be when I knew you as a yearling."

Ghost relaxed under River's calm, confident grooming until he and Anjo were grazing side by side while River untangled the stallion's mane and tail. On a whim, River unbraided several of the strips of purple ribbons from Anjo's mane, and Ghost even tolerated her braiding the brightly colored, beautifully embroidered cloth into his silver mane.

"There, now if someone from any of the Herds sees you they'll know you belong to Magenti, and we'll hear about it—how they saw a golden stallion with Magenti colors all alone on the prairie." Saying it aloud made River feel desperately sad for him. She considered tying the spear-thrower strap around his head into a makeshift hackamore, but quickly rejected the idea. "I've barely gained your trust. I know I'll lose it if I try to force you to come with me. So, Ghost, let's hope you follow us because you want to—because you're tired of being alone. This year's Rendezvous is in seven days. I'll bet you'll find your Rider there if you give it another try. You know, not all humans get Chosen their first time either. Maybe that's what happened to you—it just wasn't your time to Choose." As she spoke, River kept stroking the stallion's golden neck, rubbing his wide head, and dressing his mane in Magenti colors.

The big colt actually closed his eyes, cocked one rear leg, and napped—though if Anjo moved too far away as she grazed, Ghost woke himself to remain by her side.

When both horses had cooled and their coats were dry and shining, River checked the sky and knew that she and Anjo needed to head back to the Herd. Still moving nonchalantly, River repacked the travel kit and strapped it to Anjo's back again. Ghost snorted at the bag, but he also remained by Anjo's side.

"Progress," River said as she stroked the stallion's neck. "Let's see how much more progress we can make. We're going back to the Herd now, and we'd really like you to join us." She gave his neck one last pat before returning to her filly.

Anjo didn't hesitate, but through the strength of their bond she understood exactly what her Rider needed, and she bowed to her front knees so that River could mount her. Using only leg pressure, River turned Anjo, and they recrossed the stream and went up the little bank to the tree line.

Before heading out onto the seemingly endless expanse of green, River studied the sky, using her newly enhanced senses, which detected no imminent danger. She glanced behind them. Ghost was just a few feet away, watching them with pricked ears and what River thought was sadness in his big, brown eyes.

"Come on, handsome," she encouraged. "Come home with us."

Then River clucked at Anjo, but after just a couple of strides, the filly stopped, snorting at a section of the prairie just outside the timber line.

River knew better than to force her horse to move. Anjo was sending her feelings of concern—not fear, but there was obviously something not right close to them. And then Ghost was there, positioning himself in front of Anjo so that she couldn't keep moving forward.

"What is going on with—" River saw them! Part of a pack scurried from a clump of scrub to a fallen log, to lie in wait there.

"Yoties!" River shivered as she named them. Yoties were canine-like creatures that were about the size of grown rabbits. Individually they were annoying, with their sharp teeth and feral attitudes, but they weren't particularly dangerous. But yoties were never alone. They traveled in huge packs of as many as twenty-five or thirty creatures. Though even that many yoties couldn't fatally wound a horse—not even a yearling—horse was their favorite prey, which is why they had evolved a way to take down a full-grown equine. "Yoti holes—everywhere." Now that she'd been alerted to their presence, River could easily see them. The prairie in front of her was riddled with holes, though they would have been impossible for River and Anjo to see as they sprinted to the presumed safety of the tree line.

A terrible shiver of fear skittered down River's spine. She stared at Ghost. "That's why you herded Anjo away from here. You saved us. Thank you—thank you so much!" As if he understood, Ghost tossed his head, watching her. "Please come with us. I promise to take care of you—to help you find your Rider." Glancing at the sky, she added, "But we have to go now. It's going to be dusk when we get back as it is—we can't wait any longer." She clucked at Anjo to move out, and the filly picked her way carefully around the yoti traps.

Once free of the deadly holes, Anjo fell into a steady, leisurely trot. The pace was slow, but wouldn't stress the filly's young bones and tendons, and it would return them to the Herd by dusk. Ghost remained by their side, trotting along with them—but only until Anjo turned toward the Herd's spring campgrounds. As they made the turn, the stallion bolted in the opposite direction. Anjo paused, and she and River watched the golden horse race away until he faded into the darkening horizon.

River felt Anjo's disappointment; it mirrored her own. She sighed and clucked at Anjo to keep moving, which the filly did easily, though she threw several looks over her shoulder at the empty prairie behind them.

"I know," River told her. "But we can't force him. Well, I'll tell Mother what happened. Maybe she'll have—"

Anjo squealed and tossed her head as she flooded River with negative feelings.

Surprised, River stroked her filly's neck. "Hey, okay, it's okay. If you don't want me to tell anyone about Ghost I won't." River felt Anjo's relief, and she decided she was in agreement with her filly. "You're right. Let's keep him to ourselves. Obviously, he doesn't want to return to the Herd—for whatever reason. So, you and I will just have to keep returning to him—with plenty of carrots. Maybe someday he'll trust us enough to follow us all the way home and be reunited with our Herd."

Anjo snorted in agreement as River smiled, imagining the look on her mother's face when she and Anjo trotted into camp with the golden stallion following them. "And people say nothing happens in a Herd without the Lead Mare and her Rider knowing. Ha! Ghost will definitely be a surprise to *everyone*, even Mother and Echo!"

As the sun set, they trotted slowly into Herd Magenti's spring campground, which sprawled around the stone monoliths that marked a convergence of ley lines. These stones weren't as huge or as numerous as those at the massive Rendezvous Site, but the cave that lay at the center of the spiral was large enough to hold all of Herd Magenti, and though the beautifully dyed purple tents with the Magenti standard flying proudly were pitched outside the enormous opening into the earth, at the first sign of dangerous weather or predators the Herd, complete with every horse, could retreat to within the safety of the cave—and with supplies stockpiled within, as well as an underground river, they could remain there, invulnerable, for many months.

River meant to go directly to the private tent she shared with Anjo that had been a gift from her mother after the Choosing, but not far into the campsite several people greeted River and Anjo, "The Mother Mare's blessings on you, Wind Rider!" and as the Herd realized they had returned from their maiden ride, a cheer of celebration rolled through the Magenti.

She tried to wave off the congratulations nonchalantly, nudging Anjo to pick up her pace so that they could disappear inside their tent, and they almost made it, but just before they reached the privacy their tent promised, River saw a group of Riders spread out around the center monolith. Led by her beautiful, strong mother, they were wind dancing. In time to a circle of drums, they were practicing the intricate series of poses that kept the Riders strong but lithe, focused on the present and able to draw on that focus in times of stress and even battle. Anjo slowed as she and her Rider appreciated the graceful flow of the wind dance, as well as the difficulty of the complex movements that had the dancers' bodies slick with sweat.

Then her mother glanced above the heads of the others to see River and Anjo—and she motioned for her sister, April, to take her place, then hurried toward the newly arrived pair.

"Get ready. She's not going to be happy about this," River muttered to Anjo, whose ears twitched back to listen.

"My daughter and sweet, sweet Anjo!" Dawn gently caressed the filly's muzzle as Anjo nickered a greeting. "I see that you have completed your maiden ride. The Mother Mare's blessings on you, Wind Rider."

"Thank you, Mother."

Dawn was walking a tight circle around Anjo, inspecting the filly with her eyes and hands, making sure she was sound.

"Well?" River asked.

Dawn raised a brow at her daughter. "You know as well as I that you wouldn't be riding Anjo into camp were she not sound."

"Then why are you studying her like you think you're going to find something wrong?"

"First, out of habit. Second, because I am Rider of the Lead Mare, and I noticed that your filly shows signs of being ridden hard and fast, though I also see you took your time cooling and grooming her." Dawn rested a hand on River's leg. "What happened out there?"

Thinking quickly, River decided it was best to stay as close to the truth as possible. "We were hunted by a Flyer."

"Mother Mare! Are you well? If Anjo was even scratched by the creature the poison could cause her problems in the future. And you—did it touch you?" Dawn redoubled her inspection until River slid from Anjo's back, hooked her arm with her mother's, and made her walk with them, stilling her.

"Mother, we are well. Both of us. We were near the cross timbers when it began hunting us. We did have to sprint for the tree line, but we made it."

"Is that why you are so late returning? You had to wait for the Flyer to leave?"

River lifted her chin with pride. "No, we killed the Flyer. We're late because I made sure Anjo stood in the stream inside the cross timbers to cool her legs, and then I let her graze while I rubbed her down."

Dawn stared at her daughter and would have stopped walking had River not pulled her along.

"You killed a Flyer."

"Well, I had the help of powerful hooves," River prevaricated. "And Anjo and I are going to start practicing spear tossing—right away."

"You killed a Flyer with a spear!"

"Mother, why do you sound so shocked? I'm not a child anymore. As of today I am officially a Wind Rider."

Dawn wiped a shaky hand across her forehead, as if trying to soothe a headache. "River, I don't doubt your capability, but I worry. It is why I wish you'd take an escort with you and stop with these solitary outings. Next year completes Echo's decade as Lead Mare. You know the Herd is looking to you and Anjo as our future."

"I know that, Mother. I've never forgotten it—not for one second since Anjo Chose me. But a year is a long time. A lot can happen between now and the Mare Test. Who knows? Maybe the Mother Mare will whisper the name of another pair to the Elders. Skye and her Scout took their maiden ride before Anjo and me, and they're a well-bonded pair. Maybe the Mother Mare will tell the Elders to choose them."

"Impossible. Skye is too self-serving and Scout, while a lovely filly, is too delicate to base the bloodlines of a herd on. No, River, it will be you and your Anjo who will win the Mare Test and be named Lead Mare and Rider by the Council, with my blessing, *unless* something happens to one of you over the next year. That is why you must remember your responsibility to the Herd and be certain you and your filly remain sound."

River stopped to face her mother. "It is my responsibility to continue to learn—to experience—to grow wise, like my mother, and I cannot do that being constantly watched and protected. A cage is still a cage, no matter how well intended the jailor might be. And that is why I insist that I will *not* ride out with an escort. I must have enough experiences so that Anjo and I trust ourselves—our judgment—our decisions. Please don't make me sneak around and play a ridiculous hiding game with you."

Dawn's wise hazel eyes studied her daughter. "So, you wish to keep your own counsel?"

River nodded. "As my mother before me."

"But your mother before you knew when to listen to the Elders and to the voice of the Great Mother Mare found within the whispers of the prairie grasses."

"Who makes decisions for you, Mother?" River asked pointedly.

Her mother was surprised by the question, but she answered without hesitation. "I make my own decisions, though I do weigh the opinions of others, especially Echo's. You know that."

"Yes, I do. What I am asking you for is no different from how you live and have lived for as long as I have memory of you." River touched her mother's arm gently. "Trust that you have raised me to think before I act, and to consider more than one side of any situation. Let me grow up, Mother. I cannot do that if you smother me."

Dawn sighed. "It seems that unless I care to become a benevolent jailor I have little choice but to concede to your will." Then she added, "But give me your word on something."

"That depends on the something."

Her mother smiled seraphically before untying one of the waistbelts that draped just above her hips. This particular strand of faceted blue stones was the delicate blue of a winter sky just before snow turns it gray. Dawn wrapped the strand around her daughter's waist and then stepped back, studying her and nodding.

"Yes, you should have it. The stones look right on you."

River stared in shock at the waistbelt—the first one of her life. Waist-belts were unique to Herd Magenti Riders. Each belt of precious stones proclaimed to the world that the Rider wearing it was also a Crystal Seer and had the ability to awaken the sleeping properties within them.

"But Mother, I'm not a Seer! I have only begun my training."

Dawn pointed to the belt that now hung low around her daughter's slim waist. "What stone is that?"

"Chalcedony," River said.

"And its major properties are?"

River answered with no hesitation. "Chalcedony's major properties are that it encourages peace and brotherhood. It is a stone that nurtures, and when awakened it repels hostilities, anger, and melancholy. It draws feelings of generosity, responsiveness, openness, and a willingness to please."

"Very good. And has it warmed to you?"

River paused, concentrating on the unaccustomed weight around her hips, realizing it was, indeed, warm and pulsing faintly in time with her heartbeat.

"It has."

"Then I would ask that you give me your word that you wear it whenever you and your Anjo ride out—openly and alone—to experience life and grow into a wise leader."

River met her mother's gaze. "I give you my word that I will proudly wear it always as a gift from my mother, whom the Great Mother Mare has blessed with the wisdom to allow her daughter the freedom—"

"To learn and grow and eventually to lead her Herd wisely," Dawn finished for her.

"One step at a time, Mother," River said as she hugged Dawn.

"Tell yourself whatever you wish, but remember that the Rider of the Lead Mare is always . . ." Dawn paused, prompting River to speak the traditional words with her.

"One step ahead of the Herd," the two women intoned together.

River closed her eyes, relaxing in the familiar embrace of her mother as "one step at time . . . one step at a time . . ." played around and around in her mind in time with the heartbeat pulse of the stones around her waist.

CHAPTER 5

D rawing down the moon awakened the night sky, and the sleepy clouds cleared a little, allowing Mari enough light to do a decent job of cleaning and dressing Nik's wounds while Sora passed her clean bandages and antiseptic salve made from boiled goldenseal root. She would've liked to have sewn closed a few of the deepest wounds—the ones on Nik's shoulder and thigh in particular—but the lack of light coupled with the rocking of their little boat had Mari quickly deciding he'd be better off with a few nasty scars than the damage she could do poking around at him in the dark.

"It looks like the bleeding has completely stopped," Sora said, peering at Nik from her boat.

"It has. For right now." Mari frowned at the last wound she was dressing. "But I don't like that he's going to have to paddle for the next several hours."

"I could trade places with Nik," Sheena said. "There's room for him to rest in our boat. Sora and Rose are doing an excellent job of paddling. Add one of the other women to take my oar and they won't have any trouble keeping pace."

"I'm better," Wilkes called from where his boat was bobbing on the other side of Mari and Nik's. "Nik could take my place and I could paddle for him."

"No, no no!" Nik said. "And stop talking about me like I'm unconscious! I feel great!" He placed his hand over Mari's. "I give you my word that if I start to fade you'll be the first to know."

"Fade *or* feel sick *or* dizzy *or* like you're bleeding again," Mari insisted.

"Yes, all of those things." He lifted her hand and kissed it. "I promise, my Moon Woman."

"Mari, we really need to get going again." Antreas sounded stressed as he paddled close by. "I've had a crawling feeling along the back of my neck, and that's never good."

"Okay, well, we're as ready as we're going to be tonight," Mari said, moving to take her place in the rear of the boat.

"Good! All right, even though the clouds are letting through a little moonlight, I still believe we should remain loosely tied together—if our Moon Women have no objections." Antreas looked from Sora to Mari.

"Hey, I'm perfectly fine following your lead on the water," Sora said.

"I'm definitely out of my element here, too," Mari said. "We'll do what you recommend, Antreas."

The Lynx man nodded, then raised his voice so that the Pack could hear him. "Most of you are new at this, so we'll remain tethered together tonight. Loosely, though, and if a boat begins to get in trouble or lag behind call out immediately. It's easier to help you *before* you capsize or drift away. Understand?"

The Pack murmured agreement.

"All right. We'll reach our first obstacle by midnight. Normally, I would wait for sunrise to pass the ruins of a bridge, but I want to put as much of the river between this place and us as possible. So, whether the clouds continue to cooperate or not, my recommendation is that we light our torches and get past the State Bridge tonight. Not far from it is a good place to beach and get some rest before we begin again with first light."

"I've not traveled on the Umbria," Nik said. "Do the ruined bridges have the same runoffs as the Willum River at Port City?"

Nik's question was reasonable, but Mari could hear the stress in his voice, and she understood. It was one of the Willum River runoffs that brought him to her—and almost killed him.

"No. The Umbria has worse things than runoffs," Antreas said. "Though not in the area we'll be traveling through tonight. The State Bridge is broken in three sections. As long as we pass between those sections we'll be fine. And we must stay together."

"Can we light the torches now?" Sora asked. "I think it would make everyone feel better if we could see better."

"Not until we're farther away from the Tribe," Antreas said. "Keep in mind that torches on the water will draw attention and make us very clear targets. I'd feel better if we waited until we were near the ruins and are forced to light them."

"Might I speak?" Dove's voice was polite and pleasing.

"Yes, of course," Mari said. "We believe every member of our Pack should be able to speak his or her mind."

Even in the dim light, Mari could see that Dove's expression was delighted. "That freedom is something I will enjoy becoming accustomed to. What I wanted to say is that I must agree very strongly with Antreas. Do nothing to draw the God's attention to us. His moods are capricious and fluctuate from benevolent to cruel rapidly. I believe He will post sentries all around the Tribe's territory, and if they catch any sight of lights from the river they will report it to Death. And the one thing I know beyond all else about Him is that He always wants more, more, more."

"Which means his latest conquest won't satisfy him," Nik said grimly.

"Not for long," said Dove.

Mari found it difficult to speak. She kept replaying over and over in her mind the huge figure silhouetted on the ridge and how His eyes seemed to burn her. She was sure that His raised spear and His bellow had something to do with her.

"No torches," Sora said.

"Not until we must light them, and by that time we'll be well away from danger," Nik agreed.

"Just this particular danger," Antreas reminded them. "There are many others, which is why we will not always be able to travel at night. Nor will we always be able to use our torches, even when we are forced to travel in darkness. So, get used to staying close—*always* within sight of others."

"Pack, I want to be clear on this." Mari found her voice and stood, balancing cautiously. "It is not a cliché, but rather a fact that we are as strong as our weakest member. We will survive this journey, but only if we work together and remain together. Got it?"

"Yes, Moon Woman!" came the answer from her Pack.

"I'm proud of you. All of you." Mari's gaze swept the moonlit group that bobbed around her in their collection of little boats. "What you have already accomplished is amazing. And now we're going to keep going—keep moving ahead one day at a time until we find our new home and make our new world. Antreas, lead and your Packmates will follow!" Everyone cheered, and Antreas looked a lot less grumpy as he struck out at the head of what became a long, loose line of boats.

It didn't take long for Mari to fall into a rhythm with Nik. They remained at the rear of the line of boats, but that didn't bother Mari at all. Their pace was slow but steady, and once Mari felt more secure with her ability to paddle, she was able to look around them.

Her first shock came from how intimidating the river was. Antreas had guided them to the center of the expanse of water. He'd explained days earlier that they would have to travel upstream until they came to Lost Lake, and so Mari wasn't surprised to have to stroke against a current. She just never imagined the river would be so wide. Even with the silver light of the moon reflecting from the water, both banks were only indistinct smudges against the night.

She'd never been out on the water at night. Actually, Mari had never been in a boat at all, and she suddenly felt too far removed from the safety of the earth and the familiarity of her burrow, which had her thoughts turning to her mama.

If only Mama had lived to join us on our journey! She would be so excited—and so proud of us all.

Then with a little shock of surprise, Mari realized that her words to the Pack about how proud she was of them and how they would survive together could have—*would have*—been spoken by Leda, and she felt a wash of bittersweet happiness.

Thank you, Mama. She prayed silently. *Thank you for raising me to be ready to take on the responsibility of leadership—even when I thought it impossible that I'd ever become a Moon Woman.*

From the ballast on her right, Rigel whined, clearly feeling her inner turmoil. She shook herself mentally.

"Hey, sweet boy, all is well. It's just a lot of water."

"Yeah," Nik grumbled. "A lot."

She poked his back gently with her paddle. "Hey, I'll bet you've been out on the river many times."

"True, but not this one. Though it really doesn't matter. I hate *all* rivers."

"Hate? That's a pretty strong emotion," Mari teased.

"Strong, but honest. Actually, I hate *any* body of water that's so deep and dark I can't see through to the bottom."

"Would you rather face the river or the Skin Stealers?" Davis, who was in the boat directly in line in front of them, called over his shoulder to Nik.

"I'd rather face neither," said Nik.

Davis chuckled. "Well, look at it this way—the river, no matter how much you hate it, is getting us away from the Skin Stealers."

"And Thaddeus," Mari added.

"That's true," Nik agreed. "And I'll take the river over Thaddeus any day."

"Ah, see! A bright spot," said Davis.

"It'll be better in the daylight," said Mari.

"Yeah, so we can *see* what's going to kill us," Nik muttered.

"Hey, Jaxom, how's Fortina doing?" Mari changed the subject.

"She is beyond wonderful!" Jaxom called back.

Mari could see that the pup had finally moved off her new Companion's lap so that he could paddle more easily, but she was still pressed against him.

"I am glad she Chose you," Nik surprised Mari by saying. "I saw how Maeve was treating her. I know Maeve was infected by the sickness, but that is no excuse. Wilkes and Claudia were also infected, and they didn't turn on their Companions. Tribal law has severe penalties for anyone who abuses a canine. It shows how low the Tribe has fallen that Maeve felt free to strike and abuse that pup where everyone could see."

"It's Thaddeus," said Davis. "His hatred is contagious, though I don't understand why anyone would choose hate over happiness."

"He believes power will bring him happiness," Mari said. "And for whatever reason, enough of the Tribe believe it, too, so he now has supporters willingly following his hateful lead."

"Maeve hurt her." Jaxom's sad voice drifted with the current back to Mari. "Not so bad physically, although I know she beat my Fortina." He had to pause and clear the emotion from his throat before continuing. "It is the mental pain she caused this precious girl that hurt her the worst. Fortina couldn't understand what she was doing wrong—why her Companion hated her."

"Maeve let anger control her after Father's death," Nik said. "She wanted someone to blame. Thaddeus gave her that."

"She should've blamed Thaddeus!" Mari said, stroking the water harder to relieve her frustration. "It was his fault."

"Anger does strange things to people," Nik said.

"There has to be more to it than that," Mari said. "I was so, so angry when I walked into the Tribe tonight. Angrier than I've ever been in my life, but I wasn't filled with hate. I'm sorry we had to leave Ralina and the others who seem so decent back there with Thaddeus."

"I know about anger." Jaxom's voice was hesitant at first, but as he spoke his confidence grew, and his words reflected that. "All Earth Walker men know about anger. I believe it takes more than anger to turn someone into the kind of hate-filled monster you describe Thaddeus and his followers as. It takes self-loathing *and* self-deceit. I tried to fight the Skin Stealer disease—the anger and the hatred that festered within me with the sickness. But not all of us did. Remember Joshua?"

"I do," Mari said. It was Joshua, along with Brandon and Jaxom, who, under the influence of the Skin Stealer disease, attacked Sora not long ago. "Joshua was one of the two infected Earth Walkers Nik killed protecting Sora," she explained to Davis and Nik.

"Yes, well, we were all infected together. Brandon seemed to try to fight the disease like me, but Joshua gave in to it quickly. It was like he found pleasure in his growing anger. He tracked Sora. I say this not to take away my personal responsibility. I will spend the rest of my life trying to atone for what I almost did to Sora. But remember the kind of man Joshua was *before* he was infected?"

"I didn't know him well," said Mari. "But I do remember one thing about him, because Mama admonished him for it—he cheated at net ball."

"Yes, so much that no one wanted him on their team," said Jaxom.

"Net ball?" Nik asked. "What's that?"

"A game the Clan loves to play," said Jaxom. "I can show you the next time we make land and have some free time."

"I'd like that," Nik said.

The young Earth Walker's words piqued the interest of the healer within Mari. "So, Jaxom, what you're saying is how the Skin Stealer disease affects people might be tied to the ethics of each person. I'll have to make note of that in my journal."

"It's an interesting theory," said Davis.

"And, hopefully, one we won't need to test because we're leaving the poisoned city behind," said Nik.

"Another good thing about this river, right, Nik?" teased Davis.

Nik snorted, and Mari poked him gently with her paddle again. Nik playfully batted it away, which she was glad to see. He wouldn't be waving that arm around after her paddle if his wound had broken open and was bleeding again.

They settled back into silent paddling as Mari considered what Jaxom had said. It did make sense. Wilkes and Claudia had been infected—just like Thaddeus. But they had remained themselves—sick and dying versions of themselves, but they hadn't succumbed to hatred and anger like Thaddeus. Sora, too, had been infected, and though her anger level increased, they had been able to reason with her—she'd still been their Sora.

"Nik, you knew the Hunters and Warriors who were shooting arrows at you, right?" Mari asked.

"Yeah, of course. I grew up with them. And there was only one Warrior shooting at me—Maxim. The rest were Hunters."

"What was Maxim like before he was infected?"

Nik paused in his paddling as he considered. "He was arrogant. He used to make fun of the Terriers. He called them miniature dogs, not even canines, and encouraged his Shepherd to bully them. Hey, Jaxom may have a point. Though I liked Maeve. It was after Father died that she changed."

"Maybe not. I didn't like her," Mari admitted. "Sorry, Nik, but the night I met her and your father she was cold—distant—a lot different than how Sol greeted me."

"It does give Jaxom's theory more weight," said Nik.

"Hello, the boats!" Antreas's call interrupted their conversation.

Mari squinted, trying to make out which blob belonged to the Lynx Companion's boat.

"We're bringing up the rear, but we're all together!" Nik shouted back.

"Circle up!" Antreas said.

It only took a few minutes for all the boats to gather in a bobbing, lopsided circle. Antreas and Danita paddled their little canoe into the middle. Mari noted with pleasure that Danita seemed to already be an expert on the water as she mirrored Antreas's strokes perfectly.

"Okay, can all of you see the metal spikes sticking out of the water there?" Antreas pointed upriver.

There were still clouds in the sky, but they were more like ghosts flitting past the moon, allowing silver light to shine through. As the gentle wind parted their gauzy shrouds Mari could see two distinct hulks jutting from the river not far from either bank. Almost exactly in the center of the wide waterway another ruin protruded, though it appeared that section of the bridge had come to rest on its side, so that a wall of rust formed an ominous, watery barricade.

The Pack made nervous sounds, letting Antreas know they could, indeed, see the obstacles they faced.

"Okay, keep your wits about you. This particular ruin looks a lot worse than it truly is. First, let's light our torches."

As the Pack began producing thick, spearlike lengths of wood, Davis explained to Mari and Nik, "Look along the inside of your boat. Yours will be there."

Sure enough, Nik pulled out their torch from where it had hugged the inside bottom of their boat. Mari noted that one end of it had been wrapped in cloth that stunk like old rabbit fat. The other end was wrapped in hemp rope.

"Sora, I know you have one of the tinderboxes," Antreas said.

"I do!"

"Begin passing it from boat to boat. Each of you light your torch and then use the rope to affix it to the stern."

"Stern?" Mari asked.

"That's the rear part of your boat, Mari," Danita said.

"Exactly. Good job remembering, Danita," said Antreas.

Antreas's Lynx Companion, Bast, made the strange coughing sound that meant she was pleased, which had Mari grinning. *That Lynx has definitely chosen Danita as Antreas's mate!* And from the grin on the young Earth Walker's face, Mari deduced that that choice might be growing on Danita.

Mari was proud to see that even in the middle of the dark, treacherous river, her Pack worked together well. In no time each boat was a bobbing halo of light.

"Now, do exactly as I say," explained Antreas. "First, loose the tethers. We can be tied together through ruins, but try to keep no more than about two boat lengths between each of you. I'll help you by calling out your strokes. Those who are not paddling, help your boatmates by keeping time with me. We'll go forward single file. We are going to pass to the right of center. The current will get choppy around the ruins. Just remember, no matter what happens *do not stop paddling.* As long as you're moving forward it'll be a lot more difficult for your boat to be swamped and capsize. Questions?"

"What happens if someone does get into trouble?" asked young Spencer, sounding terrified.

"The most important thing is not to panic. All of you can swim—remember that. And I'll be watching. You'll make it through if you're steady and careful and keep your wits about you."

"Okay. I can do that," said Spencer bravely.

"We're right here with you," said Mason. He, along with the recovering Claudia and Wilkes, was in her boat.

"That's right. Wilkes and I are going to paddle as we go through the ruins. We'll be fine," said Claudia.

"I grew up on the river," added Wilkes. "We can get through this. It is scary, especially because it's dark, but we're in this together, and we'll make it out together."

"Claudia brings up an excellent idea," said Antreas. "Everyone who is able should be paddling through the ruins. Just listen to my cadence and keep your strokes together. Understand?"

There was a chorus of yesses from the Pack.

"What do we do when we're through?" Sora asked.

"Keep paddling. I'll tell you when we can stop. We have to get well upstream of the bridge to be past the sucking current. So, pay attention, and remember we're not through until we're *all* through."

"Understood!" said Sora as the Pack nodded nervously.

"Companions, relay to your canines that they need to hunker down and hold on. Strapping in your Shepherds is probably a good idea. Davis and Rose, be sure your Terriers are secure under your seats," said Antreas. "I'll give you a few minutes to get ready." He raised his brow at Bast. "You should get down from there and attach those claws of yours to the belly of this canoe."

The big feline huffed at him, but she did jump lithely from her figurehead perch to crouch close to Danita.

Mari and Nik joined the other Companions as they worked quickly to rig hemp ropes around the torsos of the big Shepherds and tie them to their ballasts.

"Companions, keep your knives handy," Nik said. "If a canine gets in too much trouble you may need to cut the rope so he or she can swim freely."

Mari's fear was a sick feeling in her stomach, but she repressed it, not wanting Rigel to pick up on her nerves.

"Ready, sweet boy?" she asked her Shepherd.

He barked twice, wagging his tail enthusiastically—and his enthusiasm was mirrored by the other Shepherds.

"They don't seem afraid," Mari said to Nik.

"Shepherds are strong swimmers," said Nik. "A lot stronger than we are. If they're worried or frightened, it's only for us. Or the Terriers."

"Wait, they can't swim?" asked Mari.

"They can," Davis told her as he tucked Cammy under his seat. "Just not very well and not for a very long time."

"How about young Shepherds?" asked Jaxom, sounding as sick as Mari was trying not to feel.

"Very young Shepherds, or Terriers, can swim, but not well. Your Fortina isn't that young anymore. She's a big, strong girl. Don't worry, Jaxom. She'll be fine."

Davis petted Fortina. They didn't have a ballast on their canoe, but she was lying under Jaxom's seat, her head poking up to give Davis a doggy grin.

"All ready?" Antreas asked.

Shouts of *"Ready!"* rang across the water.

"All right. Here we go! Stroke! Stroke! Stroke! Stroke!"

The Pack took up the cadence Antreas called until the night pulsed with their tempo.

Antreas and Danita led. The next boat behind them was one of the biggest, carrying O'Bryan with Jenna, Sarah, Lydia, Lily, and Dove. Mari kept glancing forward. She could see that everyone except the eyeless Dove was paddling, even Lydia. Mari made a mental note to check the burn wounds on her back when they stopped for the night. And with her next glance Mari noticed that even though Dove wasn't paddling, she was calling cadence with Antreas in a strong, clear voice.

Mari watched the current grab the boats, causing them to dip crazily and even spin a little, but as soon as they were past the ruins the boats shot forward, righting themselves quickly.

Mari's nerves had quieted considerably by the time there were only three boats left to cross the obstacle. They'd paddled close to the ruined bridge, where they paused, catching their breaths and readying themselves.

"All right, we're next," Sora said, glancing nervously back at Mari.

"You can do it," Mari called to her. "Just keep those puppies safe."

"Chloe isn't going anywhere." Sora patted the lump in the pouchlike carrier strapped to her chest.

"I have the rest of the pups," said Rose, who had positioned herself sitting on the hull with her Companion, the mama Terrier, Fala, crouched there with her and the remaining four pups snuggled against them.

"We've got this," Sheena said. "Just keep cadence with me."

"It's going to be okay," said Davis. He and Jaxom were directly behind Sora and Sheena's boat.

"Ready, go! Stroke! Stroke! Stroke!" shouted Sheena, and they began to row in time with the cadence she called.

Davis and Jaxom waited, giving them time to get a couple boat lengths ahead, then Davis picked up Sheena's cadence, and off they went.

"Our turn," Nik said, glancing over his shoulder at Mari.

"I'm ready." She really wasn't, but she wiped her sweaty hands on her pants, gripped the paddle, and was ready when Nik shouted "Go!"

Only he didn't shout "Go." Instead they heard a terrified scream.

It was the boat Sheena and Sora were in. As they approached the hulking ruin of the bridge, a log suddenly crossed their path. Spewed from the swirling current, it rammed into their boat, causing it to veer sideways and pitch dangerously.

"Don't stop!" Antreas's shout merged with Rose's second scream, and then Mari saw Rose *try to stand*!

The young Companion was gripping the side of the boat as it lurched, almost capsizing. She pointed behind her into the dark, frothy waters, screaming, "A puppy! A puppy fell out!" Then Rose had to grab Fala as the mama Terrier tried to jump overboard to save her pup. "Help her!" Rose shrieked. "Save her!"

"Oh, Great Goddess, no!" Mari gasped as she watched the pup's little head go under the waves and then reappear as she bravely tried to stay afloat.

"Keep paddling, Mari," Nik said. "We might be able to get close enough to her to throw in a line and snag her."

"I've got her!" Jaxom shouted, and before anyone could tell him no, he dove out of his boat, heading for the struggling pup.

"I have to keep paddling!" Davis shouted over the hysterical whines and pitiful, panicked barks that erupted from Fortina as she stood, stress-panting and looking like she was going to jump in after her Companion.

"Stop her, Mari!" Nik shouted. "Don't let Fortina go after him."

Mari concentrated quickly, sending soothing thoughts to Fortina and an image of Jaxom, safely back in the boat. She could feel the raw panic coming from the young Shepherd, but the pup didn't leap into the frothing water.

"I can't stop!" Davis yelled as his boat hit the currents by the ruins. "Gotta keep stroking!"

"I got her!" Jaxom shouted.

"This way, Jaxom!" Mari called. "Swim to us!"

Jaxom changed direction, heading toward them. Thankfully, the currents near the ruins hadn't caught them yet, and Jaxom was a strong swimmer. He reached them, and would've been swept past had Mari not stuck her paddle out for him.

"Grab on!"

Jaxom did so, and Mari pulled, helping him get close to the boat.

"Here, take her," Jaxom gasped while he held on to the paddle with one hand and almost threw the waterlogged pup into the boat, where she huddled at Mari's feet, whining, coughing, and shivering.

"Got her!" Mari said. "Your turn."

"No. I'll capsize you. Give me the rope."

"But, Jaxom, you have to—"

"He's right," Nik interrupted. "There's too much current here and our canoe's too small. He'll pull us over if he tries to get in. Here, Jaxom." Nik tossed the rope to him. "Tie this around your chest under your arms. We'll pull you through. Just keep your legs as close to the surface as possible—*not* beneath the boat. There's always wreckage waiting to snag you near these ruins."

"Got it," Jaxom yelled, treading water as he tied the rope around himself. Then, hand over hand, he made his way along the side of the canoe to position himself just off the stern. There he held on, kicking to remain as close to the surface as possible.

"The current has us. We have to go now. Stroke, Mari! Stroke!" Nik shouted.

Mari shut out everything except the cadence Nik and the rest of the Pack were calling. She gripped her paddle and used all of her strength to fight the water, battling the sucking current. She wanted to turn around and be sure Jaxom was still there—wanted to be sure they weren't dragging him under the water and drowning him—but if she did that, if she hesitated, she and Nik could capsize and join Jaxom in the seething blackness.

And then it was suddenly easier! Mari was only fighting against the usual current, and the hulking metal giant was behind them.

Mari looked to Rigel's ballast first. Her pup was there—wet, but safe. His father, Laru, looked even more waterlogged, but was also still safely strapped to his ballast.

"Jaxom?" Mari called, trying to look over her shoulder and still keep stroking.

There was a pause, and Mari saw nothing, and then Jaxom's head broke the surface as he coughed and gagged.

"Here!" he gasped. "Still here!"

"Hang on—we'll get you to the others," Nik said.

Mari's shoulders burned and the palms of her hands, wet from sweat and river water, had begun to ache in time with her heartbeat, but she kept her head down and continued to drive the little boat forward in time with Nik.

"Okay, okay, hold," Nik finally said.

Struggling for breath, Mari put her paddle down and turned. Jaxom was there, holding tightly to the rope that kept him tethered to their boat.

"Did he get her? Is she alive?" Rose was calling across the water as they joined the Pack.

"She's fine," Mari said. "Jaxom saved her. I have her right here."

"Oh, thank you! Thank you, Jaxom!" Rose said, and then she collapsed, holding Fala close as she sobbed tears of relief.

"Is Jaxom alive? Did he make it through?" Antreas asked as he paddled expertly to Mari and Nik.

"We got him. I think he's half drowned, but he's definitely alive," said Nik.

"I'm alive!" Jaxom said, and then a wave crashed over his head, causing him to gag and cough.

"I'm coming!" Davis called, maneuvering his canoe to Nik and Mari.

Antreas, too, came up beside them. "Jaxom, wait until Davis is leaning to counterbalance you, and then as smoothly as possible, lift yourself up and into the canoe."

Jaxom untied the rope from his waist and swam wearily to Davis.

"Ready!" Davis shouted, leaning away from Jaxom.

With what was obviously the last of his strength, Jaxom kicked hard, lifting himself up as he grabbed onto the side of the canoe and pulled himself aboard, where he landed in a soggy puddle. Fortina instantly began licking him as she whined pitifully while wagging the entire rear half of her body.

"That was a damn close call," Antreas said.

"Lucky. Jaxom is very lucky," said Nik.

"Not lucky," Dove's serene voice rang out. "Goddess blessed."

Mari felt a jolt of surprise as she studied Dove's serene expression. The torch on the stern of her boat cast a soft light over the eyeless girl, causing her—for just an instant—to appear as if she were glowing.

Perhaps . . . Mari thought. *Perhaps this Dove can see.*

CHAPTER 6

They transferred the waterlogged pup to Rose's boat, where Fala set to work licking and comforting her. Then the Pack bent to the task of stroking up current.

Mari missed the torches. Antreas had insisted that they extinguish them, saying that they were still too close to the cities and the turmoil they'd left not far enough behind. Mari wanted to overrule him, but she knew he was right. And she couldn't get the image of the massive God of Death from her mind. She was certain He'd seen her, and if there was any chance whatsoever that He might follow her . . . Mari's skin shivered with fear.

Better to travel in darkness for a couple more hours than to draw the attention of Death.

But enough was enough. Mari had wrapped her hands in strips of cloth she'd torn from her already tattered shirt, and still they were broken and bleeding. She had just decided to call out to Antreas and tell him that they *must* stop—if her hands were raw then others' would be, too—when from the lead position in the line of boats a torch flared, illuminating a small, brush-covered island directly in front of them. It appeared to erupt from the center of the river. After hours of fighting the current, Mari thought it was the most beautiful piece of land she'd ever seen.

Antreas raised his hand. "Pack! We're in luck! This is Spirit Island, named thus because it tends to disappear—especially in spring. I was hoping it was late enough in the season for it to be above water. So, I want you to untether yourselves and then, one at a time, stroke fast toward the island and ground yourselves. The person in the bow should get out first and help guide his or her boat in. The river is fairly shallow near the island. See those rocks and logs and such?" Antreas pointed at the island's gentle, sandy bank, which was peppered with rocks and river debris. "That's what you'll tie up with. Okay, watch me and then, one at a time, follow me in. You shouldn't have any problems. The current is mild here."

One by one, the weary Pack grounded their boats, with a little accidental dunking taking place, but no one being swept away.

Mari and Nik's boat was last, and it was with enormous relief that Mari clambered from the little watercraft to the sandy island. She wanted to curl up between Rigel and Laru and collapse into much-needed sleep. Instead she dragged herself to her feet, and while Rigel and Laru rolled in the sand, she looked around for Antreas. But before she could find him, or call out for him, there was a flurry of activity a little way down the shore as Fala rushed up to Jaxom, jumping up on him and barking with excitement.

"This should be good. Fala's thanking Jaxom," Nik said, taking Mari's hand as they approached the bemused-looking young man.

"Hey, hi, Fala. Good to see you, too."

"She's saying thank you," Rose said, hurrying up to them. She was carrying the little girl pup Jaxom had saved wrapped close to her skin, in a makeshift carrier a lot like the more permanent one Sora had rigged to carry her Chloe.

"Oh!" Jaxom squatted down closer to Fala's level. "You are welcome, little mother."

The Terrier articulated a long series of barks and whines and excited huffs, ending by jumping up on Jaxom and covering his face in loving licks. All the while Fortina was trotting around them, barking and wagging joyfully, as if to say, *Look at my wonderful, brave Companion!*

Laughing and wiping dog kisses from his face, Jaxom stood, only to have Rose hurl herself into his arms.

"Thank you so much. Fala, this little pup, and I owe you a life debt." And she kissed him gently on each cheek.

Jaxom's face blazed with color. "You don't owe me anything! I'm happy I was there and was able to catch her. Now that I have a Companion of my own, I am beginning to understand just how important these canines are to us. I know any other Companion would have tried to save Fortina, so it's the least I could do."

"You are right." Sora stepped up to Jaxom. "It does take being Chosen by a canine to understand the love and the bond that makes them such an important part of our lives, but that doesn't make what you did any less heroic. Thank you Jaxom."

Mari watched Jaxom's eyes fill with emotion, and understood it was the first time since Leda's death that Sora had spoken with empathy to him. She hoped it was a beginning for the young Clansman to find true forgiveness for himself.

The Lynx man moved as soundlessly as his big feline, and he seemed to materialize from the center of the island.

"Good job saving the pup," Antreas said as he joined them. "But you took a major risk. You *and* the pup could have drowned. Rose, let's be sure those babies are strapped in better tomorrow."

"I already have an idea for that. I'll work on weaving it tonight," she said.

"Is all the Pack on land?" Mari asked.

"Yes, I've counted everyone. No one was lost. So far—so good."

"It would do wonders for morale if we could light a fire, but only if you think we'll be safe," Mari said.

"I agree. That's why I was so relieved to see Spirit Island above water. We've been traveling steadily for almost five hours. It'll be dawn in another five. Let's build a fire on the beach, set lookouts, and rest until dawn."

Mari felt giddy with relief. "That sounds wonderful! Pack!" she shouted down the beach so everyone would hear. "Gather firewood! Light a blaze! We rest for the night here."

The shout that sounded from her Pack had Mari grinning.

"That's great news," Nik said. "I'll help unload the supplies we need for tonight. I'm starving! Should I also have O'Bryan and Davis drop a few lines in the river to see what we can catch?"

"I don't know much about river fishing, but I do know we can dig up some wapato roots and bury them in the coals."

"Wouldn't you rather have my stew and freshly baked bread?" Sora said.

"That makes me want to kiss you," teased Nik.

"Oh, I don't require kisses," Sora said, grinning. "Just flattery and devotion."

"If you can produce one of your stews *and* your bread you'll have both from me, you gracious, magickal Moon Woman." Mari bowed to Sora with a flourish that had the two of them giggling.

"It wasn't that difficult. I baked the extra bread yesterday and packed the makings of stew in the big cauldron from the Birthing Burrow. All I need do is have someone unpack the cauldron and hang it over the fire while I add water. I do hope I wrapped the bread well enough that it stayed dry."

"Show me where those things are packed and I'll bring them here," said Nik. "O'Bryan!" he shouted.

"Cuz?"

"Get that hearthfire made so that Sora's stew can simmer."

"I'm on it!" O'Bryan said.

Nik kissed Mari quickly before starting to move toward the beached line of boats with Sora. Mari called after them, "Hey, we'll need to brew some healing tea for Claudia and Wilkes."

"Yes, of course. I'll unpack the baskets with the herbs as well," Sora said.

"Moon Woman?"

Mari turned to see the young Earth Walker named Spencer approaching her shyly. "Yes, Spencer?"

"I brought as much of the mead as space would allow. Do you think it appropriate to open one of the small barrels tonight?"

"Yes! That's a great idea—but only a small barrel, okay?"

Spencer's smile was impish. "Of course, Moon Woman!" And she rushed off.

"Getting drunk tonight would be a bad idea," said Antreas.

"You're right, but a small barrel only has enough mead in it for everyone to have about one mug each. And it'll help those of us who have almost never slept outside our burrows relax and maybe actually *sleep*," Mari explained.

"Ah, right you are. I need to remember how wise my Moon Woman is," said Antreas, bowing his head respectfully to her.

"Make that Moon *Women* and you'd be right," corrected Mari. "But we're in this together, and we'll only make it by working as a team, so if you have something to say about one of our decisions don't hesitate to speak up. I don't want to make the same mistakes others before me have made."

"By not listening?" Antreas asked.

"Yes, and also by thinking that Sora and I have the only opinions that count."

Davis and Cammy approached them. Davis was carrying a full armload of dry driftwood, and Cammy proudly dragged a log that was almost bigger than the tenacious little Terrier, which had Mari laughing.

"Good job, Cammyman!" The Terrier huffed happily, but didn't let go of his log.

"Mari, maybe you should remind the Earth Walkers to unpack the new travel cloaks they wove. There aren't any trees on this island for us to hammock ourselves into with them tonight, but they're excellent to use as barriers against the ground, too," said Davis.

"Good idea, Davis," Mari said. "Go ahead and be sure the Pack understands how to use their cloaks and I'll check on Wilkes and Claudia."

"Mari, it would be a good idea for everyone to form a circle around the campfire," Antreas said.

"Okay, that sounds good," Mari agreed. "Can you let the Pack know, Davis?"

"Of course! Cammy and I will take care of it. Come on, Cammyman!" Davis headed down the shoreline toward the flat, sandy area where several of the women, along with Mason and Jaxom, were beginning to build a large fire.

"Mari! I need to hug you so I know you're real" Danita hurried up to Mari, with Bast trotting beside her. She put her arms around her Moon Woman, holding Mari close and whispering, "I was so afraid the Tribe captured you and Nik."

"Well, the Tribe, or rather Thaddeus, has a tendency to underestimate Nik *and* me. Tonight I was grateful for that," Mari said. "You seem to be getting good at maneuvering your boat. I may need you to give me lessons. Nik hates the river and I haven't made my mind up about it yet, but I'm leaning toward a respectful dislike."

"No problem, Mari! I had a good teacher." Danita smiled quickly at Antreas. "I'll try to be as good a teacher for you."

"Thank you." Mari snuck a look at Antreas. He was watching Danita with a sweet and completely besotted expression. Mari cleared her throat. "Um, Danita, would you like to help me check on Wilkes and Claudia?"

"Oh, yes! But before that, what would you like to do about Dove and Lily?" Danita asked.

"Lily?"

"Dove's friend, who is also obviously her servant, though I don't think she wants us to know that," Danita said, lowering her voice. "I helped them out of their boat. They're over by where the fire's being built."

Mari chewed her lower lip, thinking. "Well, Sora has basically welcomed them into the Pack, right?"

"Yes, but only after Dove swore to only tell her, or you, the truth," Antreas said.

"Then they're part of the Pack," Mari said firmly. "And that's a good thing. We can learn a lot from them. Let's be sure they're comfortable. This must be difficult, especially for sightless Dove. As soon as I'm able I'll talk with them and see what kind of skills they have."

"I'm going to be sure all the boats are properly moored, and then we should set the watch schedule. Would you like to assign watch duties or ask for volunteers?" Antreas asked.

"Ask. And let no one stand watch alone. They should at least be in pairs. The more eyes watching, the better," Mari decided.

"And it's harder to accidentally fall asleep if you have someone to talk to," said Danita. She scratched Bast's chin, which had the big feline purring loudly. "I'll take first watch with Bast."

"Would you mind if I watched with the two of you?" Antreas asked.

Danita's gaze met his. She didn't smile, but her expression gentled. "No, I wouldn't mind. But you'll have to ask your Lynx. You know she thinks for herself."

Antreas snorted. "Boy, do I."

Bast coughed at her Companion, but Mari thought she saw a mischievous glint in the Lynx's yellow eyes.

"Come on, Mari. I'll take you to Claudia and Wilkes. And it looks like Sora and Nik are back with a medicine basket and the food!"

Mari walked through the busy campsite with Danita, nodding at the people who called greetings to her.

"There are salves and bandages in that basket." Sora pointed to one of the tightly woven supply baskets. "As soon as the cauldron with the stew is set, I'll start brewing tea for Wilkes and Claudia."

Mari saw Nik grimace as he dragged the huge cauldron toward the fire, which was already burning cheerily.

"O'Bryan?" Mari called, and Nik's cousin dropped another load of firewood into the blaze.

"How can I help, Mari?"

"You can be sure your cousin doesn't rip open his wounds from doing too much," she said.

"Not an easy job, but I'll do my best!" O'Bryan said. He winked at

Mari and jogged over to Nik, taking the opposite side of the cauldron to help him drag it to the fire and lift it up to hang from the poles he'd already erected.

"Brew enough tea for Nik, too," Mari told Sora.

"With the juice of the poppy?" Sora asked, waggling her eyebrows.

"Definitely," said Mari before picking up the supply basket and following Danita past the fire to the far side of a circle that was forming around it where Claudia and Wilkes were resting quietly on their travel cloaks, their Shepherds curled up contentedly beside them. "How are you two feeling?" she asked as she knelt beside Claudia and began checking her pulse and feeling the warmth of her skin.

"So much better!" Claudia said, stilling Mari's hand by taking it in hers. "Thank you, Moon Woman. You saved our lives."

"Yes, Moon Woman." Wilkes bowed deeply to her. "You will always have my gratitude as well."

"I only ask for your loyalty, if you plan to stay with our Pack," Mari said.

"We do!" Claudia said. "We'd decided to leave the Tribe even before the Skin Stealers attacked."

Wilkes's shoulders bowed in defeat. "I wish I could have understood what was happening. Maybe then I could've stopped the Tribe from being taken in by Thaddeus's nonsense."

"It wasn't nonsense," Mari said as she continued to examine them. "It was hatred and disease. It seems the two are somehow working together to create a new climate of violence and a new type of Tribe—one that leaves no room for compassion. Irrational hatred is as difficult to defeat as the belief that one group of people is superior to another simply because of skin color, or where they prefer to live, and who they prefer to worship. You did what you could—you escaped. You can't be responsible for the delusions of an entire people."

Wilkes sighed deeply and lifted his arm so that Mari could begin replacing the old bandages, soggy from river water, with salve and new wrappings. "There are still good people in the Tribe. I have to believe that."

"You can believe it. I know it's true. Ralina is one of them. I wish she had accepted my invitation to join us, but she said that she must stay with the Tribe," Mari said.

"That's a mistake," Danita said as she handed Mari a fresh dressing.

"What do you mean?" Wilkes asked. "She is our Storyteller, revered by the Tribe for years. I understand why she stayed. She wants to try to record what is happening, as well as to try to uplift the remaining good people."

"I understand that, but I still say it's a mistake," Danita continued. "Good people don't make haters like Thaddeus better. They get pulled down to the level of the haters, or they get destroyed by them. Sometimes the only answer, especially when a group has been as tainted by hatred as the Tribe, is to leave hate to destroy itself—to segregate it from decent people. Hate is a lot like a disease. When it can't be cured it needs to be isolated."

"I'm afraid I agree with Danita," Claudia said.

"I was there," Mari said. "I witnessed how Thaddeus's delusions have been ingested by the Tribe along with the Skin Stealers' poisoned meat. There's no curing Thaddeus and his ilk. I tried. I asked if they wanted to be healed. Wilkes, they *like* being filled with hate. They *enjoy* making others feel less so that they can feel more. I agree with Danita, too. They should be isolated and ignored so they don't contaminate anyone else."

"I do feel for Ralina, though. She's a good person," said Claudia.

"Maybe she'll find a way to escape. Does she know where we're going?" Danita asked.

"No. Nik and I only told the Tribe that we've started a new group called a Pack and that we were leaving to find a new place to live," Mari said. "But I do hope Ralina and the others of the Tribe who are still kind and caring can escape." She met Wilkes's sad gaze. "If Ralina and those like her find us, we will welcome them to our Pack." Mari glanced over her shoulder to see that Sora was adding a smaller pot to the fire below the cauldron. "Your tea will be ready soon. Both of you are doing well, but you still need to rest. Drink the tea. Eat a large bowl of stew, and then sleep. Tomorrow Antreas and I will reorder the boats before casting off."

"I'm willing to do my part," said Wilkes.

"Me, too," said Claudia. The two Shepherds beside them wagged in agreement.

"We know that," Mari said, touching Claudia's shoulder reassuringly. "But when someone in our Pack is injured, the rest of us help them—that's one thing that makes us stronger together." Mari paused, suddenly remembering. "There is something you can do now, though."

"Name it!" Wilkes said.

"Well, you know Jaxom was Chosen by Fortina to be her Companion."

"Of course! As I said to Nik earlier, I have heard of circumstances where a canine will reject his or her Companion, though it is rare and often the canine wastes away, refusing to eat or to Choose another Companion. Did you want me to talk with Nik about it?"

"Well, yes. You could later, and I'd be interested to hear those stories, too. But I wanted to ask something else of you. When a pup Chooses, doesn't the whole Tribe rejoice?"

Wilkes blinked in understanding. "We do, indeed. And our new Shepherd Companion should know that rejoicing. Mari, would you help me to my feet?"

"Of course!"

Mari helped Wilkes to stand as Danita gave Claudia a hand. Then, moving slowly and carefully, the four of them, with their Companions, Odin and Mariah, by their sides, made their way to the crackling bonfire.

When they got there, Mari raised her hand, silencing the chattering Pack and calling everyone's attention. Nik and Laru joined them and Rigel trotted to Mari's side.

"Jaxom, would you come here, please?" Mari called.

Jaxom stepped out of the shadows by the boats, where he'd been double-checking their moorings with Antreas, Fortina close beside him. He looked nervous and uncomfortable as all eyes focused on him.

"Wilkes has something he'd like to say to you," Mari said.

Wilkes went slowly to Jaxom. He coughed and then cleared his throat before he bent to rest his hand on Fortina's soft head.

"Jaxom, this Shepherd has Chosen you as her Companion. It is a great honor and an even greater bond, which you will share for the remainder of your lives. Do you accept her and agree to cherish and care for her for the duration of her life, and beyond should the Sun require it?"

"I do! Though I don't know much about your Sun God."

"I will answer any questions you have about our God," said Nik.

"Thank you," Jaxom said. "Thank you so much. I never knew there could be a connection like this—not with anyone or anything."

"We understand," said Mari, smiling through happy tears.

"Yes, we do," said Sora.

"And so: *Pack, the pup has Chosen!*" Wilkes yelled joyfully.

"The pup has Chosen!" shouted every Companion in the Pack as every canine, including the smallest of Fala's pups, raised its muzzle to the sky and howled with happiness.

"May the Sun bless your union with Fortina!" Nik was the first Companion to step forward and take Jaxom's hand in congratulations, but he was followed by every Companion in the Pack—and then by each Earth Walker as well.

Mari looked on with pride as her Pack fully accepted Jaxom and his Shepherd.

Oh, Mama, I hope you're seeing this . . .

CHAPTER 7

It took Mari longer than she'd anticipated to make her way to where Danita had settled Dove and Lily on the fringe of the circle the Pack had made around what was now a merrily blazing bonfire. As she'd suspected, her hands weren't the only ones feeling the strain of hours paddling, so with the help of Jenna and Isabel, salve was applied and everyone was instructed to be sure their hands were wrapped the next day and cared for carefully until cracked skin and bloody blisters became protective calluses.

But mostly everyone was in good spirits, especially as the fire burned brightly and Spencer passed around mugs of mead. The susurrus of the contented Pack mixed with the scents of bubbling stew, giving the campsite the illusion of home. Rigel by her side, Mari finally approached Dove and Lily. They were positioned as part of the Pack's circle, but they also were not. No one was chatting with them. They were sipping mead, so someone had brought that to them—probably Spencer. They were sitting on woven mats and had been given a heavy hemp blanket to share, but other than that they were being ignored.

As Mari approached them, she noticed that Lily whispered to Dove, and Mari realized the girl must serve as Dove's eyes. Still, she stopped a respectful distance from them, not wanting to startle.

"Hello, Dove and Lily. I'd like to chat with you."

"Moon Woman Mari, I am pleased you sought me out," Dove said, smiling and gesturing to the ground beside her.

Sometime while she was tending to Sarah's and Lydia's wounds, Nik had wrapped her travel cloak around her shoulders, and Mari was glad of it as she placed it on the rough ground and sat with a sigh, curling the rest of it over her for warmth. Rigel lay beside her, mirroring her exhaustion with a puppyish groan.

"Oh, you have your canine with you!" Dove spoke animatedly, turning her sightless face in Rigel's direction.

"He won't hurt you—not unless you try to cause me harm. I give you my word on that."

"Then he and I should become great friends, as I have no desire to harm anyone." Dove paused. "Might I ask you something that could seem a rather odd request?"

Curious, Mari said, "Yes. But understand I have no problem saying no."

Her smile was beautiful. "I would expect nothing less from the leader of these good people."

"Sora also leads, and we make a point to listen to all of our people," Mari said.

"I like this Pack idea." Lily spoke shyly, but Mari saw that Dove nodded, encouraging her, so the girl continued with a little more confidence. "Women *should* make the rules and run things. They make life. They are more compassionate than males. It seems more natural than men running and ruining things."

"Well, I've never known anything else," Mari said. "Earth Walkers are all matriarchal."

"But your mate? Nik?" Dove asked. "He is part of the Tribe of the Trees, correct?"

"He isn't officially my mate—not yet," Mari corrected. "And he *was* part of the Tribe of the Trees. Now he belongs to our Pack."

Dove nodded her head, silently considering Mari's words before she spoke. "But the Tribe of the Trees is a patriarchy, are they not?"

"From what Nik has told me, and what I've observed, they tend toward men holding most of the leadership roles, but more attention seems to be paid to what type of canine Chooses a Tribe member than the sex of that person. Shepherds and their Companions are leaders—be they male or female."

"From listening I thought I could tell that there is more than one type of canine, and then Lily described them to me. Are there only the two types, large Shepherds and smaller Terriers?"

"Yes, that's right. The Shepherds are the Warriors and the Terriers are the Hunters. Oh, and then there's Bast, but she wasn't part of the Tribe."

"The Lynx! She sounds so interesting."

"I'm sure Antreas would introduce you to his Bast, but that feline does as she wishes. If she doesn't want to interact with you—she won't. No matter what Antreas says."

"Antreas sounds firmly matriarchal as well."

"I suppose you're right," Mari said.

"But your Nik has no problem with joining a Pack led by women?" Dove asked.

"No, he appreciates our leadership. And, like I said, Sora and I are careful to give each of our Pack members a voice."

"But yours is the final say."

"Yes, it is. What was the odd request you spoke of earlier?" Mari asked. She was enjoying talking with Dove. The girl was poised and intelligent, but also childishly animated.

"Oh, yes. Might I touch you? It is how I see, and I would very much like to *see* you."

"Touch me? You mean my face?"

"Yes, and your hair. Perhaps your shoulders and a little of your body so I can understand your size."

Mari snort-laughed. "Well, sure. I don't mind if you'd like to see me." Dove lifted her hands, as if reaching for Mari, and Mari took them, guiding them to her face.

Dove's touch was like a butterfly's wings. Her hands flicked gently over Mari's face, then to her hair, her neck, and her shoulders. Rigel watched attentively, cocking his head as if trying to understand what the new girl was doing to his Companion. When he didn't seem stressed by Dove's attention, Mari had an idea.

"Dove, would you like to *see* Rigel and one of the Terriers so you could tell the difference in them?"

"Oh! That would be wonderful!"

"Okay, let's start with Rigel. Come here, sweet boy." Mari patted the spot to her right, which was an empty space between where she was sitting and Dove. With no hesitation, Rigel jumped over Mari's outstretched legs and sat beside her. Mari sent a quick image to her young Shepherd of him lying down and allowing Dove to run her hands over him, and Rigel promptly lay down, gazing up at Dove with a doggy grin. "That's perfect, Rigel!" Mari praised. "Dove, I'll guide your hands. Don't worry, Rigel likes to be touched."

Mari gently guided Dove's hands to Rigel's head. "Shepherds have fluffy ears and a long snout with very powerful teeth. Feel his muzzle and his wet nose?"

Dove seemed to be holding her breath, but she nodded quickly. "Is it supposed to be wet, or is he upset?"

"Oh, no! He's not upset at all. And his nose is supposed to be a little wet like it is. Here." Mari guided Dove's hands along Rigel's back to his wagging tail. "Feel his tail going back and forth like that?"

"I do!"

"That means he's happy."

"Oh, he's so, so soft! I had no idea. Different from a rabbit or a deer, and nothing like a bird's feathers. Unique and soft." Dove leaned forward and sniffed at Rigel, which had him lifting his muzzle and licking her face.

"Oh, sorry. That's a canine kiss. It's slobbery, but honestly given."

"He kissed me? That is so lovely!" Dove giggled, looking very young, and very happy.

"May I touch him, too?" Lily asked.

"Of course!" Mari nodded encouragingly, and Lily leaned across her friend to stroke Rigel's fur.

"Oh! I didn't think that his fur would be so thick!" Lily said.

"May I touch him all over? I'd like to feel his paws and get an idea of his size. All of the canines sound so large when they bark," Dove said.

"Sure, Rigel doesn't mind. But you should know that he's young and only about half grown. I'll call his father, Laru, so you can get an idea of how large he will be when he's full grown." Mari paused, finding Nik over by the bonfire talking with Wilkes and Claudia, who had moved their makeshift pallets as close to the fire as possible for warmth. "Nik!" she called. He looked up, smiling, at the sound of her voice, and Mari gestured for him to join her. She saw him say something quickly to Wilkes before he made his way to her, Laru, as usual, by his side.

"Nik, do you or Laru mind if Dove touches Laru? She sees by touch, and I wanted her to feel the difference between a Shepherd pup and a mature Shepherd."

"Oh, well, no—I don't mind, and I'm sure Laru won't either."

"Thank you, Nik," Dove said politely.

"No problem. It does make sense that you'd need to touch to see. Go ahead, Laru." Nik gestured for Laru to lie beside Rigel, which the big Shepherd did with no hesitation whatsoever.

As she did for her with Rigel, Mari guided Dove's hands first to Laru's large head. From there Dove gently felt all along his body as her lips lifted. "He is so big! And strong—I can tell that from his muscles. So magnificent! And Rigel will get this big?"

"I think Rigel will even be bigger," Nik said. "He's bigger than I remember Laru being at his age."

"Do you know where Davis and Cammy are?" Mari asked Nik.

"Yeah, they were helping Sheena and O'Bryan get the food ready for the canines. Thankfully, it's almost time for all of us to eat. Want me to get them for you?"

"That would be great, thanks." As Nik and Laru headed to the shore, Mari continued. "Davis is Cameron's Companion. Well, mostly we call him Cammy or Cammyman. He's a Terrier."

"Do they like to be touched, too?" Lily asked.

"I think almost all canines like to be touched, but they each have different personalities, like people do," Mari said. "Cammy *definitely* likes to be touched." Just then a little blond whirlwind came running up. He greeted Mari first, climbing up on her lap and licking her face. "Well, hello, Cammyman! Where's Davis?"

"Davis is still helping with the food," Nik called across the sand to Mari. "But I told him why you needed Cammy, and you know how much Cammy likes attention."

"I do!" Mari laughed as Cammy licked her face, huffing happily. "Okay, hang on, Dove wants to meet you. Ready to meet a Terrier, Dove?"

"Yes, I am!"

"He's a lot smaller than Laru and even Rigel, so get ready. Here he comes." Mari picked Cammy up and deposited him on Dove's lap.

"Oh!" Dove squeaked, and her arms immediately went around the Terrier, holding him close. Cammy sat his butt down and lifted his muzzle, licking Dove directly on her mouth. She sputtered and then laughed as she ran her hands along his face and body, all the way to his tail. "He's wagging!"

"Cammy is very friendly *and* very happy," Mari said.

"His fur feels so different from the Shepherds'. Do all the Terriers and Shepherds feel the same?"

"Mostly," Mari said. "But Cammy is a blond Terrier, which means his fur is lighter in color, and I think it is a little softer than the darker Terriers', but they are very much alike. The Shepherds can have different coats, though. Claudia's Mariah has longer fur than Laru and Rigel, and Captain, Sheena's big Shepherd, has fur that is shorter and coarser than the fur on most of the Shepherds I've seen."

"And Shepherds and Terriers live well together, even though they are so different in size?" Lily asked as she petted Cammy, who obligingly licked her hand.

"Whether they get along or not seems to be a personality thing, and not a size thing. But, yes, they mostly do seem to get along well," Mari said.

"I like this little Cammy Terrier quite a lot," Lily pronounced. Then she sent a nervous look to Mari and hastily added, "Though I mean no disrespect to you or any Shepherd—they're just so big and intimidating."

"You didn't offend me. I understand. I've only been a Companion for a few months. Truthfully, I'm still getting used to their size. I was shocked by Laru's size when I met him for the first time."

A whistle came from the far side of the circle, causing every canine ear in the Pack to lift expectantly. Then Davis's voice called, "Terriers! Shepherds! Time to eat!"

Cammy sprinted from Dove's lap and Rigel looked at Mari expectantly, whining and drooling.

"Go, sweet boy!" He took off, kicking sand and dirt behind him as he barked joyously.

"They must be hungry," Dove said.

"They think they're *always* hungry," Mari said.

"Moon Woman, your stew." Jenna approached with a wooden bowl filled with steaming food and a big hunk of bread protruding from the middle of it.

"Thank you, Jenna," Mari said. "Would you please show Lily where the bowls are so that she and Dove may eat?"

"Yes, of course. Lily, come with me. Everything is over by the fire and the cauldron, and when you're done we each clean our own bowl and then repack it with the others."

Lily nodded shyly and followed Jenna. Sora joined Mari. She put her travel cloak on the ground beside her and then sat with a groan of relief. "It feels good to just sit on ground that doesn't move. My shoulders are really tired from that paddling."

"Hello, Moon Woman Sora," Dove said.

"Hello, Dove. Are you and Lily settling in?" Sora asked.

"Yes, Mari was letting me feel the canines. I believe I like them very much," said Dove as Lily returned with bowls of steaming stew and bread for them both.

"Feel the canines?" Sora spoke around a mouthful of stew.

Before Mari could explain Dove replied. "Yes, as I have no eyes the way I see is through touch."

"Huh. Makes sense," Sora said. Chloe poked her head up from the sleeping ball she'd formed deep in the pouch Sora had rigged to strap to her chest and keep her very young Companion close to her. The pup sniffed the air and then yapped insistently. Sora kissed her indulgently on the nose before dunking a small piece of bread in the fragrant stew and letting the pup lick at it.

"Is that your Companion I hear, Sora?" Dove asked.

"Yes. She isn't weaned yet, but she likes trying to eat on her own. Mostly whatever I'm eating." Sora looked at Dove contemplatively. "I would let you see her with your touch after you're finished eating if you would like."

"I would very much. Thank you." Dove paused before continuing. "You are showing great trust in me, and I am honored by that."

"You gave your word that you would be truthful with us," Sora said in a matter-of-fact manner. "When we accepted that word we chose to trust you."

"And we will trust you unless you give us reason not to," Mari said.

"W-what happens if you become angry at us?" Lily asked softly.

"Angry?" Mari said. "You mean because you're lying?"

"No!" Lily said quickly. "My mistress and I would not lie, not after she gave you her word."

"In the Pack Mari and I settle disputes. If you have problems with someone or something, you should come to us," said Sora.

"You called Dove your mistress," Mari said as Nik joined their little group, sharing Mari's cloak. "What do you mean by that?"

"I am sorry. I did not mean to—"

Dove raised her slender hand to silence Lily. "Purposefully being quiet about details of our lives before we joined these good people is the same as a lie, Lily. I will not do that." Dove turned her face toward Mari. "Lily calls me mistress because she served me as my Attendant in the Temple of the Reaper God. I was the God's oracle."

"Which god is the Reaper? That creature with the antlers you call Death?" Nik asked.

"No and yes. Before the God of Death manifested within our Champion, Dead Eye, our god was silent." Dove's sightless face turned toward Lily. "Forgive me for what I must say now, but I am sworn to truthfulness, and even were I not it is past time that I was honest with you."

Lily blinked several times, looking shocked. "Forgive you? I do not understand."

"You will, my friend. I just hope you will allow me to call you friend after this." Dove drew a deep breath and bowed her head, as if speaking a prayer to a fallen god. "Until Lily and I escaped I had never been outside the Temple of our God. I was brought there as a newborn to sacrifice to the Reaper God, but the Watchers—the old women who were believed to hear our God's words and speak for Her—decided that I had been touched by the Reaper. They spared me. I learned quickly that I had to be of value to the Watchers or they would change their minds and sacrifice me—or worse: banish me from the Temple alone to starve to death. So, from the time I was a child I pretended to hear the voice of our God."

Lily gasped, but covered her mouth quickly. Dove nodded, acknowledging her friend's shock. She wiped a trembling hand across her face, and then continued.

"But the truth our People do not know is that all of the Watchers pretended. They were all false oracles. The God spoke to no one. And then my Dead Eye strode into the Temple, cleansing it of the vile old Watchers and sparing me. Like me, he knew the Reaper God was mute—a fabrication of old women to maintain power over the People. He also knew the source of the sickness that was infecting and killing more and more of our people."

"Tainted meat," Nik said.

Dove didn't lift her head, but she nodded in agreement. "Yes, that and more. He believed the animals in our city had become tainted by our People because they had been eating the flesh of the Others and then merging it with their flesh as they attempted to cure the skin-sloughing disease."

"Which seems to be very like a disease called the Blight that the Tribe suffers from," Mari said.

"So the old rhyme is true," Sora said, looking pale. "'Of cities beware—Skin Stealers are there.'"

"I do not know of other cities. Only my own."

"Why are you and Lily not sick?" Sora asked.

"I never ate meat, especially not the meat of the Others," said Dove. "At first it was because I wasn't allowed to, and then it was because I chose not to. The thought of it has always disgusted me."

"And I was beginning to sicken before I entered Dove's service, but I am small and only a girl, so I had to wait with the old people to get my portion of meat and often that meant there was no meat left for me. I was never allowed to eat from flesh taken from the Others." Lily extended her arm and pushed up the sleeve of her tunic to reveal a few small blisters in the crease of her elbow. "These have not spread."

"And once she entered my service I made sure she ate the same food my Dead Eye did—and he only ate from the beasts he found deep in the forest. Hunting for untainted food was how he became obsessed with the Tribe of the Trees," Dove said.

"Lily, I will give you a salve that will soothe those blisters. Third Night, when we draw down the power of the moon to cleanse the Pack, is tomorrow. Then you will be healed completely of that disease."

Lily bowed her head respectfully. "Thank you, Moon Woman Sora."

"What Dove says does make sense," Mari reasoned. "The eating of human flesh is one of our basic taboos—something passed from generation to generation. There had to be a reason for it, and not just because it's disgusting. It causes sickness. So, this Dead Eye is the same person as the Death God?"

"No! He was my love—my Champion. He was kind to me and cared for me, but somehow he awakened the Reaper God—the God of Death. My Dead Eye was ambitious, but his ambition was only for what was best for our People. Forgive me for saying this, but his intention was to defeat the Tribe of the Trees and move our People to the untainted forest."

"Only now it is tainted because of him," Nik said, his voice heavy with anger.

"His original intention was not to poison the forest," Dove said. "But he changed when Death awoke within him. At first I didn't understand what was happening. I believed he was simply doing what he must to help our People leave the city. I was wrong. Death had marked Dead Eye as His and, finally, the God of Death absorbed everything that ever was my love until he was no more. Then Death began changing the People as well—flaying the living flesh of animals to their skin so that they absorbed the characteristics of the creatures, though I do not believe any so fully became beasts as did Death."

"He did that to Thaddeus when He captured him, didn't He?" Nik said. "He flayed the flesh of his Terrier to him."

Head still bowed, Dove nodded. "He did."

"And He poisoned the animals of the forest to weaken the Tribe," Nik said.

"Yes."

Nik threw his bowl aside in anger and began to stand, but Mari's gentle touch on his arm stayed him.

"So much misery!" Nik said, shaking his head. "Her people have caused so much misery."

"I never meant to harm others. Dead Eye and I only wanted a way out of our own misery."

"And you found that way. Death will defeat what is left of the Tribe of the Trees," Mari said. "Why did you not stay with your God and enjoy your victory?"

"Enjoy it?" Dove looked as if she'd eaten sour berries. "No. There is no 'joy' left among our People. There is only Death and His needs and desires. It was when I realized this that Lily and I turned to the Goddess of Life, who I believe is the same as your Great Earth Mother. She heard my prayer and led me to you."

"But you said that you pretended to be an oracle for your Reaper God. What makes you think the Earth Mother heard you, or even acknowledges you? It seems much more likely that it is just a coincidence that your path crossed ours," Nik said, his voice still bitter.

"The dream," Sora said. "Mari's dream."

"Dream?" Nik asked.

Mari nodded. "I dreamed that a dove came to me looking for sanctuary. My mother's voice told me to grant her it, but only if she swore to tell a Moon Woman the truth."

"Yes, the dream. I am grateful for it, but there is more than that," Dove said. "Death's plan is to awaken His consort within me—to have the Goddess of Life absorb me as Death did my Dead Eye—but as I listened carefully to the God, I began to realize that the Goddess might not be in agreement with His plan. So, I fled. Hoping that, perhaps, I could serve the Goddess in another way."

"As a false oracle?" Nik said.

Dove lifted her head then and turned her eyeless face toward Nik. "No. Never. I will never pretend again." She shifted to face Lily and held out her hand. Her friend hesitated, then grasped it. "Forgive me, Lily. I will never again lie to you, or to anyone else, from this moment until my last."

"I forgive you, Mistress," Lily said in a voice that broke with emotion.

"For the rest of us it will not be so easy. Especially for the rest of us who were once part of the Tribe of the Trees," Nik said. He leaned over to kiss Mari softly. "I am going to check on the canines and help Antreas set to order the first shift of lookouts." Without another word, Nik strode away.

"You should be prepared," Sora said. "Nik's reaction will probably be mirrored in many of the Pack when they learn your story."

"I am prepared. I am also prepared to win the trust of your Pack, Moon Woman Sora."

"I don't think you'll be able to win it," Mari said. "You'll have to earn it."

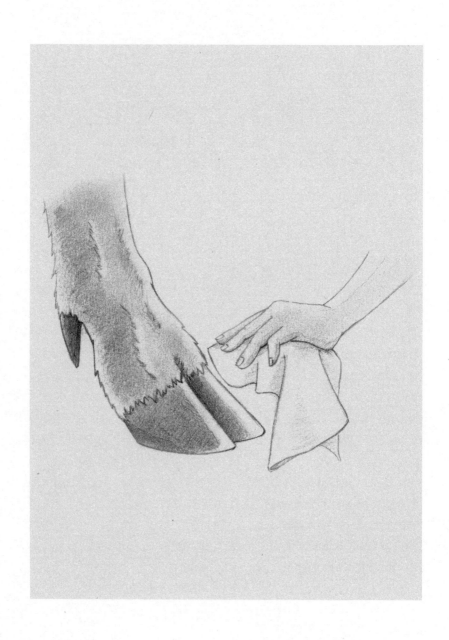

CHAPTER 8

The Pack settled in for the remainder of the short night. Arranged in a circle around the well-tended fire, close together with canines settled comfortably by their Companions' sides, those who did not have first watch slept. Mari found Nik easily. He'd created a space for them across the circle from where Dove and Lily were already sleeping. Mari unwrapped her cloak from around her shoulders and placed it on the pallet he'd made. Then she sat beside Nik as Rigel curled against her side and yawned mightily. Laru was lying on the other side of Nik, looking like he was sound asleep, but as Mari sat, he slitted his eyes and thumped his tail. She reached across Nik to caress his wide, soft head.

"Hey there, Laru. Go back to sleep. You deserve it after the day you've had," she said.

"So do you." Nik extended his arm as Mari sat so that she could lean into him. He'd placed their pallet in front of a big piece of driftwood, which they used as a backrest. "I told Antreas I'd take first watch, and like you said, we should do that in pairs, but if you're too tired I can sit watch with O'Bryan and Sheena."

"I'd rather stay awake and be with you. But do we have to move from here? It's so cozy."

Nik kissed the top of her head. "No, look." He pointed out at the dark water, which lapped only a few yards from where Nik had positioned their pallet. "I chose to put us here so that we could look out across the water. Antreas has everyone watching outward. He says lookouts need to focus on the river, as that's where the danger would come from."

Mari relaxed against Nik and gazed out at the black expanse of water. The clouds were hiding the moon again, so it was impossible to see the far bank, as it was just darkness against more darkness. She breathed deeply.

"I like the way the river smells. It's earth diluted with water plants mixed with trees and rocks to make a special scent all its own."

"Rocks smell like something?"

"Of course! They smell like rocks . . . well, and moss and pine needles and such."

"You're a strange one, Moon Woman."

"Thank you." Mari grinned. "So, you still hate the river?"

"Definitely." They laughed lightly, then Nik continued. "Mari, I want to ask you to be careful with what you say to Dove and Lily—especially Dove. I know you and Sora want to trust her, but you haven't dealt with Skin Stealers. The Tribe has. They're awful—barely human."

Mari considered her answer carefully. She knew that how she responded to Nik now would set the tone for the future, especially as they would be encountering many different peoples during, and at the end of, their journey.

"I understand why you're worried. I truly do. And I acknowledge your concern. But there's something my mama said that I've been thinking a lot about lately. She told me many times that we all must choose whether we live our lives based on love or fear. I know now why she repeated that over and over to me—because I lived most of my life based on fear. I didn't realize it, but my anger at the Clan for not accepting me was fear-based. My resentment at Mama for devoting so much of her time to caring for the Clan was fear-based. The way I used to view the Clansmen as nuisances who should stay on the fringe of the Clan was fear-based. It took losing Mama, and almost losing myself, for me to understand what she meant. Nik, now I choose to live my life based on love, and if that means I make the mistake of trusting someone who hurts me, then so be it. Can you understand that?"

"I don't know. I hear what you're saying, but I still want you to be careful."

"And I will be, but Nik, you should keep in mind if I had followed what you're saying—to withhold my trust even when my instinct tells me elsewise—I would have left you in that river to die those weeks ago."

She studied his face. She could see that he was struggling with his fear for her, and probably at his anger at what had become of his beloved Tribe. So, gently, she added, "I ask you to trust my judgment."

"I do trust you!"

"No, not just *me*, my *judgment*. Because, Nik, I do love you, but if you cannot trust my *judgment* we can never be mates. A matriarchy isn't just about women leading. It's about women being respected as equals— valued as equals—even when fear wants you to disagree with our choices, and I must have a mate who doesn't simply understand the ideals behind that way of life, but who actively embraces it by *trusting my judgment*."

Mari saw the surprise and the pain in his eyes, but she didn't move to comfort him. This was something Nik had to work through, and if he could not, no matter how much she wanted him—or how much she loved him—she truly would not accept him as her mate. She was Moon Woman, one of the leaders of their Clan, and if her own mate did not respect her then they would be an ill-fitted match that would affect her ability to lead their Pack, and that was something she could not, *would not*, live with.

"I will respect your judgment, my Moon Woman." Nik spoke somberly. "Though it will be difficult to temper my worry for you. I have lost much recently—my father, my Tribe—basically my whole way of life. I cannot bear to lose you as well."

Relief bloomed within Mari. "Loss I understand. Loss is what brought us together, but it could also tear us apart if we cannot work through it."

He nodded, and she felt him relax. "You're right, my Moon Woman."

"I love you, my Sun Priest."

"And I love you as well."

They sat in silence with their Companions and their Pack around them, gazing out at the seemingly endless river as they held each other and imagined the mysteries the future before them might hold.

Iron Fist jogged though the burned ruins of the Tribe of the Trees—silent and dark except for the sentry, Thunder, who challenged him as soon as he left the Channel and entered Tribal territory.

"Speak your name!"

"Iron Fist, Blade of the God!"

Thunder dropped from a blackened bough of a half-burned pine. "Iron Fist—Death has left word that you go to Him immediately. Keep following this stream into the burned area there before us." He pointed. "When the stream turns to the right go left and walk until you see green again. Death is waiting at the big tree with the carved platform."

"The battle is over?"

"Battle?" Thunder laughed darkly. "There was no *battle*. The Others are weak, and those who are not are eager to ally themselves with the power of our God."

"Did He kill them all?" Iron Fist asked.

"No, not yet. There is far too much work to be done, and as our God has promised, we shall rule here now, and not the pathetic Others. They are now our slaves!"

Iron Fist nodded. He was surprised that Death hadn't wiped out the entire Tribe of the Trees, but Thunder's words made sense. Why should the People struggle to rebuild the city in the sky when the original builders were so much better suited for the work? He saluted his fellow Reaper. "I go now to report to our Lord."

"May your feet be swift. Death has been asking for you."

Thunder's words goaded Iron Fist into a run. He leaped over burned logs and blackened rubble easily, feeling the strength of the boar within him. He did not know how Death had merged the mighty beast's essence with His Reapers, but Iron Fist was grateful He had. Gone were the bulbous pustules that used to cover so much of his body. Gone was the wrenching cough and the nausea that used to shadow his every moment—and he would be eternally loyal to Death for the gift of health and preternatural power.

Iron Fist turned to the left when the stream curved right. Soon he heard the sounds of celebration—the drumming and the singing—that marked a victorious battle. He followed those joyous sounds until the blackened city gave way to unscathed green. Singed tree houses that looked very much like enormous nests were now filled with celebrating People. Half-burned platforms held Reapers who were drinking and writhing in time to a sonorous drumbeat, and as Iron Fist watched, one Reaper almost fell to his death from too much revelry, though he seemed not to notice that the fast action of his fellow soldier had snagged his arm and saved him. Iron Fist frowned. It would not do to have the Reapers injuring themselves. He must speak to Death about warning the People to be more careful.

The young Attendants to the God were still back in the city, but the victorious Reapers would not be denied their pleasure. Women of the vanquished Tribe were being forced to service the soldiers. As Iron Fist watched, one Tribal woman escaped the forced embrace of a Reaper. Naked and bloody, she silently leaped from the half-burned platform high above them and landed, broken and still, not far from him.

Iron Fist didn't waste time watching further. Women were chattel. It was simply their fate to serve man. He moved on and then halted on the fringe of the main part of the celebration.

The People were spread in a great circle around a huge old pine that held multiple ornately carved platforms. Just beyond the tree, outside the circle of drinking, dancing Reapers and the suffering women of the Tribe, Iron Fist could see the beginning of a huge roped-off area. Within it was what was left of the defeated Tribe of the Trees. He wondered who was guarding them, and then ceased wondering when he recognized Spider, Deep Water, and Gully walking a slow path around the circumference of the prisoners. The three were old men too ill to be made Reapers, but not so frail that they were unable to keep watch—especially over a Tribe that was so clearly and completely defeated. Even their mighty canines lay silently beside their Companions—heads bowed in failure.

A roar drew Iron Fist's attention back to the tree in the center of the celebration, and he saw Death stride to the edge of the platform. Several huge bonfires blazed below and around the tree, illuminating the God's massive silhouette. He lifted His arms and His voice echoed with immortal power around them, easily being heard over the drums and the debauchery.

"Yes, my People! Celebrate! Dance, drink, fornicate! The night is yours—and come tomorrow we will begin building *our* city in the sky!" Cheers sounded around Him as He bellowed the great roar of a stag.

Iron Fist jogged through the People, weaving his way around Reapers stumbling with drink and triumph. He almost ran into a soldier he didn't recognize—then he took a closer look. It was a member of the Tribe—the small man who had been captured by them weeks ago and whom Death had used to spread poison to the Tribe. The man, whose name Iron Fist remembered was Thaddeus, had a drink in one hand and with the other held a young girl close to him as he forced her to dance. Her eyes met Iron Fist's briefly, and what he saw there caused the Reaper to shudder. There was no light within her gaze—there was nothing there at all. It was as if he shared a glance with a corpse.

Iron Fist hurried past her to the tree, and then sprinted up the winding stairway until he reached the platform that held Death.

"I am pleased you have returned this night, my Blade. I was beginning to think the river had swallowed you whole." As if He could see behind him, Death spoke without turning.

"No, my Lord. It would not have dared. Even the river knew I had momentous news to bring to my God."

Death motioned for Iron Fist to join him at the edge of the platform. "Do you see this?" The God ran one massive hand over the intricate carvings that decorated the balustrade.

Confused, Iron Fist glanced at the wooden railing. "I do, my Lord."

"Its beauty is impressive. I will insist that the Others rebuild our city with this much beauty."

"Yes, my Lord."

"And I shall also have a canine. One of those huge Shepherds. They fought fiercely today. What do you think of that, Iron Fist?"

"I think you are Death, our beloved Reaper God, and you should have whatever you desire."

Death clapped him on the shoulder. "Ah, Iron Fist, you give wise and true counsel. Now, tell me the momentous news you bring."

"I followed the girl. She and her man joined a group on the river. She called it her Pack."

"What size is this Pack?"

"Under fifty—mostly women."

"Do they all have canines?"

"No." Iron Fist shook his head. "I did see some canines, but much fewer than people."

"The girl who wielded fire—she has a canine Companion, does she not?"

"Yes, I believe she and her man each are bonded to a Shepherd. My Lord, she is a marvel. They cry 'Moon Woman' to her. I watched as she drew down the silver power of the moon and healed several people who were with her."

"Truly?" Death was visibly excited. "She has the ability to heal?"

"She does, my Lord!"

"And her beauty? I could not tell if she was pleasing to the eye—the distance between us was too great."

"Her skin is smooth. She is young and beautiful."

"And where is it they are escaping to?" Death asked.

"They travel up the river to a place called the Plains of the Wind Riders. There they plan to make a new home for their Pack."

"Wind Riders? I do not know of them, but I am quite sure our friends in the Tribe do. You have done well, my Blade."

"There is more. I did not just see the Moon Woman—I saw those traveling with her. Two of them were very familiar. My Lord, Dove and her servant, Lily, have joined the Pack."

Death turned slowly to fully face Iron Fist—and the Reaper shivered at the dark look in the God's eyes. "*My* Dove? The vessel for my Consort, the Goddess of Life? Are you quite sure it was she?"

"Absolutely sure, my Lord. I clearly saw her face—and Lily's as well." Iron Fist held his breath, terrified Death would somehow blame him for bringing the news of His lover's escape.

But the Reaper need not have worried. Death's expression shifted, and the God threw back His head and laughed.

"It is perfect! I felt Dove had served her purpose—that she was only a momentary diversion and unfit to be the vessel for my love, my Consort. And now I know it. I do not need a sightless child. I need a sun warrior—a Healer—a mighty Moon Woman." Death turned to face His reveling People, speaking with the solemnity that was the Oath of a God. "I shall go after this Moon Woman. Only *she* will make an appropriate vessel for the Goddess."

Ralina did her best to make the injured comfortable, though there was little comfort to be had in the section of the forest the Death God had forced them to move to. She sent a silent prayer up to the departed sun asking that the swarm stay away, as there was no way to combat them should the insects attack.

Mari had healed the Tribe of the horrible skin-sloughing sickness— or at least she'd healed those of the Tribe who had wished to be healed— but there were still many people who had been wounded in the fire, and, of course, the short but bloody battle with the Skin Stealers. After Thaddeus, the disgusting traitor, surrendered in the name of the Tribe, the invaders had forced them from the ancient Meditation Platform and the infirmary they'd created around the tree and declared it theirs, herding the weak and wounded away to a roped-off section of the forest where they had only the living canopy to protect them and whatever they could carry with them to use as pallets, medicines, and food. However, as the Tribe were forced out of their own city, the Skin Stealers randomly confiscated anything they wanted—including women.

Ralina had never been so glad that she was covered in blood and gore from tending to the sick. None of the men so much as glanced her way, and when they did her big Shepherd, Bear, showed his teeth, encouraging them to look away from his Companion.

She'd watched Thaddeus and his men join the celebration with the Skin Stealers. The traitor had even shown the invaders where the spring beer was buried, and he was currently drinking and dancing with them.

Good riddance, Ralina thought.

"Ralina, I'm so hungry!" The Tribe's Storyteller shook herself and refocused on her nearest patient—a young girl named Celeste, whose legs had been burned when she fled the forest fire.

Ralina bent and put a hand on the teenager's forehead. She could feel that Celeste's fever had broken—no doubt because of Mari's healing powers.

"I know, Celeste. You only have to wait a little longer for my soup to be ready."

"But people are eating stew—*with meat*—over there." The girl pointed to a group of weary Tribe members clustered around the main campfire they'd rebuilt inside the roped-off area Death had ordered them to.

Ralina crouched beside Celeste. "I explained to them just like to everyone else—they should not eat that stew. The meat stinks. It's tainted. You know how sick everyone was before the Moon Woman healed us. I'm sure we'll get sick again if we eat that stew."

Celeste sighed. "Okay. I'll wait." The girl looked around. "But not very many of us are waiting."

I know that and it terrifies me, Ralina thought, but she only said, "I can't force them to believe me. All I can do is let our people know what I've observed—that, added to what Mari said, tells me that the Skin Stealers poisoned us. If you do not want to get sick again, do not eat their meat. The choice is not mine to make for others, only myself."

Ralina turned back to the small campfire she'd built and the old pot she'd managed to grab when the invaders had forced them away from the Meditation Platform. It had been easy to forage edible roots, greens, and mushrooms and then add water to create a thin, but untainted soup. She stirred the soup and glanced around, counting the number of people who had joined her and were waiting like Celeste for food that wouldn't sicken them. Ralina was almost overcome with a great sinking feeling. Though the majority of the Tribe hadn't listened to her and were hungrily eating the tainted stew, those who had followed her lead were more than her meager soup could feed. She'd need to add more water and, hopefully, mushrooms.

"Celeste, keep an eye on the soup. I'm going to get more water and see if I can find some more mushrooms as well."

As she stood and began to move away from her campfire, Bear tried to join her. She knelt and took his face between her hands, speaking quietly to him and projecting an image of him lying beside her campfire. "Stay here and wait for me. I don't like how the Skin Stealers look at our Shepherds, and I don't want you to draw any attention from them."

The big canine growled low in his throat as his gaze went from his beloved Companion to one of the disgusting-smelling guards that had been stationed around their roped-off area.

"I know," Ralina whispered as she kissed his face. "They're horrible."

Bear growled again before padding back to his position beside young Celeste and the campfire. Ralina smiled and nodded at him before hurrying away—her eyes cast down as she searched for anything edible. She spotted a patch of morels and hurried to it, then dropped to her knees to harvest the meaty fungi.

His smell hit her before he spoke.

"Get back inside the rope!"

Ralina glanced up to see an old Skin Stealer, his body riddled with painful-looking pustules, his skin slick with fevered sweat, standing over her. She looked behind her, and realized she'd been too focused on the mushrooms and hadn't noticed that she'd moved under and outside the rope boundary as she harvested them.

"I'm just collecting these mushrooms for my soup. As soon as I have them all I'll go back inside the boundary."

"No, woman. You'll go back inside the boundary now." The Skin Stealer nudged her with his foot, throwing her off balance so that she fell back on her butt.

Ralina looked up at him, shaking her head in disgust. "I'm not trying to escape. I'm not trying to do anything except gather these mushrooms and feed my people."

The Skin Stealer bent and shoved his face closer to hers. "I don't care whether you and your people starve. *Get back inside the rope.*"

She shouldn't have said anything more. She'd been the one to tell Bear that he couldn't follow her because they shouldn't be drawing attention, but her exhaustion and hunger spoke before reason could silence them.

In one fluid motion Ralina stood, facing the old Skin Stealer. "Back off, you reeking wretch! I'd call you an animal, but that would be an insult to all woodland creatures. You're certainly not a man—you're a walking disease."

The Skin Stealer was carrying a sharply tipped trident, which he raised, readying it to run through Ralina. She braced herself. Her only regret about dying was that Bear would lose her and that her beloved Companion would not live long after her death.

"Ah, Ralina, here you are. I knew you'd be easy to find—always causing trouble. You're always causing fucking trouble." Thaddeus was slurring his words as he stumbled up to Ralina, shoving aside the Skin Stealer. "Don't kill her, you idiot! She's a pain in the ass, but she also knows things."

"She's outside the ropes!" the Skin Stealer said stubbornly. "I should kill her."

"Yeah, well, if you do you'll have to answer to Death." Thaddeus grabbed Ralina's arm, pulling her away from the Skin Stealer. "Your God wants to talk to her. So, take it up with Him if you have an issue." Thaddeus turned his back on the Skin Stealer, forcing Ralina to come with him.

A few yards outside the roped-off area Ralina wrenched her arm from Thaddeus's grip. "What do you want, Thaddeus?"

"How 'bout a thank-you for saving your life?"

"Traitors don't deserve thank-yous. *What do you want?*" she repeated.

"Isn't what I want, you bitch. It's what the God demands. Go ahead. Ignore Him and watch what happens."

Ralina lifted her lip in disgust. "Just take me to Him and then go away. You make me sicker than the Skin Stealer disease."

Thaddeus backhanded her so that she stumbled and almost fell, but Ralina quickly righted herself. She met Thaddeus's gaze. "If you hit me again you're going to have to kill me."

Thaddeus shrugged. "Whatever. Death might command that anyway. Just shut up and follow me. If you were smarter you'd make a deal with Him like I have."

Ralina's laughter bubbled from deep within her, rich in sarcasm. "You think you're safe? You think Death will actually *spare* you?"

"We're allies, stupid bitch!" he yelled so close to Ralina's face that his saliva rained onto her.

She wiped her dirty sleeve slowly across her face and sneered. "Oh, please. As soon as you've served whatever purpose Death has for you, He'll kill you—or, hopefully, hand you over to those of us who are still faithful to the Tribe."

"You know what? I don't have to put up with people like you and your bullshit anymore. *I'm* leading the Tribe now. And because of me we're going to finally be truly powerful—truly great again. So, shut the hell up and follow me." Thaddeus turned his back on her and weaved drunkenly toward the partying Skin Stealers.

Ralina followed him, cramming the mushrooms into the pockets of her tunic. They made their way around the group of dancing, drinking Skin Stealers. Ralina noted the Warriors and Hunters who had joined them. Like Thaddeus, they were the men who had abused their canines, flaying the living flesh from their bellies and packing it into the diseased sores the Skin Stealer poison had caused. She looked for their canines. At first she didn't see them, then she heard a whine and her gaze was drawn to the base of the ancient tree that held the Meditation Platform. The wounded canines clustered there, close together, Shepherds and Terriers—every one of them obviously in pain, and being ignored by their Companions.

Ralina turned her face away in despair. *How could they abuse their Companions?*

"Come on. Quit gawking and stay with me. He's up there." Thaddeus was heading up the stairs that led to the main Meditation Platform.

Ralina had to dodge a drunken Skin Stealer as he passed out and fell right in front of her—then she reluctantly climbed up the stairs after Thaddeus.

Death stood looking out at His people, His back turned to Thaddeus and Ralina. He held a huge wooden bowl easily in one large hand, drinking from it while He eagerly watched His men celebrating below. As Ralina got closer she smelled the strong scent of liquor, and wondered how He'd managed to find the Tribe's special stores of whisky.

"I brought you the Storyteller, Ralina," Thaddeus said.

Death didn't turn. He simply said, "Next time you come to me you will call me 'my Lord' and you will bow to me. Do you understand that, Thaddeus?"

Ralina glanced at Thaddeus. His face had gone red, but he bowed awkwardly and said, "Yes, my Lord."

"Good. Now leave us."

Ralina could see that Thaddeus wanted to argue, but reason must have gotten through the alcohol soaking his brain, and he bowed again and then took his leave, shooting her a dark look before he disappeared down the stairs.

"So, you are the Tribe's Storyteller," Death said.

"I am. My Lord," she added. It was stupid to antagonize a God—even one she hated—so she was determined to answer Him with as much truth as she could while not making Him unnecessarily angry.

"I like the idea of a Storyteller. I want my deeds recorded and retold generation after generation. It pleases me that you are here."

Ralina wasn't sure what the God expected her to say, so she remained silent.

He turned to look at her, and Ralina got her first good look at Him up close—and she had to bite the inside of her cheek to keep from gasping in shock and bolting from the platform.

The God of Death was animal and man merged to create something terrible. She'd thought the things on His head were horns, maybe fitted to Him by some kind of headdress, similar to a crown. She'd been wrong. They weren't horns—they were antlers. And they were *growing* from both sides of His head. His features were coarse—His nose wide and His brows thick. His face was clean shaven, but His hair was more like mane or fur than human tresses. It was the brown of a stag—shaggy and long. She couldn't tell for sure, but it seemed to be growing down His neck and back. And He was enormous. Easily taller than any Tribesman, or any man Ralina had ever met—and He was so muscular He looked deformed and bloated, more para-human than human. Her eyes traveled down His body, widening when they came to the cloven hooves that should have been feet.

"Have you looked your fill?"

Ralina startled and bowed her head quickly. "Yes, my Lord. I'm sorry. I didn't mean to offend you."

"You did not offend. Look, and look closely. I am a God. I know your people have never seen a living God before now, and I would have you know exactly how to answer their questions and satisfy their curiosity."

"You—you remind me of a stag," she blurted, then bit her lip, wishing her mouth had shut up.

But the God appeared pleased. He nodded, His great, shaggy mane swaying around His shoulders. "When this body was mortal, before I'd fully claimed it, it was joined with a mighty stag—a king of the forest. That stag lives on within me."

"And your men—have they all joined with stags, too?"

"No. The king of the forest was meant only for a God. My men have joined with many different forest animals. Observe them, Storyteller, and you will easily see which ones.

"And now I have a question for you. Where are the Plains of the Wind Riders?"

His question surprised Ralina, but she saw no reason to withhold this information from the God. "They are far to the east."

"How would you get there from here?" Death asked.

"Well, I wouldn't want to get there. It'd be a long, dangerous journey, and Wind Riders don't allow just anyone to settle on the Tallgrass Prairie, so even if I survived the trip there would be no guarantee I would survive the Wind Riders' scrutiny."

"Let us say that you believed you would survive the trip and be allowed to settle on the prairie. How would you get there?"

Ralina moved her shoulders, hoping beyond hope that Death was asking because He and His disgusting people were considering leaving—and with luck take Thaddeus and his followers with them. So, she thought carefully about her answer before speaking.

"I'm not an expert, but I do know stories that tell how people made the trip, though there aren't many of such stories. Few return from the Plains. To reach Wind Rider territory you must travel up the Umbria River to Lost Lake. The lake must be crossed, and from there you must find a way through the Rock Mountains. The Plains of the Wind Riders begin on the east side of the mountains."

"What are Wind Riders?" Death asked.

"They're called 'equestrians'—riders of horses." When she saw His blank look she continued to explain. "Horses—equines—they're hooved animals that are bigger than stags and can be ridden. They're swift and magnificent and dangerous."

"Have you ever seen one?"

"No. I've only seen carvings and drawings," she said.

"I would like to hear any stories you know of the journey to the Plains, and of the Wind Riders themselves."

"Yes, my Lord," she said, bowing nervously. "Now, my Lord?"

"No, not tonight, but soon. I also want you to create stories about me. So, remain vigilant and observant. When I am settled into this new forest dwelling I will call for you often and ask for you to tell me the stories of journeys to the Plains, of the Wind Riders, and, most importantly, of me leading my people to victory and prosperity. Can you do that for me, Storyteller?"

Ralina knew she had absolutely no choice. "Yes, my Lord." He began to turn His back to her dismissively, and she swallowed her fear and spoke up. "My Lord, might I please be allowed to go through our makeshift infirmary and collect the salves and bandages left behind? Many of my people are wounded. And the stew, my Lord, it is made from tainted meat. My people will sicken again if they eat it. Could our Hunters be allowed to bring game to us that is not poisoned?"

Death met her gaze, and Ralina felt as if His dark eyes were a bottomless well she would fall into and drown in should she look too long. "You say that they are your people—they are not. All of this—" Death flung out His arms in a wide circle, taking in the whole Tribe of the Trees. "*All* of this is now mine—my forest, my city, my Tribe. Yes, you may collect the supplies from the infirmary. The Hunters who are allied with Thaddeus may do as they wish. If they desire to provide game for you, then I will not dissuade them. But know this—there is a cure for the sloughing disease. I discovered it, and that cure makes those taking it stronger, faster, *more* than they were before."

Yeah, it also makes them mutate into something that isn't human or animal, she thought silently. Aloud she said, "Thank you, my Lord, but many of us would rather avoid getting sick again."

Death shrugged. "That is your mistake." Then His sharp gaze caught hers. "You say that you would rather avoid getting sick *again*. Some of you were ill and then were cured?"

Ralina bit her cheek and nodded, realizing that she had probably said too much.

"How? Who cured the skin-sloughing disease?" Death demanded.

Mari wasn't part of the Tribe, but Ralina appreciated what she'd done for them, and she had always respected Sol and his son, Nik, and expected Nik to be Sun Priest after his father. She definitely didn't want to cause Mari and Nik problems, but they were gone, and she was here—suffering Tribesmen and women were here. So, she drew a deep breath and then reluctantly answered the God.

"It was a young woman named Mari. She's part Tribe, part Scr—um, I mean Earth Walker, and she's a Healer. She cured the disease, but I'm sure if we eat tainted meat we'll get sick again."

"Indeed, I'm sure you will. And this Mari, how did she cure you?"

Ralina hated every word she spoke, and as she gave the God the information He sought she silently sent a prayer up to the sun asking that Mari's path be easy and swift, and that she hasten far, far away from here.

"Mari drew down power from the moon and cured us with it. I do not know how she did it—it's some kind of Earth Walker magick."

Death nodded His massive head. "So I hear . . . so I hear." Then He turned away from her, gesturing dismissively. "Leave me now so that I may think. Collect whatever supplies you can carry and take them back to your campsite, and as I rebuild this city I will be sure to fashion a home for you, *my* Storyteller."

Sick to her stomach, Ralina rushed from the platform and began gathering baskets and filling them with medicines and anything else she could find that might help her people, and then she hurried back to her little campfire and the few members of the Tribe who had listened to her—had refused the tainted meat and waited for what she could provide. Ralina knew one thing beyond any other—that whoever remained here, under the control of Death and Thaddeus, was doomed.

CHAPTER 9

A soft kiss and the fragrant aroma of steaming tea woke Mari. She blinked blurrily, yawned, and rubbed the sleep from her eyes as she sat. The fragrant mug was beside her, pressed down in the sand so that it wouldn't topple over. She could see that the Pack was stirring, but when she looked for Nik he was nowhere in sight.

"Nik?"

Rigel rushed up, wagging happily and licking her face. She put her arms around the young Shepherd and kissed his nose. "Good morning, sweet boy! Where are Nik and Laru?"

"They're hunting gull eggs in the interior of this mini-island," Sora said as she sat beside Mari with her own cup of tea. "He brought you a mug of tea before they took off on their hunting mission."

"Gull eggs? I've never heard of such a thing."

"Neither have I, but Nik and the rest of the ex-Tribers got super excited when Antreas announced that he'd found a gull nest with eggs in it." Sora pointed her chin at the mess of scrub, river debris, ferns, and tenacious pines that filled the interior of Spirit Island. "Apparently they're delicious, so they asked me to wait to ladle up the leftover stew until the group of them return, hopefully with eggs to poach and add to it." She sighed and leaned back against the log Nik and Mari had used as a backrest the night before. "I can't say I mind the break."

"Didn't you get any sleep last night?" Mari asked, sipping her tea.

"Oh, sure. All two or three hours that I wasn't on watch." She yawned. "Which wasn't enough. Goddess, I wish we could rest here for the day."

"You know we can't."

"That's why I said 'I wish.' And I do agree with Antreas. We're still way too close to Port City and what's left of the Tribe of the Trees to take a break. I wonder what *is* left of the Tribe of the Trees."

Mari shook her head. "It's bad, Sora. You should've seen them. The entire Tribe was infected with the skin-sloughing disease, and Thaddeus, *of course,* was rallying them under a cry of hatred and anger. But for all of their hate they were in no shape to fight the Skin Stealers. Unless the Death God takes prisoners, I can't image many of them living."

Sora met her gaze. "You sound upset by that."

"I am! You weren't there. The Tribe was suffering. Good people, bad people, the skin-sloughing disease doesn't care. It infected all of them, but some were still *good*, like Wilkes and Claudia. I really hate that the Storyteller, Ralina, didn't come with us. I would've liked to have gotten to know her better. And, Sora, the canines—they would have broken your heart. Thaddeus's men had flayed skin from them, packed it onto their own bodies so *they* healed, but they then ignored the agony of their canines. It made me angry and sick."

"That must have been why Fortina left her Companion and Chose Jaxom. She knew what her Companion was getting ready to do to her." Sora lifted her lip in distaste. "I had that horrible illness, and I can tell you that I would *never* have hurt Chloe to make myself feel better."

"Right? I'm starting to agree with the hypothesis that the Skin Stealers' disease reflects who we truly are. And there is something very wrong with many members of that Tribe—many, but not all of them."

"Yeah, it made me lose my patience and react in an angry manner, but I hated how I felt. I didn't want to be angry—I fought it."

"Maybe that's it—whether an infected person has the will to fight the anger the disease brings or not."

"Or whether an infected person actually *likes* the anger. Well, hopefully, we're leaving all of that behind us as we head into our new future."

"From your mouth to the Great Earth Mother's ears," Mari said reverently.

"Hey, speaking of new futures, what do you think of them?" Sora's gaze flicked to the spot almost directly across the camp's fire pit, where Dove and Lily were rolling up their bedding and then beginning to walk slowly toward the secluded area that had been designated as the Pack's temporary latrine.

"I think Lily is young and sweet. And I think Dove is as layered as an onion. But I have to say that I'm starting to like her."

"So, you trust her?" Sora asked.

"I'm going to trust her until she gives me reason not to. What about you?"

"That's where I'm at, too. She did swear an oath to us, and she seems forthcoming. Plus, it's obvious that her people have abused her. Her option is going back to them or wandering around the forest with Lily until something kills them." Sora sent Mari a pointed look. "Why? Are you getting pushback from the Pack about accepting them?"

"Not the Pack—Nik." Mari shrugged. "But that doesn't change my decision. Actually, it opened up a discussion about respect between the two of us."

Sora grinned. "I'll bet that didn't go well for Mr. Sun Priest."

"I'll just say that I think he has a better understanding of my leadership style now," Mari said.

Sora snorted.

"Sora! There you are!" O'Bryan called as he jogged up the sandy shore toward them with a little black fur ball chasing him.

"Chloe! My baby girl! Come here to me!" Sora gushed.

The instant Chloe spotted Sora the puppy attempted to sprint over the sand to her Companion, but her little legs kept getting caught by rocks and shells, slowing her until she began a yipping whine that sounded like someone was beating her.

"Goddess, she's loud!" Mari said, eyeing Sora, who remained seated. "Aren't you going to save her?"

"No, I can't. Rose told me that Chloe's getting spoiled by me carrying her around all the time—that she needs to develop her baby muscles—so I can't save her." Sora put down her mug of tea and leaned forward, encouraging the puppy. "Come here, baby girl! You can do it!" She clapped her hands and then stretched her arms out to her pup.

Complaining all the way, Chloe finally made it to her Companion and Sora picked her up, showering her face with kisses as she told her how brave and strong she'd been.

"That little girl definitely has a voice on her," O'Bryan said, joining Mari and Sora with his own mug of morning tea. "She was done nursing and Rose asked me to bring her here because as soon as she was full, Chloe sat her butt down and started crying for you."

Sora smiled at O'Bryan over the top of Chloe's head. "Thank you. I was just going to finish my tea and then go find Rose."

Mari watched the blush Sora's grateful smile caused as it worked its way up from O'Bryan's neck to his cheeks. Sora, of course, didn't notice. She was too busy kissing and cooing to her Chloe.

"You're not gull-egg hunting with Nik and the rest of them?" Mari asked.

"No, they have plenty of help. I was working with Jaxom and Mason to reload the boats. Antreas said we need to get back on the water as soon as we've eaten."

Sora groaned. "So soon? The sun isn't even over the trees yet."

"Hey, don't worry. Your stew will give you plenty of energy, especially with the addition of gull eggs!" O'Bryan said.

"Again with those gull eggs. I'm hoping they're worth the hype," muttered Sora.

"You know what? I *am* going to join the hunt for eggs—just to be sure you do know how delicious they are." He ruffled the top of Chloe's head, causing her to squirm with happiness, and then headed inland.

Mari raised a brow at Sora.

"What?" Sora said.

"You know what."

"No I do not. Tell me what."

"He likes you," Mari said. "A lot."

"Well, I'm likeable," Sora said.

"Humph."

"What's that mean?"

"You know what it means," Mari said.

"Enlighten me," Sora said.

"He *really* likes you."

"Yeah, you already said that. And I know he likes me. I like him, too. So what?"

"So, what are you going to do when he starts courting you?" Mari asked.

"Courting me? We just began a journey to practically the other side of the world. No one has time to court," Sora said.

"Nik does."

"That's Nik. He's weird. I've known it since the first moment I saw him."

"I'm pretty sure Antreas is courting Danita, whether she knows it or not," said Mari.

"I thought Bast was courting Danita for Antreas."

"Same thing, isn't it?"

"Well, they're weird, too—and by 'they' I mean Bast and Antreas, though I like them. O'Bryan isn't going to court me. He's too—I don't know—'unsure of himself' I guess is the best way to describe it. Plus, he's probably already figured out that it's not such a good deal to be with a Moon Woman. Our first responsibility is always to our Pack."

"We'll see. And I think you've misjudged O'Bryan. He ran back into a forest fire to save puppies—*this* puppy is alive and bonded to you because of him." Mari tickled little Chloe under her chin.

"You do have a point there, and I didn't say he lacked bravery, but he definitely lacks experience with women, and I am a woman who prefers a confident man."

"Give him time, Sora. I have a feeling about O'Bryan."

"You know, you didn't use to be so nosy," Sora said.

"You wanted to be friends, remember?"

"Can I take that back?" Sora teased.

"Nope, too late. But I promise not to say 'Told you so' when O'Bryan starts courting you."

"Drink your tea," Sora said.

Mari did, but only after she stopped giggling . . .

🐎🐎🐎

"Tell me again why we're looking in the scrub and debris on the ground for these eggs instead of in the trees," Danita asked Antreas as she trudged after him, picking her way over fallen logs and around nettle clumps.

"Gulls don't ever lay their eggs in trees. They build a mound of grasses, twigs, and really anything they take a fancy to, but they build it on the ground," explained Antreas. Bast chirped at him, alerting him to another spot of nettles. "Careful there." He pointed. "Bast says there are more stickers ahead."

"Ugh. But thanks. I hate nettles." Danita moved lithely around the sharp-tipped clump. "So, gulls just aren't very smart? I certainly wouldn't build my nest on the ground. That seems like I'd be asking for danger."

"They are smart. Remember why this island is called Spirit Island?"

"Yeah. You said that it disappears when it rains."

"Most of the winter and spring almost this entire island does, minus a few of these bigger, heartier hackberry trees, which means the island is uninhabited. The gulls wait until the spring rains are over and then they build their nests. Nothing can get them out here, except another bird."

"Huh. I guess that is pretty smart. I think I'd still build my nest in a tree, though," she said. Then her eyes were caught by a large mound of grass and dry twigs that was on top of a pile of water-whitened logs. "Hey, I think I found a nest!"

Antreas hurried to her side and followed her pointing finger. "I think you did, too! I'll climb up there and—"

"Hey, no way! I found the nest—I'm going to collect the eggs." Danita hurried to the pile of river debris and began climbing it. When she came to the spot that held the nest she reached in and then lifted a large, speckled egg. "Is this one?"

"Yes! Good job! There should be more, though."

"There are! There are three of them." Danita took the three eggs, putting them carefully in the bodice of her shirt, before she began climbing down—but part of one of the logs gave way beneath her foot and she tumbled backwards, windmilling her arms as she unsuccessfully tried to regain her balance.

Bast yowled and sprinted toward Danita, but Antreas was closer. He caught her as she fell, knocking them both to the ground, though he was careful that Danita landed on top and not under him. "I got you!" he said.

"Great Goddess, I hope I didn't break my eggs!" Danita peered down her shirt, and sighed happily. "All safe and uncracked." Then she swiveled at the waist to look at Antreas—whom she was sitting on. She grinned. "Comfy?"

"You're like a feather," he lied. "And I could lie here all day and barely notice that you're sitting on me and cutting off my breath."

Bast coughed at him, and Danita punched his shoulder. "Feathers don't cut off breathing. We're delicate and light and ever so lovely."

Antreas grinned. "Must be the eggs weighing me down."

Danita returned his smile. "*Definitely* the eggs."

Bast sat beside them to groom herself and purr as Danita and Antreas laughed.

Somewhere in the middle of their laughter Antreas realized he had never been this happy in his life—that in this moment, with Danita sprawled on his lap and Bast curled beside him, he had never felt so fulfilled, so content.

And that's when he made his mistake.

Antreas didn't think—he acted. He shifted Danita's slight weight and sat, putting his arms loosely around her so that she was snug on his lap. She turned to look at him, laughter still shining in her eyes, and Antreas kissed her.

Danita froze. She didn't pull away. Not at first. At first she simply stopped moving—later Antreas realized she'd even stopped breathing. Then slowly, hesitantly, her lips softened under his and for the space of a few breaths she melted into the kiss and her arms even found their way to his shoulders.

Antreas loved the taste and feel of her. She was sweetness and salt—and her body was warm and soft against him. Without even thinking about it, Antreas tightened his arms around her—and Danita changed instantly.

She shoved against his chest. Hard. "No, stop!" she cried, scrambling, crablike, off his lap until her back was pressed against the mound of debris she'd so recently fallen from. There she sat, her arms wrapped around her chest, staring at Antreas with big, glassy eyes.

Bast reacted first. She rushed to Danita, chirping sweetly to her and rubbing against the girl. Automatically, Danita buried her hands in the big feline's fur, obviously trying to stop their trembling.

"Danita, I'm sorry. I didn't mean to scare you," Antreas said. He stood and began to move toward her, but Danita cowered back against the debris pile and he halted, holding his hands out as if in surrender. "Danita." He spoke more slowly this time as he crouched so that he didn't tower over her. "Everything is okay. I would never, ever hurt you. You're safe. I promise. Bast promises. Do you think she'd let anyone hurt you?"

"N-no," Danita stuttered. Then she blinked, as if waking from a nightmare, and tears filled her eyes. "Antreas! I—I'm sorry. I'm so embarrassed." She turned her face from him and buried it in Bast's thick, soft coat, and began to sob.

"Hey, it really is okay. I understand," Antreas said soothingly to her.

"No, it's not okay." Danita lifted her tear-tracked face to look at him. "I do know you wouldn't hurt me, and I actually wanted to kiss you, but then everything changed and suddenly I was back *there*, with *them*—the men who raped me."

"I know, I know." Antreas felt lost. He wasn't sure what to say—what to do—to help Danita, so instead he sat not far from her and decided to just be there. "It's understandable that you had a flashback. I should've been more careful—I should've thought before I acted. This is my fault."

"No! It's *theirs*. Not yours. Not mine. But I have to live with what they did—what they have left me with—not you. I care about you and Bast so, so much, but I can't ever be your mate." She pressed her face into Bast's fur again and sobbed.

The big feline looked at Antreas and coughed.

"Danita, may I come closer to you?" Antreas asked gently.

"Y-yes." Danita's voice was muffled by tears and fur.

Antreas slid forward. Bast was on Danita's right side, so he positioned himself on her left.

"Would it be okay if I put my arm around you?"

She looked up at him, snot and tears mixing with Lynx fur and dirt from her fall. "Y-yes. I would like that."

Antreas thought he'd never in his life seen anyone as beautiful as his Danita. He put his arm around her. She stiffened for a moment, and Antreas waited, not moving, not tightening or loosening his grip on her shoulders—he simply sat there until he felt her relax against him, and then finally she rested her head against him.

"I'm sorry that I'm broken," she said.

"You're not broken. They didn't break you. They only changed you."

"Changed me for the worse."

"Don't say that! You get to decide what the change means—not me—not even Bast—not *anyone* but you."

She lifted her head from his shoulder and looked up at him. "You and Bast should stop this."

"This what?"

"This wanting me to be with you," she said, wiping her face with her sleeve.

Moving slowly and carefully, Antreas brushed aside a long, dark curl of hair that had fallen across Danita's face. "Bast and I aren't so easily frightened away."

"But you don't want a mate who can't stand your touch."

"I'm touching you now and you seem fine," he said.

"This is different. You're comforting me because we're friends, but you want more than that," she insisted.

"Don't you?" Antreas asked.

"I used to. I wanted babies—lots of babies. And now Mari and Sora say I might not be able to get pregnant, even if I could bear to be touched like that," she said.

"I'd like to swear an oath to you—right now—right here."

"What kind of oath?" Danita asked, sniffling.

"Well, it's two-part. First, I swear that I will *never* hurt you—not physically," he said.

Danita cocked her head to the side, studying him. "But what about hurting me mentally?"

Antreas's lips quirked up. "I would like to swear that as well, but over the past weeks I've realized that I really don't know much about women, which means I will definitely mess up—unintentionally—in my courting of you."

Danita's brows went straight up, and Antreas thought her gray eyes got even bigger. "You think you're courting me?"

He sighed. "See, I already messed up because I thought you knew that." Antreas watched Danita try to hide her smile. "And now you're laughing at me. I think I better go back to Sora for more lessons."

"Sora? Lessons?" Danita squeaked. "You told her you're courting me?"

"Well, sort of. She explained to me how Earth Walkers Choose their mates, which is why I know I'm supposed to court you—though it seems I'm not doing a good job of it. What have I missed?"

"Earth Walker males give a gift to the woman they wish to court," said Danita.

"Eggs! I gave you gull eggs. Did you break them?"

Danita felt the front of her shirt. "No, they're still whole, and you didn't give them to me. I found them!"

"Okay, how about those blue jay feathers I gave you before you danced your name to the Goddess?"

Danita rolled her eyes. "Bast found those for me, not you. All you did was hand them to me."

"See, I told you I was doing a bad job at this courting thing." But Antreas's heart felt lighter as Danita seemed more and more like herself again. "Maybe I'm the broken one in this relationship."

"Don't tease about it—it's awful to be broken."

"But you aren't. You, Danita, are just exactly as you should be. I would not change you if I could."

Danita met his eyes, and he saw that hers were filling with tears again.

"Ssh, don't cry. Bast and I are here. We'll always be here."

"But what about—" She broke off on a sob.

Antreas touched her face gently, wiping away a tear with his thumb. "We'll figure it out—the three of us. And that's the second part of my oath to you. Do you accept my oath?"

"If I do does that mean you think I'm accepting you as my mate?" she asked.

"No. It means you accept that I'm courting you."

Danita drew in a deep breath, and as she loosed it she said, "Yes. I will accept your oath. Though this might be the longest courtship in Earth Walker history."

Antreas's smile blazed. "That's fine with me. Bast taught me patience a long, long time ago."

🐎🐎🐎

"Antreas, you have officially made my morning," Sora said after spooning the last of the eggs into her mouth and then letting little Chloe lick her spoon. She'd scrambled the eggs the Pack had gathered and served them with the leftover stew. "You were completely right about these eggs, and I hope we can find more tonight."

"If we're lucky we will! Gulls only lay eggs for a short time once per year—and that time is now," Antreas said.

Mari smiled at the group of happily eating canines. "Rigel sure seems to love the shells added to his food. I thought you were kidding when you told us about putting them in their food, but you were right about that, too."

"I'm not sure why canines—and my Bast—like the shells so much, but they do," Antreas said.

"Must be good for them, and your Bast is certainly in excellent health," Nik said.

"She is!" Antreas agreed. "And now that everyone has eaten a warm breakfast, it is time to cast off again. Is the Pack good with the boat assignments?"

Mari's eyes scanned the Pack, taking in all forty-two people. She and Sora and Nik had worked with Antreas on the rearranging of the boat assignments, so she was especially relieved when no one spoke out or looked upset.

"Okay then—let's bury this fire and stow the rest of the bowls and get on our way. Looks like we might not get rained on today, which is nice," Antreas said.

"Why does it sound like there is a 'but' coming next?" Sora asked, making the Pack laugh nervously.

"Because you are wise, Moon Woman," Antreas said. "We have about two hours of paddling before we meet our next obstacle. As long as the light is good the broken bridge won't be much of a problem, and as it looks to be a clear day that is excellent news. The second obstacle, Bonn Dam—or rather what is left of it—is trickier. So my plan"—he paused and nodded to Mari and Sora—"if okayed by our Moon Women, is to travel a mere six hours today and then stop early and get a solid night's rest so that we can be ready for the dam crossing tomorrow."

Mari and Sora shared a glance, then Mari spoke up. "That sounds good. The break will also help with our hands." The Moon Woman addressed her Pack. "Today everyone must wrap their hands, and if your blisters break call either Sora, Jenna, or me immediately. We'll dress your wound and see if you need to be relieved from paddling or rowing—depending on the severity of your blisters."

"I would like to help with the dressing of the wounds, too," Danita said. "I'll be in Antreas's boat, and the two of us can maneuver a lot quicker than the bigger boats. I'll take some salve and bandages, and if someone needs more than just a dressing change I can bring them to one of our Healers."

"*We* can bring them to one of our Healers," Antreas corrected gently.

"You're right—*we* can." Danita shot Antreas a sassy smile before tickling the top of Bast's head. "Right, Bast?"

The big feline chirped and rubbed against Danita's legs while Antreas looked on with an amused smile.

"That's a good idea," Sora said. "And remember, all of you, keeping your wounds a secret—*any* wound—is not helping your Pack. If we don't know about it we can't fix it."

"And individual untreated weaknesses only make the entire Pack weak," Mari added. "Antreas, I would ask that we camp somewhere tonight that is not on the water. It's a Third Night, so Sora and I will be Washing the Pack, and even though I called down the moon last night while we were on the water, I vastly prefer feeling land under my feet."

"That shouldn't be a problem," said Antreas. "And I have a task for the weavers in our Pack that will probably be easier for them to begin on solid ground."

Mari thought she could almost see the ears of the Earth Walkers perking at the mention of weaving. Before they'd decided to join as a Pack, they had been part of Clan Weaver, and had grown up tending plants and weaving beautiful and functional things made from those plants.

"Remember I mentioned that we would be traveling past different types of peoples on our journey?" Antreas asked.

Intrigued, the Pack nodded.

"We will meet those peoples as we cross through Bonn Dam. They are called Tribe Saleesh and are mostly a peaceful people, but they completely control the land around the dam, as well as the river from the dam all the way to Lost Lake. In order to pass safely we must pay them a token at each of their villages, though the first is the most important."

"A 'token'? What does that mean?" Mari asked.

"A gift. For a group this size a couple of our travel cocoons and perhaps some hair decorations should suffice." He paused and then added, "They do love fragrant smoke. I forget what they call it, but they use it in their religious practices."

"I could wrap some of the dried herbs together. Lavender and sage make sweet-smelling smoke," Mari said.

"That would be perfect. Actually, their senior priest would especially like the herb sticks," said Antreas.

"Aren't the Saleesh also called Teteplates?" Wilkes asked.

"Only if you're trying to offend them. Their servants are called Teteplates—not them," said Antreas.

"Servants?" Danita frowned. "I don't like the sound of that."

"Yeah," Jenna said as she finished cleaning her bowl and packing it into her basket. "Do you mean servants or slaves?"

Antreas shrugged. "They call the Teteplates their servants. I don't know them intimately, but I have made the dam crossing several times, and even stayed the night in their camp. The Teteplates seem happy. They're free to come and go. But they do serve the Saleesh."

"What do the Saleesh give them in return for their service?" Mari asked.

"Their payment is through food and lodging. The Saleesh are incredible farmers and spend almost all their time tending their crops—up and down the river, which they use as irrigation. Their tribe is nomadic, so they never stay in one camp too long. The Teteplates don't tend crops or hunt. They care for the Saleesh—keep their homes clean, look after their children, make their clothes, and a lot of other things, but they never worry about going hungry or not having shelter."

"I don't know if that sounds fair," said Jenna.

"It's their culture, and their people—Saleesh and Teteplates—thrive." Antreas cleared his throat before continuing. "Something you all must understand is that we are not in a position to judge the practices of other Tribes and Clans. If someone is in trouble, we may help them—especially if they are injured. But it is not our business or our right to interfere in the lives of others, especially when we do not truly know them."

Jenna opened her mouth, obviously ready to argue with Antreas, but Mari's raised hand silenced her.

"What Antreas says is wise. It takes a special kind of arrogance to believe that our way is the best way—or the only way—to live, and that everyone who chooses differently is wrong or somehow lesser than us. Isn't that the kind of thinking that allowed the Tribe to enslave Earth Walkers for generations? They believed their needs and beliefs were superior to ours—yet they knew nothing about us except that we made plants grow. They saw us as childlike because they did not understand us. Let us not make their mistake."

"I agree with Mari," Sora said. "If we're asked for help, that is one thing, and we will try to give it."

"*If* giving help doesn't put the Pack in danger, correct?" Nik said.

"Correct," Mari agreed.

"But if we are not asked for help, then we should not meddle in that which is not our business," finished Sora.

"That sounds reasonable as well as wise," Nik said. "And Mari is right. The Tribe of the Trees was arrogant. We believed we were superior to others, especially Earth Walkers. We were wrong, and look where the Tribe is now—what is left of it is led by hatred. It sickens me." He turned to Mari. "I fully support respecting the ways of others and *not* judging them."

Mari's heart filled with appreciation for her lover. This was Nik publicly supporting her and showing respect for her—proving to her that he would be the mate she needed him to be.

"I agree with Nik and Mari and Sora," Wilkes said, stepping up beside Nik. "It makes me sad, but the Tribe took a wrong path some time ago, and that path allowed our people to accept Thaddeus's hatred as their rallying cry. I watched it happen from the inside, and I never want to be part of anything like that again."

"Thank you, Nik and Wilkes," said Mari. "Pack? Do you agree?"

"Agreed!" they shouted.

"All right then, we mind our own business," Antreas said, obviously relieved. "Let us cast off. The sun is just topping the pines, so the timing is perfect."

"I would ask our Moon Women if we could wait just a few moments before we cast off while those of us who choose to do so join me in greeting the sun," Nik said.

"Of course! I'm sorry I didn't think of it," Mari said. "Pack, those of you who wish to greet the sun, please follow our Sun Priest . . . where, Nik?"

"Here on the beach is just fine." Nik moved to a spot a few yards away from the water and turned to the east and the sun that was just topping the pines. "Spread out behind me and face the sun."

"Nik, do we have to be Companions to greet the sun?" Jenna asked, sounding hesitant and unsure of herself.

"No! Absolutely not! Anyone may greet the sun," Nik said.

"Well, then, I would like to try it," Jenna said. "I saw the Tribe greeting the sun while I was a prisoner. I used to wonder why a people who could be so beautiful and loving could also be so cruel."

Wilkes went to Jenna and put his hand gently on her shoulder. "We took a wrong path, but no more. Never again. Please join us." The Warrior's gaze took in the Pack, and he met the eyes of each Earth Walker. "Those of us who are here have changed—we woke up. I give you my oath as a Companion on that."

With tears filling her eyes, Mari watched almost the entire Pack spread out behind Nik and Laru and the rest of the Companion pairs.

"Want to join them?" Mari asked Sora.

Sora shrugged and tucked Chloe into the sling that held the puppy close to her heart. "Might as well. It's part of Chloe's culture. Maybe she'll like it."

Rigel bounded up to Mari, wagging eagerly. "There you are! Ready to greet the sun?"

But before they could join Nik, Mari felt a touch on her back.

"Moon Woman?"

She turned to see Lily and Dove. "Yes?"

"Might we join the greeting of the sun, too?" Dove asked.

"Of course," Mari said firmly. "Come with Sora and me." Mari watched how Lily guided Dove as they joined Nik, who frowned slightly at the two Skin Stealers, but said nothing.

Nik stood a little way in front of everyone, and even Mari held back a few steps, mimicking the other Companions. Wilkes led the way. He and his Odin chose to stand behind and to the left of Nik. Claudia and her Mariah were beside him. Davis rushed up, with Cammyman bouncing and huffing happily. Rose was next, with Fala and four of her five pups curling up in the sand.

Sheena and her Captain stepped into place to the right of Sora, with O'Bryan beside her. Then Rigel barked twice, and Mari felt his encouragement. She glanced behind them to where the young Shepherd was staring to see Jaxom and Fortina hanging back and looking very unsure.

"Please, Jaxom. Join us," Mari said.

"Yeah, Jaxom!" O'Bryan motioned to the empty spot beside him. "Come on up here by me. Your Fortina will love greeting the sun."

Jaxom's cheeks were red, but when Fortina trotted up to O'Bryan, he followed.

And then Mari watched Jenna step into place behind her. Danita joined her, with Bast and Antreas. Then it was as if the Earth Walkers collectively decided it was okay, and they all—the entire Pack—spread out across the beach.

Mari was blinking to keep her tears from leaking down her face when Nik turned. She saw him start in surprise when he realized *everyone* had joined them—and then his eyes, too, went suspiciously wet.

"Thank you." Nik's voice carried across the beach. "This means more to me than I can put into words. Just—just *thank you*."

"This would make Sol so happy," O'Bryan said.

Nik nodded and wiped at his eyes. "Yes. Yes it would. And I dedicate this sun greeting to my father, the Sun Priest Sol of the Tribe of the Trees."

"To Sol!" said the Companions.

"To Nik's father, Sol!" Mari shouted.

"To Sol!" echoed the rest of the Pack.

Nik met Mari's gaze and whispered, "I love you so much."

Mari could only smile and nod. She knew if she spoke she would burst into emotional tears.

Nik turned and faced the rising sun. He lifted his arms, and the Companions followed him. Mari lifted her arms as well, nudging Sora to do the same. Directly behind her she heard Lily whispering to Dove, describing what was happening, as well as giving her directions as everyone raised their arms as if to embrace the sun.

Nik threw back his head so that he was staring directly at the sun.

Every canine on the beach turned his or her muzzle up so that they too were gazing at the bright yellow ball of fire.

"Behold the wonder of our Pack!" Nik shouted. "Pack! Behold the first beams of our lifeline—our salvation—our sun!"

Though Mari couldn't see Nik's eyes, she knew they'd changed color, from a warm, mossy green to a shining yellow-gold that was perfectly mirrored in Laru's eyes. Nik laughed, a sound of pure joy, as he embraced the sun. She saw filigree patterns lift from within Nik's body to glow from under his skin—patterns that mimicked the Mother Plant, the enormous fern that the Tribe wrapped every infant in for the entire first year of his or her life, that magickal plant somehow absorbing into their bodies to create a mystical bond with the sun, a bond that was shared with their Companions.

Mari knew all of this intimately, because her father's blood had gifted her with the same magick, and the Mother Fern fronds he'd stolen for her and that her mother had swaddled her in as an infant had made sure that magick was awakened by the sun. Delicate fern filigree patterns lifted from her skin, and Mari threw back her head, staring at the blazing ball of light, reveling in the warmth and strength that swept from Rigel to her, further solidifying their unbreakable bond.

She heard Sora gasp, and glanced to her right to see her friend staring up at the sun, looking directly at it, as her pup's eyes glowed with light. Surprised, Mari's gaze found Jaxom. The Earth Walker, too, was staring directly at the sun, an expression of shock slackening his young, handsome features. Beside him, pressed against his thigh, Fortina's eyes blazed.

Interesting . . . Mari thought, wondering how sunlight, shared with their bonded Companions, would affect Earth Walkers, but there was no time to follow her thoughts.

"May the blessings of the Sun be with us today!" Nik turned and addressed the Pack, closing the sun greeting.

"That was really something," Mari said, as she stepped into Nik's embrace.

"We're really something! All of us—this whole Pack. Mari, I have never been this happy," he said, bending to kiss her thoroughly.

"Okay, Pack, let's get on the water now!" Antreas said. "Unless our Sun Priest and Mari Moon Woman need some *private time*." The Lynx man waggled his eyebrows at the Pack, causing everyone to laugh good-naturedly.

"Don't tempt me," Nik said as Mari stepped out of his arms and hurried to the shoreline with the Pack. "You know how I feel about that river."

"I do," Mari heard Antreas say to Nik. "But I also know how you feel about Mari. Seems she's leaving you behind."

Then there were more amiable chuckles as Nik jogged to catch up with his Moon Woman.

CHAPTER 10

ONE AND A HALF YEARS IN THE PAST—HERD
MAGENTI'S FALL CAMPSITE, OZARK PLATEAU

R emember, Riders, it is easiest to awaken the properties in crystals and stones when you are in communion with your horse. As Crystal Seer trainees, your strongest communion will be while you're on your horse's back." Dawn, the Rider of the Lead Mare of Herd Magenti and the most powerful Seer in the herd, paused and met the gaze of each of her six pupils—the young female Riders who had shown the most promise for becoming Seers. Out of this small group, narrowed from twenty young women down to the remaining six, her replacement, the next Lead Mare and Rider of Herd Magenti, might be chosen.

Though every mare in the Herd could compete for Lead Mare status, the four fillies and their Riders were exceptional, and Dawn had a very strong feeling that one of them would be the next Lead Mare. Her gaze lingered on her daughter and she was filled with pride—though she was careful not to outwardly show favoritism, she was not as neutral in her thoughts. *River and Anjo are doing so well! They excel at everything!* "If you feel ready, go ahead and mount."

The girls stood and each of their horses—four fillies and two geldings—knelt so that their Riders could easily mount them. Then the six young horses and their Riders eagerly faced their teacher.

"Here is what I would like you to do," Dawn began after mounting her own mare, the spectacular Echo, who had served almost a decade as Lead Mare of their Herd. "Each of you has a clear quartz crystal that you chose before class today, correct?"

The Riders nodded.

"You cleansed your crystals in the light of the full moon last night, correct?" Dawn knew that each girl had done as required. The six who remained were well beyond making such a simple, irresponsible mistake as not bringing the correct crystal to class or not cleansing it, but Dawn liked to reiterate each step in the awakening process, as someday one of these girls, *hopefully her talented daughter,* might be teaching her own young Seers.

"Yes," the class spoke as one.

"Excellent. Now, hold your crystal like this." Dawn placed her own well-used quartz crystal between her palms, weaving her fingers together as if clasping her hands in prayer. "If your crystal is tipped, that tip should face up. If it is not, take a moment to try different positions for it in your hands. Listen to your intuition. The crystal will speak to you. It will tell you how it should be held."

Dawn paused, watching her six students adjust their crystals. She was pleased to notice that River didn't fidget around with the crystal at all. She held it still and true between her palms, her hands clasped around it, her eyes focused down on the finger-sized shard of pure quartz she'd found the summer before in the Quachita Mountains, near the Valley of Vapors and the hot springs where Herd Magenti wintered.

"Dawn, I can't tell which way to hold mine."

Dawn shifted her attention instantly from her daughter to Skye, the Rider of a lovely dappled gray filly named Scout, who had been one of the weanlings from Herd Magenti who had Chosen a Rider from the same Herd. Often weanlings Chose Riders from other Herds, which helped to keep inbreeding to a minimum. And, truthfully, Scout was not one of Echo's fillies, though her dam's bloodlines did cross with hers far enough removed to allow her to be a serious contender for Lead Mare. The stallion that had sired Scout had been one of the minor Herd studs, allowed to breed only after the mares picked to be bred to the Lead Stallion were all covered, or impregnated.

Dawn couldn't deny that Scout was a sound, beautiful mare, and Skye was very obviously going to enter the Mare Test. She thought that there was something rather cold about the young woman, but she was intelligent and popular with the Herd, so perhaps she just didn't know the girl well enough to understand her.

Dawn studied the crystal cupped in Skye's hands. It was the size of a chicken's egg, flat on the bottom with many faceted tips pointing upward from its base. *A difficult crystal equates to a difficult student* flitted through her mind, and Dawn had to force her face to remain impassive, though she did tap Echo on the shoulder in acknowledgment of her mare's comment.

"Hold the crystal close to your heart," Dawn instructed, and Skye quickly did so. "Now, close your eyes and instead of concentrating on the crystal, concentrate on Scout. Her intuition is more highly developed than yours. Let her feel the crystal through you, and through her you will feel which way it should be held."

The girl closed her eyes and bowed her head, concentrating so hard that her brow furrowed. Suddenly she opened her eyes, smiling victoriously.

"She showed me!" Skye leaned forward to stroke her filly's smooth neck. "Thank you, Scout."

"Well done," said Dawn. "Everyone else have your crystals positioned?"

Six heads nodded.

"Quartz crystal is a stone of communication," Dawn continued. "They are the easiest of the crystals for a Seer to awaken. Skye, I will begin with you. Tell me what properties of the Seer quartz enhances."

"Quartz enhances body energy as well as thoughts," said Skye.

"True." Dawn shifted her attention to one of the two gelding Riders, a promising girl named Mist. Though not a mare Rider, so obviously not in contention for Lead Mare Rider, Mist had an aptitude for stones and Dawn was certain she would make an excellent Crystal Seer. "Mist, explain why Seers often begin their work by awakening a clear quartz."

Unlike Skye, Mist paused and took her time responding. "Quartz crystals clear a Seer's mind, enabling her to more effectively work with any other stone."

"Yes, that's right. Quartz is also a harmonizing stone—a powerful one. Cali, what does it harmonize?" Dawn asked the young Rider of an exceptional sorrel filly. The young horse was a true beauty—long-legged and wide of forehead and chest. Her Rider was an intelligent young woman, though she tended to lack confidence in herself.

Cali startled and her cheeks flushed pink. "Um, our thoughts and the thoughts of others?"

"Are you asking me or answering me?" Dawn asked, though not unkindly. When the girl simply lowered her eyes, the Lead Mare Rider moved on to another girl. "Luce, do you have a clearer answer?"

Luce, a passionate girl and the Rider of a big filly with unusual grulla markings of mouse-colored hairs on her body, shoulder and dorsal stripes, and black barring on her lower legs, was definitely one of the contenders for Lead Mare, replied quickly. "It harmonizes energies—thoughts, consciousness, and emotions."

"Yes, with what?"

"Humans," Luce said.

"Anyone else have an answer?"

River lifted her head. Dawn watched her daughter's gaze skim over the two girls who had not answered, and when they remained silent, she spoke.

"Quartz harmonizes our thoughts, consciousness, and emotions with the Universe and the Great Mother Mare and Father Stallion. A talented Seer can use quartz to tap into the will of the Divine."

"Exactly, and how does this aid a Seer?" asked Dawn.

"Well, if she can sense the will of the Great Mother Mare, then she can ask for guidance to make wise choices, and since quartz is a stone of communication, she should be able to easily pass along that Divine guidance."

"Correct." Dawn held in the rush of pride she felt from Echo, again being careful not to show favoritism for her daughter. "Today you do not need to try to tap into Divine guidance, though. Today I simply want you to awaken your crystal and have it focus your thoughts. So, first, each of you decide on a question. It can be as simple as *'Which boy do I ride out with during the next full moon?'*" Dawn paused as several of the girls giggled and blushed. "Or it can be more complex, like *'How do I become the best Rider I can be for my horse?'* But be sure you focus on one question." She paused again, waiting for her class to think of their questions before she continued.

"All ready?"

The group of six nodded again.

"To awaken your crystal, keep it clasped between your palms and raise it to touch your third eye." Dawn demonstrated, placing her crystal in the middle of her forehead, with its point touching her skin. "Once it's there, close your eyes and concentrate on your question. Your crystal will warm with awakening. When you feel its warmth you should also begin to feel your mind clear. Your concentration should sharpen. You might get an answer to your question quickly—or another question might come to your mind, one that involves the first. If that happens follow the path of the second question, as your crystal has led you there. And now you may begin. I wish you all a mare's luck."

Each of her students did exactly as she instructed. Dawn studied them carefully, automatically joining with her mare and using Echo's heightened senses to observe each of them.

Skye was struggling, which surprised Dawn. The girl was talented, but there was something about her that made her try too hard, causing many of her actions and reactions to appear forced. Dawn could even see beads of sweat beginning to dot the girl's upper lip, and she wondered what question she'd brought to her crystal. *Obviously one that was either unanswerable, or perhaps her answer wasn't what she expected.*

Not a Seer? Echo's question filled Dawn's mind with her familiar wisdom.

We can't know that yet, Dawn replied silently.

Echo snorted, and Dawn had to bite her lip to keep from smiling.

Behave! she told her mare, who swished her tail in cheeky response.

Though all Chosen Riders communicated on a psychic level with their horses, few Riders were able to hear their horse's voice. The majority of the Herd communicated through emotion. For instance, if a mare sensed danger, her Rider would also feel that danger. Sometimes a horse and Rider communicated through mental images. From the moment Echo had Chosen Dawn she had heard her voice—usually in complete sentences. Dawn had asked her daughter how Anjo communicated with her, and River had explained through feelings and pictures.

Dawn was hopeful that as the pair grew together and their bond strengthened they would also develop the ability for silent speech, though that was not a requirement for Lead Mare and Rider.

Dawn shifted her attention to Cali, the Rider of the attractive sorrel Vixen. The girl was sweet, and whether or not the pair was chosen for Lead Mare and Rider, Dawn had hopes that Cali would be drawn to the counseling aspect of being a Seer, as her kind manner and intelligence would be an excellent addition to the small team of Seers who saw to the mental health of the Riders—though in order to be successful as a counselor or a Lead Mare team Cali would have to gain confidence. As she watched, Vixen's head lifted, and then Cali's eyes opened. A smile bloomed on her pretty face and Dawn motioned for the girl and filly to step out of line and join her in front of the class, which Cali did quickly, though her cheeks blazed pink again.

"Did your awakened crystal help you find your answer?" Dawn spoke in a soft voice so as not to disturb the other concentrating Riders.

"It did!" Cali whispered.

"Then you are finished for the day. Tomorrow bring your quartz crystal to class again."

"Thank you, Mare Rider." Cali bowed respectfully before she and Vixen trotted away.

Nice girl. Like her and her filly.

Dawn silently agreed with her mare before returning to studying her students. Luce and her grulla filly, Blue, were both very still and seemed to be concentrating together. Even the filly's eyes were closed, and her bowed head mirrored her Rider.

She's a smart girl, Dawn sent to Echo.

Filly is sound and a lovely color, Echo replied, and then added, *but not as lovely as our River's Anjo.*

Dawn was agreeing with her mare when she heard a gasp, and her attention went to her daughter, whose large, dark eyes were open wide in a face that had suddenly gone slack with either shock or surprise. She motioned for River to join her.

Anjo trotted to her, rubbing her head against Echo's neck affectionately in greeting, but Dawn only had eyes for her daughter.

"Did your crystal not awaken?" she whispered to her daughter.

"No, it did. Easily," River said.

"Did you find an answer to your question?"

River sighed and Anjo snorted and tossed her head restlessly. "Yes."

"Why do you look as if someone just docked Anjo's tail?"

"Because you're not going to like the answer I got," River said reluctantly.

"Would you like to share it with me? We can talk about it—maybe you're wrong. Maybe I'll just be surprised and not unhappy."

River chewed her cheek. "Mare Rider, I would like to keep my own counsel, please, and figure this out myself."

Dawn suppressed a frustrated sigh. "Then I give you leave to go. Return tomorrow with your quartz crystal."

"Thank you, Mare Rider." Her daughter crossed her wrists over her heart and bowed formally before Anjo turned and they cantered away.

Dawn looked after her eldest and, truth be told, her favorite child. *Well, we did this,* she shared her thoughts with Echo. *We encouraged her to be strong-willed and self-reliant. Whatever were we thinking?*

Echo snorted and flooded her Rider with silent amusement.

"Going out by yourself? Again?"

River finished tying the saddle pack onto Anjo before turning to face Clayton. "Yep. Today's Seer class instigated a mission, so Anjo and I are off to complete it."

"I'd love to help—if you'd like," Clayton said. His arm was draped around his stud colt, Bard. The horse, though only two years older than Anjo, was already filling out with a thickened neck and powerful chest and rump. His solid black coat, relieved only by a white blaze on his face and four white socks, shone with health.

"Bard is really looking good." River avoided the question. "He's going to be a tough contender at the Stallion Run."

"I believe he's going to *win* the Stallion Run." Clayton patted his colt's neck affectionately. "I also believe you and Anjo are going to win the Mare Test."

"Well, thank you, but that is far from a sure thing. I'm just glad we have a year and a half more to prepare. The Stallion Run and the Mare Test are being held the same year—aren't you glad for more time as well?"

Clayton shrugged his broad shoulders. "I don't know, sometimes I'm glad—because preparing is good. The Run is tough, and no telling how many incredible stallions and Riders will enter, but there's something to be said for getting it over with, too."

"I definitely know what you mean," River said.

"So, what's this mission you and Anjo are on?"

"It's about communication. We awakened quartz crystals today. You know they're a stone of communication, right?"

He nodded and smiled. "I do. I've been studying crystals. I figured understanding them will help me when I'm Rider of our Herd Stallion."

His eyes seemed to burn into River at the unsaid rest of his thought, which she guessed had something to do with mating with the Rider of the Lead Mare—though that was absolutely *not* a given, even should he and Bard win the Run. Sure, some Lead Riders of the Herd's Mare and Stallion did become mates, but definitely not all of them. River's father was Rider of Herd Cinnabar's Lead Stallion, and different men had fathered each of her three sisters—with only her youngest sister being the offspring of their current Herd Stallion Rider, Jasper. Dawn often said that she liked to change her men with the seasons, which was more than fine with her daughters.

"That's a good idea," River said, motioning for Anjo to kneel so she could mount her. "I think more males should understand the properties of crystals. It doesn't matter that they can't awaken them—it's good knowledge to have, especially in a Herd of Crystal Seers."

"As usual, you and I agree."

River raised her brows at him, but decided that arguing with him was pointless, especially as she and Clayton did agree on many things—just not on their mutual attraction.

"Well? Can I help you with your mission?" he asked.

"No, but thank you. This is a solitary mission that Anjo and I have to conquer together."

"Aren't they all with you two?"

Clayton's voice was light, as if he were kidding around with her, but River saw the truth in his eyes, and this time instead of looking sad or disappointed, he looked annoyed and angry.

She met his gaze steadily from astride Anjo's back. "No, they aren't. Every day I do things with the Herd. Yesterday Anjo and I helped teach the children how to dress a horse's mane with ribbons. This morning Anjo and I partnered with Luce and Blue to teach the sunrise Flow class. I'm not a hermit, and there's nothing wrong with me needing and wanting alone time with my filly."

"Hey, whoa, I was just kidding. No need to snap at me." He raised his hands in surrender.

"Oh, horseshit, Clayton. Don't hide your true feelings like that. You're mad. That's easy to see. And you have no reason to be. I'm being myself. I'll always be myself. I love our Herd. I care about the people and the horses, and someday—if Anjo and I are judged worthy—I want to be the best Lead Mare Rider I can be for everyone. Nowhere in my life is there time for passive-aggressive crap and game playing."

Clayton's eyes blazed with anger. "Why do you always insult me?"

"Why do you always try to push me into a relationship that I have been very clear about not wanting?"

Without another word Clayton spun on his heels and stomped away, with Bard trotting behind him.

River sighed and said aloud, "I'm going to have to do something about him. It's been six months since he returned from Herd Cinnabar—six whole months since I told him clearly that I'm not into him like *that*. And it's not like we were lovers before he left and I suddenly changed. I've always made it clear that I am not interested in mating with him. He's just not listening."

Anjo snorted and tossed her head fretfully, sending worry to her Rider, along with a mental picture of Clayton—face red, punching a tree.

River laughed. "Well, he'll hurt his hand—that's for sure. Come on, let's go. There's a stallion we need to find and, thankfully, he's *not* bonded to Clayton."

River clucked to Anjo and turned the filly with the gentle pressure of her outside leg, and as soon as they were past the camp boundary she stepped up into a smooth canter. As she passed, she waved at a Watcher stallion—one of several Rider/stallion pairs who kept watch over the Herd, day and night. Then they headed *away*—away from the prying eyes of the Herd.

It didn't take long. It never did. How Ghost found them, River wasn't sure, though she believed it had something to do with Anjo. It seemed the filly and the stallion had bonded and she somehow called to him, though River had never known of a psychic bond happening between two horses. Anjo and Ghost's bond was so strong that the stallion had followed them from the Herd's spring campgrounds north to their summer ground, and again east to the Ozark Plateau and their fall grounds. And River was certain Ghost would also follow them to the Quachita Mountains and the Valley of Vapors and the hot springs that kept them warm and safe, even in the most terrible of winters.

Just thinking about winter had River shivering—and not for Anjo and herself. As the days grew shorter and colder, and the Herd prepared to move again, River was more and more concerned with what would happen to Ghost if he tried to weather the winter in the Quachita Mountains—outside the warmth of the Herd's hot springs valley.

The golden stallion galloped up to them, trumpeting a welcome which Anjo echoed, and River thought—not for the first time—how much she wished she could ask her mother's advice about this mysterious stallion and his connection to Anjo, and to her. But she agreed with her filly—

no one need know about Ghost. Not yet. The stigma of a Riderless horse and the belief that there must be something very wrong with him was just too great. What if the Herd decided he must be driven away? Or worse, euthanized?

"Anjo and I won't let that happen, and today I got help with how we can find an answer for what is going on with you, handsome." Ghost had paused in his greeting of Anjo to lip River's leg gently. Still astride her filly, she rubbed his wide forehead and automatically began combing her fingers through his tangled forelock. "This should be very interesting. I hope you're open for a little, um, *exploration*."

The stallion nuzzled her and then started trying to mouth her saddlebag open, making River laugh.

"Yes, I brought your carrots! I wouldn't forget them." River slid from Anjo's back and opened the pack, offering the bunch of carrots, as well as a bag of hearty feed, to Ghost, who settled in to munch contentedly. As usual, River brought a helping of grain for Anjo, too, and her filly joined Ghost.

While the two horses were eating, River prepared. This was something else she wished she could have asked her mother's advice about, but as that wasn't possible, she followed her intuition and used all of the knowledge she had already gained in her Crystal Seer classes.

From her saddlebags she took out a blanket and spread it on the ground near the horses. Then she brought out a full skin of water, a narrow length of leather cord, and the two crystals she'd been guided by her intuition to bring—the quartz crystal she'd used earlier in class that day, and the amethyst phantom crystal Clayton had given her six months before, on the day Anjo had Chosen her as Rider.

First, she washed the crystals, pouring clean water over them and then laying them on the blanket to dry. River had recharged both crystals the previous night during the full moon, before she had any idea she would be using the phantom stone.

Then she sat cross-legged on the blanket and picked up the quartz crystal. "But you made me realize the answer to my question of what to do about Ghost could be found *with him,* or at least found with him if I had a crystal that could help show us the way." River took the leather cord and wrapped it around the crystal, tying it tightly so that it wouldn't slip, before knotting the cord and slipping it over her neck, letting the clear stone rest against the skin between her breasts.

She placed a hand over the stone, pressing it against her skin and feeling it warm as it awakened for her again. River spent several minutes focusing on the crystal. She didn't lift it to her third eye—she was saving that place for the phantom crystal. It didn't seem to matter anyway. Along with the crystal warming, she could feel her thoughts sharpening and the typical mental babble in her mind quieting.

She had no idea how much time had passed when she noticed the horses had finished the carrots and the grain and were grazing lazily side by side. River called Anjo to her, and the filly trotted eagerly to River's blanket.

River concentrated on her connection with Anjo, and then she made the hand gesture that Anjo had been trained to recognize as asking her to lie down. Then she imagined Ghost lying beside her—the two of them facing River where she sat on the blanket.

Anjo immediately did as River asked, buckling her legs and lying down. Then the filly tossed her head and nickered to Ghost, who was standing close by, watching with open curiosity. He was more hesitant, but eventually he folded his legs and, with a groan that had River smiling, lay beside Anjo, facing River.

"Perfect," River praised them. "This is exactly what I needed you two to do. Now, what comes next might be nothing—or it might be very crazy. I really have no idea. All I know is that earlier today the quartz crystal made me believe I could get the answer to what's going on with Ghost by using the phantom crystal. So, here goes."

River wiped the nervous sweat from her palms and then picked up the beautiful phantom quartz. It was a warm, sunny fall day—probably one of the last of them—and the sunlight caught the amethyst phantom in the center of the crystal, turning it into a purple halo around the stone. River clasped it between her palms, just as she had done with the quartz crystal in class that day, lifted it to her third eye, and pressed the tip of it gently against her forehead. Within just a few heartbeats she felt the crystal warm and awaken. She drew a deep breath, let it out slowly, and then spoke what had been in her heart on the ride to Ghost that day, which she hoped very much were the correct words.

"Phantom quartz, I am River of Herd Magenti, Rider of Anjo and daughter of Echo's Rider, Dawn. I need your aid today. This stallion, Ghost, has left our Herd, and I do not understand why. My desire is to help him, and in order to do that, I must understand him better. What is it he seeks? How may I help him?" River phrased the questions in the same way she had heard her mother query crystals to tap into their wisdom. "I wish only for his best, and for what is best for Herd Magenti, so I ask that you part the veil between the seen and unseen worlds, and bring me the knowledge I require. It has been said!" River concluded with the ritual words that all Herdmembers used to seal a promise or anything of great importance.

Eyes closed, River waited—opening herself to the power of the phantom crystal.

Heat shot into her head. It wasn't painful, but it caused River to gasp in surprise. She closed her mouth and continued to concentrate, allowing the power of the crystal to guide her. River was filled with relief and an incredible sense of awe as images began to flash against her closed eyelids.

A great ball of fire exploded into a forest, causing a ferocious blaze. Animals fled—though not away from the burning forest, but *to* it. River realized there was something wrong with the animals, even before the fire consumed them. They were obviously sick—stumbling, salivating, and showing signs of a toxic madness.

Then the scene changed. She saw a huge wave of water, clear and beautiful. Riding the wave were a group of people, and with them were amazing animals that River recognized from drawings and descriptions passed from Herd to Herd as canines. Their eyes glowed the yellow of the sun, but not with anger—with strength and compassion. River was immediately drawn to them, so that she was shocked to her core when an enormous wall of dark blue water formed over the group of people and canines, threatening to drown them all.

Suddenly the vision changed and they were on the Plains of the Wind Riders. River even thought she recognized Rendezvous Site near the edge of the Rock Mountains. The crystal wave the people and canines had been riding washed them against a huge, verdant tree whose trunk had grown in the shape of a naked woman, depositing them safely among her branches so that they looked like beautiful birds.

And then Ghost was there! He stood before the tree, whinnying desperately as if calling for someone.

River's attention shifted from the stallion back to the tree as a second wave—the one that was sapphire colored and oozed darkness and danger—surged around the tree, battering the thick trunk as it tried to drown the people and canines.

In the vision Ghost screamed a warning, rearing as if he would strike out with his hooves to fight the blue wave, but he could do nothing against its tsunami-like strength, and it consumed the tree and the land around it, turning what was green and thriving to death and destruction, though at the last moment a small bird burst from the tree, flying erratically straight at Ghost to collapse on the stallion's back.

River was intrigued by the bird. It was small and gray—and its wings fell limp against Ghost's golden coat, exhausted and broken.

River felt the stallion's anger and despair. He *must* save the bird! But instead of running away, Ghost galloped straight for the tree, with the bird clinging tenuously to his back.

The sapphire water surged around his flanks and Ghost swam, fighting the darkness that threatened to suck him under, and as the stallion fought the current the bird rallied, pulling itself upright and singing a song that reminded River of wind sloughing through the prairie grasses. As the bird sang, Ghost's coat began to shine a brilliant gold, like fire, or the harnessed light of the sun—and the horrible water retreated from him, parting so that he could gallop to the base of the tree.

With a mighty effort, the bird flew from his back into the branches of the tree, as a great, silver moon lifted into the sky, shining down on them. Under the silver light the sticky, dark water began to retreat into the ground while the tree drank it in, growing straighter, stronger, and the trunk that was a woman glistened silver with magick as the land recovered, turning green with life again.

River gazed up into the branches of the tree to see that the people and their amazing canines hadn't drowned, but were celebrating—clapping, singing, and howling in happiness.

The little gray bird burst from the branches of the tree to rejoin Ghost. The moment she perched on the stallion's back, the bird was healed. Then the two of them, the lonely stallion and the strange gray bird, turned to look directly at Anjo and River—and River was filled with such sublime love and joy that tears flowed down her cheeks, the words *Yes! We belong together!* echoing through her mind.

Then the stone went cold and the vision ended. Shaking herself—mentally and physically—River opened her eyes to see the two horses staring at her.

Anjo immediately nickered her concern and River went to her, stroking the filly's neck and murmuring soothingly. Ghost lipped her shoulder and hair and River included him in her reassurances, telling both horses how special they were. When the three of them had calmed, River knew what she had to do.

She concentrated on her connection with Anjo, but she faced Ghost, stroking the big stallion's golden forehead.

"You were there with us—with Anjo and me—weren't you? You saw the vision, too."

Ghost went very still, turning his head so that he could meet River's gaze.

"I don't understand it—not all of it—not yet. But what my intuition is telling me is that you *must* survive. Something good is coming, and so is something equally bad—and you're part of defeating the bad, as well as welcoming the good. You can*not* die this winter. You must rejoin the Herd."

River felt Anjo's emotions—and the filly was in absolute agreement with her. Through their bond, she could feel that Anjo, too, was beseeching the stallion to come with them—to rejoin the Herd. And she could also feel Ghost's resistance.

The stallion feared returning to the Herd.

"I understand," River said somberly. "And I give you my oath as Anjo's Rider that I will not let anyone harm you—*ever*. You were part of our Herd. You know my mother is Lead Mare Rider. She trusts me; I trust her. She will protect you, too."

With a great sigh of release, Ghost stepped forward, resting his head against River, and Anjo nickered her relief as the stallion gave in.

The return ride was joyous. After Ghost agreed to rejoin the Herd it was like he suddenly became a colt again—galloping and bucking around Anjo and River as if his worries, along with his loneliness, were gone.

"Everyone is going to be so surprised!" River said, laughing as Anjo pranced, tail high. "Hey," she whispered to her filly, and Anjo's ears flicked back to catch her words. "Let's play tag with him!"

Anjo snorted and then sprinted toward Ghost, who had been bucking and kicking around them, and nipped his rump playfully before galloping off, with Ghost in pursuit.

The game continued as they came to a stream. River used her legs to guide Anjo under the branches of a massive weeping willow, hoping that Ghost would gallop past them—but the stallion was on to them, and he stuck his head within the hanging boughs, nipping Anjo's rump before he raced into the stream, splashing water everywhere.

Anjo shot after him, but River was laughing so hard that the filly had to slow, especially as they headed into the stream, to keep her Rider from uncharacteristically sliding off her back.

So, they were several lengths behind Ghost when they emerged from the water. Collecting herself, River fisted Anjo's mane and gripped her tightly with her thighs.

"Let's get him!"

That was all the encouragement the filly needed. She surged up the bank and galloped after Ghost.

Then everything changed.

A Rider burst from a clump of trees, giving chase to Ghost. Anjo startled, and River was so shocked to see anyone else that she slipped halfway off the filly's back, causing Anjo to slow again to keep River from falling.

The Rider—and his black stallion—pulled between Anjo and Ghost. River righted herself, encouraging Anjo to catch up, and when she'd drawn close enough she recognized the Rider.

"Clayton!" She shouted his name, but Bard was pounding after Ghost, and his hooves drowned her words.

Clayton began twirling a length of woven rope over his head. It happened so quickly that River had no time to even shout a warning. The rope snaked out, settling expertly around the stallion's back leg, tripping him so that the golden horse fell to the ground with a sickening thud.

At that instant River's mind was blasted with sound as she heard Anjo's voice scream *NO!*

"I got him! I got him! Great Father Stallion, I can't believe it!" Clayton was shouting and waving in victory at River.

Anjo slid to a stop beside Ghost and River was off her back in seconds, rushing to the fallen stallion. Her entire body was trembling—with anger at Clayton and with shocked excitement that she had heard the voice of her filly.

"Hey, careful, River. You know he's a rogue!"

River spun around. "Free him! Now!"

"But Bard and I just caught him."

"You idiot! I'll free him." River pulled a knife from her waistbelt and strode to Ghost. The stallion was struggling to stand, and she went to his head first. "It's okay, Ghost. It's okay, handsome boy. I'm here. I'll get that rope off you." She stroked and calmed him before moving to his rear leg and neatly cutting the rope so that the stallion stood, trembling, his sides heaving with shock.

Free! Anjo's voice rang in River's mind as she trotted to Ghost, nuzzling him and murmuring low, concerned nickers.

River felt a little dizzy and she had to reach out and lean against the stallion while she concentrated on breathing and grounding herself—though she wanted to shout, *I can hear my filly! I can hear her words!!*

"By the Great Mother Mare—you know him!" Clayton's eyes grew huge as he watched Anjo and River comfort the stallion. "That's why you go out by yourself so much. He's been hiding out here for a while, hasn't he?"

Feeling more like herself, River rounded on him. "Why are you following me?"

"I wasn't. It's a beautiful day—probably the last warm one until spring. Bard and I were out for a ride. I saw something flash gold—and it was him. Then I saw you and Anjo giving chase, and I figured you were trying to capture him. I thought I was helping."

"You're not. And since when is it okay to run down a stallion and trip him like that? You could've broken his leg!" River went to Ghost's back leg and felt the length of it, relieved that he didn't seem injured.

Sound. He is sound. Anjo's voice drifted through River's mind and she smiled with relief at the stallion. "You *are* sound, handsome boy."

"You do know him! Hey, I didn't mean to hurt him—truly." Clayton started to dismount from Bard, but Ghost squealed a warning and began backing away, ears flat against his head.

"Ssh, it's okay. I'm not going to let him hurt you. Again." River glared at Clayton while she remained with Anjo at Ghost's side, stroking and soothing him.

"Okay, okay, I'll stay on Bard. And I won't hurt him." Clayton shook his head incredulously. "He is a magnificent-looking stallion! What's wrong with him?"

"Nothing!"

"He's completely sane? I can't exactly tell right now—he's pretty upset."

"Wouldn't your Bard be? And, yes, Ghost is completely sane."

"Ghost? Wait—did he Choose you?"

"Of course not. I'm Anjo's Rider. It's just what I call him. He doesn't mind."

"Then this truly is a mare's luck. And we must take him back to the Herd," Clayton said.

"*We*—meaning Anjo and me—were just doing that before you interrupted."

"Um, River, he was running from you."

"Of course he was! We were playing tag, you fool!"

Clayton's look darkened. "How would I know that? He's a rogue stallion. I saw you chasing him. What would *you* have thought?"

"I hope I would have thought *enough* to ask you what was going on before I did anything."

"River, that's pretty difficult to do from the back of a galloping horse," Clayton said.

"Okay, yeah, I can see how you could have misunderstood the situation." She turned to Ghost, caressing his head and noting that he had stopped trembling and was standing quietly between her and Anjo—though his attention remained focused on Clayton and Bard.

"So, he was returning to the Herd of his own will?" Clayton asked.

"Yes. Anjo and I met him last spring. He saved us from a Flyer and a pack of yoties. He's followed us from campsite to campsite. We thought we'd lost him last winter, but this spring he was there again—healthy, if thin."

"And he's actually sound? And sane?"

"Do you not believe I can judge the health of a stallion?" River said, exasperated.

"Yes, of course, I'm just—just shocked. And amazed. And excited. If he can survive and thrive *without* a Rider, this changes everything."

River looked up at the beautiful golden stallion. "Yes, he can." She stroked his neck. "If he'll still come with us."

"I still have rope. We can always—"

"No!" she cut him off. "I won't force him. You won't force him. Ghost decides—not us." River looked to Anjo. "Will he come with us, pretty girl?"

Anjo and Ghost touched muzzles. They nuzzled each other and rumbled low, reassuring nickers back and forth, and then River was filled with a tide of happy relief from Anjo as her voice sounded in her Rider's mind. *He will come!*

She grinned up at the stallion and threw her arms around his neck, rubbing her cheek against him. "You're so brave and smart. You can always trust me, Ghost. I promise," River whispered to the stallion.

"So, he is returning to the Herd?" Clayton asked.

"Yes. On his own terms—not tied and frightened and forced," River said. She turned to Anjo, and the filly knelt so that River could mount her. Then she met Clayton's gaze. "Stay on my right. Ghost will stay on my left."

"Sounds like a good idea."

The small group headed east, and just before they came to the well-traveled path that would take them to Herd Magenti's fall campsite, River dismounted, telling Clayton, "I almost forgot. I have to do something, but it'll only take a few minutes. Go ahead if you want, but please don't say anything about Ghost until we arrive."

"Leave you and miss entering the camp with him?" He jerked his chin at Ghost. "Not a chance. I can wait." As River dug through her saddlebags he asked, "What is it you're doing?"

River held up a wide-toothed wooden comb and a handful of purple strips of cloth embroidered with Herd Magenti's crystal symbol. She and Anjo hadn't seen Ghost in almost a week, and the ribbons she'd braided into his mane had come loose. "I'm going to dress Ghost's mane and tail with our colors so that there's no question whether he belongs to our Herd or not."

"That won't stop them from questioning."

"Maybe not, but I'm going to begin this as I want it to end—with Ghost accepted as part of Herd Magenti."

It didn't take long for River's experienced hands to braid the ribbons into Ghost's mane and tail. The stallion looked spectacular! The bright purple of the ribbons flashed against the white of his mane and tail— an undeniable, unmistakable sign that he belonged to the Herd Magenti.

Clayton couldn't keep his eyes from Ghost. "River, if they're wrong about him—then what else are they wrong about?"

"What do you mean? And who's 'they'?" she asked as she worked.

"The Mare Council, of course. They make all the laws. And—no disrespect meant to your mother—but maybe it's time we change things," Clayton said.

"Change how?"

"Well, maybe more people should have a say in Herd law."

"Every Herdmember has a say in Herd law," said River.

"There has always been a Lead Mare and her Rider, and they're always in charge—with the *Mare* Council's blessing and backing," said Clayton.

"Yeah, that's what I was saying. The entire Herd votes in the Mare Council."

"Well, maybe some of us want more than a vote. Maybe it's time more people have a say."

River felt a chill spider down her spine. "And by more people you mean men."

River hadn't phrased it as a question, but Clayton didn't seem to notice and answered anyway.

"Yes, and that sounds good to me!"

"I'm sure it does." Again, Clayton paid no attention to the tone of her voice.

"And, thanks to you, *he's* going to be what begins the change." He pointed at the stallion, who gave him a suspicious side-eye look.

River said nothing as she finished dressing Ghost's mane and they took the well-kept path that led to Herd Magenti. Clayton kept spewing traitorous thoughts all the rest of the way back, as if plotting to supplant generations of leadership and Herd stability was a good thing—a normal thing, a thing everyone was talking about. River's stomach tightened. What if she didn't know about it because no one wanted to say anything around her? River's anger began to simmer.

We won't let him destroy our Herd, River told Anjo.

No. We will not, sounded her filly's already familiar voice in her mind.

CHAPTER 11

Mari was amazed at how much easier it was to paddle up the river during the day, especially during a day with no wind and a cloudless, cerulean sky. There was even one point when the Earth Walker women began a spring growing song, teaching the words to the rest of the group so that eventually everyone was singing along.

It felt good. It felt like family.

"Is it a bad thing to admit that I'm having fun?" Mari asked Nik's back. The Pack had been rearranged and divided into boats so that strengths were spread around and weaknesses were compensated for, but the two of them still shared one of the smaller boats—the kind that was outfitted with paddles instead of oars and had ballasts on either side so that Laru and Rigel could ride comfortably.

"I'm glad someone is," Nik muttered, but he shot a smile over his shoulder at her and added, "If I have to be on the water, there's no one else I'd want to be with."

She used her paddle to splash a little water on him. "You do truly loathe the water, don't you?"

"I absolutely do," he said firmly. "When we get to the Wind Rider Plains I hope I never have to be on the water again."

"You will bathe, though, won't you?"

"For you, Moon Woman, I will continue to bathe."

Laru sneezed and made a low, sarcastic sound in his big chest, causing Mari to laugh. "I think he's saying you smell."

"Traitor," Nik teased his Shepherd.

"How do your wounds feel?" Mari asked.

"Sore, but not terrible. And nothing has broken open. I am looking forward to a real rest tonight, though." Nik's voice lifted. "Hey, it's Third Night, isn't it?"

"Yes, it is."

"Good. I love it when you draw down the moon. It's magickal to watch, and even more magickal to be on the receiving end of the Washing."

"There was a time not so long ago when I couldn't imagine ever saying this, but I love it, too. I wish Mama were here. She used to tell me over and over how wonderful it was to draw down the moon for the Clan, and I refused to believe her. Back then I resented anything she did for the Clan. I'm sorry about that. I'm sorry I never got a chance to tell her she was right."

"She knows," Nik said. "Just like I believe my father knows Laru is safe and happy with me, and that I have found my home with you and our Pack."

"Our Pack—our family. We made the right decision to leave—to start new."

He glanced over his shoulder again at her. "Were you questioning it?"

Mari shrugged. "Yes and no. And certainly not after the Skin Stealer attack. No one in that forest is safe anymore. But it's hard to leave everything I've ever known—and harder to be responsible for leading a whole Pack to leave everything they've ever known. But I feel a lightness in my spirit that tells me we're headed in the right direction."

"Yeah, *away* from the God of Death," Nik said.

"Well, yes. But we could've headed to the coast, or north to the Winterlands and the Whale Singers, or even far south to where they never see snow. We could've found an isolated place to call our own. There's just something about the Plains that feels right."

"For as long as I can remember I've dreamed of seeing a horse and meeting the Wind Riders. Hard to believe it's actually going to happen."

"Maybe you'll make friends with one of the Riders and you'll actually get to sit on a horse's back," Mari said.

"Ha! Now *that* makes paddling down this river worth it," Nik said.

"Hey! Heads up!" Antreas's deep voice carried across the water, and the Pack quieted their private conversations and gave the Lynx Companion their undivided attention as he paddled up and down their loose line of boats. "The next ruin is not far ahead. This one is minor, but only because the river is so wide and deep here. Most of the bridge is well beneath the water. As long as you follow directly behind me you will pass safely. Do not hesitate. Do not stop paddling." Antreas, in his small boat with Danita, put his paddle down near the larger boat that held Rose, her puppies, Sora and Chloe, O'Bryan, Sheena, and her big Shepherd, Captain. "Rose, are the pups stowed?"

"Yes!" She held up a slinglike contraption that was similar to the one Sora tucked Chloe away in close to her chest, like a pouch. "Everyone has a puppy snuggled into one of these." Rose quickly demonstrated—securing the sling around her and then stuffing two puppies into it. Their little black heads were barely visible, but their bright eyes peeked out.

"They look like baby owls!" Danita said, making the Pack laugh.

"Safely tucked away baby owls!" Rose said. "Don't worry. I won't chance losing another pup." She looked around until she spotted Jaxom in a nearby boat. "Thanks to Jaxom I get a second chance at keeping this little one *inside* the boat." Rose beamed a grateful smile at the young Clansman as his cheeks flushed pink.

"Okay, then, is everyone ready?" Antreas asked.

"Ready!" the Pack responded.

"Follow me!" Antreas and Danita sliced the water, expertly propelling their boat to the front of the line as the Pack bowed their backs, focusing on staying in their wake.

Antreas had been right, of course. Now that she was looking for it, Mari could easily see the disruption in the glassy river that signaled a ruined bridge. As she squinted against the sunlight she spotted sections of metal stuck up out of the water, but that was really all there was to see—just a swirling of currents and a few metal shards. Antreas and

Danita glided between two of the protruding pieces of metal easily. They paddled several yards upriver and then paused, turning to encourage the rest of the Pack through.

Nik and Mari chose to bring up the rear again, and they paddled through the ruin with no problem. If she ignored the metal ruins of the bridge, Nik's white knuckles on his paddle and the tug of a strange current were the only things that marked this section of the river as dangerous, and Mari—along with the rest of the Pack—was feeling very confident as she joined the rest of the boats.

"We all made it safely!" Rose said, lifting a puppy victoriously.

"We're getting great at this!" Isabel called from one of the large boats she shared with Davis and his Cammyman, Spencer, Dove, and Lily.

"Yes we are!" Danita lifted her paddle over her head as the Pack cheered—unbalancing her boat. She, along with Antreas and Bast, would have been dunked in the river had Antreas and Bast not quickly counterbalanced.

Suddenly all boats went silent as Danita hung her head in shame.

"Everyone—don't get over overconfident," Antreas said, but not before taking Danita's hand and smiling kindly. "It's okay. It's very easy to capsize these boats, especially the little ones."

"I thought I was doing so well," Danita said, lifting her head, but still looking miserable.

"You are!" Antreas assured her. Then he turned his attention to the watching Pack. "You *all* are doing well. You were cautious and attentive, and you did exactly what I asked of you." He paused, his eyes scanning the river behind them. Finally he pointed, and the Pack turned to follow his finger. "See that big ball of roots and debris?"

Mari held her hand over her eyes against the sun. "I see it!"

"The Tribe calls those sweepers," Nik said, disgust clear in his voice. "They're dangerous. There's usually a lot more debris and roots invisible under the water. I've seen a man get tangled up in one and drown. We should paddle out of its way."

"Sweepers are tough. I agree with Nik," Sheena said. "Let's avoid it."

"It's following in our wake. Just watch and wait," Antreas said.

Mari watched with the Pack, and it didn't take long for Antreas to be proven right. As soon as the sweeper came to the ruins it began spinning erratically as the strange current quickly took hold of it, pulling it off course until it suddenly was sucked beneath the swirling water, disappearing completely.

"Where is it?" Jenna asked, scanning the river with the rest of the Pack.

"Stuck," Antreas said. "The current took it, pulling it underwater. It's being held there—either because it got caught on a piece of wreckage, or because it is being held under by one of the unpredictable currents that haunt every ruin on the river."

"That's terrifying," Danita said. "It could've happened to any of us."

"Do you understand now why I don't want any of us to get overconfident?" Antreas took Danita's hand again and squeezed it affectionately.

"I do. I'll be more careful."

"Be careful and watchful, but that doesn't mean I want us to lose the joy of traveling up this magnificent river on a beautiful day," Antreas said, meeting and holding Danita's gaze. "Don't lose your joy—but also don't lose your balance."

Danita grinned at him, her embarrassment completely gone. "I won't!"

Mari loved watching Antreas's exchange with Danita. She felt so proud of the Lynx Companion. Just weeks ago he had been aloof and closed off—and now here he was, being unashamedly compassionate with Danita in front of the entire Pack.

"Maybe he is worthy of her," Mari said softly, more to herself than to Nik.

"That's almost exactly what I was thinking," Nik said, sotto voce. "And I don't need to be a Clansman to see that he is definitely courting Danita."

"And she's definitely accepted his courtship," Mari whispered back. "I think it's wonderful."

Nik leaned toward her, and she met him halfway so they could share a long kiss that had Rigel's and Laru's tails thumping in unison against their ballasts.

"Hey, you two, be careful!" O'Bryan called. "Those ballasts won't save you from tipping."

"But a dip in the river will cool you two off!" said Jenna, giggling.

The Pack chuckled and Mari used her paddle to throw water at Jenna, which only made her giggle harder.

Smiling, Antreas held up his hand, and the Pack quieted. "We have five more hours of travel to go, which will take us to a place where we can safely beach for the night. It will only be mid-afternoon when we get there, so we'll be able to rest, pitch camp, and maybe even do a little fishing before moonrise. Mari, Sora, you did say it is a Third Night, did you not?"

"We did!" Sora called, and Mari nodded in agreement.

"Good! Then it should be a magickal night," said Antreas. "Ready to paddle on, Pack?"

With an enthusiastic cheer and quite a bit of barking, the Pack continued upriver.

Though they beached early, the Pack was dragging after seven concentrated hours of steady river travel. They'd gone from singing and laughing to silently bending their backs to the task of propelling the boats ever forward when Antreas finally shouted, *Follow me to beach the boats straight ahead!*

The relief that ran through the Pack was almost palpable. One boat at a time, they wearily grounded on a tongue of flat, silty beach at the base of a huge gray monolith of a rock that jutted into the sky. They quickly made camp, creating a fire as their central point, and then spreading out around it. O'Bryan and Mason baited hooks and waded into the river, trying for fish to add to Sora's stew. Several of the Earth Walkers began digging for fresh wapato, and Sora promised to part with some of her precious salt stash to add savory flavor to the fibrous roots.

The rest of the Pack were resting and chatting easily. A few of the Earth Walkers were giving weaving lessons to Lydia, Sarah, and—surprisingly—Dove and Lily as they finished the travel cloaks they would gift the Saleesh people with the next day when they entered their territory. Mari had been shocked by Dove's interest in weaving, but she had explained that she could feel the patterns with her hands, and she seemed content to sit with the other weaving women and work. Mari thought that she almost appeared to be part of the Pack. Almost.

Done checking on the wounded members of the Pack, Mari sat beside Sora. Little Chloe was lying between Sora's feet gnawing on a waterlogged stick. Mari ruffled the fur on the top of the puppy's head and the little girl wagged her small tail and greeted Mari with a quick lick before going back to chew on her stick.

"I don't think I'll ever understand why canines like chewing so much," Mari said.

Sora smiled down at her pup. "It is strange, but O'Bryan told me that it feels good to young canines to chew because it helps their teeth to come in."

"I suppose that makes sense. Rigel's certainly obsessed with chewing. I wonder if we could come up with something better for our young canines to chew on than sticks and rocks and whatever else they can fit into their mouths," said Mari.

"That's a thought. Maybe we could weave a smaller version of a net ball and offer that to the pups. At the very least it wouldn't splinter in their mouths," said Sora.

"I'll talk to some of the older women about it. They can weave almost anything into being," Mari said. Then they sat in easy silence as Sora added herbs and handfuls of dried vegetables to the stew she was preparing. "I like watching you cook," Mari told her friend.

"Does that mean you're actually paying attention so that your dismal cooking skills get better?" Sora asked.

"Absolutely not. I like watching you like I watch the river. I enjoy gazing at the mystery—not trying to become the mystery."

"I'm going to take that as a strange compliment," Sora said.

"It was meant as one." Mari tilted her head back and looked up at the rock that dominated the landscape almost as much as the wide river did. "That thing is enormous. It gives me a weird feeling. I'm not sure I like it."

"Antreas told me they call it Rooster Rock, though I am not sure why," Sora said, looking up at the rock with Mari. "Of course, I don't have any idea what a rooster is, so it might have looked just like that."

"I kinda like it," Danita said, plopping down beside them after kissing Chloe on the top of her head. "It looks so strong and wise. Antreas told me a rooster is a bird. He said they have them on the Plains of the Wind Riders and their eggs are almost as delicious as gull eggs."

"Oooh!" Mari's attention instantly shifted from staring at the hulking rock to Danita. "Did he say there might be gull eggs here? They were delicious."

"He and Bast went to look. Antreas didn't sound hopeful, but Bast did."

"Then I will happily plan for gull eggs. That feline knows things," Sora said.

"She sure does," Danita agreed.

Mari and Sora shared a glance, then Sora cleared her throat and said, "So, Danita, it appears as if Antreas is courting you."

"Yes," she said, but Danita's gaze went down and she picked at the pebbles around her feet.

"You accepted him?" Mari asked.

"Yes," Danita said, her eyes still downcast. "But I shouldn't have."

"Do you not like him?" Sora said.

"No! I mean, yes. I like him. A lot."

"But as a friend? You're not attracted to him?" Mari asked.

"I'm attracted to him," Danita said softly.

Sora and Mari shared another look before Mari spoke gently. "You can talk to us. It might help."

Danita lifted her head. Tears pooled in her eyes. "I like him. I may even love him. I know I love Bast. But it was selfish of me to accept his courtship, because I can't ever be his mate."

"Because you're afraid you can't have sex with him?" Sora asked.

"Sora!" Mari said.

"What? I'm just saying what we're all thinking."

"Sora's right. It's what I've been thinking, because it's the truth," Danita said miserably.

"Hey," Mari said. "It's only the truth right now. It doesn't have to be the forever truth."

"I know a little of what you're feeling," Sora said, stirring the bubbling cauldron. "Thanks to Nik I was attacked, but not raped. I think I understand as much as anyone who has not lived your experience can. Even though logic tells me Jaxom was not himself when he and the other two Clansmen attacked me—and I know Jaxom. I've known him all my life, so I also know that in his right mind he would *never* hurt me. Still, I can barely look at him without being filled with anger. And I have not allowed a man to touch me intimately since that horrible day."

"Do you think you'll ever be able to be touched by a man, by a mate, again?" Danita asked.

"I know I will. I'm not going to let violence and hatred win. This is how I look at it—if what happened to me stops me from opening myself to the love of a mate, then all that was terrible about that day wins."

"Danita, you have to give yourself time to heal," Mari said.

"But my body feels so much better," she said.

"It isn't just your body that needs to heal. It's your mind, too," Mari said gently.

"But how do I heal my mind?"

"By talking. By letting us help you. By being kind to yourself and not pushing for too much too fast."

"Sora's right. If you keep all your fears and anger inside and don't share them, they'll get bigger and bigger," Mari said. "I haven't been attacked like the two of you have, but I do know about what happens when you keep sadness and anger and fears inside. They eat away at you. I did that after Mama died. I disappeared into my grief. Thankfully, Rigel and Sora wouldn't leave me alone. They forced me to open up and rejoin the world. Danita, I give you my word as a Moon Woman that I will *not* leave you alone."

"You have my word as well," Sora said. "We're going to help you heal—mind and body."

"Do you really think there's a chance I can be normal again? That I can be intimate with Antreas?"

"Yes," Sora said.

"Absolutely," Mari said.

Danita quickly wiped away her tears. "Thank you, Moon Women. Thank you so much."

Making her unusual coughing sounds, Bast padded up to Danita, sniffing her wet face and rubbing against her while she sent Mari and Sora yellow-eyed looks that said she was blaming them for the girl's tears.

"I'm fine. No, everything is okay." Danita caressed the big feline, kissing her nose and rubbing her face in Bast's soft ruff.

"What's happened?" Antreas jogged up, brow furrowed and breathing hard. "Bast took off. Told me Danita's upset."

"I'm fine. I was just talking with Mari and Sora about, um, my problem," Danita said without making eye contact with Antreas.

"Hey." Antreas crouched before Danita. "It's not a problem. Nothing about you is a problem."

"That's pretty much what we've been saying, too," Sora said.

"Moon Women are wise. I think you should listen to them," Antreas said.

"I'm listening. And I'll keep listening." Danita took Bast's face between her hands and gently chided, "And you shouldn't worry him like that."

The Lynx coughed and then settled down to groom herself beside Danita.

"For those of you who do not understand Lynx-speak, let me translate," Antreas said. "Bast is definitely not done worrying me about Danita."

"I got that. How 'bout you, Mari?" Sora teased.

"Loud and clear," Mari said.

"Hey, I found something for you. Hold out your hand," Antreas said to Danita.

She held out her hand. The Lynx Companion reached into his pocket and then plopped a dappled gull egg in the middle of her palm.

Danita gasped happily. "You found a gull egg!"

"Thankfully, I found a lot more than one," Antreas said. "They're in nests that cover the side of Rooster Rock. It'll take a little climbing, but there are enough for the entire Pack to have them for breakfast."

"I told you that feline knows things," Sora said.

"Antreas, you just made me look forward to the morning," Mari said.

"I think we can spare a little garlic and onion to add to the morning scramble," said Sora.

"That's going to be delicious!" Danita clapped happily.

"Is this a party that I'm missing?" Nik asked as he and Davis joined them, with Laru, Rigel, and Cammy trotting at their heels.

"No, just girl talk," Mari said.

"Antreas isn't a girl," Davis said.

"What?!" Sora gasped in mock surprise, causing Danita to giggle.

"Hey, Sora, how long do we have until dinner?" Nik asked.

"That depends on whether O'Bryan and Mason are having any success with catching fish."

"We just checked in with them, and they are," Nik said.

"They need more time, though," Davis added. "They said another hour and they'll have enough fish to fill the stew."

"And I saw the women digging the wapato," Antreas said. "They should be bringing you a very large pile soon. I believe after they wash the roots they're going to collect leaves to wrap them in for baking."

"Good." Sora squinted up at the sky. "Then I'd say another couple hours and it'll be sunset. We'll Wash the Pack then. Afterwards it'll be time to eat."

"Fantastic!" Nik's eyes glittered with excitement. "That's definitely enough time."

"Absolutely! I'll go get Wilkes, Claudia, Sheena, and Rose," Davis said before he and Cammy sprinted off down the beach.

"What are you two planning?" Mari asked, smiling at her lover.

"I'm planning to show you how to shadow-dance with Rigel," Nik said.

"Shadow-*dance*? What does that mean?" Mari asked.

"It's a game the Tribe plays, but it's really more than a game. It's about the bond between human and canine, and it's about fun," said Nik.

"Can Chloe and I play, or is she too young?"

"Chloe Chose a Companion, which means she's old enough to play, but you could check with Rose to be sure," said Nik.

"What about Bast and Antreas?" Danita asked.

"Have you ever seen a shadow dance?" Nik asked Antreas.

"I have. Several times, actually."

"Did you and Bast join in?" Danita asked.

Antreas looked surprised. "Well, no. We were never invited to join."

"I can change that right now. Antreas, would you and your Companion like to join us in the shadow dance?" Nik asked.

Antreas shared a long look with Bast, and the feline chirped at him, making Antreas grin. "I'd like to accept half of your invitation. Bast wants to dance, but not with me. She wants to dance with Danita."

"Me?" Danita squeaked.

"Why not? You danced your name to the Goddess. You're good at dancing," Antreas said. Bast circled Danita excitedly, rubbing against her and purring.

"Is their connection strong enough?" Nik asked.

Antreas, Mari, and Sora answered together with a resounding "Yes!"

Nik chuckled and shook his head. "Mari and Sora, you two have never seen a shadow dance. How do you know Danita's connection with Bast is strong enough for it?"

"Nik, Bast was hunting eggs with Antreas. Danita was here talking with Sora and me. She was upset. Bast knew it even though she could not see or hear Danita," Mari explained.

"Well, to be completely fair, Bast's eyesight is remarkable, so she might have been able to see Danita, but I stand by my answer. My Bast's connection with Danita is strong enough for the dance," Antreas said. His gaze found Danita again, and his whole face changed and softened with affection. "You and Bast can do it. I know you can. And I will love watching."

Mari watched Danita closely to see if Antreas was being too pushy, but the pleased smile that lit her face told the truth—Antreas wasn't forcing her into anything. Danita was quite clearly falling in love with the Lynx man.

"I'm not sure what I'm getting myself into, but I'll try," said Danita.

The rest of the Companions joined them then. There was a festive air about them, and even Laru was wagging and showing puppyish excitement.

"A shadow dance! It has been far too long," said Claudia. "Right, Mariah?" The beautiful Shepherd barked in happy agreement.

"This is going to be fun!" Davis said as Cammy jumped around him, huffing merrily.

"Could someone watch Fala's pups so she and I can join the dance?" Rose asked.

"Dove and I would very much like to take care of Fala's puppies." Everyone turned to see Lily leading Dove up to them.

Mari held her breath, wondering at Rose's response.

Rose and Fala shared a long look, and then Rose began unwrapping the sling she'd taken to wearing since the girl pup had fallen into the river the day before, and walked over to Lily and Dove. She carefully handed Lily the pouchlike carrier and the four squirming pups within. "Take good care of them, please."

"Oh, we will!" Lily said.

"Thank you, Rose," Dove said. "Thank you for trusting us with Fala's babies."

"We share a boat, and I've watched how tender you are with them," said Rose. "They like you. Both of you."

"We like them!" Lily gushed, kissing one of the puppies.

Mari released her breath, and with an audible sigh, so did the Pack. Even the Earth Walkers, who knew almost nothing about canines, understood that Rose had just taken an important step in trusting the two

Skin Stealers with the puppies, which filled Mari with hope for Lily and Dove's future with them.

The rest of the Pack began moving to form a circle around the campfire, talking with one another and openly wondering about the shadow dance.

Sarah limped up, supported by her sister, Lydia, and as soon as they heard "shadow dance" they began grinning and talking with the Earth Walkers. Mari overheard the words "beautiful" and "graceful," and grew even more curious.

Jaxom and Fortina jogged up, looking confused but curious. "Fortina told me we needed to get back to camp, but I did find these first." He shyly offered Sora the basket he carried.

She took it without looking at Jaxom, and her face registered happy surprise. "Mussels! They're going to be wonderful with the fish stew. Thank you, Jaxom."

Jaxom's cheeks pinkened, but he waved away her thanks. "Fortina found them. Her nose is amazing. So, what's going on?"

"Good timing, Jaxom," Nik said. Then he bent to pet Fortina. "That's a good girl, Fortina. You and your Jaxom do need to join us in the shadow dance."

Immediately Fortina began wriggling with glee.

"What's a shadow dance?" Jaxom said.

"That's what we're all asking," Mari said.

"I could explain, but it's easier to show you," Nik said.

"We need music," said Davis.

"We have musicians," Sora said.

"Drums are a must," Nik explained. "Any other instruments are a plus."

Sora stood and cupped her hands around her mouth to shout, "Drum circle! We need you!"

The Pack was scattered all along the beach, working on projects, unloading supplies, or simply resting, but when they heard Sora's call several Earth Walkers stopped what they were doing, unpacked their drums, and joined the growing group around the campfire.

Nik and the other ex-Tribers were clearing an area close by, removing large rocks, washed-up branches, and any big pieces of river debris. When they seemed satisfied, Nik approached the Earth Walkers, who waited patiently with their drums.

"It would be good if you sat here." He pointed to a spot in front of the campfire within the area of beach he and the others had just cleared. "We're going to dance there." Nik gestured to the cleared area. "The rhythm of your drumbeats really doesn't matter, as long as it's consistent, but a four- or eight-count beat is best."

"They should start with a four count," Wilkes said, and Mari thought that even that gnarled old Warrior looked eager to dance. "That's easiest to learn."

"You're right," said Nik. "How about something with a four-count beat, about at this speed." Nik clapped his hands in a rhythm that was brisk, but not difficult to follow.

"Like this?" asked one of the Earth Walkers, repeating Nik's rhythm on her drum.

"That's perfect! Okay, keep that up." Nik turned to Davis, Wilkes, Claudia, Sheena, and Rose. "Ready?"

"Yes!" they shouted, and their canines barked eagerly.

"Take your places. I'll do some explaining and then we'll start." Nik faced the Pack. By now the entire Pack had gathered, even Mason and Davis, who had finished fishing and were cleaning their catch riverside, but also watching the proceedings closely. "The shadow dance is a way canines and Companions practice silently using the bond between them. When it works well, our canines can read our minds as well as our bodies. When we dance together we give no verbal cues to our canines." Nik paused and nodded at Bast. "Or our felines." Bast chirped at Nik as if to thank him, causing the Pack to chuckle. "The goal is to move as one with the beat of the drums."

"Are there rules we have to follow?" asked Jaxom nervously.

"None except not speaking, but you can communicate mentally with Fortina—and you will. It's something our canines do naturally. Just relax and open yourself to her, and don't forget to have fun. We'll start, and then when you feel comfortable, please join us. You, too, Sora and Mari."

"Rose? Is Chloe too little?" Sora called to Rose, who had already taken her position with Fala.

Rose considered for a moment, and then shrugged. "I've never known a pup so young to join the shadow dance, but that's because I don't believe a pup so young has ever Chosen her Companion before. Chloe is special. Fala and I agree that you should try the dance with her."

"I'll stir the stew so you and Chloe can move closer and watch," said Spencer.

Mari made a mental note to give the girl more responsibility. She seemed to always be willing to help, and she liked her bright, happy eyes.

"Thank you, Spence." Sora picked up Chloe and moved to a place where she and the pup could see more clearly.

Mari and Rigel, with Jaxom and Fortina beside them, followed her.

Nik and Laru took a place in the center of the others. He shot a grin at Mari and then nodded to the drummers. "We're ready!"

The drumming began—a sonorous beat that was to the count of four. The drumbeats echoed off the river, which turned the sound liquid and lovely.

Mari forgot about the drums and the river and everything but the Companion pairs before her as they began to move together. Her breath caught at the grace of the canines as they easily mimicked the movements of their Companions. Nik's feet tapped out a pretty pattern in time with the beats of the drums, and Laru shadowed him so closely and completely that it seemed the two were one. The group moved in a circle, slowly at first, using easy steps, and then Claudia lifted her hands, clapping in counter time to the drumbeats as she turned in quick, graceful circles. Mariah's gaze was locked on her Companion as the Shepherd mirrored each of Claudia's movements.

Then Rose did the same thing, clapping with Claudia and twirling around—even faster—as Fala agilely stayed with her, little black paws blurring with speed.

Davis whooped and began a series of jumps and side steps that Cammy copied perfectly as he grinned a tongue-lolling canine smile.

Nik broke from the group, sprinting to Mari and taking her hand. His face was flushed and he was breathing fast—and joy radiated from him. "Come on! You and Rigel will be great!"

Mari wasn't so sure they'd be "great," but she was eager to try. As she and Rigel joined the shadow dancers, Mari saw Rose gesturing to Sora to join her. For a moment Jaxom and Fortina were left standing by themselves, looking lost. Then Claudia rushed to him, taking the young Earth Walker's hand and pulling him into the circle with her as Fortina barked with happiness.

"How do I start?" Mari asked Nik.

"Just let the beat of the drums guide your feet. Think about Rigel. He'll be watching you and he'll also be inside your mind." Then Nik began moving with the drumbeat, and Laru fell into step beside him, dancing with a light-footedness that belied his size.

"Let's do this, sweet boy," Mari said to Rigel. She stared down at the half-grown pup and felt him there, joined in her mind. She began dancing, and Rigel matched her every step. As they moved around the circle with the others, Mari realized the Pack had joined in—they were clapping with the drumbeats. Then there was the lilting sound of a flute trilling with the drums and, finally, women's voices, singing wordlessly with the rhythm that filled the air, creating a lilting melody.

Mari felt as if she and Rigel were flying! She spared a quick glance at Sora and Chloe. Sora was moving more slowly than the other dancers, but the tiny pup was keeping up with her—and Sora's face was radiant with joy.

She looked quickly to find Jaxom and Fortina dancing nimbly between Claudia and Sheena—and her heart swelled at the smile that blazed from Jaxom's face.

Mari had forgotten that Danita had agreed to dance, but the gasp from the Pack pulled her attention to the very center of their circle. Danita danced there with Bast. Unlike the canines, the Lynx wasn't beside the girl, pressed to her side. Instead the feline stood in front of Danita, facing her, and every step Danita took, Bast mirrored. Danita moved with a beauty that reminded Mari of willow boughs swaying with impossible grace, especially when her long, dark hair floated around her like a halo. Bast was every bit as exquisite—her preternaturally sharp yellow eyes never leaving Danita.

Then Nik and Laru were beside her again. "I know you can communicate with Laru. Do you think the four of us—you, me, Laru, and Rigel—can dance together?"

"Let's try!"

They did more than try—they succeeded in a graceful joining that filled Mari with an indescribable lightness. Soon Mari threw out her arms and laughed. She couldn't remember the last time she'd known such a sense of completeness and hope for the future. It wasn't just the dance—it was the joining the dance signified, as well as the voices and instruments of her Pack as they *all* celebrated their togetherness.

This feeling is almost like the one I get when I Wash our people, Mari thought as she danced. And then she realized how dark the sky had grown and her feet faltered, understanding before her mind that soon the Earth Walkers would be suffering with Moon Fever, and her Pack would, once again, need to be Washed.

She was near the drummers and could see that even though the women kept beating out the basis of the melody, their expressions had gone from happy and open to strained and serious. And Mari could see the sickly gray tint begin to creep over their skin.

Her gaze sought out Sora, who had picked up the panting, happy Chloe and was kissing her and continuing to dance with the pup in her arms. Mari caught her eye, and pointed up at the darkening sky.

Sora's eyes widened in surprise, and she nodded, dancing her way out of the circle.

"Nik, I have to get ready to Wash the Pack with Sora," Mari said. He and Laru and Rigel paused with her. "No, you and Laru keep dancing. There's still a little while until sunset."

Nik kissed her cheek, and then he and Laru danced away together.

Mari met Sora by the campfire. As she'd made her way through the Pack, people murmured compliments, and several people reached out to stroke Rigel affectionately. *It's happening. It's really happening! Our Pack is becoming one.* Even Lily and Dove weren't being ostracized. They were sitting beside Spencer, who was adding hunks of fish to the stew from a basket Mason and Davis had given her—as well as sneaking small scraps of meat to the puppies that were contentedly sprawled on Lily's and Dove's laps. Everywhere Mari looked, she saw her people integrated with those who used to be called enemies. *Maybe we've left the darkness behind us.*

"Great Mother Goddess, that was fun!" Sora said, wiping sweat from her flushed face as she tucked Chloe back into her sling. "I hope we can dance more after we Wash the Pack."

"I'm sorry I let us dance for so long. I lost track of time," Mari said.

"So did I," Sora said. "Gloriously!"

Mari smiled. "I love that you were having so much fun that not even Moon Fever could spoil it."

"Moon Fever? It can't be that late. I'm not feeling anything." Sora looked up at the sky, and her brow furrowed. "Mari, the sun is setting."

"I know. That's why I pulled you out of the dance." Then realization hit her, and her gaze flew to Jaxom. *Oh, Goddess! He's out there close to Danita!* Mari wasn't worried that Jaxom would suddenly attack Danita or anyone. When male Earth Walkers came under the effect of Moon Fever their anger increased, but that anger was rarely directed at anyone but themselves. The moon acted on female Earth Walkers in a slightly different way. Un-Washed by a Moon Woman, they would fall into dark depression and would, eventually, succumb to it, to either waste away in a catatonic state or take their own life.

Mari was the only Earth Walker not affected by Moon Fever—thanks to her father's Tribal blood and the fact that he had made sure Mari was swaddled in the Tribe's magickal Mother Plant—a sacrifice that had cost him his life.

"I have to get Jaxom before he frightens Danita," Mari said, beginning to move toward the dancing circle.

Sora held her wrist, stopping her. "Mari, wait. Something is happening—or rather, something is not happening."

Mari turned to her friend. "Sora, we can't let Jaxom—"

"Moon Woman, we need you," Davis's tremulous voice interrupted. Mari and Sora turned to see that Davis had his arm around Mason, supporting the young Earth Walker, whose skin had taken on the gray tinge that signaled the beginnings of Moon Fever. "Mason started acting strange—angry—and he went really quiet. Then I remembered it's a Third Night, and I brought him to you."

"You did the right thing, Davis. But know that Mason isn't dangerous. Help him sit over there and we'll get Jaxom and begin Washing the Pack," Mari said.

Sora, who still had hold of Mari's wrist, pulled her so that she had a better view of the dancing circle. "Look at Jaxom."

Mari did. The Earth Walker was still dancing. Joyously. With absolutely no sign of Moon Fever.

"But, I don't understand," Mari said.

"I think I do!" Sora was so filled with excitement that her body was trembling. "Look at me. Look at my arms."

Mari studied Sora, and as she began to understand what she was seeing, she lifted her friend's arm, studying her for signs of Moon Fever—and finding none.

"How do you feel?" Mari asked.

"Fantastic. Incredible. *Normal.*"

"But, how can that be?" Mari asked.

Tears spilled down Sora's cheeks as she answered. "I believe it's Chloe. Something happened this morning when we greeted the sun. I—I *felt* it: the power of it—the beauty of it. I've never felt anything like it—not before Chloe—never until this morning."

"And this morning was the first time you greeted the sun with her!" Mari was catching Sora's excitement.

"Yes! Jaxom was there, too. And Jaxom is now a Companion. He's not showing any sign of Moon Fever either. Mari, it's our canines. They can keep us from getting Moon Fever!"

CHAPTER 12

S till the drums, please!" Mari called to the drummers, and they fell silent, followed by the women playing the flutes and singing. As Mari strode to the center of her Pack, with Sora by her side, she noted how exhausted the Earth Walker women looked. Mason, the only Earth Walker male besides Jaxom, was sitting a little apart from the others, head bowed and shoulders slumped. Davis remained by his side, hand on his shoulder, talking soothingly to him.

The dancers were much more animated—jubilant even—but the only Earth Walker among them was Jaxom, who appeared like Sora—totally untouched by Moon Fever.

"Ready to Wash your Pack, Moon Women?" Nik's face was shiny with sweat and he was smiling happily.

"Almost," Mari said. "First, we need to understand something. Jaxom, could you please come here?"

Jaxom had been crouched by Fortina, petting his Companion, but he quickly approached the two Moon Women, Fortina by his side.

"How are you feeling?" Mari asked as the Pack watched with openly curious expressions.

"Great!" He grinned, then the smile slid from his face as he noted the solemnity of the way she and Sora were studying him. "Is something wrong? The disease isn't returning, is it? I haven't felt it—not at all." Fortina began to whine fretfully and press against his side, and Jaxom bent to comfort her.

"No! It's nothing like that," Mari said quickly. "I should have been more specific. Are you feeling any signs of Moon Fever?"

"Well, no, but as soon as the sun sets I'm sure I—" Jaxom's words broke off as his gaze found the dark sky. Confused, he shook his head back and forth, back and forth. "I don't understand." He lifted his arm, pushing up the sleeves of his shirt to expose his skin—his brownish-colored skin that was completely absent of any of the signs of Moon Fever. "Wait, this doesn't make any sense. Mason? Where's Mason?"

Mari touched Jaxom's arm gently. "Mason is with Davis. He'll be fine as soon as we Wash him."

"Why isn't he getting angry?" Nik asked, moving closer to Jaxom to stare at him. Nik gestured to the Earth Walkers surrounding them. "I can see the tint of their skin changing. I can see sadness taking them over. Why isn't it happening to Jaxom?" Nik's gaze went to Sora, and his eyes widened. "And Sora, too?"

"Sora, too." Then Mari raised her voice. "Earth Walkers, if any of you are *not* feeling the symptoms of Moon Fever, please step forward immediately."

There was some shuffling around as people looked at one another, but no one stepped forward.

"Isabel, Danita, Jenna, all of you are feeling the effects of Moon Fever?" Sora asked.

"Yes, of course." Danita was closest, as she had been dancing with Bast. She and the feline came to Mari.

"My skin is gray and I feel awful," said Jenna.

"Me, too, as always," answered Isabel as she and Jenna joined Danita.

"Do you know what's happening?" Nik asked Mari.

"I think we do," Mari answered, sharing a look with Sora.

"Jaxom, this morning when you were greeting the sun with Fortina, what did you feel?" asked Sora.

"I felt good! Really good. Fortina and I liked it a lot." He paused and looked as if he would like to say more, but pressed his lips closed instead.

"No, don't keep quiet about it. This is important. Tell us everything," Sora encouraged.

"Well, I wasn't going to say anything because I thought I was just imagining it, or maybe feeling what Fortina felt and not actually what *I* felt, but my body got warm in a strange way. Like the heat of the sun was actually pumping through me."

"With your heartbeat!" Sora said, nodding in agreement. "Like your blood had turned into sunlight and was spreading that light all over your body!"

"Yes! Exactly!" Jaxom said.

"That's how it feels when Rigel and I greet the sun," Mari said.

"Bloody beetle balls! Neither of you have Moon Fever!" Nik blurted, and the Pack gasped.

Sora spread her arms wide, showing her untainted skin. "I do not have Moon Fever!"

O'Bryan, Wilkes, Claudia, and the rest of the people who used to belong to the Tribe of the Trees pressed closer as the Pack stared, gaping, at Sora and Jaxom.

"It's their Companions," O'Bryan said. "It has to be."

Nik nodded vigorously in agreement, raising his voice so that all the Pack members could hear him. "That must be it! Through our connection to our Companions, we share the power of the sun. Our ancient stories say that long ago, before the world changed, canines lived much shorter lives, but after the miracle of the Choosing happened between canines and humans, their lives extended to what they are today." Nik was speaking directly to the Earth Walkers in the Pack. "We've always believed that is because of the power of the sun—that through us we share it with our canines—but maybe that isn't completely accurate. Maybe it's the other way around—our canines channel the strengthening power of the sun through *them* to *us*." He turned to Jaxom and Sora. "And now, because you've become Companions, bonded body and spirit to your canines, they are sharing the power of the sun with you."

"And it somehow prevents Moon Fever," Mari finished for Nik. She faced the Earth Walkers. "You know what that means? You could *all* be free of Moon Fever!"

Rose was suddenly there, beside Mari. "May I speak to the other Earth Walkers?"

"Yes, of course," Mari said, motioning for Rose to take her place.

Rose cleared her throat and looked nervous, but determined. "I do not know if this will help, but I feel I need to tell you in case, even in some small way, it does. In the Tribe everyone raised each litter. We *all* handled puppies. Not as soon as they were born—that would've overwhelmed them—but around this age." She lifted one of the pups, whose tail wagged as she wriggled in Rose's arms. "Now, when they're older and able to walk around, awkwardly, by themselves—now is when the Tribe begins handling them. We do not know why a pup Chooses a particular person. We do not know if handling the pup makes any difference, but we do know it doesn't hurt. So, I am inviting you to handle Rose's pups. Spend time with them. Get to know the little canines, because if they really can stop you from suffering from Moon Fever, well, then, I'd like them to be part of that miracle—just like Sora's little Chloe is."

"Thank you, Rose. That was very generous," Mari said.

"Rose, I—" Overcome with emotion, Sora hugged Rose tightly, until the pup she'd been holding *and* Chloe complained.

"We know Chloe Chose Sora earlier than any pup has ever Chosen anyone from the Tribe," said Isabel. "But what is the normal age that they begin to Choose their Companions?"

"That's a good question," Rose said. "And I want the Pack to know that if you have any questions about canines—any at all—please, just come to me and ask. Pups are usually ready to be weaned and leave their mother at about eight weeks old. Between then and about six months old, all pups Choose their Companions."

"How old are Fala's pups now?" Jenna asked, tickling the pup Rose was holding under her chin.

Rose smiled and handed Jenna the puppy. "They're almost five weeks old now."

"Wow, so they're going to start Choosing soon!" Jenna said, cuddling the puppy as it licked her face.

"And those of you who used to be part of the Tribe won't mind if the pups Choose Earth Walkers?" Isabel asked.

Nik's chuckle was echoed by the other Companions. "What we mind or don't mind has very little to do with it. A pup's Choice is his or her own. In the Tribe we learned long ago that it can't be predicted or rushed."

"Or changed," Wilkes added. "Well, except for Jaxom's Fortina."

"You said you heard of it happening before," Jaxom said. "A canine leaving his Companion."

"Yes, I used to enjoy talking with our Storyteller, Ralina." Wilkes hesitated as sadness shadowed his face. Then he shook himself and continued. "We discussed many things, and once she told me a story about a Shepherd leaving his Companion after that man betrayed his family and his Tribe."

"That woman hurt my Fortina," Jaxom said darkly.

"I remember the day Fortina Chose Maeve," Nik said. "Father and I spoke of it in private. Maeve didn't want to accept the pup's Choice because the pain of losing her first Companion was too great. Father had to encourage her. Perhaps her heart wasn't able to love more than one Shepherd."

"I saw Maeve strike Fortina," Mari said. "I'm glad the pup left her."

"She's with me now, and no one will ever hurt her again," said Jaxom, putting his arms around the young Shepherd as she leaned into him.

"You saved her, and in return she saved you," Sora said. "Just like my Chloe saved me."

"It is a miracle." Jenna spoke in a hushed voice before she kissed the pup she was holding.

"Yes, a miracle," Danita agreed.

Mari smiled at Nik and raised her voice to project throughout the Pack. "It's a miracle born from the joining of Tribe and Clan!"

"It is!" The Pack turned as one to look at Dove. She was standing before the campfire, silhouetted in its orange light, her long hair lifting in the warm eddies of air.

"What do you know of it?" Nik asked, his voice hard.

"I know that in speaking I have offended. I apologize." Dove bowed her head slightly to Nik and reached out for Lily to lead her away.

Mari motioned for Lily to wait. "You may speak freely here, Dove."

"Freely and truthfully," Sora added.

"I have given you my oath to only tell the truth, and I will not break it," Dove said. "Mari, as you were questioning Jaxom I felt the answer rise within me, only it did not come from me. The answer seemed to come from the earth beneath me, and the forest around me. The Great Goddess has a hand in this. I cannot tell you how I know it, but I believe it with every fiber of my being."

"Did you not lie about being an oracle of the—" Nik began, but Dove raised her hand, cutting him off.

"Yes. I did lie before. I had no choice. I had to survive. I have a choice now, and I choose to live a truthful life. This change that has happened to Jaxom and Sora—it is a gift from the Goddess. I know it. Believe or do not believe, but I have not lied to any of you—nor will I."

"Dove tells the truth!" Davis called from his place at Mason's side. "I feel the rightness of it as well. It is a miracle gifted to us by the Great Earth Mother in partnership with the sun. It is like our Pack—a joining that makes everything better."

"I choose to believe," Sora said. "Think of it! Someday in the future there is a chance that none of us will ever suffer from Moon Fever again."

"And that means none of our children will suffer, either." Nik put his arm around Mari. "Because we have the Mother Plant to swaddle them."

"And canine Companions to love them," Mari added.

"Yes!" Nik cried.

"Yes!" the Pack echoed.

"But until then, your Moon Women will Wash you," Sora said. "Ready, Mari?"

"I am. Isabel and Danita, please join us in Washing our Pack," Mari said. "Pack, ready yourselves for your Moon Women!"

And as the Pack arranged themselves into a circle around the campfire, Mari whispered to Nik, "I think we're going to need a lot more puppies."

"Oh, don't worry about that. It'll take a little time, but where there are boy and girl canines, there *will* be puppies, and right now we don't need to limit the breedings. So we're going to have puppies—*lots* of puppies."

Mari and Sora stood side by side before the campfire. Danita was on Mari's left, and Isabel took position on Sora's right, their Pack circled around them.

As one, Mari and Sora lifted their arms high to the night sky, facing the rising moon. Mari began the invocation.

"Moon Woman I proclaim myself to be!"

Sora continued, *"Greatly gifted, I bare myself to thee. Earth Mother, aid me with your magick sight. Lend me strength on this Third Night."*

Mari took up the call with, *"Come, silver light—fill us to overflow, so those in our care your healing touch will know."*

Together, the two Moon Women finished the invocation.

"By right of blood and birth channel through me
The Goddess gift that is my destiny!"

Mari turned first to Danita as Sora faced Isabel. Both young women were on their knees, their heads bowed. Mari and Sora placed their hands on each girl's head, saying, "I Wash you free of all sadness and gift you with the love of our Great Earth Mother."

Then, Washed and whole once more, Danita stood and linked her hand with Mari's while Sora and Isabel joined hands, too. Then the Moon Women separated, each with their willing apprentice, and began to move around the circle Washing the Pack.

"You're doing well, Danita," Mari encouraged as together they touched the bowed heads of their Pack brothers and sisters.

"It's still really cold, but I'm learning to let it slide through me, like water off a gull's back," Danita said.

"That's right. Keep that image in your mind," Mari said. "It'll help. Just remember, save only enough to heal yourself. The rest we share with others."

They came to Antreas, and he met Mari's eyes with a lopsided smile. "I'm not sick, and I don't get Moon Fever, so there's no reason to waste our moon magick on me."

"It wouldn't be a waste," Mari said. "But it is your choice."

Beside Antreas, Bast chirped and batted him gently with one of her giant paws, which made Danita giggle, though she covered it with a cough.

Antreas cleared his throat. "Well, it appears that Bast would like me to be Washed." He met Mari's eyes, and she saw sweet shyness hiding there. "Mari, I respect and admire you, and absolutely do not want to offend you, but would it be okay if Danita Washed me?"

"Of course, and you do not offend me at all."

Antreas sank to his knees.

Mari nodded at Danita, who moved into position in front of Antreas. As she placed her hand gently on his bowed head, Mari concentrated on channeling the silver cascade of moonlight through herself and then from her hand into Danita. She saw the Lynx man's body jolt in surprise as the cold power filled him.

"I Wash you free of any sadness your life has brought you, and gift you with the love of our Great Earth Mother." Danita spoke the invocation with warmth and confidence.

Antreas raised his head. His eyes were shining with unshed tears. "That was incredible! Thank you, my precious Moon Woman," he said to Danita.

Mari thought Danita's answering smile was so bright it could've started another forest fire.

The last person Mari washed was Nik, who was waiting on his knees patiently, with Rigel on one side and Laru on the other. Both canines behaved with somber decorum—even Rigel remained seated, though his whole backside wiggled along with his tail.

Mari placed both hands on Nik's bowed head. "I Wash you free of all pain and injury, and gift you with the love of our Great Earth Mother," she said softly.

Nik lifted his head. "Thank you, my precious Moon Woman."

The look in Nik's eyes filled Mari with warmth that not even the silver power of the moon could cool.

Then, from across the circle Sora shouted, "All have been Washed! All have been blessed! And now we eat!"

The Pack cheered and everyone began to jostle to form a line for the fish stew that was bubbling aromatically over the fire. And as the Pack filled their bowls and found places to sit in little clusters, Mari noticed that several women, and Mason, chose to be near Rose and Fala, and the four pups, who had yet to Choose their Companions.

"Someday we won't remember a time when it was Earth Walkers and Tribe of the Trees," Nik murmured in Mari's ear. "Someday we will all simply be Pack, with no more Moon Fever. Canines will play among our children, and we will thrive as a people. I believe that with everything inside me."

Mari turned and stepped into his arms. "I believe it, too." She kissed Nik as she realized that she had never in her life been as hopeful as she was at that moment.

The rest of the night was peaceful and filled with a sense of contentment that Mari thought was almost palpable. With Mari and Sora by his side, Nik checked on the starters—appropriately called "pups"—from the Mother Plant that he had brought to the Pack at great risk to his life.

"They thrive!" Nik exclaimed, gently touching one of the green fronds of the magickal fern.

"Of course they thrive. Earth Walkers are caring for them, and as long as we do they will always thrive," said Adira, an older woman who at first hadn't seemed excited about leaving the burrows of Clan Weaver. But as the trip progressed she had taken charge of the plants that they'd brought with them—cuttings, seedlings, bulbs, and even dried fruits and vegetables. Along with being in charge of the plants came caring for the Mother Plant pups, which were, indeed, thriving.

Nik bowed his head slightly, but respectfully, to the older woman. "I am in awe of your ability to grow plants. It's impressive. And I appreciate it very much."

Adira's stiff expression relaxed slightly. "You are welcome."

"The future children of the Pack will appreciate your care with the Mother Plant, too," Mari added pointedly, "as the fronds from the mature plants will swaddle our infants and, perhaps, aid in ending Moon Fever forever."

"That *and* being bonded to a remarkable canine." Sora smiled affectionately down at Chloe's little black-furred head poking out of the sling she carried her pup in.

"I admit that seeing you and Jaxom free of Moon Fever has brought many of us hope we've never dared to feel before," Adira said. She sent Nik a sideways look that Mari couldn't quite read. "After almost a decade of being enslaved by them, I suppose I am in the odd position of needing to thank someone from the Tribe of the Trees."

"No you're not." Mari spoke before Nik could. "There are no Tribal members here. We are all a Pack."

"A Pack," Nik said. "There's something about the sound of it that I've liked from the beginning. Yes, Adira, as Mari said, I am a proud member of this Pack."

"I stand corrected, Moon Woman," Adira said. "And I meant no offense."

Nik gently rested his hand on the older woman's shoulder. "I understand. What my people did to you and your people was wrong. Very wrong. And it will take time to forget it."

Adira met Nik's gaze. "Our enslavement won't ever be forgotten. Nor should it be. But it can be learned from and, eventually, forgiven."

Nik answered solemnly. "Then I will look forward to earning your forgiveness."

The sounds of drums and flutes drifted down the beach to where the three of them were standing, making Mari and Sora smile as they recognized the familiar melody. Mari's foot had just begun to tap in rhythm with the music when O'Bryan rushed up.

"Oh, good! There you are, Sora. The shadow dancing has been re-placed by something they're calling the Weaver's Tune, and everyone's dancing. Well, all of the Earth Walkers are dancing—in a line—all the same. I tried to follow their steps, but it's too complicated. Claudia and Sheena sent me to find you because all the Earth Walkers are saying you're the best dancer of the Pack."

Sora flicked back her thick, dark hair. "All the Earth Walkers are correct."

Mari snorted.

"What? You know I'm an excellent dancer," Sora said.

"Well, if she didn't know it I'm sure you'd tell her," Nik mumbled.

Sora skewered him with her sharp gray gaze. "You realize that I know herbs to sprinkle in your stew that will make your bowels turn to liquid, don't you?"

Nik ducked behind Mari, saying teasingly, "Save me, Moon Woman!"

O'Bryan turned his back to Nik. "Ignore him. Will you teach us the steps?"

"Of course I'll ignore him. And, yes, I'll teach you."

O'Bryan shouted victoriously and grabbed Sora's hand, pulling her back to the campfire and the cluster of waiting Companions.

"A Moon Woman should be treated with more respect," Adira said.

"He isn't disrespecting her," Mari explained gently. "He just isn't treating her as if she is a far-off Goddess who must be revered." Mari purposefully took Nik's hand in hers, weaving her fingers intimately with his. "You know what happens when you're revered?"

"Yes, of course. You are treated with the utmost respect," said the older woman.

"Not really. See, I understand this subject intimately, as I grew up with my mother's loneliness as our constant companion. When someone is revered she is also isolated, treated as untouchable—unapproachable. Did you know I was Mama's only friend?"

Adira's brow rose in surprise. "That could not be true! We all loved your mother very much."

"Yes, I know you did. She knew you did. But you also revered her so much that none of you were close to her. Our burrow was isolated—and we were isolated. I grew up believing my only choice was to be alone, and not because I was half Companion, half Earth Walker. I believed it because all of our Moon Women and their daughters are kept separate from the Clan. But no more." Mari gazed up at Nik as she squeezed his hand. "I prefer less reverence and more happiness."

"As do I, Moon Woman." Nik lifted her hand and kissed it.

Adira was staring at them. "I must consider what you have said. I never imagined that Leda, or any other Moon Woman, could feel isolated or lonely. And the thinking of it now saddens me."

"Don't be sad, Adira," Nik said. "Those times are over. None of our Pack should ever be alone again."

"You mean Moon Women will live among us when we finally make our new burrows?" Adira said.

"Oh, Sora and I—along with Danita and Isabel—will definitely live among our Pack, but whether we'll be in burrows will be decided when we get there," Mari said.

"A mixture would be nice," Nik said.

"It's definitely something to think about," Mari said. She turned to Adira. "Thank you for the care you're taking of all the plants. We value your skills." Then she and Nik began to head back to the campfire.

"I think that went pretty well," said Nik.

"It'll definitely give the rest of the Earth Walker women, especially the older ones, something to talk about," said Mari.

"Which is exactly why you just had that conversation with her."

Mari looked up at him. "How did you know that?"

Nik slid his arm around her shoulder, drawing her closer to him. "Oh, I know things, Moon Woman. *Lots* of things."

"Oh, really?"

"Really. For instance, you want the women talking about the changes you and Sora are making so that as you make them they're not too shocking."

"I hope it's a good strategy," Mari said.

"I think it is."

They joined the group around the campfire, who were watching Sora try to teach the Companions the intricate steps to the Weaver's Tune, which O'Bryan seemed to be picking up quickly.

"Your cousin has skills," Mari said. "That's a tough dance."

"I think his skills have something to do with his beautiful teacher," Nik said.

"You think Sora is beautiful?" Mari didn't ask out of jealousy. She was truly curious. Earth Walkers and Companions had several differences in their appearances. Earth Walkers were shorter, with darker skin, hair, and eyes, as well as thicker features. The Tribe of the Trees people were tall and predominantly blond, with more delicate features. Mari thought both peoples were beautiful, but since she was a child she'd heard her fellow Clansmen remark on the light-skinned giants and compare them to long-limbed praying mantises, or even fish-belly-colored spiders. And she knew Tribesmen belittled Earth Walkers, calling them Scratchers who were barely human and too ugly to live aboveground.

"Sure. Sora is pretty, but it's my cousin who I've heard describe her as beautiful. You look strange. Is something wrong?"

"No, I just suddenly wondered how you Companions see us Earth Walkers," Mari said.

Nik gently turned her to face him, his hands resting on her shoulders. "I see you as unique, exquisite, and more beautiful than the moon you can draw."

"But I'm part Companion. I look different than the rest of the Earth Walkers. It's why I had to hide my appearance for so many years."

"Well, O'Bryan thinks Sora is a great beauty. And I heard Sarah and Lydia flirting openly with Mason today. Does that answer your question?" Nik asked.

"Actually, it puts my question to rest." Her hands went up around his broad shoulders. "Would you like me to teach you the steps to the Weaver's Tune?"

Rigel and Laru rushed up, their evening meal all finished. They were wagging enthusiastically, and Rigel even whined as he gazed longingly at the dancers, sending Mari waves of emotion that basically translated to *Please please please please please let's dance!*

"You think you can teach them, too?" Nik ruffled the fur atop both Shepherds' heads.

"Them—yes. You—I'm not so sure . . ." Mari said.

The Pack didn't dance long into the night, as they would have had the safe familiarity of their burrows been close by, but when it was time to bed down, there was a sense of happy hopefulness that remained with them, allowing those whose turn it was to sleep to drift off contentedly, and those who took first watch to do so with smiles and shared conversation.

So it was shocking when the night neared the midway point, all was dark and quiet, and the Pack's serenity was shattered by Dove's terrified scream.

Several things happened at once. Every canine alerted—tails up, ears pricked. Growls rumbled across the campsite as sharp noses tested the air for intruders.

Bast was at Danita's side, her sharp yellow eyes scanning the area around them as she hissed a warning to the night.

Antreas was calling for the Pack to gather with their backs to the enormous stone monolith that stood sentinel at the edge of the beach.

With Rigel and Laru beside her, Mari rushed to Dove and Lily, who had made their pallet not far from the campfire.

"What's happening? Where is the danger?" Mari snapped.

Dove reached out blindly, and Mari took her hands. "Forgive me, Moon Woman! The danger is not living. Please, tell everyone to return to their pallets. I am so, so sorry."

"Not living?" Nik asked, rushing up to join them. "Explain!"

Dove raised her pale face. "Spirits. They came to me in my dream. They were all around us—watching."

"But dead, right?" Mari asked.

"Yes, dead. I give you my word," Dove said.

"Can they harm us?" Mari said.

"I—I think they can, but I sense that they will not." Dove answered slowly, as if considering each word.

"Antreas! All is well. Everyone may return!" Mari called up the beach to where the Pack had gathered with the huge stone behind them.

They muttered and sent Dove dark, confused looks, but the Pack made their way back to their pallets and their watch spots. Mari sat cross-legged before Dove, still holding the girl's cold hands.

"If it's okay with you, I'm going to take Laru and Rigel and walk the perimeter of the camp," Nik said.

"That's a good idea," Mari said as Nik left and Sora hurried up to the women.

"What was all of that about?" she asked.

"It seemed so real, but it must have only been a dream. Forgive me, Moon Women," Dove said, her hands trembling in Mari's.

"What kind of dream?" Antreas asked, joining them without Bast. Mari glanced around, finding the big feline curled up beside Danita in the pallet she shared with Isabel and Jenna.

"Terrible. They were pressing all around me. Watching. Always watching. Always near the river. Cold. They made me so cold." Dove shivered, and Mari rubbed her hands.

"Her skin is freezing," Mari said.

"Lily, I have tea brewing for those taking the second watch. It would help warm Dove if you got her some," Sora said, sitting beside Mari and studying Dove closely. "No dream has ever made me lose my color and my warmth."

"It wasn't a dream. Or not just a dream." Antreas sighed, and looked at Mari. "I didn't think I needed to say anything until we were farther upriver, and then I was only going to warn you and Sora. I didn't believe anyone else would be intuitive enough to feel them."

"Who are they?" Dove asked, her voice still shaky.

"Spirits of the ancients," Antreas said, his voice low so that it wouldn't carry. "This land that runs along the river is lush, well irrigated—an excellent place for a Tribe or Clan, or even a Lynx Chain to settle. But the Saleesh are the only people who live near it."

"The spirits must tolerate them," said Dove.

Lily returned, and Mari guided Dove's hands to wrap around the wooden mug.

"That's what the Saleesh say," Antreas explained.

"And you were going to wait until *when* to tell us this river is haunted?" Sora frowned at Antreas.

"Until after we passed the Bonn Dam tomorrow. I have never led anyone who could sense the spirits this soon. Truth be told, in all my journeys I have only had two other people who sensed them at all, and that wasn't until we were just before the entrance to Lost Lake, where they are strongest. I've *never* sensed them."

"So they aren't dangerous?" Dove asked.

"Only if we attempted to settle by the river," said Antreas.

"Then what would happen?" Lily said, her voice tremulous.

"Crops would fail. Babies would wither in our wombs. We would go mad. We would go mad." Dove's voice took on a strange, singsong rhythm.

"Good thing we're not settling here." Mari spoke matter-of-factly. She stood, brushing the sand from her. "Sora, let's walk among the Pack and let them know that all is well."

"Please tell them how sorry I am," Dove said.

"I will not," Mari said sternly. "You have nothing to be sorry for."

"True," Sora said. "And you just proved that you are some kind of oracle—or at least have a connection to the spirit world."

"And that could be a very good thing for our Pack," Antreas said. "Wind Riders hold those who can communicate with the spirit world in high esteem. There is an entire Herd whose leaders commune with crystals. They are strong and prosperous and called Crystal Seers. I think they would be very interested in Dove."

"Truly?" Dove said as Lily took her hand and blinked tears from her eyes.

"Truly. You could be one of the reasons they allow us to settle in their territory," said Antreas.

Dove bowed her head. "Oh, thank you, Great Earth Goddess, Giver of Life."

"Sora and I will let the Pack know that you sensed danger, but that danger will not come to us as long as we keep moving," said Mari.

"The Pack will be grateful to have a Seer with us," said Sora. "Because we *are* grateful."

As the two Moon Women moved away, heading to spread the news to their Pack, Mari spoke quietly to Sora. "So, a Skin Stealer with no eyes can see ancient spirits and may be the reason we'll be able to make our home in a magickal land where people ride the wind and speak to crystals?"

"Yeah. Proving once and for all the Goddess has a rather strange sense of humor," said Sora.

"That's what Mama used to tell me, and I never believed her," Mari said.

"Leda was right," Sora said.

"I wish I could tell her," Mari said.

Sora bumped Mari gently with her shoulder. "She knows, Moon Woman. I promise you, she knows."

CHAPTER 13

The morning began bright and early, with the Pack breaking their fast with leftover baked wapato roots and scrambled gull eggs with a pinch of Sora's precious salt. Then, led by their Sun Priest, Nik, the Pack—the *entire* Pack—faced the rising sun and joyously greeted it.

Mari loved watching Sora and Jaxom absorbing the powerful rays of the sun alongside their Companions. She also loved the fact that the Earth Walkers were now eagerly interacting with the canines, especially Fala's puppies.

The boats were packed and everyone was ready to cast off when Antreas raised his hand and drew the Pack's attention.

"We have about six hours of river travel before we come to the ruins of the Bonn Dam. This part of the river is wide and, at this time of year, mostly placid. We will pass the ruins of two ancient ships, but it is easy to steer well clear of them. Other than that, there are no major obstacles until we reach Bonn Dam and the home of the Saleesh."

"Antreas, did you say that we are going to have to leave the river to pass the dam?" Mari asked.

Antreas nodded. "Yes. The river turns to white-water rapids around the dam. The Saleesh are the only people who understand how to traverse it. We will beach the boats on this side of the dam. The Saleesh will greet us and we will gift them with our offerings." He paused. "We *do* have offerings for them, correct?"

Adira spoke up. "Yes! We finished weaving two new travel cloaks last night—the kind that can be used to overnight in the boughs of trees like cocoons."

"And the women did a perfect job with them," O'Bryan said, smiling warmly at the older woman. "They are even better made than our old ones."

"Why, thank you, O'Bryan. You were an excellent teacher," Adira surprised Mari by saying.

"And this morning I woke early and finished these." Sora held up a woven basket that held several fat sticks of dried lavender, sage, and pine that she'd bound together.

"Will those gifts be enough?" Nik asked.

"I believe they will," Antreas said. "The Saleesh aren't greedy. Actually, they are quite wealthy in their own right. The gifts they expect are a sign of respect, and these cloaks and the smudge sticks should be very well received."

"What happens after we beach the boats? Will we have to drag them across the ground until we get past the ruins of the dam?" Mari asked.

"No. The Saleesh pilots will take over for us. There is a narrow passageway that only the Saleesh can successfully traverse. It goes through the dam area, the rapids surrounding it, and then past the ruins of an extremely dangerous bridge they call Of the Gods—and it's white water the entire way. They will steer the boats through the passage while we travel across ground—through their campsite—and meet the boats on the other side of the dam, where the water is calm again."

"Are there any rules we should know about the Saleesh? Anything we might accidentally do to offend them?" Mari asked.

"They're patriarchal. Each of their villages is led by an elder priest they call Father."

Sora narrowed her eyes. "You didn't say anything about that before. Are they going to have a problem with the fact that two women lead our group? Are we going to have to pretend to follow around behind you and Nik and the rest of our men?"

"No. We won't be spending much time with them. We beach the boats and then travel through their village, and keep following the pathway along the river until we're clear of the rapids and the ruins. We'll do that several times in different villages as we continue upriver. And I didn't mean to imply the Saleesh women are abused. As far as I've been able to tell, they are loved by their men and treated with care."

"But they have no say in the governing of themselves or their people?" Mari asked.

"No. I do not believe they do," Antreas said.

Sora snorted.

"What else should we know?" Mari said.

"The Saleesh are a deeply religious people. They have a distinctive greeting," Antreas explained. "They will say *'Blessings be with you,'* and the correct response is *'And also with you.'* It's more than just *'Hello, how are you?'* to them. They literally are blessing their visitors and asking for the same in return. Also, don't stare at the Teteplates. The backs of their heads are distinctively flattened, which they see as a sign of great beauty. I know that we've discussed this before, but remember that the Saleesh and the Teteplates exist together, as one people. Yes, they do have a caste system, but they say it works for them—for *all* OF THEM. Also, remember that they are a devout people. They worship Mother. You'll see idols of her throughout the village. It is a sign of respect to leave an offering before an idol, so if you feel compelled to, the Saleesh will be appreciative, but it is not necessary. The worst thing you could ever do to one of the Saleesh would be to desecrate one of their Mother idols—so, keep that in mind."

"'Mother'? That is the name of their Goddess?" Davis asked.

"That is all I have ever known them to call her by. The idols are really quite beautiful. Oh, blue is a sacred color to them, but you'll see that for yourself. Any other questions?"

"How are they with canines?" Mari asked.

"As long as you keep them from urinating on their idols, they're just fine with them. I've led several small groups of Companions through their village with no incidents."

Mari ruffled the fur on Rigel's head. "You hear that? No leg-lifting on the idols."

Around her, the Pack chuckled.

"Also, the Saleesh are great traders, known for their silver jewelry, their blue cloth, and their carvings. We aren't going to linger in their village, but if you have anything you'd like to trade—like one of your woven baskets—be sure you take them from your boat and bring them with you as we walk through their village."

"Are there any rules to the trading?" Sora asked.

"Only to be fair," Antreas said.

Mari was just about to speak—to inform the Pack about what Dove had discovered last night—but the girl beat her to it.

"I do not have a question, but I would like to say something. Moon Women, might I speak?"

The Pack turned to stare at Dove. She stood beside Lily, her hand resting on her friend's arm.

"Yes, of course," Mari said.

Dove bowed her head slightly to Mari before drawing a deep breath and addressing the curious Pack.

"Last night I was visited in my dreams by spirits of the ancients. I am truly sorry that I disturbed everyone. That was not my intent, but I am new to communicating with the spirit world, and it was quite a surprise."

Dove smiled shyly, and Mari thought, not for the first time, how truly beautiful the girl was and how strange it was that her beauty seemed enhanced, rather than marred, by her lack of eyes.

"Why did the spirits come to you?" Spencer called from her spot across the beach beside the boat she shared with Davis, Isabel, Dove, and Lily.

Dove didn't hesitate in her answer. "To warn us."

"Well, I was going to do that as soon as we passed Bonn Dam," Antreas said. "The river is haunted. Or more specifically, the land on both banks is haunted. No one settles successfully here except the Saleesh and their Teteplates."

"So, we aren't in danger unless we try to settle along the river?" Wilkes asked.

"Correct, though I also wouldn't stay in one campsite for more than a few nights. A storm trapped a group I was leading several years ago. We had to spend ten days waiting just a few miles upriver from a Saleesh settlement for the weather to clear enough for us to get back on the river, and by day ten my skin was crawling and everyone was more than eager to leave, though no one was harmed."

"Then it seems odd that the ancients would feel the need to come to Dove to warn us," Nik said. "They must be acquainted with you, which means they would recognize you as a guide and not a settler."

"The warning was not about settling," Dove said.

Mari felt a cold finger trace a line down her spine. "Then what were they warning us about?"

Dove shook her head, causing her long, straight hair to wave around her waist. "I do not know. I only know that there is much more to it than warning us not to settle here."

"Maybe they'll come to you again," Mari said.

"And if they do you could try to communicate with them—ask them what it is they're warning us about," Sora added.

"Moon Women, I will try. I will do my best for the Pack," Dove said, bowing her head reverently.

"That is all Sora and I ask from any of our people," Mari said. Her gaze swept the Pack. "Is that it? Are we ready to launch now?"

The Pack members nodded their heads and, with Antreas leading, began to launch the boats. The day was almost completely cloudless and there was little wind, which meant the current wasn't too terrible to struggle against. Mari could already see that the Pack was growing increasingly more confident with the boats—herself included—and she was able to look around as she matched Nik stroke for stroke.

The land on either side of the incredibly wide river was mountainous, rocky, and covered with enormous pines. In the clear day they looked like jewels crowning the land, and Mari imagined how cool and inviting it would be under their protective canopy.

"Wow, a beautiful City in the Trees could be built anywhere along here," Mari said, more to herself than Nik.

"I was thinking the same thing myself," Nik mused. "It's odd that this was never spoken about among the Tribe, especially as we had outgrown the ridge. Before everything went sideways when Thaddeus killed Father, the Elder Council was planning to expand farther west into the higher elevations. That's what brought me to the Skin Stealers' city the day they attacked and almost killed me—I was on a salvage mission to try to find more metal for the pulleys and lifts required for the expansion."

"Your father must have known about the ghosts."

"He had to have—and so must the Council have—though they didn't speak publicly of it."

Mari gazed around them at the pristine forest. "It's so lovely. I wonder why the ancients haunt it. I hope Dove can find out."

Nik snorted.

"Hey, give her a chance—the same chance we'd give to anyone else," Mari admonished.

"I do not think you'd give an enemy, someone like Thaddeus or even Maeve, a chance," Nik said stubbornly.

"You're right. Both of them have used up their chances with me. Dove has not. So, I'm giving her a chance. Do we have to argue about this? Again?"

Nik sent a chagrined look over his shoulder to Mari. "Sorry. You're right. I'll work on my attitude."

"Thank you," Mari said.

Antreas and Danita's small boat paddled smoothly up to them, and Antreas said, "Mari, Nik, after the next bend in the river the current is going to get rough. We have about another hour of stroking against it before we reach the Saleesh checkpoint. We can stop for a break before tackling it, but the truth is the sooner we get to the checkpoint the better. We'll need all the light left today to get through the village and past the Of the Gods ruins."

Mari and Nik had maintained their position at the rear of the Pack, so Mari gestured to the boats that were spread out in front of them, skimming along the river. "I think a full night of rest last night is working well for us today. I say we keep going. What do you think, Nik?"

Nik nodded. "We've been keeping a good pace—not so fast that the Pack is worn out, but steady. I think we should just push through."

"Good, I'm glad to hear it," Antreas said.

"But I think Antreas and I should let everyone know that it's going to be rough going for the next hour or so, don't you? It's better they know what's ahead, and that there's an end to it," said Danita.

"That's a good idea, Danita," Mari said. "Let the Pack know—and tell them that soon we'll at least be on dry land."

"Thank the Goddess," Nik muttered.

The next hour was horrible. Antreas hadn't exaggerated. As soon as they turned the sharp bend in the river, the current came at them, battering the boats and slowing their progress. Mari was instantly glad they'd decided not to take a break, though by the time Nik pointed to a signal fire ahead on the right bank, sweat was dripping from her arms, rolling down her back, and getting in her eyes. She made a mental note to be sure to check everyone's hands, as her own were aching with sweat and blisters.

"Beach here!" Antreas was standing waist deep in water near the bank, helping a group of strangers guide in the Pack boats and help people from them and onto dry land.

Nik and Mari brought up the rear, so as she was waiting their turn to beach their little boat, she studied the Saleesh. They were a handsome people—tall, skin the color of the fertile earth that bordered the river, long, straight dark hair that had streaks of blue within it. Tattooed into their smooth skin in deep sapphire were intricate symbols that Mari couldn't decipher, but that intrigued her. She saw no women—only barechested, muscular men.

"Mari! Nik! Your turn!" Antreas called.

It only took a few minutes to paddle to the beach and depart the little boat, with Rigel and Laru splashing through the water beside them. A tall Saleesh man, whose long dark hair was streaked with silver along with indigo and whose lean body was covered in a long, free-flowing tunic that trailed the ground and had big, bell-like sleeves, nodded his head slightly to Mari.

"Mari, I'm going to remain with the boats and be sure everything is securely tied down. I'll join the Pack on the other side of the village," said Antreas. "You'll be in good hands with Father John."

"Do you need help?" Nik asked.

"No, not at all. The Saleesh know what they're doing. I just like being extra careful."

"Okay, see you on the other side," Nik said.

"I am Father John, senior priest for all of our villages." He spoke respectfully, addressing Mari. "I will lead you to the rest of your people, who are waiting just ahead. Friend Antreas says that you are Mari Moon Woman, and the other leader of this Pack. Blessing be with you, Mari Moon Woman."

"And also with you, Father John," Mari said. "This is Nik. He is our Sun Priest."

Father John nodded to Nik as they began up the rocky path that seemed to run parallel to the river. "Blessings be with you, Nik Sun Priest."

"And also with you," Nik intoned.

"Come this way, please."

They climbed the steep, rocky path with Father John, joining the rest of the Pack where they'd stopped to stare at the Saleesh village. Mari's breath caught as she took in the incredible sight. The Saleesh village spread out around them, beginning at the end of the path and climbing in magickal tiers up the side of the pine-covered ridge. The colors were what struck Mari first. The pines were brilliant green and stood out in stark relief against the brown front of wooden homes that appeared to be built directly into the ridge. As far as Mari could tell from her initial look, each home had an intricately carved idol standing at the doorway, and it was those idols that held the most striking of the colors. Even from a distance, Mari could see that the idols were all female, though each of their bodies were completely covered, head to toe, in a hooded robe the color of a cloudless summer sky. Blue flowers cascaded from hanging baskets, and wind chimes of precious blue glass tinkled musically from the arms of the pines. All across the ridge tongues of smoke curled from braziers hanging from intricately carved posts, so that the entire village smelled of sweet incense and flowers.

"It's amazing, isn't it?" Sora's voice was hushed as she moved through the Pack to join Mari and Nik.

"And I thought the City in the Trees was breathtaking," Mari said. "But this—this is beyond even that." She turned to Father John. "Your village is spectacular." She breathed deeply. "And it smells wonderful."

Father John's lips tilted up. "That is our incense—something sacred to the Mother."

"Then you're going to love the gifts Sora made you," Mari said.

"We very much appreciate your offerings. Please come to the chancel so that you may leave them on the altar." Father John moved through the Pack so that he could take over the leadership from one of the younger men who had guided the boats to docking, and that young man immediately jogged back down the path to rejoin the others.

The Pack, walking single and double file along the narrow, rocky pathway, followed Father John to an area that looked like a marketplace, which is when the women and children began to appear.

The Saleesh women filled the market. Most of them were working with fabrics and hides in various stages of being dyed their distinctive blue, and each woman wore a long, flowing tunic that brushed the ground—usually of a light color, from white to yellow—and over their long tunic they each had a shawl, draped around their shoulders and sometimes even over their heads. Unlike the men, they weren't tattooed—or at least none of the tattoos could be seen—but they were swathed in jewelry.

There were children everywhere—running around the marketplace, playing at rolling a leather ball with sticks, dancing and skipping around flat stones in what looked like a complex game of tag, singing in a circle with adult women—with the younger children toddling around and just generally being underfoot.

"I've never seen so many kids," Mari said.

"I've never seen so many things that sparkle," Danita whispered to Mari, making her laugh.

Bast was by Danita's side, which didn't surprise Mari. One look at the half-naked, powerful Saleesh men and Mari would've done the same thing Antreas obviously had done—told Bast to stick close by. The Lynx prowled beside the girl, her intelligent yellow gaze continually scanning around them for signs of danger.

"My mother had a necklace made from Saleesh silver," Nik said, keeping his voice low as well. "My father gave it to her as a mating gift. He told me how he'd had to trade two crossbows and a piece of glass for it, but it was incredibly beautiful—silver wire holding a blue stone carved in the shape of a heart. She wore it always, and when Father placed her on her funeral pyre, she wore it to greet the sun."

"Your father came here?" Mari asked.

"Yes, when he was a young man. I never thought I'd see this place for myself—especially with my aversion to river travel—but I'm glad I'm here. I like walking in Father's steps."

Father John faced the Pack. "Friends, the chancel is there, guarding us from the river. You may place your kind offerings before the Mother. Then if you feel so inclined you may make trade with our women. You have but a few minutes to tarry, as you will need to meet your boats more than a mile upriver, but know you are welcome here."

"Thank you, Father John," Mari said. "Your hospitality is greatly appreciated." She glanced at Sora and under her breath said, "Who has the gifts?"

"Isabel has my herb sticks." Sora sniffed the air and then sneezed. "I can smell that they're going to like them. A lot. And Jenna is carrying the travel cloaks. Would you mind if you went with them to the chancel? I brought one of my extra slings." Sora lifted the length of material that was a match to the one wrapped around her torso and from which

Chloe's little black head poked as her shining eyes peered curiously around. "I thought I might trade it for some cooking herbs and spices."

"Sounds like a really good idea," Mari said. "Sure, I'll go with Jenna and Isabel."

"I'll stay with the Pack and keep an eye on everyone," Nik said.

"Do you sense trouble?" Mari asked quietly.

"No. And I want to keep it that way."

Mari nodded. "Jenna—Isabel," she called into the Pack, and the two girls turned their heads in her direction. "Please come with me to the chancel to leave our gifts—I mean, our offerings."

The girls hurried to Mari as the rest of the Pack scattered, stopping to admire the blue cloth and the groups of women making sparkling jewelry.

"Mari, might Lily and I join you at the chancel as well?"

Lily had led Dove through the Pack to stand before Mari and Rigel. "Sure, I don't see why not."

Together, Mari and Rigel walked with Isabel, who was carrying a tightly woven basket filled with the herb sticks Sora had finished just that morning, and Danita, whose arms were filled with two neatly folded travel cloaks. Behind them, Lily led Dove in their wake.

As they began to walk through the market, Mari noticed women who were not swathed in tunics and shawls. These women wore long black dresses that were trimmed in white at the seams. They were more fair-skinned than the Saleesh, and petite—much shorter than the women they were serving. They moved gracefully among them, refilling wooden mugs, bringing what looked like dried fruits and fragrant flatbread rolls to the working Saleesh women, and herding children out from under-foot. Though they moved silently, the Saleesh thanked them, and Mari saw that they smiled and seemed content.

"Are those the Teteplates?" Jenna whispered.

Mari was about to say she didn't know, that their faces seemed longer and their heads maybe a little bigger, when one of the black-robed women turned, giving them a clear view of first the side, and then the back of her head—which was definitely flattened, as well as oddly elongated.

"Yes," Mari whispered back. "They must be."

"I think they're pretty," said Isabel softly.

"I think you're right," said Mari.

The Teteplate women were strangely beautiful. They wore their hair piled in intricate swirls atop their elongated heads, giving them an alluring elegance.

"They remind me of the cranes that come to the lowlands in the spring," Jenna said. "Father used to take me there to collect their feathers—remember how he used to braid them into my hair?"

"I do." Mari squeezed her friend's hand. "Xander always kept your hair so pretty when you were a little girl. Mama used to say he did a better job than most of the women."

"He did!" Jenna blinked quickly to keep the tears that had suddenly pooled in her eyes from spilling over. "This village would amaze him."

"It sure amazes me," Isabel said. "Part of me is jealous, and wants to stay here. It's so beautiful, and everyone seems so nice."

"Things are rarely as they seem on the surface." Dove's sweet voice drifted over from behind them.

Mari turned her head, looking from Dove to Lily, and then studying the village with new eyes. "Do you sense something?" she asked the eyeless girl quietly.

"Is the day still bright and clear?" Dove asked.

"It is."

"In my mind it is not—not anymore. In my mind there is a great storm clouding the sky."

Mari, Jenna, and Isabel all turned their eyes skyward.

"There isn't one cloud up there," Isabel said.

"Wait. It's coming," Dove said firmly. "And when the storm hits, we do not want to be here."

"Really? You can't see it, Dove, but their homes are fantastic. They have wooden fronts with life-sized carved goddesses standing watch. And it looks like the back of the homes are more burrow than not, built right into the ridge. I'd sure rather be snug inside there than out on that river," said Jenna.

"I'm not speaking of the kind of storm that brings rain," said Dove solemnly.

"Well, then, let's get these offerings dropped off and gather the Pack," Mari said as Jenna and Isabel went pale. "I don't like the sound of a metaphoric storm."

The young women hurried to the chancel, but once there they couldn't help but pause to admire the beauty of the altar. It had been built of layered flat rock to create a halo-like effect surrounding a larger-than-life statue of a serene-faced woman. She'd been carved from a stone that was brilliantly white. Her face was tilted down and her arms were spread wide, as if to embrace the river that raged far below. Mari could hardly glance down and down to the white water and jutting hunks of debris that was the ruin of Bonn Dam. The roar of the white water lifted from below, creating a disconcerting hum in her ears, so she turned her attention back to the statue.

Like the Saleesh women, their Goddess was wearing a long, light-colored tunic that pooled around her feet. Over it was a blue shawl that had been painted. It covered the idol's golden hair and draped to her bare feet. Around her neck hung strand after strand of glistening round beads. Mari peered closely at them, marveling at the exquisite workmanship. All about the Goddess offerings had been left; they were around her feet as well as placed in niches in the stone wall behind her, everything from bright pieces of blue cloth to glistening crystals and small candles—many, many small candles.

"She's incredible," Jenna said.

"I wonder what she was carved out of. I've never seen stone so white," said Isabel.

"It is called marble. Our people mine it. It is only used to create idols of the Mother." Father John seemed to materialize from behind the altar.

"She is exquisite," Mari said. "We, too, worship a Goddess—the Great Earth Mother. Though we form her idols from the earth itself."

Father John tilted his head, considering. "I would very much like to see one of your Great Earth Mother idols."

"Well, after we settle on the Wind Rider plains, maybe you will come visit us," Mari said.

Father John's smile flattened. "Oh, no, Mari Moon Woman. Thank you for your kind offer, but the Saleesh never travel far from their river. We cannot. We must not. The Mother wishes us to remain and keep the spirits at peace."

"But they aren't at peace," Dove said. "They are restless and sad—as if they're waiting. Always waiting, and never arriving."

Father John's eyes narrowed. "Who is this eyeless young one?"

Mari spoke the words that lifted from her heart. "She is our Seer. Her name is Dove."

"Ah, so, Sister Dove—you have no eyes, but you see."

"I try to," Dove said.

Father John turned and reached into a long, wooden chest that sat behind the Mother idol. It was intricately carved with the same symbols that were tattooed on the men's bodies, and Mari suddenly noticed that the symbols were all the same—large letter Ms, surrounded by ornate decorations. The old man pulled out a brazier that was a miniature of the larger ones that hung before the Saleesh houses, giving off sweet smoke. He took a long, thin twig and held it to one of the candles, then used it to light the clump of dried herbs within the brazier.

Then he went to stand in front of Dove as he wafted the brazier back and forth, back and forth—causing the smoke from the herbs to drift around Lily and her. Mari recognized the earthy scent of burning sage.

"Sister Dove, breathe deeply. Open your mind to the sacred smoke. Then tell the Mother what it is you see with no eyes."

Mari watched Dove startle as the smoke engulfed her. She coughed delicately, and then breathed deeply. Lily was watching Dove as if she was going to pull away from Father John at any moment—and then Dove's posture changed. Her back straightened. Her chin lifted. Her head turned so that if she'd had eyes, she would have been staring out at the river. When she spoke, Mari recognized the singsong tone her words had taken on the night before.

"I do not need to tell the Mother, for she already knows. Great darkness is coming—like a tide of shadows. I see it drowning the Saleesh. And when the tide ebbs, I see no Saleesh and there is a silent keening in the land as those who are enslaved mourn for what could have been."

Dove coughed and then sneezed, wiped her nose with the back of her hand—and just like that she was herself again, a slight, pretty girl who had no eyes. Her face turned from looking out at the river to Father John.

"I'm sorry. I know that sounds awful, and I'm not even sure where those words came from, but I believe them. Something bad is coming—something that has waited a long time to be awakened. It will destroy the Saleesh if you do not leave here. You may return safely—I feel that strongly. But first you must leave for an entire cycle of the seasons."

"Leave? We are the Saleesh. We do not leave our river."

"But you can, right?" Mari said. "It's spring. You have time to move inland. And as Dove foretells, it isn't permanent, but only for one cycle of the seasons."

"The Mother will protect us. We will remain, as we have always remained. We survived the destruction of an entire world. The Mother made certain we thrived when others perished. We remain under her powerful protection."

"But the Mother knows what is coming. I believe this warning comes from her," Dove said.

"That is absurd. Why would the Mother not warn me, her chosen Priest, directly? Or any of our people? Why would she choose the voice of a stranger?"

When Dove only bit her lip and remained silent, Jenna spoke up. "Maybe she *has* been trying to warn you, and you wouldn't listen? I don't mean that with any disrespect. It's just that I know what it's like to have overlooked the truth because I didn't want to see it." Jenna met Mari's eyes and mouthed, *I'm sorry.*

"Father John," Dove said. "Think back on your dreams and on signs and portents you might have either overlooked or misinterpreted during the past several months. Perhaps then my words will hold more meaning."

"You must go. Now." Father John's voice was flat and emotionless—like the edge of a knife.

"I—I did not mean to offend," Dove said.

Mari touched the girl's arm, silencing her. "Father John, Dove only did what you asked of her. She looked with no eyes and told you what she saw. I have not known her long, but she has given me her oath to only tell the truth. I believe her, and I think you should, too."

Father John met her gaze, and Mari saw complete denial there, as well as simmering anger. "Place your offerings at the feet of the Mother. I will gather your Pack. You will leave. Now. You will not speak to any of our people. Do you understand me?"

"I do, and we will leave. But first, I would like to meet with your Elder Council, or whatever governing body is in charge of your people," Mari said as Isabel and Jenna hastily deposited the gifts at the feet of the Mother idol.

"I am Father John, Senior Priest. I speak for the Saleesh. If you wish to rejoin your boats you will leave. Now. And for the rest of your journey on our river you will not utter one word of what that woman said to any Saleesh. Ever." He pointed accusingly at Dove. "I have eyes and ears in each of our villages. Should I hear even a rumor of the nonsense your eyeless Seer spouted I will declare that your people are not to be allowed passage on our river."

"But we only wanted to—" Mari began. This time it was Dove's hand on her arm stilling her.

"It will do no good. He has eyes, but does not wish to see, and in his blindness he has doomed his people."

"I have eyes, and I know evil when I see it. You bring evil here. I should have expected no less from unchaste women who play at leadership. You speak of shadows and death, but our village is a place of light and beauty. We guard the river and the Mother guards us. We keep the spirits at peace. *We are Saleesh!*" Father John spat the words at Dove. "Now leave us or I will order your boats to be broken and sunk to the bottom of our river for your blasphemy." Then he turned on his heels and, robes flapping in his wake like a foolish old bird, he strode into the marketplace, calling for the Pack to gather.

"His people are going to die," Dove said softly.

Dove's words pressed against Mari's skin, lifting the small hairs on her arms and the back of her neck. She gazed around at the peaceful, prosperous village filled with women and children, and Mari felt a terrible sinking within her—like she was drowning in the shadow tide that would come. "I have to do something."

"You just did, Mari," Jenna said. "Or, you tried to. All four of us tried to."

"Yeah, Dove warned him—he's their leader—and not only is he refusing to listen, but he threatened us," Isabel said.

"I could try to talk to him again," said Dove.

"Or we could get one of the Saleesh women alone—maybe one of the older women. We could tell her. Maybe she would listen to reason," Jenna said.

"That's not going to work. Remember what Antreas said about the Saleesh being patriarchal," Isabel said.

"But he also said they love and care for their women," said Jenna.

"Loving and caring for their women is not the same as respecting and valuing their opinions." Mari sighed. "Look at them." She pointed to the marketplace. Father John had flapped his way through it, telling the Saleesh women that they were to close trading with the Pack. "There is no discussion. No questioning. Nothing. Father John gave an order and all the women are leaping to respond. They won't listen to us, and why should they? He's their leader, not Dove. Not me. No. I won't risk the Pack. Let's get out of here, like he said—now."

The Pack was quickly gathered up with no explanation. Father John disappeared, leaving a somber, younger man called Brother Joseph to lead the Pack through the village and up the narrow, winding trail that ran along the steep bank of the river.

"You must move swiftly, please. Father John wants you to camp on the far side of the Of the Gods ruins this night. So, come! Come! Follow me."

His robes weren't as voluminous as were Father John's, but Mari thought he, too, looked birdlike as he gestured and pointed.

"Excuse me, Brother Joseph. Antreas, our guide and the Companion to the Lynx, Bast, was going to meet us here in the village," Danita said.

"The Lynx man knows the way. There is no need to wait for him, and it is not permitted. As I said, Father John insists you leave. Now. Follow me." The tall young man turned and rushed to the front of the Pack, gesturing for them to follow him.

"Antreas will be fine," Mari told Danita. "He has been here—several times. Don't worry. And if for some reason he doesn't meet us tonight, I promise you little Cammy will lead Davis right to him."

"You would do that? Send Davis to find Antreas? Even after Father John threatened us?" Danita said.

"We're a Pack. We don't leave our people behind."

Nik and Laru joined them then, with Sora close behind. Nik lowered his voice. "What happened?"

"The short version is Dove had a vision because Father John asked her to, but he didn't like what she saw. When we tried to talk with him about it, he kicked us out," Mari said. "Sorry if that messed up your trading."

"Not mine. I was mostly just looking," Nik said. "They have an amazing selection of trade goods. I'd just found some excellent-looking charcoal pencils I thought you'd like for sketching, when Father John proclaimed the market closed and that was that. No one spoke except to call the children. They just closed everything up and turned their backs on us."

"Literally!" Sora said. "Thankfully, I'd already traded for a nice supply of spices and salt." She lifted a piece of cloth that had been fashioned into a bag that was bulging with spices.

"Moon Woman, is all well?" Adira fell back beside Mari. "We were trading with the Saleesh women when suddenly they stopped speaking to us and closed their shops. Mari, Sora, did we do something to offend them?"

"Nothing except tell them the truth," Mari said. They'd passed through the village and were winding up the trail beside the river.

"It was me, and not any of you," Dove's voice drifted over from behind Mari, where she walked carefully beside Lily, keeping her arm linked tightly with the younger girl's.

"No. That's not true. It wasn't you, Dove. Father John asked you for a vision. It is not your fault that he didn't like what you saw," Mari said.

"What did she see?" Sora asked.

"The death of the Saleesh, if they do not leave the river for a full cycle of seasons," Dove said.

Nik glanced over his shoulder at Dove, his eyes wide with surprise. "What kills them?"

Dove shook her head. "I couldn't see that. I only saw a tide of shadows, like mist and darkness, and I *knew* with certainty that the tide would drown them if they did not leave here."

"That is horrible!" Adira gasped. "There are so many children in the village. The women must know about the danger."

"We tried to talk with Father John about the vision, but he wouldn't listen," Mari said.

"He threatened us," Danita said.

"What?" Nik motioned for Wilkes to fall back with them.

"Dove had a vision their priest didn't like. That's why everything got shut down so fast. And Father John threatened them," Nik caught Wilkes up.

The older Warrior's eyes narrowed. Beside him, Odin growled deep in his chest, and Wilkes's hand rested on the Shepherd's broad head.

"Warning the women won't do anything," Mari said, careful to keep her voice low, even though Brother Joseph was at the head of the group, many yards away from them, and still moving at a pace so brisk the Pack almost had to jog to keep up. "They don't have a voice in the leadership of the village."

"It is true none of them said so much as a word after Father John ordered them to stop trading," said Adira.

Sora snorted. "It seems the leadership of their village isn't all they don't have a voice in—not if they have to be silent whenever that priest speaks."

"That's pretty much what Antreas told me about them. Men make the rules. Women obey. He said the women don't believe they should have a say. They believe their priest knows best because he speaks to the Mother for them," said Danita.

"But she's a goddess. Why would they believe what she says must be interpreted by a man, and only a man?" Isabel said.

"Because that's how they've been raised. Look at them—they're prosperous, swathed in jewelry. Their children are healthy. I saw not one thin, sickly person in the entire village, and I asked if there was an infirmary that might need our help. There is not," said Sora.

"Wait, *no one* in that village is sick *or* injured?" Mari said. "I find that hard to believe."

"The woman I traded with said that they have a maternity lodge and midwives, but that they rarely need any other type of Healer. They insist they already have everything they need." Sora shrugged. "Good for them, but I would not live silently."

"Is it such a bad trade?" Adira said. "Compliance for safety and prosperity?"

"Safety and prosperity?" Jenna responded quickly. "It's suppression and slavery. Shouldn't the question be, Is it such a *good* trade: safety and prosperity"—her voice was thick with sarcasm—"for the freedom to have a say in their own lives, their own governing? How much different is that village from the floating cages the Tribe of the Trees locked us in?"

"Yeah, and how safe and prosperous are they going to be when the shadow tide Dove saw drowns them?" Isabel said. "They don't get a voice in deciding what should be done about the vision, but they sure will pay the consequences for the decision that was made for them."

"Do you want Wilkes and me to slip back into the village and try to warn someone else?" Nik said. "Maybe their response would be different if the vision was told by a man."

"Father John said that if we mention the vision to any of the Saleesh people upriver he would find out and declare that we are not to be al-

lowed passage," Mari said grimly. "It might be selfish, but I'm not willing to risk our people on the outside chance someone will stand up
against Father John."

"How about I feel out Brother Joseph?" Nik said. "He's younger. I'll
strike up a conversation about Dove's vision, like I believe he already
knows about it, and see what his response is."

"That's a good idea. But if he reacts like Father John back off right
away," Mari said.

"Oh, I will. I agree with you completely. We can't risk our Pack for
people who will not listen." Nik jogged off toward the front of the group,
with Laru padding silently beside him.

"Jenna, I understand your point, though I must say that I do not agree
with it." Adira spoke up as they watched Nik hurry toward Brother Joseph. "But you are very young, and you have not had to worry for your
next meal and be terrified for your safety for decades."

Jenna stopped and faced the older woman. She put her hands on her
hips and shook her head. "No. You cannot use my youth as a way of jus-
tifying that." She pointed back at the village. "I've known hardship. My
mother died. My father raised me—a father with Moon Fever. He was
killed in front of me. I watched Tribesmen sink arrows into him as he
tried to save me. Then I was enslaved. Not as long as you, but I've known
captivity, and I'm telling you that believing you're better off—safer—if
someone else takes care of you and makes decisions for you is a step back
into captivity. Not for me—never again for me."

"Then we shall have to agree to disagree," Adira said before she walked
away, disappearing into the line of Earth Walkers following them.

"Is it immature of me to say that I'll remember that Adira is fine with
following orders as long as she thinks she's being cared for next time I
need an unpleasant job done?" Sora asked.

Mari held her response as Nik jogged back to them, his face grim.

"Father John told him the unchaste blind woman is not to be listened
to, and that our Pack is doomed because we allow women to rule us,"
Nik said.

"'Allow!'" Sora almost spat the word. Her gray eyes found the back of Brother Joseph, and she looked as if she would like to push him off the trail to the white water that raged far below. "We are Moon Women! No one 'allows' us to lead. We *are* leaders."

"And our men are not silent, subjugated shells," Mari said.

"They are also not doomed to a terrible death because they will not see," Dove said. "Pity them, Moon Women, and then release them from your minds. You cannot save people who do not wish to be saved."

"Dove's right. Let's leave this place and these people to their ways," Mari said.

"And to the consequences of their ways," Sora added.

"And to the consequences of their ways," Mari agreed.

"If Antreas doesn't join us tonight, I'm going to take them all down," Danita said grimly.

Mari put her arm around her friend. "You won't have to. Do you really think Bast would be here beside you, relaxed and happy, if Antreas were in any danger?"

Danita grinned up at her, looking relieved and youthful. "Moon Woman, you are absolutely right. As long as Bast is fine, so am I."

The Lynx punctuated Danita's comments by purring contentedly.

CHAPTER 14

R iver loved the winter camp. Of course winter had its dangers, and she would never underestimate the power of the elements, but it was difficult to worry much about snow and ice when Herd Magenti was snug and secure *and warm*. The Valley of Vapors was River's favorite place in all of the Herd's wide territory. The trek to get to it was always treacherous, and this year had been no exception. As they traveled through the narrow passage of the Quachita Mountains it had begun to snow, almost trapping the rear half of the Herd, but once they were through the pass and into the mountain valley, everything was green and growing again as the vast system of hot springs kept the valley perpetually verdant.

This was the only place in the Herd's territory that they inhabited any of the ruins of the long-dead ancients. Here the lofty marble and stone buildings that fronted several of the steaming springs were cared for lovingly by members of Herd Magenti who were not Riders. Those who had never been Chosen by a horse could decide if they wanted to live the nomadic life of a Wind Rider and move from camp to camp, or if they would rather remain at one of the Herd's large campsites, keeping it in working order, planting and harvesting crops, and generally living a comfortable but stationary life. One of the most popular sites for permanent habitation was the Valley of Vapors. Herdmembers who lived in the valley year round kept vegetation cleared from the regal columns and high ceilings of mysterious, beautiful buildings that had been converted to stables and living quarters for the Herd to wait out the winter.

The valley wasn't big, just barely large enough to hold the five combined branches of Herd Magenti, but no one minded being crowded. It was like they passed the winter in a bubble of springtime, surrounded by life-giving waters, while they slept inside marble palaces of the past.

River sat at the edge of one of the reservoirs that bubbled up from the side of the eastern ridge that framed the valley, her feet dangling just above the steaming water. She lazily braided her long, dark curls into one thick plait, smiling to herself about how the rising mist from the hot spring caused escaping locks of her hair to curl around her face. The humidity of the springs annoyed some of the girls and had them complaining about what it did to their hair, but since she had been a child River had embraced the thick riot of her black mane as beautiful and she loved that the springs gave her a halo of curls—whether she tried to tame it or not.

Once in a while she'd dip a toe into the aromatic water, but not for long. The thermal springs that heated the valley and drew an entire Herd through treacherous mountains were life giving and healing, but they were also so hot that they had to be diluted by the nearby lake water to be bearable to the touch.

"I thought you'd be here. Scoot over. This isn't just *your* favorite place."

River scooted over, but she also leaned down and flicked hot water at her sister.

"Don't be immature," April said, sitting beside River.

"You're sounding more and more like Mother," River said.

"I'll take that as a compliment."

"I didn't mean it as one." River butted her sister with her shoulder, and both girls laughed.

"Who's working out today?" April lifted her hand, squinting against the bright winter sunlight at the muddy scene below them.

The girls were sitting on the top lip of a tier of basins that cascaded steaming thermal water down, down, down, to a reservoir below. Long ago Herd Magenti had built a mud trap beside the reservoir—a long strip of earth that ran the length of one side of the rocky water catch and was the width of six horses. The mud trap was mixed with sand gathered from the lake and tilled daily—and daily it was also drenched with thermal water, diverted from one of the cascading basins, so that it was a sucking, muddy mess that required a lot of strength and tenacity for any horse to cross. All winter Riders brought their horses to the mud trap, exercising them so that their stay in the warm, comfortable Valley of Vapors did not make them soft.

But with the Mare Test coming the last day of spring and the Stallion Run the last day of summer, both the following year, this winter the mud trap was a proving ground for the next leaders of Herd Magenti.

"Clayton has Bard down there, of course," River said.

"I see him. That big white blaze is hard to miss, even mud-spattered," April said. "He is a good-looking stallion. And fast, too. Do you think he'll win?"

"I hope not." The words left River's mouth before she realized she'd spoken them.

Her sister studied her. "Because of Clayton and Skye?"

River rolled her eyes. "Not you, too."

"What do you mean—not me too? Hey, the whole herd knows that until you brought Ghost back to us Clayton had been following you around for years, totally love struck. There was even a rumor last year that you were the reason he left to spend those months training with Herd Cinnabar."

"He trained with Cinnabar because they're the best warriors, and Clayton thinks that training will help him guide Bard into winning the Stallion Run. Anything more than that is stupid gossip."

"Stupid gossip that spread through the herd," April said.

"I can't help that."

"True, but he was back to following you around when he returned—until Ghost. Then something changed with him, and Skye slipped right in where everyone thought you would be—mated to Clayton: you the Rider of our next Lead Mare, and him the Rider of our next Herd Stallion."

River made a rude noise that sounded a lot like Anjo blowing snot from her nose.

"Okay, tell me if I'm wrong."

"You're wrong. At least you're wrong from my perspective. Clayton and I have been friends since we were children. He wanted more. I didn't. It's been hard for him to accept it." River moved her shoulders restlessly. "But I can't force myself to feel more for him than I do, and I wouldn't even if I could."

April turned to face her sister, drawing her knees up and hugging them. "River, have you ever had feelings of 'more' for anyone?"

River sighed. "No. Not yet. And I'm tired of people asking me about it. Maybe that's why Ghost found Anjo and me—because I understand what it feels like to have everyone obsessed with who I'll choose. Why can't we not choose anyone except ourselves? What's so wrong with that?"

"Hey, sorry. I didn't mean it like that—like I'm one of the gossips lurking around watching every time you so much as talk too long with any one guy or girl. The truth is, I want to be more like you than her." April jerked her chin in the direction of the mud trap, where Skye had just appeared and was already giggling breathlessly at something Clayton was saying.

"If Skye spent half the time working with her filly as she does simpering at Clayton she might very well challenge Anjo and me for Lead Mare and Rider," River said.

April shook her head as they watched Clayton knee Bard into rearing in the middle of the mud trap, apparently just so Skye and the group of girls joining her could coo and clap.

"Sometimes I think we should go back to the way it was generations ago, when men were only allowed in our camps when they were invited by women who wanted babies," River said. "It's hard for me to believe how ridiculous girls act when a cute boy pays attention to them."

"Girls who take other girls as lovers can act silly, too," April said.

"Not *as* silly."

"So, you think Clayton's mad at you for not wanting him and that's why he's stirring up so much talk?"

"I don't know. He's been really angry since Mother allowed Ghost to winter with the Herd, and he knew I didn't feel more than friendship for him before I found Ghost. April, he knew it well before he left to train with Cinnabar. It's just that me finding Ghost made the knowing finally sink in. I'm not sure why."

"Uh, River, it could be because Ghost obviously hates Clayton, and you obviously like Ghost more than him."

River shrugged. "Horses Choose their own Riders, as well as their own friends. I wish Clayton and Skye well."

"Why?"

River's brows went up. "Because I don't want him, so why shouldn't Skye find happiness with him?"

April sighed. "No, that's not what I meant. I meant if you don't have any feelings of jealousy, why don't you want Clayton and Bard to be the Herd's next Stallion and Rider? But I also think it's weird that Ghost dislikes him so much."

River blew out a long breath. "I'm not surprised Ghost dislikes Clayton. He can probably sense how irritating it is that Clayton wouldn't take my *No I don't want you—I just want to be friends with you* as a true no. Well, that and the fact that Clayton roped and tripped Ghost the first time they met—which definitely wasn't a good start for them. I do think it's strange that Clayton so clearly dislikes Ghost, especially when he spouts all that crap about the Riderless stallion heralding change for the Herd. Maybe he thinks I'm bonded to the stallion, which would mean I could compete against him for Rider of the Herd Stallion."

"But you're not bonded to Ghost, right?"

"Right. We're just friends. If he's bonded to anyone it's Anjo," River said.

Anjo raised her head from where she was grazing nearby and nickered softly at her Rider, and River blew her a kiss in return.

"Ghost and Anjo would make gorgeous foals. Can you imagine? Makes me wish Anjo could be bred to him in time to have a weanling for the next Choosing."

River studied her sister. April was the sister closest in age to her, and at this spring's Rendezvous she would be sixteen, which made her a first-time Candidate for the Choosing. Over the past year she and River had gotten close, which made River unexpectedly happy as she realized her sister was smart and funny, and very loyal. River needed loyalty—especially with the talk of change that kept being whispered through the Herd.

"Are you nervous already?" River asked her.

"Not yet. More looking forward and anxious for it to hurry and get here, but I know how nervous I'll be at the Rendezvous, so I don't *really* want it to hurry and get here. Know what I mean?"

"Exactly."

"So, you think Clayton changed toward you because he's worried that Ghost can beat Bard in the Run?"

"Ghost *can* beat Bard. I don't have any doubt about that, but it doesn't matter. Ghost doesn't have a Rider. He can't compete."

April looked around them, and even though they were alone she lowered her voice. "You know there's talk about letting him compete."

"Ghost? That's impossible."

"Under the current law, yes. But there's a whole group who think it's time to change those laws," April said.

"I know Clayton's part of that group, but he's not going to be for allowing Ghost to compete." River shook her head. "I wish Mother would shut down the rumors, but she acts like they mean nothing," she added.

"Maybe because they don't mean anything. Mother has ruled for almost a decade. She's wise. She wouldn't just ignore something that needed to be dealt with. And you know there's always crazy talk when the Lead Mare *and* Herd Stallion are stepping down in the same year."

"I know, but it's still annoying."

"Hey, you didn't answer me. Why don't you want Clayton and Bard to win?"

"I think Bard is a fine stallion—not better than Ghost, and maybe not better than a couple of the other contenders, but that'll be decided by the race. I don't want Clayton to be Lead Stallion Rider because he wants to rule," River said.

"But that's what a Herd Stallion Rider does."

"No. He *leads* the other stallions in service to the Lead Mare and the rest of the Herd. I know Clayton. He doesn't want to serve the Lead Mare. He wants to *rule* over her."

April made a rude noise. "That will *never* happen!"

"And yet Clayton and his supporters, including Skye, who believes she can beat Anjo and me for Lead Mare, follow him—and they're getting more and more vocal about their desire for change."

April shook her head. "I don't get it. Our horses are strong and beautiful. Our people are healthy and prosperous. The Wind Rider lands have been a place of peace for centuries. And it's not like any other Herd is going to listen to them. I just don't understand why Clayton and his friends suddenly want change."

"I don't think it's sudden. And I don't think it's only happening here, with our Herd. Clayton used to say little things I thought were off, or strange sounding, but when I'd ask him to explain what he meant he'd shrug away his words and change the subject—*until* he returned from Herd Cinnabar last spring. Since then he's been blatant about his ideas. April, I didn't start avoiding him just because he was pressuring me to be more than friends. I avoided him because I didn't like what I heard coming out of his mouth."

"So, it'll truly be bad for the Herd if Clayton wins."

"Yes, truly. Or at least bad for the Herd as we know it," River said.

"He'll need a strong mare-and-Rider team to keep him under control. You don't think Skye and Scout can beat you and Anjo, do you? The Great Mother Mare knows Skye would give in to anything Clayton wanted. I mean, look at them down there," April said, worrying a long piece of grass between her fingers.

Both girls gazed below. Skye was now perched on a rock at the edge of the mud trap. Even from their high vantage point River could see that

Skye's strawberry-colored hair was dressed with streams of purple ribbons braided in the same fashion as her filly, Scout. As River watched, Clayton, who was on Bard's back as the stallion trotted determinedly back and forth along the length of the mud trap, his deep, muscular chest frothy with sweat, shouted something to Skye, and her flirtatious laughter drifted up with the rising steam from the reservoir. Several lengths behind Bard, Scout struggled through the mud, Riderless and ignored.

"Skye's not the only person who doesn't ride in the mud trap," River said.

"Yeah, I know, but if I were lucky enough to be Chosen, especially by a horse as wonderful as Scout, I'd be out there with her and not posed on a rock flirting with a boy."

River looked at her sister. "You mean unless Brax and Kanth were down there?"

April's face flamed. Brax was a year older than her, and at the last Rendezvous was Chosen by a sweet bay gelding named Kanth.

"Brax and I like each other—maybe a lot—but I wouldn't let my feelings for him turn me into that." April pointed down at Skye, who had tossed back her long hair and was clapping and cheering Bard on, as her Scout continued to labor behind him, mud-spattered and breathing hard.

Disgusted by Skye, River's gaze went to the girl's filly. "Scout's a fine horse, but she's not as fast as Anjo—no mare is except Echo, and that was when she was in her prime."

"Don't let Mother hear you say that." April bumped River with her shoulder.

"Oh, don't worry. I'd never disrespect Echo like that."

"But I agree with you. Anjo is fast."

"She is! I'm sure Luce and Blue are going to compete in the Mare Test, and they're actually a stronger team than Scout and Skye. Blue can definitely outrun Scout. And don't think that Skye and Luce and I will be the only Riders entering the Test. Anyone can enter as long as their mare isn't older than ten—and that includes a lot of amazing teams in our

Herd and the other branches of Magenti. Pairs will come from all of our Herds, and the competition will be tough. You know the Test is about a lot more than speed. There will be choices we have to make as a team out there. I don't know what the tests will be—no one except the Mare Council know—and since every Mare Test is different, not even Mother can help Anjo and me prepare."

"Yeah, and the only witnesses will be the Council judges hidden all around the course—well, at least until you cross the finish line, where *everyone* will be waiting and cheering. I know all that—we all do. But do you think you can win?"

"Anjo says we can, and that's good enough for me," River said.

"I think you can, too," April said firmly.

"Hey, you realize that if I'm Lead Mare Rider that means you and whatever filly Chooses you probably can't be, don't you?" River asked her sister. Lead Stallions held their position no longer than eight years— sometimes a lot less if they were injured or otherwise unable to father foals. Lead Mares led the Herd for ten years—unless injury or illness forced them to step down—and no mare over the age of ten could apply for the Mare Test, which meant that unless something unexpected happened, any horse who Chose April would not be eligible for Lead Mare.

April looked at her sister, surprise clear in her hazel eyes. "Of course I know that! Riv, I've never wanted to be Lead Mare Rider. I watch Mother. She and Echo have so many responsibilities. They have to figure out which mares should be bred to which stallions and when. They have to decide on the backup stallions, and the order they stand in for the Herd Stallion after he has been bred to the max. They sit in judgment and hear all the Herd disputes—*all of them*—then she and Echo decide the outcome, and sometimes that means enforcing penalties and even banishing Riders from the Herd!" She shuddered. "I can't even imagine! And then there are all of the formal trade gatherings they oversee, as well as deciding which campsite we move to and when—and that's just *part* of their responsibilities. It's exhausting just listing them."

April shook her head firmly. "No. I have no desire to lead, and you have *always* wanted to. Plus, you're Mother's choice—not me, not Amber, and not Violet."

"Violet's only four. She can't be chosen for anything yet," River teased.

"True. But me—no way. I'll be content to be bonded to a horse. Any horse. And to serve my Lead Mare Rider." She bowed her head only half kiddingly.

"Thank you," River said soberly. "I mean it."

April met her sister's gaze. "I mean it, too. And you're welcome. Now, why don't you take that gorgeous filly of yours down there and see if you can splash some mud on Skye?"

"That's really petty," River said.

"Yes, it is."

River dimpled. "But it sounds like fun. Want to come with me?"

"Absolutely!"

River wiped her feet off in the grass beside the basin, and then she and April walked over to Anjo.

"How about we go to the mud trap and get some exercise?" River asked Anjo as she rubbed her filly's wide forehead.

Anjo snorted and bumped River playfully.

"She's more than ready!" April said, kissing Anjo on the side of her face.

"She likes competition a lot more than I do," River said.

"Because she knows she's the best—just like Echo," April said as she walked beside her sister and Anjo down the steep, winding path to the reservoir.

By the time they reached the mud trap it was no longer early morning and the exercise ground was filling with young Riders and their Companions. River noted right away that Skye remained seated on the rock beside the trap, and that several young girls—some already Riders, and some not—had taken seats around her. Those who had horses sent them into the trap to exercise while the girls remained comfortable, almost as if they were holding court around Skye.

There were a couple fillies laboring away in the mud trap, but most of the spectator attention was focused on Clayton and Bard, who were both covered with sweat and mud and sand, still struggling against the sucking ground while Scout held her own with them, though no one seemed to notice the hardworking filly.

"Do you see that?" April whispered to her sister while River braided Anjo's long tail so that it would be easier to wash free of mud afterwards. "Those girls are taking their cues from Skye and just sitting around while their fillies exercise."

"I see, and I do not approve," River said darkly.

"Mother should know about this. It's the laziest thing I think I've ever seen. If this is the *change* Clayton and his friends are for, well, they need to be stopped!" April hissed the words under her breath to her sister.

"We don't have to bother Mother. If I'm going to lead our herd I can't be calling on my mommy to help me."

"Are you going to yell at them? Tell them how lazy and stupid they're being?"

River smiled at her passionate little sister. "No. I'm going to do what our mother would do—lead by example. If they don't follow, well, then, I'm the wrong leader."

"Or they're the wrong followers," April muttered.

River laughed as Anjo knelt so that she could mount. She, like the other Riders exercising in the mud trap, were riding bareback. Actually, River preferred to ride Anjo bareback. She liked the skin-to-skin contact, and Anjo was so sensitive to her every movement that River could direct her filly without using their mental bond, and instead just nudged her slightly with thigh, calf, and heel pressure.

"Either way," River said to her sister, "I only know one way to lead. So, here goes."

"A mare's luck to you," said April.

Crowded today. Anjo's sweet voice filled River's mind. She reached forward, stroking her filly's strong neck.

"Would you rather wait until they clear out?" River asked her.

Anjo swiveled her head back and forth, taking in the whispering girls perched around Skye, the two stallions laboring under their Riders, as well as the fillies who—Riderless—were sloughing determinedly through the mud trap.

Your decision. I can beat them all.

River grinned and stroked Anjo's slick neck, loving her filly's confidence. She touched her briefly with both of her heels, a sign the filly knew meant to stand still and wait while her Rider assessed the situation.

Clayton and Bard were still working, though River thought they were coming close to overdoing it. Only one other stallion had entered the mud trap. Red, a big sorrel who was several years older than Bard, was well proven and respected by the Herd. His Rider, Jonathan, sat confidently on his back as the stallion trotted determinedly through the mud trap, his coat already slick with sweat.

Two fillies had joined Skye's Scout—Luce's grulla filly, Blue, and Cali's delicate sorrel filly, Vixen. There was an older black mare she recognized as Xanthos, whose Rider, Cybill, had been Chosen the year before Anjo had Chosen River. She was surprised to see that Cybill had joined the group around Skye.

"Cybill usually shows better sense than that." River spoke softly to Anjo, whose ears twitched back to catch her words.

Xanthos is a fine mare. Cybill is a follower. She follows Skye.

River didn't say anything more, but she began to feel uneasy. She didn't like the changes she was seeing in the Herd.

"Let's show them how this is done," River said to Anjo.

Yes—let's!

Anjo moved into the mud trap, choosing the lane that was empty of another horse, but also closest to the reservoir, which meant it was the wettest and the toughest. But the powerful filly didn't falter. She arched her head, gathered herself, and, as River murmured encouragement, attacked the mud, working her muscles to move her long, fine legs like pistons. River didn't look to the left or right. She concentrated on her filly, knowing that she was extra weight and that if she shifted her balance she could throw off Anjo's stride. The Rider and filly worked together, moving as one, and soon River was sweating along with her horse.

She knew that Anjo was approaching and then passing the Riderless fillies, but River didn't shift her concentration. From her peripheral vision, she could tell that Anjo was moving up beside Red, the first of the two stallions.

Anjo passed him without even straining herself.

They came to the far end of the mud trap, and Anjo turned neatly to head back. She paused at the end, dancing in place, which River understood was a little showoffish, but she couldn't blame her filly. Though River didn't so much as glance over at the group of girls surrounding Skye, she could feel that their attention was riveted on her.

"They should be paying attention to their own horses—like, actually *riding* them." River spoke quietly to Anjo, who snorted her agreement.

"They like the show."

River looked up, shocked to see Clayton on Bard, who was breathing heavily. The two were standing just outside the mud trap, taking a well-earned break.

"I'm not here for your show." River turned her attention from Clayton. She quickly tucked several escaping curls behind her ears and wiped the sweat from her face with her sleeve before clucking at her filly to keep going. Anjo enthusiastically set out again, easily lapping the fillies and Cybill's black mare, as well as Jonathan's stallion.

Alone on the return trek, River concentrated on her filly, being sure Anjo was gathering herself correctly so that she wouldn't strain a misused muscle, or twist a leg.

They challenge.

Anjo's warning came just before the noise of sucking mud and laboring breath told River a rider was coming up beside them. She glanced to her left to see Bard gaining ground on them.

This is stupid, River thought. *His stallion is way too tired for games.*

Then River heard the cheers.

"Pass her, Clayton!"

"Go for it, Bard!"

"Beat her!"

They have chosen the wrong horse to cheer. Anjo's voice blasted through River's mind, and she took a deeper seat, gripping her filly's sweat-and-mud-slick sides with her thighs as excitement bubbled up from within her.

"We're fresher, younger, and a lot less foolish. Let's lead by example, perfect girl. *Do not let Bard beat us to the end of the trap!*"

It was as if River's words had broken a dam, and strength poured throughout the filly's body. River could feel it pulse against her skin as Anjo's muscles worked.

Bard had pulled up beside them. River didn't so much as glance his way.

"Just stay with me! You and me—we can give them a great show!" Clayton said.

River didn't look at him. Instead she said, "When are you going to learn I mean what I say? I am *not* here for your show." She bent low over Anjo's neck and urged, "Anjo! Go!"

The filly surged ahead, easily pulling away from the weary stallion and spattering him with mud and sand.

"That's right, Anjo! Go! Go! Go!" April shouted from the sidelines.

And Anjo went. She pulled one length ahead of Bard, and then another—which is when the cheers for Clayton and Bard began to be drowned out by a tide of voices calling, "Anjo! River! Anjo! River! Anjo! River!"

River still didn't look around. She was utterly focused on maintaining her balance and riding low so that her filly didn't have to waste energy correcting her balance or dealing with wind drag.

Suddenly startled gasps came from the crowd. River still didn't look around, believing the spectators were simply shocked that Anjo was leaving Bard so far behind.

Ghost comes! I will beat him, too.

Ghost! River did glance to the side then. Sure enough, the golden stallion was plowing through the mud. He easily caught and passed Bard, who snorted and squealed his rage, but Clayton's stallion was simply too tired and could not challenge Ghost.

And then Ghost pulled up beside Anjo. She laid her ears back flat on her head and surged forward, breathing deeply and evenly. River clung to her back, ignoring the shouts from the crowd. She could see the end of the trap between Anjo's flattened ears—and it was only yards away.

"Go! Anjo! Go! You can do it!" River shouted, and her filly responded with an added burst of speed that left Ghost behind her, mud flying into his face, as Anjo vaulted out of the mud trap—the indisputable winner.

The filly turned to face the slack-mouthed crowd.

Hold tight, she warned River seconds before she reared, pawing the air and trumpeting in victory. River clung to her back, gripping her mane tightly, and finding that she didn't mind her filly's display of dominance, especially when she noted that the crowd had grown, and her mother was front and center, smiling proudly and clapping.

Skye was still on her rock, though now standing instead of posing perfectly. River expected the girl to be glowering at her, and she was definitely glowering, but at Ghost, not her. The golden stallion had climbed from the mud trap and joined Anjo, who touched muzzles affectionately with him.

Bard was still several lengths behind them, laboring through the mud and sand. The rest of the exercising horses had paused at the far end of the trap to watch the show.

River threw her arms around Anjo's neck and hugged her filly. "You are the best, smartest, fastest, strongest horse in the world!"

World? No. Herd? Perhaps, came Anjo's confident response.

River laughed and sat up. "Ghost, that was quite a race." She was reaching over to stroke the handsome stallion's neck when his demeanor abruptly changed.

The stallion's head went up. His ears went back. He pawed the ground with one muddy front hoof, and then with a war trumpet, he surged forward, parting the shocked group of watchers as he bolted at Skye.

"Stop him!" Clayton cried while Bard finally struggled from the trap. The stallion tried to chase Ghost, but he'd passed the limits of his great strength, and stumbled, almost falling to his knees. "Stop him!" Clayton repeated. "He's going to kill her!"

River couldn't move. She was utterly shocked, but she heard Anjo's voice, calm and sure, *Ghost will not harm Skye.*

People screamed as Ghost sprinted to where Skye was standing, apparently as frozen as River, atop the rock. From the corner of her eye, River saw a dappled gray blur that could only be the exhausted, mud-coated Scout racing for her Rider.

And then the golden stallion was at the rock. His head whipped down, ears still pinned flat against his head, the whites of his eyes showing. He slid to a halt as he reached out and snagged something from the ground in his powerful jaws. Skye screamed while the stallion shook his head, severing the thick, dark body of the lethally poisonous water moccasin before he dropped it and, squealing, stomped it flat with his hooves.

Scout, sweat-drenched sides heaving and body trembling, stumbled to a stop in front of Skye's rock. Her muzzle reached out to touch her Rider, who was staring in silent shock at the dead viper. Then Scout faced Ghost. Slowly, they touched muzzles before the filly closed her eyes in obvious relief, and bowed her head to him.

As if what he'd done had been an everyday occurrence, Ghost nuzzled the filly before trotting back through the staring crowd, pausing before the Lead Mare Rider. The magnificent stallion bowed deeply to her, and Dawn rubbed his muddy forehead, speaking so that everyone watching could hear.

"Well done, Ghost. You have shown us a Herd Stallion's place, which is to protect his Herd. Just as River's Anjo has demonstrated the traits of a Lead Mare—strength, intelligence, and a respectful, loving partnership with her Rider." Dawn's gaze found Skye. "Sadly, I cannot say the same for any other filly Riders here today." She turned back to Ghost, saying affectionately, "May a mare's blessing be with you, and may you always have a mare's luck."

Ghost nuzzled Dawn gently, wiping mud all over her tunic, which had the Lead Mare Rider laughing and shaking her head as Ghost trotted back to Anjo's side.

Clayton looked from the stallion to River. "I've never seen anything like that."

River straightened her back and raised her voice. "Get used to it, Clayton.

Things are changing, but not the way you and your gossips think they are. Come on, Anjo, Ghost—let's get you wiped down and cooled off."

As the crowd watched, Anjo pranced from the mud trap viewing area, tail high, neck arched, and ears pricked—with the golden stallion trotting contentedly behind.

CHAPTER 15

A stench hung over the forest. Ralina had decided it was part decay and part despair. Death had claimed the top platform of the old pine for himself. He'd had his Reapers bring the rest of the Skin Stealers from Port City. More soldiers, in various stages of the macabre animal-human mutation the God had begun calling The Cure, had joined his already transformed Reapers. Currently, they weren't so much restoring the blackened City in the Trees as moving into any of the nests that were still even semi-habitable and gutting the rest of them.

They reminded Ralina of maggots, crawling in and out of decomposing bodies.

A bevy of young women and girls had joined the Reapers. The youngest and prettiest were always in attendance to the God—lounging about Him, feeding Him, often by hand, and, of course, coupling with Him, as his appetite for everything seemed insatiable.

Death had ordered braziers lit all around him on the platform, as well as surrounding the tree he'd moved into permanently, commanding the firepots to be constantly filled with sweetly scented herbs and pinecones. But the fetid smell that hung over the Tribe found its way into the smoke, mixing with pine and mint and lavender to form a revolting sick-sweetness that tainted every breath Ralina took, causing her stomach to heave.

One good thing about not eating much—I don't have much to throw up.

"Why do you stop? That could not be the end of your tale. The big Alpha Shepherd, Raphael, has not yet reached the children. I must know what happens! Continue!"

Ralina mentally shook herself, and then lifted her chin, trying to reclaim even a small part of the Storyteller pride she used to hold so dear for herself, and for her Tribe. Her voice found the singsong rhythm the end of the story called for, and she concluded.

"Helpless, the girls clung to the ice in fear.
They screamed their need, though no Tribesmen were near.
But the Alpha, born to protect, did hear.

He knew the ice would break
He did not hesitate
His body made the path
Bloody paws striking with wrath.

He reached the children and to him they clung
Weeping with relief—salvation had come!

Sides heaving—breath leaving—the Alpha stroked on
He kept swimming, even after his strength was gone.
They reached the shore by his blood and his brawn
He saw them safe before the last of his breath was drawn.
That is why always and still
The Tribe remembers mighty Alpha Raphael."

Ralina bowed her head and crossed her arms over her chest to signify the end of her tale, and the God laughed and clapped.

"Ah, I do so love a story that ends in death! I am eager to hear how you will begin my tale, and I have been considering where you should start. Perhaps not with my victory over the Tribe of the Trees. Perhaps you should begin as I awakened. What are your thoughts, Storyteller?"

You would kill me for my thoughts. Aloud, Ralina said, "Great God, it would be difficult for me to begin your tale by describing something I was not there to observe, especially as I know you would want me to be as accurate as possible."

"Hum, you make an excellent point, Storyteller, though I mourn that the beginnings of my tale will be lost." Death sighed sadly as one of the girls He called Feather rubbed His cloven hooves, and another whose name Ralina had never heard Him speak hand-fed Him pieces of rabbit.

Ralina had to keep herself from glaring at the God. She could smell that the rabbit meat was untainted, and could be safely fed to the Tribe, but the God hoarded every bit of untainted meat for Himself. Ralina was beginning to understand that Death's intention was to infect them all— every one of them.

I must figure out a way to stop Him—and to do that I need to know more about how He went from a sleeping God to one that walks the earth, bringing misery and pestilence.

"My Lord, there is an alternative," Ralina said.

"Speak, Storyteller!"

"It is just a thought, and I do not mean to overstep, but if you explained to me in detail what happened, how you were awakened, I could recount your tale accurately, and it would be told over and over again throughout the ages."

Death nibbled a piece of succulent rabbit from the girl's hand, licking and sucking fat from her fingers while He considered Ralina's words.

The Storyteller's empty stomach roiled, and she averted her eyes from His greasy lips and the disgusting noises He made as the girl fed Him.

"I like this new idea of yours very much," He said as He chewed noisily.

"I would need access to you during the process of researching your tale, though, my Lord. Would that be something you might allow?"

"Of course! Anything to immortalize my story! I shall let Iron Fist know that he is to pass word to all Reapers that you are given leave to come and go freely." Then the God glanced around the platform, as if just realizing something was missing.

"Where is your handsome Shepherd? What is his name again?"

"Bear, my Lord." Ralina forced her voice to remain emotionless. She purposefully left her Companion in the roped-off area where Death had segregated all members of the Tribe who had not accepted The Cure. She didn't like how the God stared at the Shepherds, especially the large males.

"Yes, Bear! Aptly named. He is one of the largest of the Tribe's canines, is he not?"

"There were several males larger than Bear, but none are with us anymore," Ralina prevaricated.

Death's gaze hardened along with His voice. "Then there is no need to speak of them! Bring your canine with you next time you come. I enjoy observing them."

"Yes, my Lord," Ralina said, as terror clenched her heart.

Death was watching her closely. "Storyteller, you do not appear to be ill."

"I am not, my Lord," she replied carefully. "Or at least I am not at this moment."

"It would be interesting to see what a magnificent being you would become should you fall ill and take The Cure. Merging your flesh with that mighty canine of yours—why, you would be even more powerful than the beloved Raphael of your old tale!"

"I will keep that in mind should I fall ill, my Lord."

"I will keep that in mind as well, *when* you fall ill, Storyteller."

Ralina had to swallow quickly to keep from vomiting.

"Now, you asked about how I came into being, and I shall tell you. But first I am curious about how Shepherds and even those small, insignificant Terriers first began bonding with your people. Thaddeus tells me there is a tale called 'Endings and Beginnings.' Is that true?"

"It is, my Lord." Ralina's answer was flat, but she wept inside. She'd thought her heart couldn't break any more, but Death's question had her remembering the last time she'd performed the "Tale of Endings and Beginnings" before their wise Sun Priest, Sol, and their prosperous Tribe. She longed to recapture those days when she stood before an eager Tribe in her rabbit fur cloak and her tunic that had stories beaded into it for decoration.

"Well, then, what is it you wait for? Or must you get your canine to tell the tale?" He didn't wait for Ralina to answer, but as usual, barreled on without a thought for anyone but Himself. "That is a splendid idea! You have my leave to get your canine and then return to—"

Feet scuffing the circular stairs up to the God's platform interrupted Death, who brushed away the piece of rabbit the girl was trying to feed Him as He turned to glare at whoever was interrupting.

Ralina had to school her face as Thaddeus entered the platform. In just three days, the Hunter had changed drastically. He no longer hid his preternatural abilities, but stalked through the campsite, remind-ing her of a rabid dog that needed to be put down for his own good. His body had changed. He had always been short, but powerfully built. Now there was a hunch in his back; his increasing muscle mass had apparently bowed his spine as it attempted to accommodate the man's unnatural strength. His hands were more claw-like than finger-like. It seemed he'd quit bathing completely, and his eyes were perpetually red.

"My Lord!" Thaddeus dropped to one knee before the God of Death.

"Thaddeus, why do you interrupt my storytelling time? You know how important it is to me."

"Forgive me, my Lord, but I assumed you would want a status report on the tainted meat."

Death sighed. "Yes, yes, of course." He pulled his hooves from Feath-er's grasp. "Girl, find Iron Fist and bring him to me." As she scurried away the God added, "You should know this as well as my Blade. Be cer-tain you tell your Warriors and Hunters that the Storyteller is free to come and go as she wishes."

Thaddeus's cruel eyes found Ralina. She stared back at him steadily, trying to focus her disgust for him in her gaze.

"Do you think that wise, my Lord? Ralina has long been—"

Death came to His feet, planting his cloven hooves wide so that he towered over the much smaller man. "Did you just question me?"

Ralina watched the exchange eagerly. *Kill Thaddeus*, she wished silently. *Without his traitorous leadership we might be able to form a true resistance.*

But as usual when Thaddeus was confronted by someone stronger than him, he backed down. Bowing deeply, Thaddeus said, "I apologize, my Lord. It is just that you do not know the Tribe as well as I do, and I thought it wise to warn you that the Storyteller has been known to—"

"The Storyteller is under my protection. Is that clear enough for you?"

"Yes, my Lord. Of course." Thaddeus sounded servile, but when his gaze flicked to Ralina she saw raw hatred smoldering there.

"My Lord, I must see that Bear is fed, and I'm sure you and Thaddeus have things of great import you must talk about. Might I have leave to go?"

"Not quite yet." Death smiled at Ralina. "If Thaddeus does have something of importance to discuss with me, you should hear it. Perhaps you could devote an entire scene to our conversation. Just sit quietly and listen."

Ralina nodded. She backed to the railing and finally allowed her legs to give way so that she slid to a seat. The God's smile did not fool her— nor did His proclamation of protection.

His happily ever afters all end in death.

"Now, Thaddeus, go ahead with your status report."

While the God sat and nibbled more succulent rabbit from the girl's fingers, Thaddeus paced before Him, speaking in quick, short sentences. Ralina almost expected him to start yapping like his poor, dead Terrier, Odysseus.

"People are being reinfected. Each day more and more. Though my Hunters go deeper into the forest for game, they only find tainted animals."

The God shrugged His massive shoulders, causing the deer pelt he wore as a cloak to fall from Him so that His naked chest and back were visible. Ralina had to stifle a shudder. *His chest is covered with the fur of a stag.*

"Why should this interest me?" asked Death.

"The people sicken. Your people. My people. And there are more fights. Daily. My men are stronger and faster, but it is getting difficult to control those infected. There are just too many of them."

"Then use my Reapers. They can control them."

Thaddeus ran his fingers through his greasy hair. "It isn't just that. My Lord, you know my first position was as Hunter to the Tribe, and that now I perform the same service for you."

"Yes, Thaddeus, I know that." Death's tone was of a father talking to an annoying and rather stupid child.

Thaddeus stopped pacing and faced the God. "I believe the animals of the forest have been irrevocably poisoned with the skin-sloughing disease."

Death cocked His head to the side, His mighty antlers casting bizarre shadows against the trunk of the tree behind Him. "Truly? I assumed the tainted animals would die and the disease would fade. Is that not what is happening?"

Thaddeus was visibly relieved that the God was listening to him. "No, my Lord. The tainted animals go mad. They attack anything in their path before they die, infecting whatever their blood touches. From what I have observed, it is taking longer and longer for the animals to die. Some even appear to be living with the disease." Thaddeus shuddered.

Ralina's mouth went dry as she imagined what could be so terrible to make that angry, evil little man shudder.

"Ah, the disease mutates." Death nodded as if this didn't surprise Him.

"I do not believe the forest will ever be the same," Thaddeus said.

Death sat up straight, knocking the girl's slender hand roughly away from His face. "So, what you're saying is that this forest is no longer an escape from the poisoned city."

Thaddeus nodded. "What I am saying is that the forest has *become* the poisoned city."

The sadness in Thaddeus's voice made Ralina want to gag. *This is your fault, you traitor! You could have warned us! We could have attacked Port City before they caught us unaware and reeling from the fire. All of this death and disease could have been prevented if you hadn't been so filled with anger and hatred and the need for power!*

Thaddeus's proclamation had a much different effect on the God. He seemed to swell with excitement.

"Then we must leave this poisoned place for a land untainted, where I can awaken my Goddess and rule far away from the pestilence that is this forest," Death said.

"Leave the forest?" Thaddeus shook his head. "The Tribe will not do that."

Death stood abruptly. His voice shook the platform. "Then the Tribe can stay here and die!" The God shook back His long mane, pulled the cloak up around His shoulders, and sat, motioning for the girl, who was cowering on the floor before Him, to continue feeding Him. "But your Warriors and Hunters—those who have taken The Cure—shall come with me. And many canines. Especially the Shepherds. They must come as well."

"To where, my Lord?" Thaddeus asked.

"To the Plains of the Wind Riders, of course," Death said. "It is a fortunate coincidence that I have property there that I must reclaim, and it is there that I will awaken my beloved Goddess." Death smiled as He gazed off into the distance, as if He could already see their future.

"The Plains of the Wind Riders? To get there we must travel up the Umbria River, then cross Lost Lake and the Rock Mountains. We would have to begin almost immediately to make it through the mountains before snow closes the passes."

Death shrugged. "Then we will leave very soon. Who among your Tribe knows the way?"

"No one! Only the Lynx guides know the way there," said Thaddeus.

"Then bring a Lynx guide to me and let us begin our next adventure!" Death said.

"I can light the signal fire. If there is a guide available, he will come," said Thaddeus.

"Do so immediately. As you said—there is no time to wait."

"I will, my Lord." Thaddeus hesitated, and then added, "What of the people who are infected?"

"Offer them The Cure if you believe they are worthy. If they have no canine Companion, they may substitute the flesh of any living animal—except people." Death sighed and shook His head. "I do not understand why it does not work with the flesh of people, but no matter. Any animal will do—even an infected one."

"And the ones who refuse?" Thaddeus asked.

Instead of answering, Death turned to Ralina. "Storyteller, do you know why I call those who follow me 'the People'?"

Ralina had to clear the bile from her throat before she could answer. "No, mighty God. I do not."

"It is because those who follow me are the only 'people' I acknowledge. All others are inconsequential—fit only to be servants, if that. Be quite sure you mention that in my tale."

"I will, my Lord," Ralina said. *And I will mention so, so much more, so that future generations will know exactly what a monster you are.*

He swiveled His head to look from Ralina to Thaddeus.

"Nothing," Death said.

"Nothing?" Thaddeus shook his head, confused.

"Yes. Nothing. As I said, do *nothing.* Those who refuse The Cure will die. Let them. Do not waste time or resources on them. Simply herd them into that fetid penned-off area and let them die. It is the natural way of things, isn't it?"

Speechless, Thaddeus stared at him.

Ralina thought, *This will do it. Children have been infected. Nursing mothers have been infected. Even petty, angry little Thaddeus must understand now just how dangerous this creature is—and just how much we must work together to try to defeat Him.*

But as a feral smile began lifting the corners of Thaddeus's thin lips, Ralina realized how very wrong she was.

"It is, my Lord. Why bother with those too weak to save themselves and too stupid to understand the power that there is in The Cure." His gaze slid to Ralina and she refused to look away—refused to cower before his appalling callousness.

Death clapped Thaddeus on the back. "Yes! Good man! You understand. Begin separating the sick from those who are uninfected, or who are taking The Cure. Put the sick in the pen. The rest, if they have sworn loyalty to me, may find shelter among the trees, though not for long. Soon we will be on our way."

"The boats!" Thaddeus said darkly. "That bitch and Nik destroyed what they didn't steal."

"Then set the Tribe to repairing them."

"Yes, they can be repaired, and I believe in time, but it will take too long to build more." Then before Death could comment, Thaddeus's slick smile widened. "But we won't be taking everyone with us—so we won't need many more boats. And don't your Reapers know how to build rafts?"

"I have said from the beginning that you are a quick learner, Thaddeus. You understand. Yes, repair the damaged boats. Yes, my Reapers are expert raft builders. I will command Iron Fist to set the People to building. Now, go. You have much to do."

"My Lord!" Thaddeus bowed, sent Ralina a sneering smile, and then hurried from the platform.

"Storyteller! I am pleased that you were here to witness the beginning of what will be a grand new adventure."

"I cannot tell you how pleased I am, too," Ralina said. *Because knowledge is power, and I need all the power I can get if I am to rid the world of you.* "My Lord, may I be granted leave to go, now?"

"To care for your Companion, correct?"

"Yes."

"Then you may take your leave. The sun is setting and I find I am hungry for more than rabbit." Death snagged the wrist of the girl who'd been feeding Him, and pulled Her onto His lap. "But return to me tomorrow at the same time, and when you do—be quite sure you bring your Companion."

"Yes, my Lord." Ralina bowed and exited—her stomach tight with fear. *I will not let that monster harm Bear. And I don't know how, but I'm going to stop Him. I swear it by the Sun and by the memory of what used to be our glorious Tribe.*

The sun was setting when Antreas finally rejoined the Pack. They were camped on the bank of the Umbria, east of the ruins of the dam and a huge bridge that was broken but still semi-intact—so that it looked like the skeletal remains of a long-extinct monster.

Brother Joseph had left immediately after they'd arrived at the campsite. No one had been sorry to see him go.

As the sun sank below the horizon Danita began pacing and staring down the darkening trail while Bast groomed herself close by. About halfway to the campsite Bast had suddenly stopped, yowled as if she'd been in pain, and even limped for a little while, though Danita couldn't find anything wrong with her paw. Dinner had been made and eaten, and the Pack congregated in small groups as they worked on weaving projects. The boats were docked nearby. All seemed well with them. Only one paddle had been lost, and there were several extra, so it was easy to replace. The Mother Plants had survived the white water well—very well. They, along with the rest of the cuttings, seedlings, and young plants had been thoroughly drenched in the crossing, soaking them all with life-giving water. Relieved and full of fish stew seasoned with the very delicious almond butter Sora had managed to trade for, before Father John had closed the market, the Pack—except for Danita—had settled contentedly for the night.

Bast's head suddenly went up, and she coughed at Danita several times. The big feline rubbed against the girl's legs before speeding silently down the path and disappearing.

"Is it Antreas?" Mari asked. She'd been keeping a close eye on Danita since Bast had had her limping spell. Mari had no doubt that Antreas was well, and would catch up with the Pack soon—the fact that Bast had recovered quickly and been so relaxed all evening was testament to the fact that her Companion remained safe. But the phantom soreness of her paw had been worrisome.

"Oh, Goddess, I hope so. I can't imagine what's taking him so long! The boats were here when we arrived hours ago."

"Hey, he must not have joined them on the boats, which means he had to travel overland to catch up with us. He's fine. Bast would be the first to know if something were wrong."

"But what happened to her paw earlier? I swear I couldn't find anything wrong with it."

"Maybe it was nothing. Maybe she twisted it. Or maybe Antreas smacked his hand against something and Bast felt it. The two of them are awfully close. But she settled down fast, and I don't believe she would have if he'd been really hurt."

"I know. I just, well, I don't want to lose Antreas," Danita said quietly.

"You won't. He and that feline love you."

Danita's gaze shot to Mari's. "Did he tell you that?"

Mari laughed. "He didn't have to. It's obvious."

"I keep worrying that something happened to him and that I've never told him how I really feel about him—how much I want to be with him and with Bast, forever. I've been so worried about him touching me that I've kept walls up and tried to make it seem like I—like I wasn't falling in love with him." Danita paused and wiped away a tear. "I would hate myself forever if I never saw him again and he didn't know."

"Know what? And why are you crying?" Antreas seemed to materialize out of the darkness, with the yellow-eyed feline at his side.

"Antreas!" Danita ran to him and threw herself into his arms.

The Lynx man was laughing as he lifted Danita off her feet, twirled her around, and kissed her—quickly. Mari noted that it wasn't a demanding, passionate kiss, but a sweet hello, and she was pleased to see Danita didn't cringe back or step out of his arms.

"Bast and I were so worried about you! What took you so long? I was starting to think—" Her words broke off as she caught sight of the bloody bandage covering his thumb. Danita tried to reach for his injured hand, but he pulled it from her grasp.

"Hey, it's nothing. Just a torn thumbnail. It'll grow back," he said. Antreas nodded hello to Mari.

She returned his nod, but also went to him and, with her usual no-nonsense attitude, lifted his hand and began unwrapping the bandage.

"It really is nothing. Sore, but not lethal," he said.

"Sore and not lethal can easily turn into infected and deadly, especially if you ignore it." Mari winced as she unwound the last of the bloody bandage and saw that his thumbnail had been completely ripped off—and that included the talon that rested dormant under his nail. "That looks nasty. How did you do it?"

"Oh, it's not a big deal. And it'll grow back—quickly. It's part of being a Companion to Bast. My, uh, *extra* attributes, like the claws I can unsheathe and my enhanced sight, regenerate fast if something happens to them."

Danita was peeking around Mari's shoulder at Antreas's hand. "That looks terrible!"

He grinned at her. "A scratch like that can't get me down," he said, but sucked in his breath as Mari poked and prodded the wound.

"There's nothing caught in there, and I don't think you've broken anything. Actually, the wound is very clean—almost like someone pulled your claw off." Mari watched him carefully as she noted to herself that he hadn't answered her question about how the injury had happened.

Antreas shrugged. "Guess I'm just lucky that it broke off easily. It'll be fine. I promise."

"It definitely needs to be cleaned and freshly bandaged," Mari said. She paused and then added, "Antreas, did Father John do this to you?"

"No!"

"Then what took you so long to get here?" Danita asked.

"It just took me a while to get out of the village. I'd planned on doing some trading, and by the time the boats were all launched the market had been closed down." Antreas's gaze found Mari. "Father John didn't do this to me, but he was not happy. Apparently, he doesn't like you very much."

"Father John does not impress me with his leadership skills," Mari said.

Antreas barked laughter. "That's a nice way to put it."

"Did he tell you what happened today?" Danita asked.

"His version, which was easy to see through. I gather Dove had a vision that the priest didn't like," Antreas said.

Mari and Danita quickly described what had happened, and Antreas shook his head in disgust. "So he asked for the vision, and then discounted it and insulted you. That's narrow-minded, even for Father John."

"Is there anything we can do? Any way we can warn the Saleesh people farther upstream?" Mari asked.

"There's only one way, but it means that the Saleesh might never allow me or anyone I guide to travel this river again," Antreas said.

"Are you planning on leaving when we get to the Wind Rider Plains?" Danita's pretty face had suddenly gone pale.

"No," Antreas said firmly. "I am no longer a solitary Lynx Companion. You and Mari and Nik and everyone else have accepted me. I'm Pack."

"You sure are," Nik said as he joined them. "Good to see you back where you belong, my friend." Then he winced as he saw the Lynx man's thumb. "Damn! That looks sore."

"It is, but being home is the best medicine for it," Antreas said. At the word "home" his gaze met Danita's, and the girl's smile blazed while Bast's purr rumbled around them.

"So, what's this talk about leaving?" Nik asked.

"Oh, no. I'm not going anywhere. All I meant was that if for any reason we need to return this way—go back to the Earth Walker burrows or the Tribe of the Trees—I more than likely wouldn't be allowed passage."

"Ah, Father John." Nik shook his head. "I'm still having problems trusting Dove, and even I am shocked at how ignorantly he discounted her vision."

"And if Dove's vision *is* true, which I do believe, the Saleesh will be killed. I don't mean to sound callous about it—I'm just repeating her vision. So whether we offend the Saleesh might not matter in the future, because there's a good chance they will no longer control the river." Mari said.

"Yeah, and no one should be traveling along this river for an entire cycle of seasons because something really bad is going to happen here," Danita said.

"But if we are not accepted by the Wind Riders . . ." Antreas began.

"We will be," Mari said. "I feel positive about it, but I'm not going to be a fool like Father John, blinded by my own beliefs. If the Wind Riders reject us we will find somewhere else to make our home, and that can't be back in our forest."

"Yeah, there's no returning," Nik said. "But there's a big world out there, and if the Wind Riders don't see our worth, we'll find another land—another place."

"Without going backwards," Mari added.

"Okay then, here's what we can do. From here it'll take about two weeks to reach Lost Lake. At the entrance to the lake are the worst of the rapids, as the currents of the river shift. There used to be a mighty dam there. The Saleesh call the ruins Day Dam. Something happened there during the time when the sun destroyed the world of the ancients and the earth shook, tearing apart bridges and dams. It changed the route of the Umbria River, flooding a huge section of land and covering many cities of the ancients. At the entrance to the lake is also where the last of the Saleesh villages are located. If we say nothing about Dove's vision all the way to Day Dam, Father John will believe he silenced us," Antreas said.

"But we won't be silenced," Mari said. "We'll speak out loudly and clearly, in front of as many people as we can—men *and* women."

"They'll be warned, and we won't need their access to the river anymore," Nik said. "Good plan."

"Should we prepare for the Saleesh to attack us when we speak?" Mari asked.

"Yes, and we'll have to choose when we speak carefully. We must be sure our boats are all past the rapids, and under our control," Antreas said.

"But we will warn them, and that's important. Even if we risk a fight," Danita said.

"That's how I feel, too, but I'll have to talk with Sora," Mari said.

"You have two weeks to figure it out," Antreas said. That settled, he sniffed the air appreciatively. "Any chance there's some of Sora's stew left? Father John was not in the mood to feed me."

"Yes, I saved you some," Danita said. "But first I'm going to clean that thumb and redress it."

"I find that I like it when you worry about me." Slowly, the Lynx man offered his arm to Danita. "After you clean up my little wound, would you sit with me while I eat?"

"Always," Danita said as she slid her arm through his and they walked away, heads tilted together, with the Lynx padding happily behind them.

"That cat really is a good matchmaker," Nik said.

Mari bumped his shoulder. "You're going to be really sorry if Bast hears you call her a cat."

Nik grinned and put his arm around her. "That's why I waited until she was gone to say it. Hey, I thought that maybe we'd take second watch tonight. Is that okay with you, or are you too tired?"

"No, I'm great! Getting a full night's sleep last night did wonders for me."

"Good—then I have something to show you." He held out his hand, and Mari took it, giving him a curious look.

"Where are we going?"

"Not far. You'll see." With Laru and Rigel beside them, Nik led Mari up a narrow trail that opened to a ledge overlooking the beach. It was just big enough for a pallet and a small fire, which was burning cheerily to one side. Rigel and Laru plopped down at the entrance to the ledge. Curled close together, father and son looked almost identical as they yawned and finally began to relax for the night.

"Ooooh! Nice view from up here. How'd you find it?" Mari took a seat on their travel cloaks, which Nik had already placed over a mattress of pine needles and fern fronds.

"I didn't—Laru and Rigel did." Before Nik stretched out beside her, he uncovered a wooden mug that he'd carefully stowed under a flap of a travel cloak. "Would you like a little spring mead?"

"Yes!" Mari reached eagerly for the mug and took a big drink, sighing happily before she handed it back to Nik. "How'd you talk Spencer into giving you some?"

"I told her the truth—that I was going to use it to ply favors from my Moon Woman."

"Nik! You did not say that. Did you?"

Nik laughed. "No. But I did tell her it was for you." He took a sip and handed the mug back to Mari, moving closer to her and pulling her into his arms. "And I *am* going to try to ply favors from you."

Mari sipped the mead—her eyes smiling at him over the mug. "What kind of favors?"

Nik shifted so that he was behind her, and he began to massage her shoulders. "Only the kind of favors you'd like to give."

"Oh, Nik, that feels *so good*. I don't think my shoulders have ever worked this hard, or been this sore."

"How sore are you? Too sore for this?" Nik kissed the side of her neck, letting his lips linger on her skin.

Mari sighed in contentment. "No, definitely not too sore for that."

"How about this?" Nik kissed the other side of her neck. This time when his lips lingered, they made a trail of heat down her neck and along her shoulder, causing her to shiver with pleasure.

"Not too sore for that either." Mari gulped the last of the mead and put the mug down, turning to face Nik. She wrapped her arms around his neck. "I'm not too sore for *anything* you have in mind, Nikolas."

Mari pulled him down to her and their lips met—searching and finding the same completion that their bodies soon found together as they made love slowly, languorously, learning each other's needs and desires, speaking softly to one another and sharing the language of love while they discovered anew how perfectly they fit.

Davis stood before the sturdy little pine, gazing in wonder at it. Cammy sat beside him, uncharacteristically quiet. The pine was at the far edge of the beach, just at the point where brave little trees began to dot the steep ridge that lifted up to the plateau the Saleesh claimed. Slowly, Davis approached the pine. He unloaded the pile of rocks he'd gathered, carrying them in his tunic like they were wapato roots. Then he sat and began placing the rocks, one atop another, beginning with the largest, until he had a stack of them resting at the foot of the tree. Then, after he was sure that the rock pile was sturdy enough to last—at least until the stormy season came—he placed the final rock atop the stack. It was small and almost as flat as the rest of them, but this rock was perfectly heart shaped.

Then he and Cammy scooted back a few steps and Davis gazed up into what he believed was one of the faces of his Goddess, and prayed.

"Thank you, Great Earth Mother, for being here with us. I know you are here. You drew me to this tree. I feel you, and it fills me with wonder. I make you this offering of this cairn, topped with my heart, so that everyone who passes through here might know that your people love you—cherish you—believe in you. And, please: I know that they do not worship you, but I would like to ask that you watch over the Tribe of the Trees, and if there are still people there who are good—who have not been poisoned by Thaddeus and the God of Death—please help them. Strengthen them. Allow them to survive and, someday, to thrive again as a better people—a kinder people." He touched his fingers to his lips and then pressed them to the foot of the trunk. "Thank you, Great Earth Mother."

A twig snapped behind them and Cammy whirled around, showing his teeth and growling deep in his chest. Davis was slower to react, turning just as a Shepherd trotted up to greet the little Terrier, who instantly changed from growling to huffing a welcome.

"I am so sorry!" Claudia said, hurrying to catch up with Mariah, who was nose to nose with Cammy as their tails wagged happily. "I did not mean to interrupt you. Mariah kept telling me there was something I had to see, and wouldn't settle down for the night until I followed her." Claudia stopped abruptly as she caught sight of the little pine. "Oh! That's beautiful! It looks just like a woman."

"Or a goddess," Davis said softly. "She is beautiful, isn't she? And you didn't interrupt. I've already made my offering and prayed." He smiled shyly at the beautiful young woman. "Cammy obviously likes the company, and so do I. I think something like this needs to be shared to be truly appreciated."

"I've seen shapes in the trees before—who hasn't?" Claudia said as she moved closer to the pine, studying it. "But I've never seen anything like this. And you're right. She's more goddess than woman." Gently, Claudia stroked the bark of the tree with her finger, tracing the perfectly formed face that seemed to look so serenely at them. It seemed the figure's arms were raised, morphing into branches. The trunk curved to show breasts, a slender waist, and generous hips. Even her legs could be seen, and it seemed she was mid-dance, whirling with her arms joyously raised as she gazed out at the world. As Claudia took in the entire vision, she found the small stone cairn. "That's lovely. Did you make it?"

"I did."

"And that heart?"

"It's my offering," Davis said. "I hope the Goddess likes it."

Claudia turned to look into Davis's face. "She does. She must. I would, were I a goddess."

Davis's breath caught. He wished it were easier for him to speak his mind to Claudia, but even back in the Tribe her beauty and her confidence had seemed to freeze his mind—at least whenever they spoke about anything except their canines. His eyes found her young Shepherd and he blurted, "Mariah is looking really good."

Claudia's lovely face seemed to radiate pleasure as she smiled down at her Shepherd, ruffling Mariah's fur affectionately. "Little did I know before, but Mariah is an excellent traveler. She actually enjoys the river."

"You don't?" Davis motioned at a water-bleached log that had washed up close enough to the tree that they could sit on it and still look at the Goddess image. Claudia sat beside him while Cammy and Mariah played tug with a stick.

"No. I'm a homebody." She sighed. "I miss my nest."

"Yeah, I understand that, but I'm really glad you're here with us," Davis said.

"I am, too. I shudder to think about what's happening back at the Tribe—so I don't think about it at all. It's the only way I can stand it."

"I petition the Goddess in prayer for the good people we had to leave behind. I believe she hears me, and even though I have not known her long, I trust that she is too kind to allow those who are not like Thaddeus to suffer without hope."

Claudia turned to him. "I've been meaning to tell you how much I respect that you've embraced this Mother Earth Goddess. It took a lot of courage to open yourself to a new way of worshipping. You really do hear her, don't you?"

Davis's gaze found the tree again. "I do. Her voice is everywhere—in the wind and the river, the grasses and the sky. She is powerful, but kind. I feel as if I've known her my whole life."

"Maybe you have. I'll bet she's known you. I mean, she's a Goddess, right?"

Davis smiled. "Right."

"Which watch do you have tonight?" Claudia asked.

"Second. You?"

"Second. Would you and Cammy like to watch with us?"

Davis blinked in surprise. He felt his cheeks heat, and was glad that the wan light of the moon kept them in silver shadow. "I would." Cammy barked and jumped against his leg, causing Claudia to laugh. "I mean, yes, *Cammy* and I would like that. Very much."

Claudia reached down and scratched Cammy's big blond ears as he wagged and huffed in pleasure. "I've always liked your Terrier, Davis. He has a big personality for a little canine. Did you hear him growl when he thought Mariah and I were sneaking up on you?"

"Yeah, he's a tough little guy," Davis said. Mariah finally got tired of her stick and joined them, unexpectedly resting her head on Davis's thigh. He stroked the Shepherd's thick fur. "Hey, pretty girl."

"She likes you," Claudia said. "And she *really* likes to be scratched right here."

Davis happily complied, scratching the Shepherd while Claudia tickled Cammy's ears.

"I like being around you," Claudia said abruptly. "I thought at first it was because you remind me of home, but if that were true I'd feel like this around Wilkes or Sheena or Rose, or any of the other Tribers with us." She met his gaze. "I've decided you make me feel good because you're kind. Truly kind. I think that's why your Goddess speaks to you, too."

Davis's heart felt all fluttery. "She could be your Goddess, too," he said softly.

"Do you think so?"

"I know so," he said.

She smiled. "Oh, that's right. She talks to you."

"She does, but that's not why I know she would accept you," Davis said.

"Then how do you know?"

"Because you are truly kind, too. And it makes me feel good to be near you as well." Davis held his breath.

Claudia stared at him and then slowly, she leaned forward to softly, but intimately press her lips to his. "I think that's the nicest thing anyone has ever said to me." Then she stood. "Come on, Mariah. Let's go get some sleep so we can be wide awake to keep watch with Davis and Cammy. See you two cuties soon!" Claudia bent to ruffle Cammy's ears once more before she blew a kiss at Davis, and she and her Shepherd disappeared into the darkness that led to camp.

It was only then that Davis allowed himself to breathe. He looked at Cammy. Cammy looked at him.

"Did that really just happen?" he asked his Terrier.

Ruff! Cammy barked, and wagged his tail so enthusiastically that his whole body wiggled.

Davis's gaze returned to the Goddess tree. "If that was you—thank you. Thank you so much."

As he and Cammy made their way back to camp, Davis was sure he heard the Goddess's happy laughter echoing in the wind around him.

First watch ended at midnight, and Danita yawned widely as she stumbled sleepily to the pallet she'd made up with Antreas. Last night she'd slept with him and Bast—with Bast stretched out between them like a warm, soft barricade. Danita liked being close to Antreas, especially during the darkest hours of the night, but the thought of sleeping pressed against his big, strong, decidedly male body made her stomach feel funny. Sometimes that was good, and sometimes it was scary. But worrying about Antreas that day had shifted something within her. Not that she was ready to have sex with him—she was *absolutely* not ready for that— but maybe, just maybe she was ready to try more intimacy.

Danita hadn't stood watch with Antreas that night. She'd been helping Sora and Isabel sort herbs. Then Isabel had found a whole clump of aloe plants close to the temporary campsite, so they'd been busy making up a new batch of healing salve, as well as carefully harvesting a few intact aloe plants, which joined the other medicinal cuttings and seedlings they carried with them.

Antreas and Bast had gone to check the boat line and serve first watch from the waterside. Wilkes and his big Shepherd, Odin, had joined them, and Danita was amazed at how fast time passed when Antreas was suddenly there, smiling at her and going from awake group to awake group, letting everyone know it was time for a change of watch.

Danita hoped it was time for more to change than just the watch.

She was sitting on her pallet with her legs pulled up to her chest, resting her head on her knees, when Bast appeared, chirping and rubbing against her.

"Hey there! I missed you, too. Oh, ugh! You have fish breath." She giggled and pushed the big feline's face away playfully.

"She and Odin decided to go fishing and they shared their catch." Antreas dropped heavily to the pallet beside her. "Wow!" he said around a yawn. "I'm beat."

"How's your thumb?"

Antreas let her take his wounded hand in hers. "You tell me. You're the Healer."

"Not really. I'm just a Healer-in-training. But I did make you some aloe salve and some goldenseal wash. I'd like to clean it again and put on a fresh bandage, if you don't mind."

"If *you* do it I don't mind," Antreas said.

She grinned at him. "Good, because I was going to tell Mari on you if you minded."

"No need to bother either of our Moon Women. I will happily allow you to fix me."

Danita unwrapped the bandage and carefully dunked his thumb in the mug of goldenseal, swishing it around.

"I like that it's stopped bleeding. Are you going to be okay to paddle tomorrow?"

"Of course! It's really not bad—just sore."

"Here, the aloe will help with the pain. Do you want me to brew you some poppy tea to help you sleep?"

"No, I wouldn't waste that tea for something so minor. Plus, I'm exhausted and won't have any problem sleeping."

Danita finished dressing his thumb and then she lifted it to her lips and kissed it, quickly and gently.

His eyes widened with surprise. "What was that for?"

"Extra healing."

Bast chirped and curled up at Danita's feet, purring loudly.

"She says kisses work for healing," Antreas said. "Maybe we should do more of them."

Danita's brows went up. "Bast said we should kiss more?"

"Well, not exactly. But she said it works. I, uh, added the part about doing more kissing."

Danita studied him, and then she slowly leaned into him until she gently pressed her lips against his. When she sat back, her cheeks were burning.

"That is a very nice start," Antreas said. "Makes me wish I'd hurt myself here, here, and here." He pointed to each of his cheeks and then his lips.

"Don't talk like that!" Danita said, only half kidding. "I don't even like to *think* about you or Bast getting hurt."

"Oh, don't worry, Dani. Bast and I are practically indestructible—especially now that we have a family to live for."

"A family?" she asked softly.

He nodded. "This Pack is a family. Bast and I like belonging to it. And, if it's okay with you, we like belonging to you, too. A lot."

"It's okay with me," she said.

And then they said at the same time:

"I wanted to ask you if—"

"I wanted to ask you if—"

They grinned at each other. "You first," Antreas said.

"Okay." Danita cleared her throat, feeling unexpectedly nervous. "I wanted to ask you if I could sleep with you."

Antreas cocked his head to the side. "Isn't that what you did last night?"

"No. I slept *near* you last night. Bast slept between us. Tonight I'd like to sleep beside you—*with* you. But I'm not ready to do more than sleep. I mean, I know you want more, and I do like kissing you. I just can't think about anything more yet without—"

"Hey, ssh. It's okay." He touched her face and brushed back her hair. "I would love *nothing* more tonight than for you to sleep *with* me, *beside* me—as close to me as you'd like. And, here's a little secret." Antreas make a show of looking around, before lowering his voice to a whisper. "I'm too tired to do more than sleep. Even kissing, as much as I like kissing you, would be better another night. Tonight sleep, with you, is perfect."

Danita visibly relaxed. "Your turn," she said. "What did you want to ask me?"

Antreas sat up straighter. He reached into his pocket and took out a long, delicate silver chain. From the center of it hung a smallish, white thing with a pointed end. The top of the object had been beautifully wrapped in silver, so that it glinted, catching the campfire, which was close enough to lend light to their pallet.

"That's really pretty. What is it?"

"I hope it's yours," Antreas said. He met her gaze, and within his eyes Danita saw a new world open before her—one filled with love and understanding and perhaps even restoration and passion. Bast had moved from being curled up at Danita's feet to sitting beside her as Antreas held the necklace out, offering it to Danita. "Dani, I would like to officially court you. Please accept this gift." Bast coughed and Antreas added, "Oh, yeah, this is one of Bast's baby teeth. I've kept it all these years—carried it like a talisman. It's what took me so long in the village today. I had to persuade Father John to let me trade with a jeweler. She made this for you. Bast and I hope you like it and will wear it—for us—for the three of us."

Danita's hand trembled as she took the necklace from Antreas. It was warm from his body. She looked closely at it, marveling at the way the jeweler had wrapped the silver around the top of the tooth.

"This is wonderful! I love it so, so much." Danita threw her arms around Bast, hugging her close. Then she turned to Antreas. "I accept your courting gift."

His face came alive. "Really? That means I'm officially courting you now?"

"Yes. That's exactly what I mean. Oh, Antreas, it is the perfect, *perfect* gift." She lifted it, putting it over her head so that it hung between her breasts. She touched it gently. "Thank you, Antreas."

"You're welcome," he said. Then he fist-pumped the air. "We did it, Bast! She likes it! And she likes us!"

"Ssssh, silly!" Danita giggled and shifted so that she could snuggle beside him as she studied her necklace. "This is an amazingly big baby tooth. Bast, you have some very sharp teeth."

"You think *that's* big? Show her, Bast," Antreas said.

The Lynx complied, baring her teeth in a mock snarl, and Danita pretended fear as she clutched her heart and fell back against Antreas, which had Bast padding to her and rubbing against her while purring manically. Then the feline settled next to Danita, so that she was securely sandwiched between Lynx and Lynx Companion.

Danita sighed happily and put her head on Antreas's shoulder. "Hey, how did you talk Father John into letting you trade? He was really mad when he basically kicked us out of the village."

Antreas shrugged. "It was no big thing."

Danita turned so that she could look up into his face. "But how did you do it?"

Antreas's gaze slid away from hers, making her sit up and stare at him. "Antreas?"

"I traded the jeweler some more of those jay feathers. You know, like the ones Bast gathered for you. The Saleesh *love* anything blue. Hard to believe I got all that silver for a few blue feathers, huh?"

"Antreas. Why are you avoiding my question? How did you persuade Father John to let you trade with the jeweler? You didn't hurt him, did you?"

Antreas looked shocked. "Of course not!"

"Well then?"

Antreas sighed. "I just gave him something I knew he wanted. A lot. And he led me to the jeweler. Not hospitably, mind you."

"Antreas! Stop avoiding my question."

"Okay. Sorry. I gave him my claw."

Danita felt sick. "Great Goddess! You cut off your finger for this!" She started to pull the necklace over her head, but Antreas's hand stopped her.

"Please don't. Please keep it. Dani, I didn't cut off my finger. I just cut off a claw—more like the tip of my finger."

"That's horrible!"

"No, it's not. I did it willingly."

"Antreas, do not ever do something like that again. I will *not* have you hurting yourself for me. Ever. Promise?"

"I promise," he said. "Will you wear it? For Bast and me?"

"Yes, but only because you promised." She let the necklace settle around her neck again.

Then he lay down and opened his arms to her. Danita lay beside him, within the embrace of his arms, her head resting on his muscular chest and the warm, soft length of Bast pressed against her back. That night, for the first time since Danita had been raped and nearly beaten to death, she slept soundly, without one nightmare.

The morning dawned clear and cool, with a brisk breeze that would, thankfully, be at their backs. Mari splashed water on her face, shivering and gasping with the cold, and then brushed her teeth with a willow stick. Beside her, Nik did the same. They were at the edge of the river, where they'd moved after they'd reluctantly left the privacy of their hidden ledge, though the intimacy they'd shared the night before clung to them.

Nik dried his face with his shirt and sniffed the air. "Is that eggs? Gull eggs?"

"Oh, Goddess, I hope so! Antreas said egg season is short, but I hope that doesn't mean it's over yet. Let's go see."

As she turned to hurry back to the campfire, Nik snagged her wrist, pulling her against him. "Last night was perfect," he said after he'd kissed her thoroughly.

"Yes, it was." Mari leaned into him, thinking how much she loved being close to him.

Laru ran past them, carrying a huge stick, with Rigel on his heels, barking like a crazy creature as they threw sand on their Companions.

When Mari opened her mouth to tell them to behave, Nik pressed his finger to her lips, and then kissed her again quickly.

"Let them play. They need to burn off energy. They'll be lying on those ballasts all day. It must get old for them."

"I hadn't thought about that," Mari said as she and Nik made their way to the campfire, hand in hand. "But you're right. The canines do need to keep up with their exercise. Do you think they might do some swimming beside the boats?"

"That's a good idea. After we greet the sun, I'll talk to Antreas about it. In spots where the current is placid and there are no ruins, I think it would be a great way for them to exercise."

Nik and Mari joined the Pack where they were circled around the campfire. Sora was poking some wapato roots that were cooking in the glowing coals, and Mari was thrilled to see a large pile of gull eggs sitting beside the cauldron.

"Oh, good! There you two are," Sora said. "I didn't want to start the eggs until after we greeted the sun. They're best steaming hot."

"Just talking about it is making my mouth water!" Jenna said, clapping happily around one of Fala's pups that she'd snuggled in her arms.

"Is everyone here?" Nik asked, looking around to be sure all the Companions were present.

"I don't see Davis or Cammy," Mari said. "Oh, wait, here they come."

"Yeah, with Claudia and Mariah," Sora added, winking surreptitiously at Mari.

Surprised by Sora's wink, Mari watched closely as Davis and Claudia approached from up the beach. They walked so closely that their hands and arms brushed against one another. They were talking, their heads tilted together. Mari's eyes widened as Claudia laughed flirtatiously and touched Davis with easy intimacy. Behind them, Cammy and Mariah walked side by side, as close together as their Companions. Mari thought Cammy's tail might possibly wag off his body, and Mariah's mouth was open in a very pleased-looking canine grin.

"When did that happen?" Mari whispered to Sora.

"Recently," Sora whispered back.

"What happened? When?" Nik said.

"Nothing!" Mari and Sora answered together.

"We're all here now," Wilkes said as Davis and Claudia joined the rest of the Pack.

"Then let us greet this beautiful morning!" Nik led the ritual, and Mari loved hearing the joy in his voice as he welcomed the sun into his body, his Companion's body, and the body of the Pack.

Then, as the Pack turned eagerly to the campfire and Sora moved to prepare the gull eggs, Davis and Claudia approached Mari and Nik.

Davis cleared his throat. Mari thought he looked nervous, but there was also a very real sense of excitement surrounding him.

"Sun Priest and Moon Women—and Pack." Davis raised his voice, drawing everyone's attention. "Claudia and I have something we must tell you—tell all of you."

"Okay, go ahead. We're listening," Mari said, smiling encouragement at the nervous young man.

"Last night Mariah and Cameron mated."

The sentence dropped like a stone in a still pond, sending ripples of gasps throughout the Pack, especially throughout the members of the Pack who used to call themselves the Tribe of the Trees.

Laru immediately padded over to Mariah. The two canines greeted each other, and then the big Alpha male sniffed the smaller, younger female Shepherd before returning to Nik's side.

It was evidence of Laru's surprise that Mari caught the image he transmitted to Nik.

"Puppies!" Mari blurted, causing the Pack to erupt in sound.

Nik raised his hand, and the people went silent. He stared at Davis and Mariah, and it seemed to Mari that he was struggling to find the right words.

Claudia spoke into the silence. "Well, it happened more than once, so, yes, I would expect puppies."

She shared a very intimate look with Davis, whose cheeks flushed pink, but who also looked inordinately pleased with himself—so pleased that Mari realized Claudia wasn't just talking about Cammy and Mariah!

"Wait, say that again," Wilkes said, stepping up beside Nik.

Davis met the older man's gaze and spoke slowly and distinctly. "So there is no misunderstanding I will repeat myself. Mariah, the Shepherd, and Cameron, the Terrier, mated last night. Several times. I believe Laru's sense of smell, as well as the lack of reaction from Rigel and Odin, tells us Mariah is pregnant." Davis shifted his attention from Wilkes to Nik. "Claudia and I did not mean to overstep. The truth is we were surprised."

"Yes, I can usually tell when Mariah is coming into estrus, but I completely missed the signs. It could be because I've been so sick, or because we're traveling, but I do apologize, Nik. I would've come to you had I known."

"But she didn't. Well, she didn't until it was obvious, and then it was too late," Davis added. "I am sorry, too, Nik."

"Why are you sorry?" Sora asked. "Puppies are a good thing. We were just talking about that yesterday—about how wonderful it would be if everyone in our Pack was a Companion to a canine and no one would have to worry about Moon Fever again."

"Yeah, why aren't we congratulating them?" Mari asked Nik as several other Earth Walkers murmured agreement.

Nik looked uncomfortable, but he nodded and drew a deep breath. "Okay, Pack, I'll explain. In the Tribe all canine breedings are approved by the Alpha and his Companion."

"That sounds awfully controlling," Jenna said.

Mari remained silent, waiting for Nik's answer, though her first thought was to agree with Jenna.

"It is controlling, but think about what would happen if every female canine who came into estrus mated with whomever she desired, whenever she desired. Canine litters usually range from about five to ten puppies. Canines would overpopulate. And then there's inbreeding to worry about. You see how healthy and strong all of our canines are?" Nik gestured to Laru, Rigel, and several other canines while the Pack nodded. "They aren't that way accidentally. The Tribe had an excellent breeding program. My father spent long hours in discussion with the Elder Council deciding which male should breed with which female to bring out the best traits from both."

"That does make sense," Mari said. "But we have a lot fewer canines here, and we would like a lot more—so breeding is a good thing."

"It is," Nik said. He ran his fingers through his hair, looking increasingly uncomfortable.

"I'll help Nik," Davis said. "He's having such a problem knowing what to say because never in the history of our Tribe have a Shepherd and a Terrier been allowed to breed. There have never been mixed puppies in the Tribe. Ever."

Mari's gaze swept her Pack. Those who used to be Tribe of the Trees looked as uncomfortable as Nik—well, except for Davis and Claudia.

They looked stoic and kept sharing glances that were easily read. They knew they were in trouble, but didn't appear sorry. The Earth Walkers were watching the proceedings with open curiosity.

Mari decided right then that she'd had enough.

She moved to Nik's side and in a voice that carried throughout the beach said, "Isn't it about time they did mix? How is that any different than us? *Than me?*" She looked up at Nik. "Than our children?" She made a gesture that took in the whole Pack. "We're a mixture of Tribe and Clan and Chain, and even Skin Stealer. We're making this journey so that we don't have to be bound by the archaic, narrow-minded rules of the past. Don't you agree, Nik?"

Nik stared at her, and Mari saw the struggle in his eyes—she understood it, too. It was difficult to let go of the beliefs and taboos, but necessary. So, so necessary. And she knew if Nik could not accept this surprise, if he could not move past it and open himself completely to a new way of life, she could not continue to open herself to him. It would break her heart, but Mari would not love a man who wasn't able to leave behind toxic beliefs that had damaged all of them—and would continue to do so if they allowed it.

Nik's expression suddenly cleared. He put his arms around Mari and hugged her tightly. "Thank you for being a voice of reason," he spoke softly into her ear. Then he strode to Davis and Claudia. "I agree with Mari. May the Sun bless this mating and the incredible puppies that will come from it!" As the Pack cheered, Nik embraced Davis and then Claudia, who was wiping her eyes and crying happy tears.

Mari went to little Cammyman, who was sitting quietly beside Mariah. She knelt before the two canines. "Let me be the first to congratulate you two. Puppies are a blessing." She laughed as Cammy licked her face and Mariah swept the sandy beach with her thick tail. Then Mari stood and repeated with a shout, "Puppies are a blessing!"

But Davis wasn't done with surprises for the day. He held up his hand, calling for silence.

"Thank you, Sun Priest. And thank you, Moon Women, for blessing our unusual, but happy news. I have one more thing to say, and

I'd like to follow Clan tradition with this, because I believe it is a good thing." While the Pack watched, Davis went to Claudia. Cammy rushed to his side, acting much more serious than was his norm. Davis went to his knees and Cammy mimicked him, lying down. He reached into his pocket and pulled out a crystal shaped like a heart, which he held out to Claudia. It sparkled, catching the morning sun beautifully. "I keep finding rocks and crystals shaped like hearts, and I keep leaving them as offerings to the Goddess, but this morning I realized the Goddess was gifting them to me for a reason. Claudia, you are that reason. Before the Pack I would like to ask that you accept my proposal to formally court you. It is tradition that this be completely your choice. It is also tradition that you be given a gift. This one is from the Goddess and Cammy and me. I hope you accept us, because no person on this earth has ever made me feel as alive as you do, and I want that feeling for the rest of our lives."

The Pack was so still that Mari decided they must have all been holding their breath.

"Oh, Davis, of course I accept you—you adorably sweet, sexy man! Ooooh! And I also accept this gorgeous crystal." While the Pack laughed and clapped, and Cammy and Mariah barked joyously, Davis took Claudia in his arms and kissed her in front of everyone.

"So, how long before Mariah has puppies?" Mari whispered to Nik.

"*That's* your only question? Oh, no no no. I have way more questions than that," Sora said, keeping her voice low as she tried not to laugh. "Like *how* did little Cammy mate with Mariah? Did he use a stump? A ditch? And what are those puppies going to look like?"

"I'll answer the easy question first: Mariah will give birth in about two months. As to Sora's questions, well, the only one I can answer for sure is the last." Nik grinned at the other Moon Woman. "The puppies are going to look like love, Sora, pure love, and I couldn't be happier about it."

🐎🐎🐎

After the Pack broke their fast they launched the boats and resumed paddling upriver with a brilliant sense of hope. The news that Mariah would be having puppies before they reached the Plains of the Wind Riders was such a good omen that everyone shared in the excitement that carried them upriver, even as the days began to blend together into an endlessness that had them all so accustomed to the rhythm of the river that the nights they were able to make camp, and not just tie up anchored together on the water, their legs felt strange—as if they'd forgotten how to be land creatures.

Their bodies hardened along with their resolve to make a new life for themselves. As one, the Pack believed they would make it to the Plains, and they would build that new, harmonious future there—together. Passing the checkpoints controlled by the Saleesh only cemented their resolve, especially as they watched children play happily and innocently. No one—not one person in the Pack—wanted to imagine what would happen to all of those beautiful, innocent lives if their mothers never learned of Dove's vision and never had the opportunity to choose for themselves if they would remain, as Father John insisted, or flee.

As the sun set the evening before they would reach Day Dam, the Pack turned somber, knowing that the next day would test them, perhaps to the breaking point. But they could not remain silent. They had to warn the Saleesh, even should that warning prove fatal to some of them . . .

CHAPTER 16

My Lord! I present to you Dax and his Lynx, Mihos." Thaddeus bowed to the God and then stepped aside so that the Lynx Companion got his first full view of Death.

To his credit, the Lynx man's only sign of shock was that the color drained from his face. His Lynx stayed close to his side, yellow eyes fixed on the God. Dax bowed deeply, following Iron Fist's example.

"My Lord, I come in answer to your signal beacon."

"Ten days! It has been ten days since the signal fire was lit calling for a guide from your people." Death faced the Lynx Companion, who had been led to the platform in the tree that the God rarely left.

"I apologize for the delay, but spring is a busy time, my Lord," Dax said after he took several steps back, looking startled and out of sorts. The fur on his Lynx's back lifted, though the big male feline remained eerily silent. "Mihos and I came to you as soon as we completed our previous job."

Ralina felt sorry for Dax, whom she knew because he was one of the older mercenaries who had been hired by the Tribe several times over the past decade. She'd been called to the God's platform to witness this next chapter in Death's obscene conquest of the Tribe, and she sat in her usual shadowy corner of the platform, with Bear lying behind her while she attempted to shield him from Death's too curious gaze. But this evening Death only had eyes for Dax—and was more interested in His plan to flee the poisoned forest for the untainted lands of the Wind Riders than He was about obsessing over male Shepherds.

Death's attitude shifted instantly, as His mercurial temperament was wont to do. Ralina's stomach clenched. She knew His smile always foretold something terrible.

"Ah, I have been too passionate. Dax and Mihos, you are welcome here, among my People. Please, sit." Death gestured to the floor of the platform in front of Him, and after only a slight hesitation, Dax sat, Mihos at his side.

Death was, of course, the only person on the platform allowed a chair. He'd had an enormous, water-whitened log dragged up to the platform for Him. Its bleached white roots reminded Ralina of the skeleton of a throne. On it the young women who were Death's Attendants kept a pallet of pelts so that He could recline in comfort while everyone else either stood or was forced to sit at His feet.

Just looking at Him sickened Ralina.

"I do understand how frustrating it is to wait for a guide," Dax said.

It seemed to Ralina that the Lynx man was doing his best to recover quickly from what must have been a terrible shock at being brought into what he had to have thought was a normal job for Sol and the prosperous Tribe of the Trees. Finding the city decimated, the Tribe either poisoned and dying or healthy and mutated, and Skin Stealers with their God of Death in charge, was surely a blow, and Ralina wondered how much Thaddeus had told him on his way to meet Death. And then Ralina really *looked* at Thaddeus, and she realized what was happening. The Hunter was wearing a cloak that covered much of his body, with a hood pulled up to shield his face.

Thaddeus is hiding his visible changes, and the only other people on the platform, or even close by, are Death's young female Attendants—none of them have taken The Cure. A man claiming to be a God should look like a strange, hybrid creature, but they're purposefully hiding the mutations happening here from Dax until he's given his word and accepted the job. Ralina felt a new wave of nausea. *I wish I could've warned him, but there were too many Skin Stealers on the lookout for the Lynx man. To-night . . . I will get to him later tonight . . .*

Dax gazed around him, taking in the vastly altered state of the Tribe of the Trees. "Is Sol no longer even Sun Priest?" he asked.

No one so much as moved.

Death's sharp gaze caught Dax. "The Tribe of the Trees is no more. I rule here. And now that the People have a living God, there is no need for any priest."

Dax's gaze slid to Thaddeus, who stood beside Death, staring out at nothing.

"Then there is also no Elder Council I need to meet with in order to formalize any agreement you and I come to?" Dax asked.

"I am a God! I am not ruled by a council!" Death roared.

Dax flinched back and his Lynx pressed against his side, his back beginning to arch.

"I did not mean to offend. I only wished to hurry the process of my hiring. You have waited long enough for me to get here. I don't want you to wait any longer."

"Indeed! Indeed!" Death sat down, nodding. "I understand your reasoning. Fear not—I am the only authority here. Dax, would you like some of the Tribe's beer? Or, perhaps, something stronger? And if you hunger I can have my women bring you some delectable stew."

Ralina had to bite a bloody hole in the side of her cheek to keep herself from shouting, *Don't eat anything he offers you!* But the Lynx man was far from stupid. He bowed his head cordially and replied.

"Spring beer would be refreshing. Thank you, my Lord. Mihos and I ate our evening meal just before we entered your territory. It is Lynx tradition not to arrive hungry when summoned for a job."

"Excellent tradition," Death said, motioning for one of the Attendants to bring Dax beer. "It is always wise to arrive without need; then you can focus on what others need from you."

Dax nodded. "And what is it you need from me?"

"Right to the point. I already like that about you, Dax." Death paused as an Attendant gave Dax a wooden mug of beer. "I require that you guide my People and me to the Plains of the Wind Riders."

Dax choked on his beer. He swallowed quickly, and wiped his mouth. "Surely you aren't planning on taking that journey this year."

"I most surely am," Death said.

Dax shook his head. "You would be cutting it too close. There will already be snow in the mountains by the time you reach them, and once it begins snowing it does not stop. It may be the shining end of summer on the Plains, but in the Rock Mountains it will be the beginning of winter—and the closing of the passes."

"Then we will leave immediately and travel quickly."

"Immediately?"

"I commanded the People to begin preparations to travel the day the signal fire was lit. Thaddeus, how much longer before we will be ready to leave this forest?"

"No more than five days, my Lord."

"There you have it, Dax. Five days. Then we will begin our journey."

"But, my Lord, you run a very real risk of getting trapped in the mountains. If anything happens on the river leg of the journey—if you are delayed at all, something that is easy to happen, especially as we cross Lost Lake—you will not make it through the mountains."

"I am not overly concerned about delays. They are for those weaker than the People and me. You will be surprised at the strength of my People. We leave in five days, and because of the lateness of the season, I will agree to pay you five times your normal fee."

Ralina's heart sank as she saw Dax lean forward, steepling his hands while he considered.

"How many people will be traveling?" Dax asked.

"Two hundred," Death said. "There will be canines with us as well."

Ralina's breath stopped. *Two hundred! That is less than half of the number of Tribe members still alive, but it was almost exactly the number of Reapers in His disgusting army. He's leaving the Tribe to die, along with many of His own People. He is despicable.* Ralina swallowed down bile as she continued to listen silently.

"And you have boats to carry that many, and supplies that will last the entire journey?"

"As you and I have just met I will not take offense at your questioning of me." Death's look darkened dangerously.

Dax swallowed hard, obviously uncomfortable. "I do not mean to offend you. It is just that the journey could take up to three, even four or five months. The first leg is the easiest, and there is nothing easy about paddling up the Umbria River, and then over Lost Lake. After that you either ditch the boats, or adapt them to litters to use in the second leg as we make our way through the Rock Mountains. It is an arduous, difficult trip."

"I understand that, and we will be ready to depart in five days," Death said.

"Well, then, I will guide you if you do pay me five times more than my usual fee, plus a bonus of a brace of my choice of pelts when we reach the Wind Riders—whether they accept you or not," Dax said.

"Accept me or not? Whatever do you mean?"

"Wind Riders rarely accept outsiders. They only allow them to remain on their Plains if the settlers can prove that they have skills the Wind Riders need. Even then the acceptance is sometimes more whim or feeling than need. The horse people are proud and strong and independent—and they are sole rulers of a huge area of land."

Death threw back His massive head and laughed. As if they had no will of their own, Thaddeus, Iron Fist, and the Attendants all echoed the God. Death wiped his eyes and, smiling his terrible smile, said, "Oh, Dax, let me worry about being *accepted* by the Wind Riders. I agree to your terms. We leave in five days. Please, be my guest until then."

"Thank you," Dax said. "I can help Thaddeus be sure that your People are bringing the proper supplies."

"That would be helpful," Death said absently, as if He had no real concern for whether or not they brought the proper supplies with them. Then His expression became much more animated. "Dax, I know little about the peoples we will encounter on the journey, but I assume there are many settlements along the river."

"Not as many as you might imagine. The lands bordering the Umbria and Lost Lake are not welcoming to settlers, except for a river people called the Saleesh. Part of what I will discuss with Thaddeus is the fact that we will need to pay the Saleesh a form of tribute as we pass each village."

"And why do these river people deserve tribute?" Death asked, sounding more curious than angry.

"Well, they control the most difficult parts of the Umbria. Without their permission to pass, and their help getting your boats through the ruins around which they build their villages, you would have no chance of making it to the Rock Mountains in time to cross. It would add months onto your journey."

"Are the Saleesh such great warriors?" Death said.

"Truthfully, I don't know how adept they are at fighting. I do know that they are expert river men. I've traveled far, and never met any people who have greater knowledge of waterways, except perhaps the Whale Singers, though they understand the seas, and not so much rivers."

"Ah, I understand. And are there many rivers on the Plains of the Wind Riders?"

Dax looked surprised at the question, but he answered it smoothly. "That depends on which part of their territory you're asking about. There are rivers that begin in the mountains and spill down to the Plains. The eastern boundary of Wind Rider territory is an enormous river called the Missi, and there are a few others as well."

Death nodded his enormous head and scratched his chin contemplatively. "So, the Saleesh would be excellent additions to my People."

"Well, yes, they probably would be, but I have never known of any Saleesh to leave the banks of the Umbria. They marry into other Saleesh villages, but it is usually the women who move. The men almost always remain in the village in which they were born for their entire lives."

"You might be surprised at how persuasive I can be." Death waved away Dax's response. "And what types of peoples will we encounter in the Rock Mountains?"

"Not many," Dax said. "There are some odd, reclusive mountain people, though they are only seen when they want to be. And, of course, there are several Lynx Chains that call those mountains home, but as the snow begins to fall they only leave their dens to hunt and trade."

"Fascinating . . ." Death said.

Ralina's nausea rose again. She understood exactly why Death was asking those questions. She spent so much time shadowing Him that the God tended to forget she was present and spoke freely around her—especially to His disgusting Blade, Iron Fist and Thaddeus. She hadn't thought her loathing of Him could be any greater, but the past ten days had proved her wrong. The God of Death was a merciless, despicable, manipulative tyrant bent on destroying everything and everyone who did not bend to His will. Ralina had to force herself to breathe slowly and deeply, and to remain silent. *I can do nothing to stop Him if I'm dead,* she reminded herself.

The sound of Dax's voice broke into Ralina's dark thoughts.

"My Lord, if I have your permission, I would like to retire for the night. Mihos and I traveled far and fast to reach you today."

"Of course! Iron Fist, show our guest to the nest we prepared for him, and be sure that he has plenty of food and water," Death said.

Dax wasted no time. He quickly followed the Skin Stealer from the platform, still throwing the God of Death glances of shock mixed with curiosity.

Ralina waited until the God and Thaddeus had their heads together, speaking in low, animated voices. Then, moving quickly, she remained hugged to the shadows, making her way silently to the stairway.

His voice stopped her just before she reached the exit.

"Storyteller, I did not give you permission to leave."

Ralina turned to face Death as Bear stepped silently behind her. "My Lord, I did not wish to interrupt you and Thaddeus, but I wanted to collect my thoughts and order my words. Today marks an important chapter in your story."

"It does, indeed," Death said. "And you are right to give today's events special attention. I do grant you leave to go."

"Thank you, my Lord." She bowed to him.

"Have you moved into that nest I assigned to you?" Death asked her before she could escape down the stairs.

"I was planning to do that tonight," she lied. She'd had no intention of leaving her sick and dying people to rot away in the repulsive holding pen area Death had designated for all who were ill or injured and refused to take The Cure. But this night the move that Death had ordered fit perfectly with her plan—desperate and unlikely to succeed as it was.

"Good. Be sure you do. That is where I will call for you on the morrow, when you will observe the next chapter of my magnificent tale. And, Storyteller, you are looking too thin. I am concerned for you. Do I need to send you special cuts of meats so that I can be sure you are eating enough?"

Ralina's mouth flooded with saliva, and she had to swallow several times to keep from vomiting. *Of course I'm thin. I have to forage for roots and berries and vegetables. Thank the Sun God canines don't seem to be able to be infected by eating tainted meat, or Bear would've starved by now.* Finally, she was able to smile and say, "Oh, no, thank you. I tend to lose weight while I am creating a new tale. It's part of my process. The more important the tale, the more I focus on its creation. If I eat too much it makes my brain sluggish. I'm sure you understand that, my Lord."

Before Death could respond Thaddeus spoke. "Strange that I don't remember you getting thin when you wrote our stories."

"Strange that I don't remember you paying much attention to me at all before now, Thaddeus. We were not friends. We were not intimate. How would you know anything about my creative process?"

"Well, I—"

Ralina cut him off. "And I have never been entrusted with a tale of this importance. Of course it is going to require special concentration." She looked from Thaddeus to meet Death's dark gaze. "My Lord, would you rather that I fatten up or I that I create your tale authentically?"

"Thaddeus, do not question her again," Death said. "I give you the freedom to do what you need to do, Storyteller."

"Yes, my Lord." Ralina fled down the stairs, silently urging Bear to hurry before He changed His mind—again—and made her stay with Him longer, or listened to Thaddeus more than He listened to her.

She and Bear jogged to the holding pen. The Skin Stealer standing guard near the area where Ralina had built a rickety shelter and pallet barely glanced her way as she ducked under the rope barrier no other Tribesman or woman was allowed to cross. She hastily gathered her few meager items—a wooden mug, clothes she'd managed to salvage, a bowl for Bear, and a few precious piles of paper that Death had commanded be brought to her the instant He'd understood she recorded her tales on them. She rolled the items carefully in her pallet, and then left the holding pen area. Again, the guard paid no notice. Death had made it clear that she could come and go as she wished, and not one person in the camp would dare to cross Death.

Well, not one person except Ralina, Storyteller of the Tribe of the Trees.

She knew where she was going, but had ready the excuse of *It was dark and I got lost trying to find my new nest.* No Skin Stealer would question her. Most of them were too animalist and didn't seem to think about much of anything except fighting, eating, and fornicating, but the Warriors and Hunters who followed Thaddeus—who had ripped living flesh from their canines and merged it with their own—were a different story. They were mean *and* cunning. Ralina avoided them as much as possible.

Thankfully, the excitement of the Lynx guide's arrival had brought on a celebration that drew Skin Stealers and Thaddeus's followers to the God's tree, where they were drinking and dancing themselves into an orgy-like frenzy. It was simple for Ralina to slip from shadow to shadow in the darkness until she reached the tree the God had commanded be prepared for the Lynx man several days earlier.

Ralina had to steady herself before she hailed Dax from below. The nest they'd prepared for him used to belong to Cyril, Lead Elder of the Tribe, and though the tree had been damaged in the fire, and the nest blackened, it was still recognizable enough that homesickness washed over her, threatening to drown her in sadness.

"Hey, aren't you the Tribe's Storyteller?"

Dax's voice startled her and Ralina whirled around, Bear hugging the side of her leg and growling low in his deep chest.

Dax backed a step, his hands held up, palms out. His big Lynx was beside him, almost invisible except for his yellow eyes. "Sorry. I didn't mean to startle you. Mihos needed to go out before we bedded down for the night."

Ralina recovered quickly. "My fault. I was lost in the past for a moment, but I'm back now. Yes, I am Ralina, Storyteller for the Tribe of the Trees—though that is now an extinct position."

"Things have definitely changed." Dax glanced around as if to see if anyone else was near.

"I need to speak with you. Privately," Ralina said.

"Well, then, come on up." Dax motioned to the lift that was on the far side of the tree, and they entered it, working a pulley mechanism that took them up fifty feet and into the arms of the huge old pine.

Cyril's nest had been completely gutted—which made Ralina relieved and sad at the same time. The only thing left in it was a bucket for Dax's overnight wastes, a pallet, and a small brazier.

Ralina wasted no time. "Have you eaten anything since you arrived in the forest?"

Dax was lighting the brazier, and he looked over his shoulder at her in surprise. "No, not yet. What I said to your leader is the truth. Mihos and I ate before we crossed into Tribe of the Trees territory. Why?"

"First, the God of Death is *not* my leader. He's my jailor. Next, do *not* eat the meat of *any* animal in this forest. Too many of them have been tainted."

"Tainted? You're going to have to explain. And is that guy really a god?"

"Yes. I have seen enough to believe that He is truly the God of Death. He is horrible beyond imagining. He defeated our people by poisoning the animals of the forest. The Tribe ate the tainted meat and was infected with the disease of the Skin Stealers."

Dax grimaced in disgust. "That horrible skin-sloughing disease? Great Stormshaker! Is that the stench I smell? I thought the Tribe was tanning hides—that's why I asked for pelts as my bonus."

"What you smell is the stench of disease and death. It's why the God is insisting we leave the forest. It's poisoned—probably forever."

"People need to be warned about this," Dax said.

"People need to be warned about a lot more than just the disease. Listen to me carefully—you *must not* guide Death and his people anywhere."

Dax sighed. "I tend to agree with you, but I've accepted the job. If I renege on the deal my Chain will punish me, and it will be almost impossible for Mihos and me to get any other job."

"What would your Chain say about you guiding an invading army up the Umbria? An army that can procreate and swell in size on the way as they poison everything they touch—and that means you as well. One bowl of stew and you will be infected and be faced with the same choice my people had—take The Cure and mutate into something unthinkable, or die. And as you will be our guide, I promise you Death won't give you a choice."

Dax looked pale. "We are forbidden to get involved in wars. My people would never agree to guide an invading army anywhere."

Ralina felt some of the tension in her body begin to relax. "Thank you. You can't imagine how glad I am to hear that."

"Hold on. I need to know more." He studied her carefully. "You don't look ill. Did you take The Cure?"

Ralina shook her head. "No! And I will never. It's vile. I'm only healthy because I refuse to eat meat."

"Why is The Cure so horrible?"

"When a person is infected, part of the symptoms are pustules that form at the creases in our bodies, like at our elbows, wrists, and knees."

Dax nodded. "Yes, I know that. Years ago I had a run-in with Skin Stealers while I was guiding a small party up the Willum River. I've seen what you're talking about up close, and it isn't pretty. But what about The Cure?"

"To cure the disease Death flays strips of flesh from the body of a living animal and packs that flesh inside the pustules."

Dax grimaced in disgust. "And that actually works?"

"Depends on what you called 'cured.' It stops the progression of the disease. It also changes the person, drastically—and from all I've seen, not for the better."

"Is that why the God looks like he's the human version of a stag?"

"Yes. The God brags often about how the mighty king of the forest, a huge stag, sacrificed himself for Him. Didn't you wonder why you saw only one Skin Stealer with the God, and why the others were kept at a distance?"

"Thaddeus explained that on the way into camp. He said that he and Death were in charge, and that the Skin Stealers were basically servants. So, it made sense that I didn't see many Skin Stealers—except those serving the God."

"Lies. Everything that comes out of Thaddeus's mouth is either a lie or a manipulation. The Skin Stealers are called Reapers, and they make up the bulk of Death's army. If you saw a group of them up close, you would never have entered camp—or at least you wouldn't have entered it of your free will. They're all taking on animalistic characteristics."

Dax shuddered. "Skin Stealers have always disgusted me. I was shocked when Thaddeus said their God was now leader of the Tribe of the Trees."

"The Tribe is no more. And it isn't just the Skin Stealers who have mutated. Thaddeus kept his cloak on and his face partially hooded. Had he not you would have seen an oddness about him that is the perversion of a Terrier mixed with a man."

"Are you telling me Thaddeus took strips of flesh from his Companion and packed his own flesh with them?"

"I am. He did it, and many Hunters followed him, as well as far too many Warriors."

Looking like he was either going to be sick or pass out, Dax slid down the side of the nest to sit hard on the woven floor. "Great Stormshaker!

It is almost unbelievable." His gaze caught Ralina's. "I didn't see Thaddeus's Terrier. Did the flaying kill him?"

"I'm not sure what killed him. None of us witnessed his death. I wouldn't be surprised if the God had a hand in it. It was Thaddeus who surrendered our people to the Skin Stealers—Thaddeus who caused Sol's death, as well as the forest fire that made the Tribe vulnerable to invasion."

"Sol was a wise leader." Dax shook his head. "This is bad. Very bad." He wiped a trembling hand across his face, and his Lynx pressed into his side, staying always within touch as he tried to comfort his Companion. "He has created an army of monsters."

"And Death will make more!"

"That's what He was talking about when He said I'd be surprised at how persuasive He could be. He isn't going to persuade anyone. He's going to *infect* them!"

"Yes. I don't know how or why, but it all started with Him. People have to be warned. Get to the river people, and the mountain people, and even the Wind Riders. Warn everyone. And tell all of the Lynx guides to hide in their dens or flee—but be sure the God doesn't capture any of your people."

"My people would die before anyone—even a Death God—could force them to torture their Lynxes to save themselves."

"You might be surprised. The Skin Stealer disease affects people differently, but all of them behave in a manner unlike themselves."

"Noted. Don't worry. I'll go straight to my Chain and call an emergency meeting. I will tell them everything. We will take to the North Shore Mountains and to the deep, hidden dens only our Chains know of. Death won't be able to find one Lynx team to guide His abominations."

"I don't think it'll keep Him from going to the Wind Riders, but without a guide He might be delayed long enough for you to spread the warning—and for me to figure out a way to get rid of Him," Ralina said.

"Kill Death? That doesn't even sound possible. Stormshaker! What are we going to do? He could poison the entire world!" Panic colored Dax's voice, causing Mihos to chirp in concern and press even closer to his Companion.

"Okay, no, listen. Panic won't help. Death can't die, but I've heard Him say over and over again that He is going to awaken the Goddess of Life like He was awakened, so that She can reign at His side. He slept once—for eons—and He can be put back to sleep." Ralina paused, then added, meaningfully, "He made me His Storyteller."

"You think you can get him to reveal how to make him sleep again," Dax said.

"It's part of His story, which means He'll eventually reveal it to me."

"Ralina, you must not remain here. Think of your Companion if not yourself. Come away with me now—this very moment. Our Chains revere Storytellers. You would be welcomed and respected."

Ralina rested her hand on Bear's broad, intelligent head. The big Shepherd gazed up at her, sending her waves of strength. He knew what they must do—even if it cost them their lives.

"Thank you, Dax. I will always remember your kindness, and I would be honored to be Storyteller for a Chain, but I cannot leave. You were right to be afraid. Death could poison this world. I have begun to believe He did it once before, when the ancients and their way of life died. It might be fated to happen again—the destruction of our world and our peoples—but if there is even a slight chance that He can be stopped, I have to try. I have to stay. And you must leave. Now."

Dax nodded somberly and picked up his travel pack, strapping it to his back. Silently, the four of them lowered to the ground in the lift.

"Head there—through the part of our city that the fire completely destroyed. Everyone avoids it. Stay within the tree line until you get past the Channel lookout platform. My guess is Death will command Thaddeus to have his Hunters track you. They're fast, Dax. They have the heightened senses of Terriers. You have to move, and move fast."

Dax flexed his hand open, and the ghostly light of the moon illuminated the Lynx man's claws. "They are not the only ones with heightened abilities—only I did not get them through disease and torture. No Terrier could catch Mihos; no Hunter will catch me."

"May the Sun bless and keep you safe, Dax and Mihos," Ralina said formally.

"And may our Great Stormshaker lend you strength. You will need it, Ralina." Dax retracted his claws, and then gently, kindly, took her hands in his. "I am no Storyteller, but I give you my oath that I will tell your story—over and over. Your bravery will be known everywhere. I hope we will meet again." Dax bent and kissed her softly on her forehead. Then he and his Lynx turned and disappeared into the fire-blackened forest.

Slowly, Ralina and Bear made their way to the nest Death had insisted she take as her own. Once inside, the Storyteller dropped to her pallet, put her arms around her Companion, and sobbed brokenly into his thick fur, crying out her fear and loneliness and despair until exhaustion claimed canine and Companion and they finally slept.

CHAPTER 17

The sun hadn't climbed far in the sky when the roar of the water sounded throughout the forest. Mari and Nik stood side by side, their Companions beside them and the Pack spreading out along the bank of the tumultuous river.

"I know Antreas described this to us, but I didn't expect it to be so big," Mari said.

"Or so loud," Nik said.

"It makes me feel strange—afraid and drawn to it at the same time," said Sora.

"It's like a monster in one of the old myths Mama used to tell me about," Mari said. "Its name was Charybdis. It was a great, sucking whirlpool creature that devoured entire ships."

"Seems pretty accurate," said O'Bryan.

They'd arrived at the Day Dam ruin not long after sunrise, docked their little boats with the Saleesh, and then followed the path that ran along the bank overlooking the incredible ruin.

The river was almost unrecognizable here. Until they'd reached the area surrounding the Day Dam ruins the Umbria had been a wide waterway flanked on either side by tall banks filled with verdant forests. As they got closer and closer to the dam the land had changed—become arid, with the only sections of green being big squares of crops the

Saleesh grew and irrigated by harnessing the mighty wind that blew down the gorge to pump river water over the otherwise dry land. And as they drew nearer to the last river ruins they would traverse, the Umbria became deeper and wider, lifting to meet the banks, which were green with corn and grapes, cotton, hemp, and other valuable crops. Now that they were overlooking the confluence of the Umbria and the entrance to Lost Lake the water level had risen to within just a few yards of the path that ran along the bank, and the sound of the churning river was deafening.

"Come! Come!" Father Job, the dour priest who'd met them at the final crossing, waved his arms, motioning at the Pack to follow him along the riverbank.

"Why do they always look like angry birds?" Sora asked Mari.

"Just a guess, but it could have something to do with the fact that they subjugate an entire gender of their people. You'd have to be angry to do that," Mari said.

"Good answer," Nik said. "Accurate, too. Think about Thaddeus."

"I'd rather not," Mari said, only half teasingly.

Nik grinned. "I'm just using him as an example. He wanted to subjugate everyone, and he's probably the angriest person I've ever known."

"That's an excellent point," Sora said. She glanced around them, but the only Saleesh in view was Father Job, who was marching swiftly at the front of the Pack. "Do you think we're ready for this?"

Antreas had jogged up with them. He'd already decided at this last crossing he would remain with the Pack instead of watching the boats. He'd explained there was really no need. The Saleesh never allowed any river travelers to watch them traverse the whirlpool, and they would shoo him away quickly.

He ruffled the top of Bast's furry head and took Danita's hand before responding to Sora.

"Do you mean are we ready for Lost Lake, or for what's going to happen when we get to the Saleesh village?"

"Both!" Mari and Sora said together.

"I can't speak for the Lost Lake part, but we're definitely ready for the village," Nik said. "We've run through it the past several nights. Don't worry. The Pack will do well."

"And I'd say we're as ready as we're going to be to cross Lost Lake," Antreas said. "We've carved as many extra arrows as possible and stockpiled supplies."

"Don't forget our slingshots. They can be deadly," Mari said.

"In your hands a slingshot is deadly. In mine it's pathetic," Sora said.

"Hey, don't worry. I've got your back," O'Bryan told her. "Well, yours *and* Chloe's." He scratched the puppy under her chin and she wiggled in the sling Sora carried her in. "She's getting so big. She'll be walking beside you soon."

Sora kissed her pup on top of her curly head. "I'm not sure whether I'm excited about that or sad that she's becoming such a big girl." Then she shifted her attention to Antreas. "I'll admit that I'm nervous about this lake crossing. Just thinking about being on water for fifty days has my stomach feeling queasy."

"Like I said, there are a few islands we'll be able to camp on," Antreas said.

"If it doesn't rain too much," Danita added.

"Yes, well, there is that," Antreas said. "But when we finally make land we will be at the foot of the Rock Mountains, and our days of water travel will be over."

"Thank the Sun," Nik muttered.

"Don't forget that the current will be with us all the way across the lake," Antreas said. "It shifts here." He nodded out at the seething water.

"It's so strange." Nik stared out at the island-sized whirlpool. "I wonder how it happened?"

"The story I've heard told is that one of the great earthquakes that toppled cities ripped apart the dam that was here, and when it did it tore the earth with a sound like a million people screaming. Water spouted from the earth, creating the whirlpools and altering the course of the river. The water that came from the earth spewed eastward, covering entire cities and drowning everyone in its path."

"Which means more ghosts, I'm sure," Sora said.

"Spirits have never bothered me during a crossing," Antreas said. "I can tell you, I'd rather deal with ghosts than the Mouths and Monkeys that are all too real and haunt any area of the lake that has exposed ruins or is close to one of the green islands."

Danita shivered. "'Mouths and Monkeys.' Those names are disgusting."

"They fit the creatures well. The Mouths are mostly just that—fish with gigantic mouths."

"And they can really swallow a child whole?" Mari asked.

"Or a canine—or Lynx." Antreas shot Bast a glance. She hissed, clearly showing her dislike of the Mouths. "I didn't exaggerate."

"The Monkeys work with them, but they're land animals?" Nik said.

"They were land animals that somehow survived when the cities were flooded. Now they're more amphibious, though you can tell that they're mammals. They give birth to live young and they nurse them, even though they've developed webbed feet and toes and gills in their necks. Their swimming skills put the big, clumsy Mouths to shame. And they're smart. Really smart. They have to be to have formed a partnership with the Mouths."

"You almost sound like you like them," Danita said.

"Oh, I can't stand them. They're dangerous nuisances. But I do have a healthy respect for their abilities. They serve as bait for the Mouths' prey. They float low in the water, with only their faces above the surface. They can imitate almost anything. I've heard them sound like a crying child, several types of distressed birds, and once even a Lynx."

Bast hissed again.

"But the point to their cries isn't to draw the Mouths, right?" Mari asked, trying to remember all the information Antreas had been sharing with them for almost the past two weeks in preparation for crossing Lost Lake.

"No, they don't need to call the Mouths. The Monkeys are only found in the waters around city ruins that are above water because that's where the Mouths hunt. They mimic creatures in distress to draw others to them. When they're successful they're very successful. For instance, the

Monkeys begin calling like they're seagulls blown off course and floundering with weakness. Other gulls come to investigate and the Mouths rise to the surface, using their long, tentacle-like whiskers like rope. They have incredible control over them. I've seen Mouths shoot their tentacles out of the water and into the air, wrap around a gull, and pull it under so quickly the other gulls didn't even realize what happened."

"And the Monkeys feed on the scraps," Nik said.

"Exactly. They also steal things. Whenever we have to cross over a city with ruins partially above water, everyone will have to be on alert. The Mouths are completely carnivorous, but the Monkeys eat anything. They will be trying to steal our plants and supplies."

"And our puppies," Sora said grimly, wrapping her arms around Chloe and holding her so tightly the pup whimpered.

"Yes. The Monkeys would definitely steal a pup, and the Mouths could eat a canine—even a Shepherd—whole."

"And we're completely sure crossing Lost Lake is a good idea?" Nik asked.

"We can cross the lake in fifty days—even less if the weather cooperates. If we went around the lake it would take us at least twice that. There's no way we'd make the mountain crossing before winter closes the passes," said Antreas.

"We don't have any choice," Mari said. "Even if we wanted to wait the winter out in a temporary camp at the foot of the mountains, Dove's vision says something bad is coming to the Saleesh, and they are entirely too close to Lost Lake."

"I know. I'm with you. I just had to ask," Nik said.

"Again," Antreas said with a half smile.

"Yeah, well, I don't like water."

"Really, my friend? I don't think you've mentioned that before," Antreas said sarcastically, breaking the tension talking of Mouths and Monkeys had caused as everyone around Nik chuckled.

It took most of the morning for the Pack to walk past the sucking maelstrom that hundreds of years before had been a functioning dam, and they arrived at the last Saleesh village when the sun was almost directly overhead. This village hadn't been built on top of a high bank, as were the other Saleesh settlements. Instead it spread out around the entry to Lost Lake and was almost as large as Father John's village. It, too, was tidy and prosperous—filled with women laying out trade goods and children playing among their Teteplate nannies.

The statues to the Mother were particularly beautiful. The main public altar was in the center of the village market. Candles were lit all around her feet, and her body was swathed in a beautiful blue wrap that had been covered with shells. Incense wafted from braziers dangling from the porches of well-cared-for houses.

The Pack's cluster of boats was already there, docked in the calm beach at the mouth of Lost Lake just beyond the center marketplace.

"After you place your offering at the feet of the Mother you may make trade with our women, but do not dally. I am quite certain you will want to be well on your way before sunset," announced Father Job as the Pack paused in the center of the market.

Mari had noticed that since Dove's exchange with Father John, the village priests had been decidedly short with the Pack, though each of them had opened their market to the travelers. Antreas had explained that the Saleesh had a swift messenger system. They used the river, often at night, to glide up and down from village to village, passing information and trade goods—and Father John had definitely warned his people to make short work of helping the Pack.

While the Pack made a show of looking at the market goods, Mari and Sora went to the central statue of the Mother. Sora placed a newly woven basket at the idol's feet. She'd gathered long grass found beside one of their early river stops. It had a beautiful blue tint and Adira, one of the most talented weavers in the Pack, had woven into the lovely green basket a blue image that looked remarkably like the idols the Saleesh cherished.

"That is spectacular," Father Job exclaimed. "A most worthy offering." He even nodded his head in a small bow. "I do wish our women had this skill."

"Well, in all fairness, many of us are from a Clan called Weaver," Sora said, not unkindly. "We have been weaving baskets for countless generations."

"Perhaps I will speak with your men about the possibility of one of your women remaining with us. She would have a comfortable home and be well cared for—and her arduous journey would be at an end."

"Men do not lead our Pack," Mari said. "Sora and I do."

The priest's eyes narrowed slightly. "Ah, I had forgotten your strange way of doing things."

"And to answer your question—no. None of our women would like to remain here. Our women prefer to rule themselves." Sora raised her voice so that the Saleesh women in the marketplace turned their heads to listen. "Though we would be happy to offer any of your women a place with us—and with us they would also have a voice."

The priest drew himself up to his full height and glared down at Mari and Sora. "Our women have a voice."

"Really? Let's test that, shall we?" Mari said. From across the marketplace she met Nik's gaze and nodded. She watched for just a moment as he spoke to Sheena and Wilkes—and they began passing word through the Pack, who immediately stopped their pretense of shopping and headed for their beached boats.

"What do you mean, young woman?" Father Job asked.

"Come on. We'll show you on our way out of your village," Sora said, grinning like she was having a wonderful time.

Scowling, the priest followed them as Mari and Sora walked quickly through the marketplace until they reached their gathered Pack. Then they turned to face Father Job and the curious Saleesh women, who must have been wondering why their trading had been interrupted.

Lily led Dove up to stand beside Mari. Nik moved to her other side. Sora stood beside him, with O'Bryan next to her. Wilkes, Claudia, Sheena, Jaxom, Mason, Rose, and the rest of the Pack spread out in a crescent-shaped group, canines beside them and their backs to the boats, facing the village.

"This is Dove," Mari said, lifting her voice so that it carried across the market. "She has no eyes, but the Goddess gives her visions. She has seen the destruction of the Saleesh people." Mari ignored the priest, who was already blustering for her to be silent and calling for his "Brothers" to come to him.

Mari focused on the Saleesh women, who were staring at her with eyes wide with shock. "But you are not doomed. Dove's vision showed that if you leave your village for one complete passing of the seasons you may return and continue to live in safety. We tried to warn you back at the first Saleesh village, but Father John refused to listen—or to share what Dove saw with the women of the village. If any of you would like to join us, we would welcome you, and if you would like to ask about—"

"We do not listen to the hysterical words of women or children!" Father Job's face was florid and spittle flecked his lips as he shouted over Mari. Then his gaze found Wilkes and Adira—the two oldest members of the Pack. He focused on Wilkes. "You there, are you going to allow children and women to lead you?"

The corners of Wilkes's lips turned up. He crossed his arms and studied Father Job as if he'd never seen a priest before. Then his answer echoed in the listening silence.

"I respect Mari and Sora. They are far better leaders than those we left behind at the Tribe of the Trees—who were all men. Who better to be led by than young people? They are our future. If you can't see that, then perhaps it's time you became extinct."

As the priest sputtered Mari met Nik's gaze and nodded. As they'd already decided, Nik stepped forward and addressed the priest, speaking clearly so that the listening women were sure to hear.

"If you will not listen to Mari, then maybe you'll listen to the words of a man—a fellow priest. I am Nikolas, Son of Sol, Sun Priest for the Pack. Dove's vision is true, and the reason I believe her isn't hysteria. It's logic. Dove knows she has a safe home with us. We didn't invite her to join us because she is a Seer. We had no idea about her abilities when we accepted her. We invited a refugee to join us. Dove doesn't *need* to lie to be respected and treated like an equal among us."

"That only means she's secure to say or do anything without repercussions," Father Job scoffed.

"I am not secure to say or do anything." Dove stepped up beside Nik, her hand reaching out and finding his arm, which he offered to her. She continued in a voice that filled the marketplace. "The one condition the Pack had for me at my joining was that I give my oath that I will never lie. If I break that oath I lose my place among these good people I have come to care so very much about. I can assure you that I would not say anything that put my home with the Pack in jeopardy."

"A woman's words are as changeable as the wind." The priest waved Dove away.

"Then consider this," Nik said. "What does Dove—what do any of us—have to gain by telling you to leave your villages? It has caused us all sorts of problems with your people. Right now we know that you will probably not help any of us pass this way again should we desire to return to our forest. It would have been easier for Dove not to speak—and it would definitely have been better for our Pack if we'd silenced her." Nik stared down at Dove's open, honest face with sudden realization. "There is *no reason* not to trust Dove except for ignorance, arrogance, or prejudice. I trust her." Nik looked up, meeting the gaze of the women who had not fled the marketplace. "Mari and Sora, our spectacular Moon Women leaders, offered you sanctuary with us. That offer stands. We will accept any of you who wish to leave and live."

"Our women are going nowhere! Brothers! To me!" Father Job bellowed.

Young men wearing long, belted robes and carrying barbed lances rushed through the marketplace to line up beside the priest, effectively blocking any woman who wanted to leave. With one gesture from Father Job, they raised their spears at the Pack.

As one, the Pack drew their weapons. Some of them held loaded crossbows. Some hefted slingshots and began twirling them, so that the air was suddenly filled with the humming of angry bees.

And then the canines and Bast stepped forward—each one of them growling deep and baring their teeth menacingly.

The line of Brothers faltered—their faces paling at the might of the Pack.

"Women! Call out if you wish to join us!" Mari shouted.

"We will grant you sanctuary!" Sora cried.

Mari tried to make eye contact with the Saleesh women, as well as their Teteplate servants, though the majority of them had fled the marketplace with the children as soon as Mari began speaking. It broke her heart, but what she saw in the women's eyes ranged from irritation and disbelief to a kind of nothingness—like they were unable to think for themselves.

Then one Saleesh woman stood and with a surety echoed by the woman closest to her, and then the rest of the women in the marketplace, she turned her back on Mari and the Pack—utterly rejecting them.

Disgusted, Mari shook her head and faced Father Job. "It seems your women have too long allowed others to think for them. But should that change"—Mari lifted her voice again and kept peering through the line of Brothers at the women, who had all begun to leave the marketplace, their backs turned to the Pack—"should you wish more out of life than being treated like cosseted children, follow us. We will grant you sanctuary and you will know a life of—"

"Leave this place! I never want to see any of your faces again!" Father Job roared.

"Oh, you will not." Dove's sweet voice cut through the marketplace. She was perfectly serene as she spoke the priest's death sentence. "Father Job, very soon you will see no living faces ever again—and all who follow you will suffer the same fate."

"She threatens me!" the priest sputtered.

"No, I do not threaten. I prophesy. I would pity you were you not leading so many into darkness."

"Blind bitch!" Father Job curled his lips and spat at Dove.

"That's it. Let's go," Mari said, and the Pack immediately started back to their boats.

"I wonder what happened to those women. Why are they like that?" Jenna asked as she helped push her boat off the beach.

Adira spoke up. "They chose security over freedom. I was wrong before to have thought that was a good trade."

The women of the Pack nodded grimly in agreement.

After almost two weeks of practice, the launching process was quick and efficient, and soon they were skimming over the placid lake, leaving the angry, doomed Saleesh in the distance.

PRESENT DAY—TRIBE OF THE TREES

Ralina hadn't thought she'd be able to sleep at all that night, but moving from the soggy, open ground and a makeshift fern-roofed shelter to a nest—even a nest that smelled of smoke and sadness—lulled her into the first full night of sleep she'd had in weeks. She was shocked when she woke slowly, well after dawn, snuggled with Bear, warm and safe high in the trees. For several sleepy breaths Ralina was transported back to a time before disease and Death destroyed her beloved Tribe, and she woke filled with warmth and contentment.

Then her stomach growled, waking her memory, and she sat with a sigh, rubbing her eyes as Bear stirred and then stretched before nuzzling her good morning.

Ralina hugged him, hating how many of his ribs she could feel through his thick coat. The God and his Reapers had destroyed all of the rabbit warrens, slaughtering the breeding stock for soup pots. Recently, Ralina and Bear had made the decision together that he would not eat poisoned meat. At first it had seemed as if canines were immune to the horrible skin-sloughing disease, but after a week of eating tainted game, Shepherds and Terriers were falling ill—except those whose flesh their Companions had already flayed for The Cure.

Ralina would never, ever do that.

Instead, she had been surviving by eating only berries and a stew she made from mushrooms and greens, with some wapato roots added when she managed to find time to dig for them. Ralina had also hidden a fishing line and hooks near the Channel, and as often as possible she snuck to the water and caught a few fish, which she gave to Bear.

"You know what? Let's leave this nest and go to the Channel right now. The God will be preoccupied as soon as He discovers Dax is gone—and

I don't think He'll want me to document the fact that a Lynx guide was so horrified by what has happened here that he broke oath and snuck away in the night."

Bear's bushy tail was wagging with eagerness as they made their way to the lift which would take them to the forest floor, when Hunters suddenly rushed past, heading toward the God's tree.

"They know he's gone," she whispered to Bear as the lift touched down. She and her Companion were just stepping to the forest floor when Iron Fist rushed up.

"Storyteller! My Lord commands your presence!" he snapped at her before he rushed away.

She looked at Bear and sighed. "Maybe you should stay here. I'll get away as soon as I can and we'll forage for something to eat."

The big Shepherd's response was immediate. He pushed against her mind with a definitive *No* and pressed himself to her side.

Ralina patted his broad head. "I know. I hate being separated from you, too. Okay, come with me. He's going to have to let us eat sometime."

Walking swiftly, it took them little time to get to the God's tree. The atmosphere was like a lightning storm. Attendants milled around—some cooking rancid-smelling meat, and others wringing their hands as if they were unsure of everything. Reapers circled the tree, looking feral as they paced. There were no Hunters or Warriors present. As had become Ralina's new normal, she ignored Attendants and Reapers—and they parted to allow her access to the entrance to the God's platform.

As soon as she was in His presence Ralina bowed low, and Bear took his place in the shadows behind her.

"My Lord, you sent for me?" She looked up at Death, expecting to see in Him a reflection of the chaos below, but He was sitting on his driftwood throne, gnawing on what looked like a hunk of deer meat that one of His favorite Attendants, Rabbit, held for Him, looking completely serene.

"Ah, Storyteller, there you are. Have you heard the news?" Death asked as He motioned for Ralina to sit.

"No, my Lord. I just woke. The first person I spoke with was your Blade, and he commanded I attend you."

"It seems our Lynx guide absconded in the night."

Ralina's Storyteller training made it easy for her to appear surprised—after all, a great storyteller must also be a great actress.

"Oh, my Lord! That news is unexpected and hard to understand. It seemed the guide accepted your job." She knew she shouldn't antagonize Him, but Ralina couldn't resist one little jab. "I have never heard of a Lynx team reneging once acceptance has been made."

The God's eyes narrowed, but He shrugged nonchalantly. "I sensed last night when I met him that he was inauthentic. Today I seem to be proved right. Again."

"You are very wise, my Lord." Ralina had learned over the past weeks that Death demanded flattery—though He pretended not to. She considered it a ridiculous charade—one more fit for a child than a leader, and especially not a God. But Death's petulance and the small cruelties He liked to mete out like crumbs before birds were always lessened if He was well plied with meaningless compliments.

"And you are very perceptive, which is why I wished you close by me—so that you could observe and record the events of this magnificent day."

"You don't seem overly concerned by Dax's absence," she said.

And then realized her mistake as soon as the God's dark eyes skewered her. "You use his name. How well do you know him, *Ralina*?" He drew out her name, as if it were a secret that had been whispered only to Him.

"Not well at all." Ralina kept her voice calm, as if she and the God were talking of nothing more important than the color of the sky or whether it might rain the next day. "He was hired by the Tribe several times. I'm not sure how many. Thaddeus would probably know. As a Hunter he probably would have consulted with any Lynx guide being tasked by the Tribe. Hunters often accompanied guides on short journeys to be sure they weren't slowed down by carrying too many supplies." She sat up straighter, as if she'd just had a thought. "Have you asked Thaddeus where he believes the Lynx man might have gotten to? I'm sure he's worked with Dax in the past."

"Thaddeus is leading our Hunters on his trail. I would not be surprised if he returned any moment with the Lynx man."

"I will be sure to note Thaddeus's hunting prowess in this chapter of your tale, my Lord." Then Ralina waited for the reaction she knew her words would evoke—which came in the space of a single breath.

"If you mention Thaddeus it should be that he followed my command to return the forsworn Lynx man to face his punishment," Death scoffed. "Thaddeus is not terribly good at thinking for himself, and without his canine he is no longer much of a Hunter."

Death's dismissal of Thaddeus had Ralina feeling a rush of hope. Getting rid of Thaddeus wouldn't restore the Tribe of the Trees, but it would rid them of a constant and malicious voice who was as cruel as Death, and even more petty.

"It will be as you say, my Lord." Ralina bowed her head.

"Did you not say you came to me directly from your nest?" Death asked.

Not sure where He was taking the conversation, Ralina was instantly on guard. "Yes, my Lord. I seem to have overslept, and would like to thank you for the nest you provided for me."

He waved away her thanks. "While we wait for Thaddeus and the Hunters to return, join me in breaking your fast." He pushed away the bloody hunk of fetid meat the Attendant had been feeding Him, and wiped His greasy mouth on the back of His hand. "Little Rabbit, scamper over to Ralina and give her and her magnificent canine some of these choice cuts."

Ralina's stomach revolted as Rabbit stood. "No, thank you, my Lord," she said quickly. "Bear and I will eat after I finish recording this day's tale."

"It was not a request, Storyteller. It was a command."

Ralina put her hand up, palm out, halting Rabbit—who looked frightened and confused. She'd known this day was going to come. Ralina had thought long about what she would say—how she would convince Death to listen to her. She didn't know if what she'd decided on would work—but she did know she had one shot at it.

If she failed, Ralina had already decided that she would kill herself and her beloved Bear, rather than cut living flesh from her Companion and turn herself into a monster.

"My Lord, I must ask a great favor of you."

That got the God's attention—as she knew it would. Death loved to appear magnanimous, often granting favors to those loyal to Him. Of course, He took away those same favors, and much more, the instant He perceived a lack of loyalty.

"Speak, Storyteller. I will consider granting the favor you beseech of me." He steepled His fingers and leaned forward, His foul breath smelling of rot.

"I ask that you allow me to be free of the sloughing disease until I have finished your tale."

"And why would I allow that? You will be stronger, better, after joining your flesh with your Shepherd's."

"That is true, my Lord. But it is also true that sometimes confusion—even delirium—fill the person who has been infected. I have noted that those symptoms can last even after The Cure has been initiated. I must have a clear head if I am to record your glorious tale. Though I am looking forward to the added strength I will have after joining with Bear," she lied, "your story is simply too important to risk not being able to tell it well."

Ralina held her breath and waited.

After a pause that felt endless, Death said, "I can see the logic in what you say. Were you not my only Storyteller I might test your theory—for joining with your Shepherd could also enhance your abilities. And perhaps you *need* your abilities enhanced. I have not heard any of my tale. All I have heard from you are stories not my own."

Ralina's empty stomach threatened to revolt and she was afraid for a moment that she would spew bile all over the God's platform. She swallowed quickly, willing herself to be calm.

"My Lord, I have told you that I do not like to speak any part of a tale that is incomplete. Often I must revise and change it—especially the beginning—to better reflect the end. I know you wouldn't want—"

"I am a God! You know *nothing* of what I want except for what I tell you—and I tell you that I want to hear the beginning of my tale—*now.* Or, if you'd rather, you may break your fast with me." His cruel blue eyes glittered maliciously as he stared at her.

From below there were several shouts, and then the Hunters and Warriors who had accepted the change burst into view below.

The God said nothing. He sat staring at Ralina while the men rushed up to His platform. Only when Thaddeus stood before Him, breathing hard and bowing deeply, did Death take his eyes from Ralina.

"I do not see the Lynx or the man with you," Death said.

"My Lord, we could not track him." Thaddeus spoke in angry bursts. "The bastard and his cat used the trees as their pathway—not touching the ground, leaping from pine to pine. They reached the Channel. We picked up his trail there, but he stole a canoe and headed into the river. It is impossible to track him on water."

Death nodded. "It is as I suspected."

"I should have posted a guard outside his nest. I shouldn't have counted on him keeping his word—those cat men have no honor, no allegiance but to their own," Thaddeus said.

Ralina pressed her lips together to keep from shouting at Thaddeus, *You just described yourself, you disgusting traitor!*

Death seemed unconcerned. "Yes, you should have, but I forgive your lack of care—this one time. Now, I have just asked the Storyteller to recite the very beginning of my tale. I am glad you and the other Tribesmen are here. I would like you to hear it as well."

"You want a *story* at a time like this? We should be heading to the northern Cascade Mountains and flushing those Sun-be-damned Lynxes from their cowardly dens!" Thaddeus blurted.

Death was on his feet, with such preternatural quickness that Ralina's sight blurred. The God backhanded Thaddeus, knocking the little man off his feet and against the balustrade, where He stood over him, teeth bared like an animal's.

"You do not speak to me thus!" Death roared, causing everyone on the platform, and on the forest floor surrounding it, to cringe back in fear.

"I am a GOD, you fool! I only played with the idea of a Lynx guide so that I could see what would happen after I infected him and gave him The Cure. I need no guide but my divinity!" Death stomped one cloven hoof so close to Thaddeus's head that it caught in the Hunter's hair. In a lower, but no less frightening voice, the God demanded. "Now beg for my forgiveness."

Thaddeus tried to get to his knees, but Death kept his hair trapped so that he had no choice but to grovel before Him.

"I beg your forgiveness, my Lord," Thaddeus said.

"Louder—so those below us can hear."

"I beg your forgiveness, my Lord!" Thaddeus shouted, his every word filled with raw anger.

Death smiled and moved his massive hoof, freeing Thaddeus. Then He offered the man His hand. Slowly, Thaddeus took it, and the God pulled him to his feet.

"I accept your apology—this one time." Death's voice filled the forest. "Cross me again and I will end you." Still smiling, the God returned to His throne. "Now, have a seat and let us listen to the Storyteller. Then you should get to work. We leave in four days for the Plains of the Wind Riders." Death's dark gaze found Ralina. "Now, Storyteller. Speak!"

Ralina stood. She had to hold on to the balustrade to keep from falling, and her head was dizzy with hunger and fear, but she drew a deep breath, then strode, tall and proud, to take center stage in front of the God.

Ralina was not afraid. She trusted her abilities, and she had planned for this moment. She knew what Death wanted—flattery and twisted truth. It sickened her, but Ralina was going to give Him what He wanted. She wished she had her beautiful rabbit cloak, and her shift, which had been lovingly decorated by the women of the Tribe with a rainbow of beads and mirrors and shells. But those things, as well as her Tribe, had been destroyed by fire and disease. So, Ralina used the only thing she had left—her voice. She threw back her hair and began, her voice falling into a melodic rhythm that was almost hypnotic.

"My Lord, I title your tale 'Death Awakened.' And it begins ..."

He came like a spring storm; vanquishing all
Mighty—divine—with power beyond words
The forest answered His immortal call.
Magnificent Death was all that they heard.

The City in the Trees stood 'gainst His will
They battled His People for one day long
But His strength won; enemies He did kill
Reapers, Attendants—sang His victory song.

Death is a stag—magnificent and pure
His mantle like the night; endless and dark
Death is a God—our Leader strong and sure
Antlers are His crown; cloven hooves His mark.

A new era begins with our Death God
World! Watch, listen, wait—prepare to be awed!"

Ralina bowed so low to Him that her hair pooled on the platform around her feet. She stood there, bent and unmoving—waiting—her heart beating like ocean waves crashing against the beach.

His clapping was deafening, and immediately echoed by everyone on the platform, as well as those surrounding the tree.

Ralina knew that He stood over her, but she remained submissively bowed until He did as she'd envisioned so many times. Death gently lifted her. His smile was terrible and filled with dark joy.

"You are, indeed, remarkable," Death said. "Now, go. Break your fast at your leisure. You are right. I will not chance ruining my tale for the novelty of seeing what you and your Shepherd might become together." Then He planted a burning kiss on her forehead.

Branded by Death, Ralina and Bear left the God's tree. She did not vomit bile onto the forest floor until they were well out of His presence.

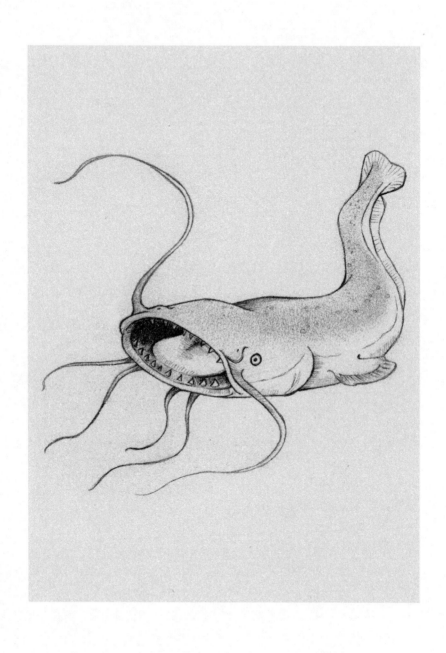

CHAPTER 18

Though they were supposed to leave the forest and cast off on the Channel at dawn of the fifth day, it wasn't until mid-morning that the ragtag collection of patched boats and hastily built rafts were loaded and ready to enter the water.

Ralina had watched Death's Reapers and Attendants loading the boats with meat they'd hastily smoked over the past five days—every bit of it tainted—as she and Bear dug through the mud along the Channel bank, uncovering wapato roots and filling basket after basket. She even crossed the rusted bridge to Farm Island, where she dug through the weed-choked fields and harvested early artichokes, baby carrots, potatoes, and beets. After she filled as many baskets as she could, Ralina began foraging for mushrooms.

She had unexpected help from Renard, a young Warrior she'd hardly known before the forest fire. He'd just passed his twenty-first winter, which meant he was almost a decade younger than the Storyteller. So, it wasn't unusual that Ralina hadn't been acquainted with him before the tragedy. Men that age tended to worship the beautiful, charismatic Storyteller from afar, but up close could rarely put a complete sentence together—let alone say anything that Ralina might find interesting.

But Renard had behaved differently than the others that fateful night Mari had healed much of the Tribe and then fled with Nik and Fortina, who was at that time Maeve's pup. He was one of the few Warriors who had listened to Ralina when she encouraged the Tribe not to eat any tainted meat. Renard and his sole surviving family member, his father, Daniel, immediately cut meat out of their diet, though they did it quietly, as Death's Reapers liked to report back to their God about Tribe members who didn't sicken. If they were Warriors, it was likely that their meatless stews were "accidentally" tainted, so that they were forced to either accept The Cure or be sickened, rounded up, and herded into the pen—the place where the Tribe went to die.

Renard did neither. He, his father, and Renard's big black Shepherd, Kong, kept an extremely low profile. They made themselves useful helping the Reapers scavenge supplies from the rubble that the forest fire left, and basically just stayed out of the way of Thaddeus and the men who had taken The Cure and followed him.

Renard and his little family had become so good at avoiding conflict and blending in with the Reapers that it hadn't been until the day after Death announced that they were going to leave the forest and head to the Plains of the Wind Riders—without a Lynx guide—that Ralina had realized the young Warrior was free of the skin-sloughing sickness. She had literally run into him as she and Bear were heading to the Channel to begin collecting as many roots and vegetables as possible to take on the journey. Renard and his Kong had been ambling along in the shadows, heading into the blackened ruins of the Tribe of the Trees to continue to forage useful items from the nests. Ralina had been on her hands and knees, digging for morel mushrooms in the pine needles of the forest floor, when Renard had tripped over her.

One look at him had told Ralina that he was dirty, tired, and too thin, but completely uninfected—and from there they had formed an alliance. She did know his father, an adequate carver who specialized in making arrows for crossbows. After she and Renard talked, Ralina formed a plan.

From that day until the mid-morning launch, Renard had helped her collect roots, vegetables, mushrooms, and berries, which they packed away in any kind of travel basket or container they could scavenge. She told his father to carve arrows—a lot of arrows—and then the two of them were to follow her lead, as she was determined to help them.

And that is exactly what they did on launch day.

"Storyteller! Where are you?" Death bellowed.

Ralina had been standing to the side of the crowd of Reapers and Thaddeus and his followers as the boats and rafts had been loaded. She had already chosen her boat—a small craft that she'd found half submerged just off the Farm Island bank when she'd been harvesting crops. Renard and his father had helped her repair it, added two ballasts—one for Bear and one for Kong—and then the two men had silently paddled it across the Channel the night before the planned launch. That morning the three of them had packed it full with their food, the few bits of clothing and pelts that had survived the fire, and Daniel's carving tools and arrows.

When Death called Ralina's name, she turned to Renard and Daniel. "Okay, remember, just follow my lead, but try not to say too much. Death's moods are unpredictable. He changes His mind constantly, but He needs me. All I must do is be sure He knows I need the two of you."

Renard reached out as if he wanted to touch her shoulder, but he stopped short—still shy and unsure around her. "Don't put yourself in danger," Renard said. "Father and I can stay here."

"Indeed, Ralina," Daniel said. "We will go north after everyone launches. We can join another Tribe. All will be well."

Ralina remembered the odd, pungent scent of rendered fat that had suddenly permeated the air around the circumference of the Tribe of the Trees, as well as the mounds of dry pine boughs that Death had ordered His Reapers to pile along the Channel edge of the Tribal territory. Death wouldn't speak of what He was doing, which was alarming. The God liked to tell Ralina every tiny thing He was thinking and doing because He'd said He wanted her tale to be true.

So, what was He hiding? Whatever it was couldn't be good for those being left behind. Ralina's intuition was telling her to get Renard and Daniel out of the forest—and she was determined to listen to her intuition.

"Storyteller!" Death shouted again.

"Follow me. Quickly." Ralina hurried to the center of the beach, where Death was directing His Reapers to launch the flotilla of hastily made rafts. She jogged to the God and bowed deeply. "My Lord, I am here."

"It's about time. My raft is loading and I would that you join me." He turned His back to her and began striding toward the largest, and most well made of the rafts, where several of His favorite Attendants already waited aboard.

"My Lord, I have a favor to ask of you."

Death stopped and turned neatly on His cloven hooves. Ralina saw a sly curiosity in his gaze. His lips tilted up. "I do enjoy granting favors to those who serve me well, and you serve me well, little Storyteller. What favor may I grant you—but keep in mind that a favor granted is a debt acquired."

Ralina swallowed her fear—met the God's eyes—and spoke calmly. "I understand that, my Lord. The favor that I ask is that you allow me to travel in my own boat."

"But you cannot possibly be strong enough to keep up with the rest of us, so that is impossible. Ask me another favor, Storyteller, and I will try to grant it to you."

"My Lord, I will not be paddling at all. I will be working on your tale, and to do so I need more solitude than I would find on your raft. You understand this, as you already granted me my own nest so that I might create in peace. I asked one of the Warriors, Renard, and his father, Daniel—who is an excellent carver—to repair a small boat and ready it for the trip. They have done so, and agreed to do all of the paddling so that I can be left in peace to write your tale." Ralina motioned for Renard and his father to step forward, which they did, bowing low.

Death studied them carefully, His eyes quickly finding Kong and Bear where they lay silently behind the three people.

"You may rise," Death commanded. He cocked His massive head to the side, in a posture Ralina recognized as the God contemplating whether there was any gain to Him in what she proposed. "I do not recognize either of these men." Death paused and shouted over His shoulder toward the side of the beach, where Thaddeus was loading his men and their Companions into the patched boats. "Thaddeus! Come to me!"

Ralina watched the Hunter sigh and frown, but she knew he would dare not disobey one of Death's commands—though his expression was sour as he jogged up to the God.

"Yes, my Lord. We are almost all launched."

Death waved away the Hunter's words. "Of course you are—it is what I commanded." Then He pointed at Renard and Daniel. "Do you know these men?"

Thaddeus glanced at them. "Yeah. Renard is a Warrior. And that old man is his father."

"And are they of use to you?" Death asked, and Ralina's stomach tightened.

Thaddeus shrugged. "Renard followed me when Wilkes betrayed his Warriors and fled the Tribe. His father is a carver." Thaddeus spoke as if the two men weren't standing right there. "Sure, we can always use another carver, but I don't remember Daniel being particularly good at making crossbows."

Ralina stepped forward. "Daniel doesn't make crossbows, my Lord," she explained. "He makes the arrows they shoot. Show him."

Daniel stepped before the God, bowed again, and opened the woven mat he'd been carrying, letting a large cache of arrows spill out.

Death's thick brows lifted as He bent to pick up and inspect an arrow. "This is well done."

Daniel bowed low again. "Thank you, my Lord."

"Yeah, that's great, but he can't carve a crossbow," Thaddeus said dismissively.

Death frowned at Thaddeus. "It matters not if we have bows if we do not have arrows to shoot from them."

"My Lord, forgive me if I speak out of turn, but I *can* carve crossbows. They will be simple and free of ornament, but they will be serviceable." Daniel said.

"Then why didn't you carve them before now?" Thaddeus asked, narrowing his hard gaze at Daniel and Renard, who stood perfectly still, heads bowed.

"Because the Tribe had several Master Carvers and we preferred bows made with beauty as well as function." Daniel's voice took on the tone of a teacher schooling a child. "But you know that already, Thaddeus. I do not understand why you would want to disparage my work. I am doing my best for our new Lord, just as you are."

Thaddeus opened his mouth to spew something vile, but Death cut him off with one raised hand.

"Silence! The carver makes an excellent point. He may join our army." Death's attention shifted to Renard. "Warrior, come closer."

Renard lifted his head and did as the God commanded, stepping up to stand beside his father. Death studied him for a long time before speaking.

"It appears you are not ill. Yet I do not sense that you have accepted The Cure." Death's gaze went from Renard to Ralina and his eyes widened with understanding. "Storyteller, have you been sharing your meatless stews with this young Warrior?"

Ralina tossed back her hair and lifted her chin. She called on the best of her acting skills and added a coquettish smile to her façade. "Yes, my Lord, I have."

"You're doing what?" Thaddeus sputtered. "You're interfering with the food my Warriors eat?"

Ralina rounded on Thaddeus. "I wasn't aware the Warriors were yours. I thought they, like all of us, belong to our God."

"Well put, Storyteller," Death said.

"I apologize for my poor choice of words," Thaddeus said as he scowled at Ralina. "But the Storyteller obviously did interfere with this Warrior's food."

"Can you explain that interference, Storyteller?" the God asked.

"Yes, my Lord, easily." Ralina moved up to stand beside Renard. Seductively, she snaked her arm around his waist. She could feel his body jolt with shock, but when she smiled up into his surprised eyes he relaxed enough to put his arm around her in return. "I have taken Renard as a lover. I find he helps my *creativity*." She smiled flirtatiously and then met Death's gaze. "And I do not want a sick lover."

"And you didn't think you needed to ask Death's permission before you kept a Warrior from choosing The Cure?" Thaddeus said spitefully.

Instead of answering Thaddeus, Ralina ignored him and spoke directly to the God. "No, I did not. Because I knew our God would want me to be at my very best when creating His tale—and this young lover keeps me at my very best."

Death threw back His head and laughed. "Storyteller, the more I get to know you—the more I find I have in common with you. I, too, am at my best surrounded by young, healthy lovers. I understand your need, though you are only mortal and therefore can only handle one lover at a time." The God's gaze slid to Daniel and He lifted one brow questioningly.

It was Ralina's turn to laugh. "Oh, my Lord, I prefer my lovers *much* younger. Daniel has remained free of the sickness so that he can keep carving arrows for your army. He and Renard share the same stew, and as they forage for the roots and vegetables together I have found that leaves much more time for me to concentrate on you and your tale."

Death nodded, His massive antlers throwing bizarre shadows along the beach. "All of this makes sense to me, Storyteller. I grant your favor. Thaddeus, free one of the smaller boats and gift it to Ralina."

Thaddeus's face was turning red with anger, and Ralina hesitated just long enough before speaking that his anger became obvious to the God.

"Oh, my Lord, that won't be necessary. Remember that I said I asked Daniel to repair a small boat I found? It is loaded and ready to launch. I wouldn't want to take anything from one of *your* Warriors," Ralina said with syrupy sweetness.

Death laughed again. "You do amuse me, Storyteller." Then His look darkened. "See that I do not regret granting you this favor."

"I will not disappoint you, my Lord," Ralina said.

"Renard, Daniel, you will keep Ralina's craft near mine at all times. My Storyteller must always have access to her muse."

The two men bowed deeply as they said, "Yes, my Lord."

"Thaddeus, you may return to launching *my* Warriors and Hunters.

And you should smile more. Your expression is always so dour," the God said.

The comment almost made Ralina snort with laughter, which she covered in a cough while Thaddeus bared his teeth in a strange semblance of a smile before he bowed and returned to the men waiting for him down the beach.

Ralina and her small group bowed, too, before hurrying to their boat.

"That was well done." Daniel spoke softly to Ralina.

"You both played along well," Ralina responded in kind, glancing at the shy young Warrior she was just getting to know. He met her eyes and smiled—and Ralina was attracted to the kindness in that smile. "I'm sorry I didn't warn you about, well, claiming you as my lover, but I didn't realize that was what I was going to have to say until the moment it happened."

"You have nothing to apologize for," Renard said. "And I certainly do not mind people believing we're lovers."

While Ralina was trying to come up with a reasonable response, Death bellowed from His raft, which was already launched and floating just off the beach in the Channel.

"Hurry, we need to get out there next to his raft before he changes his mind," Ralina said.

Bear and Kong took their places on the ballasts as Ralina settled in the middle part of the little kayak and Renard and his father launched them into the Channel.

As they paddled to Death's raft, Ralina looked back at her forest. Standing at the tree line were the Tribe members Death was leaving behind. He'd announced five days earlier that only those who took The Cure, and who had something to add to his army, could join Him—effectively deserting any of His People who were ill, as well as the Tribe's old people and children, who had survived so much. They stood there, silently, watching friends and family leave them. Ralina could see that many of them were weeping, sick with disease and fear and loss. It broke her heart, but she'd spoken to as many as would listen to her, for even a moment, and told them to get north—go to another Tribe—leave the poisoned forest.

Few listened to her. And even fewer refrained from eating meat and were still healthy, but if only a dozen or so made their way out of the diseased forest, the Tribe lived and perhaps someday Ralina could find her way back to them.

She wiped tears from her eyes and bit her lip to keep from sobbing aloud.

"My People! My army! Today we begin an adventure that will give us the world!" Death shouted. He stood in the middle of His raft, surrounded by the youngest, most attractive of His Attendants. At the oars were a dozen Reapers. Their bodies boarlike, they hunched over the oars, massive muscles preparing to follow their God's command. Death raised His arm, which held a strange-looking spear. The end of it wasn't tipped in flint, ready to kill, but wrapped in a rag that looked wet. "But to properly begin anew, we must rid ourselves of the old." Death dipped the cloth into a brazier that stood on metal legs in the center of the raft. When He raised it again it was on fire.

Ralina opened her mouth to shout a warning, but her voice wouldn't work. Later she realized that even had she been able to speak it would have been too late. Death had planned too well.

He threw the spear. It sailed above their heads and over the beach to embed itself in a pile of dry pine boughs that formed a semicircular pile of rubbish at the tree line. With an ominous *whoosh,* it lit and spread.

And Ralina realized why the forest had smelled like rancid lard. Death's Reapers had poured rendered animal fat all around the Tribe so that everything—blackened trees, half-destroyed nests, piles of dried pine boughs and forest debris they'd gathered and arranged carefully to circle the people—*everything* caught fire.

Death's voice carried over the sounds of the screaming Tribe.

"Ah, but every happy tale ends in death—it is natural. And where there is death, there is also a new beginning. Let us be off!"

Renard and Daniel paddled with their backs to the Tribe. Their expressions were mirror images—blank with shock as silent tears cascaded down their faces, making them appear as if they were past and future versions of the same person. Bear and Kong whimpered and dropped their heads, turning away from the horrors behind them.

Ralina wouldn't let herself turn away. She stared. She watched it all. Everything. Every unspeakable horror. Until they were far enough down the Channel that she could see no more, and even then the Storyteller kept staring at the cloud of black smoke that lifted from the pyre of the Tribe of the Trees. She had to. She was recording everything.

I will survive. I will tell this story—the true story—so that everyone will know what happened here.

Finally, when the smoke cloud was no longer in view, Ralina bowed her head and sobbed.

THE PACK—LOST LAKE

It wasn't until mid-morning on the fifth day that they reached anything resembling land. Antreas had said that the first set of islands they would encounter were called the Payettes, and that they—like the rest of the "islands" they'd pass as they crossed Lost Lake—weren't really islands at all. Before the huge lake had been formed they'd been a mountain range.

Mari found that easy to believe. What jutted out of the seemingly endless lake looked nothing like an island, but instead it appeared that shards of earth had pushed up out of the lake—almost like teeth.

"I was looking forward to getting a chance to walk on dry land again—even if it was just for a little while," Mari told Nik as she eyed the Payettes in the distance. "But how do we even beach the boats? Maybe we're too far away still, but those islands don't look very hospitable."

"They aren't," Antreas said as he and Danita expertly paddled close to Nik and Mari's little boat. "Everyone circle up!"

Maneuvering their boats with much more skill than when they'd begun their journey, the Pack quickly circled around Antreas.

"I'd still rather be going to the island," Antreas began by saying.

"But you understand why we outvoted you," Mari said.

Antreas sighed. "I do. And you're right. If something happens to me you have no guide. It is that dangerous, though. You know, we have enough supplies. We could pass by these islands. There will be another grouping in a few more days."

"You said there are wild potatoes and blackberries growing there right now, correct?" Sora asked from the boat she shared with Sheena, Rose, and O'Bryan.

"There are," Antreas admitted.

"You also said as long as we're careful everything should be fine," Mari said.

"I did say that."

"Which is why Wilkes and I are going to accompany Jenna, Spencer, and Mason," Nik said. "We're not going to let the Mouths get any of our people."

"Or yourselves," Mari added.

Nik touched her cheek. "Or ourselves."

"Okay, I don't like that you're going into danger, but I do agree with Sora—fresh food that is not fish will be excellent for morale and our stomachs. So let's go over this once more, and then let's *all* be careful," Mari said.

Nik began. "Wilkes and I are going to temporarily trade boats with Antreas and Danita. They don't have any ballasts as Bast stays in the boat with them—and our canines are going to wait with the Pack." Laru grumbled low in his chest, voicing his displeasure. "Hey, big guy, it's going to be fine—but it won't be if I have to worry about a monster fish snagging you with its tentacles and pulling you under." Laru sneezed in disgust and grumbled some more, causing the Pack to smile.

"And because Spencer and I are the fastest berry pickers, we'll go straight to the area Antreas described as holding the blackberry brambles," Jenna said as she and Spencer held up several big baskets.

"And I'm going to dig potatoes," Mason said. "I'm good at it, and fast."

"The potatoes are up and to the left of the blackberries," Antreas reminded him.

Mason nodded. "Don't worry. I'm a big fan of new potatoes. I could spot them with my eyes closed—well, almost."

"While you're harvesting, Nik and Wilkes will wait in the boat—that will be the quickest and easiest way to get out of there when you're done,"

Antreas said. "Lynx guides built something resembling a dock many years ago, for that purpose."

"But Monkeys like to use the dock to sun themselves," Sora said.

"And Mouths like to hang around under it," Mari added.

"Exactly," Antreas said.

Almost as if Antreas had invoked them by saying their names, a scream split the morning air, causing the whole Pack to startle.

"That's one of them, isn't it?" Mari said.

"It is. Monkeys have excellent eyesight—almost as good as Bast's." From her place in the boat, Bast hissed.

Danita ruffled the big feline's fur and laughed. "He said *almost*."

"They'll be on the dock as you approach, and they're smart, which is why I want you to shoot an arrow over their heads as you paddle up," Antreas said. "They've had enough run-ins with humans to know that arrows can kill them."

"And we'll take our slingshots with us," Spencer said, holding up hers while Mason and Jenna nodded.

"As I said before, Monkeys don't usually attack humans on land. They're small, and out of the water they're slow. Plus, they're cowards. And the reason there will still be blackberries and potatoes for you to harvest is because Monkeys move awkwardly on land—so awkwardly that they're easy prey to one of the main predators on the island."

"Rattlesnakes," Jenna said with a shudder.

"Yes. It's early in the year, so most of the snakes are still in their holes. Later in the summer it would be stupid to try to harvest anything without a team of Warriors going ashore with you as protection. Still, be vigilant, and if you hear anything resembling a rattle load your slingshot and get ready to fire."

"Don't worry. We'll be careful," Spencer said.

"At least we won't have to worry about the Monkeys while we're on land," Mason said.

"On land you won't, even though they'll probably call to you from the trees and try to get you to come to them."

"Why would they do that if they're so awkward on land?" Mari asked.

"If they can get you under the canopy of one of the trees, every Monkey in that tree will drop on you. Awkward or not, their teeth are sharp. A group of them can definitely kill you."

"Not going anywhere near the trees," Mason said.

"In the water they are vicious little thieves. Keep the boat at the dock. Monkeys live in dens they make either in the ruins of a city where some of the buildings are still above water, or here, where there isn't a city, and where they build dens at the waterline. They can only be accessed underwater. Strange but true fact—one of the staples of their diet is Mouth eggs. The Mouths lay them in shallows near islands or in the ruins of cities. Monkeys devour more than half of them every season. And from about now until midsummer Mouths will be laying eggs, which means the Monkeys will be fat and lazy—especially on land."

"That's a good thing," Nik said.

"It is. Remember, you're going to be in the most danger when the group comes back and loads the boat. Move fast. Nik, Wilkes, don't help them. Let Mason do that. The two of you, don't take your eyes off the water around you," Antreas said.

"And on the return trip Spencer, Jenna, and Mason will paddle while Wilkes and I continue to be ready to shoot," Nik said.

"Yes. The water is clear here, which works in your favor, but the Mouths are dark colored and many times look like shadows, or even ruins below the water," Antreas said. "Watch for their tentacles. They're easier to spot."

"Because they're light colored, right?" Mari asked.

"Well, the bottom side of their tentacles are white. The top of them are the same dark color as their bodies, but when they lift them from the water you'll be able to see the white. Don't wait. Shoot."

"Aim for their eyes," Nik said.

"Or their open mouths," Antreas said. "But the eyes are the best shot. Their skin is so thick you can rarely get a fatal shot, but their eyes aren't on the sides of their heads like most fish. They're on top so that they can see their above-water prey."

"Don't worry. I won't miss," Nik said grimly.

"Well, save your arrows unless one of the damn things attacks," Wilkes said. "You might get lucky and they will have already fed. They only hunt when they're hungry—though the Monkeys are always bothersome. Unless a group of them can trap you they won't kill, but they will steal from you, and they'll also attempt to unbalance your boat. My best advice is if the little bastards start messing with you—shoot one. Kill it. The Mouths will feed from it and the Monkeys will take off."

"We've got it," Nik said.

"We'll handle them," Wilkes added.

"Are all of you ready?" Mari asked.

When the five of them nodded, Antreas and Danita paddled to the boat Wilkes shared with Mason and Spencer. Danita quickly switched places, and Bast nimbly jumped from one boat to the other. Then Wilkes, Mason, and Antreas paddled to pick up Jenna before heading to Mari and Nik.

Mari took Nik's face between her hands. "Do *not* die. And I'd prefer it if you didn't get hurt, either."

"I'll do my best," Nik said, kissing her soundly before he and Antreas changed places.

"Okay, head straight at the island from here. You'll see the dock. From there the blackberries and potatoes aren't far. Like I said before, they're just up from the beach, but well outside the tree line. I'll take the Pack past the island and then we'll circle and wait for you," Antreas said. "Be smart and be safe."

Laru grumbled again as Nik and Wilkes began stroking against the lake, aiming the boat for the island.

Just the thought of wide-mouthed, tentacled monsters lurking under the water had Nik's nerves on edge, but the sight of land, closer than it had been for five whole days, steadied him.

A scream echoed around them, sounding exactly like a young woman being tortured.

"That is so disgusting," Jenna said.

"It makes my skin shiver." Spencer peered down into the water surrounding them. "It's especially horrible that they're trying to lure us to those giant Mouths."

"Nik and Wilkes won't let them get us," Mason said. "And we have our slingshots for the snakes—don't forget that."

The girls nodded somberly, checking and rechecking their supply of rocks and being sure their slingshots were easily accessible.

"I see the dock! It's straight ahead." From his position in the front of the little boat, Nik squinted against the glare of the sun off the lake and could see the small wooden structure jutting off the side of the steep bank to the island.

Monkeys covered the dock. They were about the size of Terriers—had the canines walked upright. As they got closer Nik could see that except for their faces they were covered with fur that was a strange color—brown with a green tint.

"They look just like the water," Jenna said.

"That's why they're that weird greenish-brown color," Nik said. "Camouflage."

"Mason, take my paddle," Nik said, handing it to Mason, who was sitting directly behind him in the crowded canoe. Then Nik raised his crossbow, sighted, and let an arrow fly over their heads, so close to the Monkeys that it almost grazed three of them.

The creatures began screaming—this time they sounded like animals instead of terrorized girls. Most of them jumped into the water and disappeared under it. A few others waddled from the dock and awkwardly made for a grove of pines not far inland.

"Wilkes, steer us up to the dock. Mason, keep paddling for me. I'm going to watch the water—and what's beneath it," Nik said, reloading his bow.

The water was clear and deep. Nik estimated that he could see about ten feet below the surface, and then everything got dark. Shadows moved within shadows, and the sunlight captured strange shapes that Nik was sure were Mouths, though none rose to the surface.

They steered the boat easily to the dock, stopping beside it. The wooden structure was small and, like Antreas had described, it jutted from the steep side of the island to rest along the surface of the water. It was only wide enough for a couple of people to stand side by side, and it was covered with Monkey excrement.

"Bloody beetle balls, that's repulsive," Nik said, wrinkling his nose at the smell.

"We're going to do this fast," Jenna said, looking from Spencer to Mason. "Are you two ready?"

Spencer and Mason nodded.

"Remember everything Antreas said," Jenna continued. "We stay within eyesight of each other. We do not go into the trees. We look and listen for snakes. And we hurry." As Jenna spoke, she and Spencer were wrapping their hands and getting out their little harvesting knives, which were really just sharpened flint set in wood, but worked perfectly for snipping clusters of blackberries from the thorny bushes.

"I'm ready," Spencer said.

"Me, too," Mason said.

Mason had one of the precious shovels the Clan had salvaged decades before—and all three of them had as many nesting baskets as they could carry. When they took the baskets apart to fill, there were straps attached to them so that they could be carried over their shoulders.

"Okay, don't forget—if the Monkeys come too close give Wilkes and me a shout and we'll shoot more arrows at them. Hell, if they won't leave you alone, I'll kill one of them," Nik said grimly. "That'll keep them away from you."

"Thanks, Nik. We know we can count on you and Wilkes," Jenna said.

Nik thought Jenna had grown up a lot in just a short time. She was proving to be a valuable member of the Pack. Actually, all three of them—Jenna, Spencer, and Mason—were Pack members Nik was proud of. Spencer had a gift for brewing and fermenting. She'd even managed to trade in the Saleesh villages for several bushels of apples, and had talked Mari and Sora into letting her keep a few of the bushels so she could create something called cider, which Nik was really looking forward to trying.

Mason was always willing to lend a hand to help any Pack member, and except for Third Nights, when Moon Fever had ahold of him, his face was rarely lacking a smile.

"I like them," Wilkes said, and Nik realized the older Warrior was also staring after the three teenagers as they jogged up from the bank.

"I like them, too, but we need to watch the water *and* them," Nik said.

"You're right. Ah, the girls found the blackberries." Jenna turned and gave the boat a thumbs-up before she and Spencer bent to the task of harvesting berries. Wilkes continued, "I'll watch them and give you updates if you keep your eyes on the water."

"Will do," Nik said. "It's not like I can look away from it without getting a creeping feeling up my spine."

"Your dislike of water comes in handy right now," Wilkes said with a smile, though his attention was focused inland on the kids. "Okay, Mason just waved, and now he's digging."

"And while I'm staring at the water looking for fish that can swallow canines whole, I'm going to think about all of the delicious things Sora is going to do to those potatoes," Nik said.

"She's impressive," Wilkes said. "Both of our Moon Women are impressive."

Nik nodded, squinting at a dark shape under the water. He couldn't quite decide whether it was a shadow from the dock or something more ominous.

"I like that you're saying 'our' Moon Women. I was worried about you being unhappy away from the Tribe," Nik said.

"Honestly, I was, too—at first. But there's a freedom to being with the Pack that we didn't have in the Tribe. Women are the lawmakers, and I find I like that—a lot." He glanced at Nik and shrugged before returning his gaze inland. "They're kinder than we are, and they're also more intuitive. Mari and Sora are making good decisions—not 'hysterical' at all, as the Saleesh priests would describe them. They showed excellent judgment with how they handled Dove's vision. The Saleesh people were warned—men *and* women—and they didn't do it like impetuous children would have. They made sure we were safe and we had a plan. *Then* they confronted the Saleesh. That's good decision making."

"I agree. And this journey—though it has, of course, been difficult—also *hasn't* been filled with the kind of bickering and backstabbing that had seemed to be commonplace in the Tribe the past several years."

"Thaddeus . . ." Wilkes spat into the water as if to get the taste of the word out of his mouth.

"He played a major role in the change in the Tribe, but it wasn't just him. Think about the Elder Council. Those men had been making decisions for the Tribe for decades."

"Yeah, once appointed to the Council you're on it for life," Wilkes said.

"Exactly. We only had one point of view in the Tribe for a long time, and it was an old, stagnant one. Father and I discussed it often. Sometimes he agreed with me on the changes I talked about, but more often he'd tell me that I'd understand after I was made a Companion. Well, I'm a Companion, and I still believe the Tribe had become tunnel-visioned and stuck only seeing one point of view, which was usually a male's and a Companion of a Shepherd's."

"How long does a Moon Woman lead?" Wilkes asked.

"I'm not sure. I know that Mari's mother had chosen Sora and Mari as her apprentices shortly before she died—and she wasn't much older than you," Nik said. "Mari and Sora are already opening the Moon Woman training to others—something that breaks with their Clan traditions."

"Mari seems to like breaking traditions," Wilkes said, and Nik could hear the smile in his voice, though he didn't take his eyes from the water.

"She does, but she also values lessons that were learned in the past. I like that balance."

"As do I," said Wilkes. "I hope the Wind Riders agree."

"I'd be surprised if we actually joined a Herd," Nik said. "It's more likely that we create our own settlement, but I'm really looking forward to seeing a horse. It's hard to imagine an animal so big it can be ridden."

"We're going to have a lot of new things to learn. It'll keep me young,"

Wilkes said. "Nik—Monkeys to the east in the trees. I can see them watching the girls."

"Keep an eye on the water. I'll look," Nik said.

Nik studied the grove of big old pines, and easily saw a whole group of Monkeys filling the branches of the two trees closest to where Jenna and Spencer were harvesting berries. The girls hadn't noticed them. Their backs were bent, and even from the distance of the boat Nik could see that they were moving quickly and had already filled two of the baskets.

He glanced at Mason, who was west of the girls. He, too, was completely focused on what he was doing. As Nik watched, Mason reached down and lifted a handful of potato vines, shaking the dirt from the little red nuggets of new potatoes before he pulled them free of the vines and put them in the waiting baskets.

A scream came from the trees, and everyone's head turned to see the Monkeys jumping up and down on the boughs, causing the pines to look like they were shivering. One of the creatures threw a pinecone at Jenna. It fell short, but Nik didn't hesitate. He sighted his crossbow and let an arrow fly. It embedded in the bough the Monkey was standing on, causing a dozen of them to scatter while they jabbered and shrieked.

"They're getting restless," Nik said.

"Hey, what's that?" Wilkes pointed to a dark shape under the dock, not more than five feet from them.

"I think it's a Mouth," Nik said. "I noticed it before, and couldn't decide if it was a shadow or not. When they come back I'll watch it. The only things feeding today are going to be our Pack."

"Did I hear Antreas right when he said we only have a few hours left to paddle today and that we'll actually get to be on dry land tonight?" Wilkes said, still staring at the darkness beneath the dock.

"You did. He said we're stopping at a place called Flatrock."

"Does that mean we're going to be fighting off Monkeys all night? Not that I'm complaining. It'll be good to sleep on land."

"According to Antreas the island isn't more than a big rock that's flat on the top. Nothing grows there, and it's literally a rock, so Monkeys can't build dens at the waterline," Nik said.

"And no Monkeys means no Mouths, either," Wilkes said.

"Exactly."

"The girls are done! They're helping Mason with the last of the potato digging," Wilkes said.

"Good, I'm ready to get away from this stench," Nik said.

"Okay, they just waved and they're strapping the baskets over their shoulders," Wilkes reported.

He and Nik kept eyeing their respective targets, but they also arranged their arrows within easy reach. Just touching the barbed tips calmed Nik. He'd been the best bowman in the Tribe for years, and he had no doubt about his ability to take out any Monkeys or Mouths that threatened them.

"On their way back—heads up! The Monkeys are also on the move," Wilkes warned.

He hadn't needed to. The Monkeys weren't subtle. Chattering to one another, they waddled from the trees and dove into the water, morphing into expert swimmers before disappearing beneath the frothing waves.

Jenna, Spencer, and Mason returned smelling of sweat and earth, and making Nik long for the end of their journey.

Mason was the first into the boat. He stood, balancing, as Jenna and Spencer handed him their laden baskets. The dark shape that had been lurking under the dock moved, and Nik caught sight of something that looked like a snake. He aimed his crossbow and spoke quickly.

"Get in the boat. I see a Mouth. It's there—under the dock."

"Last basket in!" Mason said. Then he lifted each of the girls and practically tossed them into the cramped little boat. "Okay, we're loaded. Let's go! Let's go!"

The paddling was left to Mason, Jenna, and Spencer. Wilkes and Nik sat at opposite ends of the boat, crossbows raised, sighting into the water.

They were only a few yards from the dock when Spencer shrieked and said, "I just hit something with my paddle!"

Wilkes turned in time to see a Monkey diving beneath the boat. "Monkey—under us."

And then from the opposite side of the boat came a shriek that perfectly echoed Spencer's—sounding exactly like one of the girls had fallen overboard.

"Don't let it shake you," Nik said, sighting down into the water.

"Oh, no you don't!" Jenna shouted as a furry webbed hand glided silently up out of the water, grabbing one of the straps of a basket filled with blackberries. She lifted her paddle over her head and brought it down on the creature's wrist sharply. The Monkey cried out and the water writhed as it tried to swim away, but it didn't let loose of the strap. Jenna bent a little out of the boat so that she could swing at the thing again, this time rapping it on the knuckles of its webbed hand. It squealed, dropped the strap, and dove under the surface.

At that moment a tentacle slithered up out of the water in the exact place the Monkey had been, reaching for Jenna.

"Nik!" Spencer screamed.

"Get back!" Nik swiveled, trying to get a clean shot of the huge fish. He could see it clearly now. It had to have been twenty feet long—almost bigger than their boat. Its body was black and wide, and its enormous oval-shaped maw was open. Rows of teeth glistened wet. They weren't sharp, like a canine's incisors. Instead the teeth looked like rough-tipped bumps that were barbed so that once the Mouths bit something it was almost impossible for the prey to escape. Tentacles, like massive white-bellied snakes, grew from either side of its mouth. It seemed they moved with sentience of their own—and they were all reaching for Jenna.

Spencer lunged for Jenna, wrapping her arms around her friend's waist and pulling her backwards as one of the tentacles missed the girl's arm, instead wrapping around her paddle and jerking it out of Jenna's hand to pull it into its mouth.

"I got it!" Wilkes said, firing his bow into the water, but the arrow skittered off the creature's wide head.

In one movement Nik stood, aimed, fired—and the arrow embedded itself in the feathers in the creature's eye. The behemoth under the water exploded in an agony of movement, its thick black tail striking the canoe and causing it to tip precariously. Blood and gore poured from the creature's eye, staining the water—calling to the Monkeys. They came like a school of deadly fish, slithering through the water slick and silent, closing on the dying Mouth and the boat.

Nik aimed and shot a Monkey through the forehead, causing the group to falter as they shrieked and chattered at one another—and then several stopped their projectile-like swim toward the fish and began tearing apart their fallen comrade.

"Paddle! Paddle! Get us out of here!" Nik shouted.

Mason, Jenna, Spencer, and even Wilkes grabbed paddles and bent their backs to stroking against the seething water. The little boat shot away from the convulsing body of the Mouth as the pack of Monkeys reached it.

Nik could only watch for a moment. Like they were a swarm that formed on water, they covered the fish and began reaching into its wounded eye with greedy, webbed fingers, pulling out great hunks of bloody goo. Gagging, Nik looked away. He put down his crossbow, picked up a paddle, and got the hell out of there.

That night, belly full of potato stew and blackberries, Nik pulled Mari into his arms. Flatrock was just that—a huge rock that lifted from the water. There was no vegetation on it except strange, scrubby bushes that looked more dead than alive, but he didn't care. He was just glad the hardness he lay on wasn't bobbing in the water.

"It was even more awful than you described, wasn't it?" Mari murmured against his chest.

"It was horrible. I'm not sure which was worse, the Monkeys or the Mouth," Nik said.

"Jenna's still pretty shaken. Sora brewed cannabis tea for her—and Spencer and Mason. Are you sure you don't want some?"

Nik tightened his arms around her. "You're the best medicine I could have right now." He sighed. "It's hard for me to imagine being on this lake for another forty or more days, especially when making land between here and the other side means dealing with more of those creatures."

"Well, Antreas says there are a few other spots we're going to stop that are like Flatrock—where it isn't possible for Monkeys to build their dens, so we don't have to be worried about Mouths or Monkeys." She snuggled into him. "We'll make it, Nik. I know we will. Our Pack is strong, and getting stronger." Mari lifted a little so that she could look into his eyes. "We're going to have puppies!" And then her smile faded. "Wait, how long will Mariah be pregnant? Oh, Nik, please tell me that canine will not have to give birth in a boat."

"She'll carry the pups for about sixty days—give or take a week or so. It's going to be close, but don't worry. The Tribe has been watching over birthing canines for generations. If Mariah has to give birth in a boat, all will be well. Claudia will help her—and so will Rose." Nik chuckled. "And Laru and I will help Davis and Cammy to not lose their minds. I think you'll find that, like humans, birthing canines and the women who help them show a lot more sense about it than the men watching and waiting."

"Those puppies are a great blessing," Mari said.

"New life ushering in a new season for our Pack," Nik agreed, kissing Mari on top of her head.

"Oh, that reminds me. Did you realize tomorrow is the last day of spring?"

Nik startled in surprise. "Wow, I've lost track of time. I had no idea summer was so close."

"Yeah, me too. Antreas reminded us—and he also reminded us that we need to pick up the pace to be sure we get through the mountains before summer is over," Mari said. "But we'll do it. I know we will."

"I believe you," Nik said, tilting Mari's chin up so he could smile into her beautiful gray eyes. "I feel like I can do anything with you and our Pack beside me."

Then Mari kissed him, washing the horrors of the day away with her scent and taste and touch—and her love.

CHAPTER 19

O n the last day of spring River woke well before dawn to ready
herself for the Mare Test. Truth be told, she was amazed that she'd
had to wake. She hadn't expected to sleep. At all. But sometime after
moonrise River had slept soundly enough to have a strange dream. She
and Anjo and Ghost had been on the prairie, aimlessly searching for
someone. River couldn't quite understand who was missing, but in the
dream she felt that person's absence deeply—almost as deeply as if Anjo
had been missing. Ghost felt it, too, and was even more upset by it; River
knew him well enough by now to read his moods, even if she didn't have
the same connection with him she had with her Anjo. The stallion was
depressed, and as they searched the prairie he became more and more
agitated, neighing with heartbreaking sadness and loss, until tears leaked
down his face, as they had at the Presentation when he didn't Choose a
Rider. They searched on and on, until they came to the Rendezvous Site,
which was near the base of the Rock Mountain range.

Suddenly a dove flew from the mountains, heading straight at Ghost.
The stallion's ears pricked forward, then he lifted his magnificent head
and called a greeting that shook his whole body. The dove landed on
Ghost's back, perching there and rubbing its beautiful head against the
stallion's silver mane while Ghost nickered happily.

Then the dove turned its head to face River and Anjo, and River was overcome with emotions. She'd never seen such a lovely bird. Its feathers were all the colors of a mother-of-pearl shell. River felt a wash of incredible tenderness for the bird, and was instantly drawn to it—and at that instant she realized this was the same gray bird she'd seen in the vision the phantom quartz had sent her, the bird that had been wounded and chased by the evil blue wave. River's heart hurt for the little dove. She wanted to keep it safe—to cherish it—and that was even before she noticed that the sweet creature had no eyes.

"Dove?" River called out in her dream, and that's what woke her.

"Oh, good, you're up." April hurried into the small tent River shared with Anjo during bad weather. That night the weather hadn't been bad, but the mare had slept inside with River anyway, as Anjo understood that her Rider was anxious about the coming Test and rested better with her mare near.

Anjo raised her head and blinked sleepily at April, nickering a greeting under her breath.

"Good morning to you, too, Anjo. I've put your grain mash in a feeder next to Deinos. She'll keep you company while you eat," April said.

River sat up, rubbing sleep from her eyes. "Thank you, April. And, Anjo, don't forget—no grazing. Just eat the mash and then drink a little water and come back here so we can wrap your legs and dress your mane and tail."

Anjo nuzzled her Rider, lipping her hair playfully.

River giggled and kissed her muzzle. "Yes, I know you're not nervous, but I am. So, hurry back." The gorgeous mare trotted out of the tent, leaving the sisters alone.

"Anjo does look magnificent. She's completely shed her winter coat, and I love that she's such a beautiful mixture of gray and white that she looks almost as silver as Mother's Echo. And the black up to her knees is distinctive. I hope her foals have her coloring," April said as she handed her sister the tray she'd carried into the tent. April stared at the oatmeal and nuts and the healthy dollop of honey in the center of it.

"She does look good, and she's in peak shape." River stared at the bowl. "I don't think I can eat this."

"You have to. You'll need the energy—just like Anjo. And do not forget that about midday you need to eat the apples and nuts in your travel pack, and give Anjo—"

"A few handfuls of the molasses grain," River interrupted, speaking through a big bite of oatmeal. "I know, I know. And I'm eating. Promise."

"I think I'm more nervous for you today than I was before Deinos Chose me."

"Stop it! My stomach is already turned inside out. April, what if we do a terrible job? What if we don't just lose, but lose *badly*?"

Hands on her hips, April turned to face her sister. "What does Anjo say about that?"

River snorted, sounding a lot like her mare. "She says we're not going to lose."

"Well, mares know things. Didn't she tell you she knew I was going to be Chosen at my very first Presentation?"

"You know she did, because I told you that."

"See—mares know things. Especially Lead Mares."

"She's not Lead Mare," River said.

"Yet," April said.

"But we're so young, Anjo and me. I counted seven teams that arrived from the other branches of our Herd—*seven teams,* April. And all but one of them are older than Anjo and me. Do you know that Alani and her Doe have entered?"

April sighed. "I do. They're a strong team from the Herd Magenti East."

"Strong and experienced. Doe is ten, and that makes Alani twenty-six. They know a lot more than I do."

"But they aren't you and Anjo. No one else is—you two are special. Now get over here so I can work on your hair."

"I don't know why we bother." River sat in front of her sister, and April began combing out her thick raven's-wing-colored curls. "Anjo and I are going to look like a mess by the end of the Test."

"Of course you will, but everyone understands why. Forty miles and whatever insane tests the Mare Council has for you over the course of those miles will take a toll. But the Herd will remember how you looked when you and Anjo pranced to the starting line and shot off, leaving everyone behind."

"Hey, don't expect Anjo to set the beginning pace. Didn't you hear that Willow and her Gontia decided to join the Test? Gontia can beat Anjo in a sprint."

"In a sprint, sure. But not over forty miles," April said.

"They're strong competition. Willow is two years older than me. She's had two more years to condition her mare," River said. "Luce and Blue are a strong team, too. They're passionate about winning. I've watched them preparing. Ever since that day in the mud trap Luce has made Blue's conditioning a priority. Add that competition to the seven teams from the other Magenti Herds, and I'm really worried."

"Riv, pull yourself together. You're forgetting something really important. No one knows more about what it takes to be a Lead Mare Rider than you. Well, except for Mother, who is *actually* our Lead Mare Rider. You've been watching Mother for a decade. And for the past three years, since Anjo's Choosing, you've been accompanying Mother as she goes about Herd business. This year you even attended the Mare Council with her. Our people know that. They've watched you earn the leadership role you've grown into, *before* the Mare Test. And you know Herd members seek you out, especially for your opinion on their horses."

"Yeah, that's true. But I would be one of the youngest Riders ever to win a Mare Test."

"Youngest doesn't mean that you also wouldn't be qualified. Look, Riv, our Herd, Magenti Central, is the largest of all five of our branches. We hold the best of the Magenti territory—we have the strongest, smartest, fastest horses. You know what you're doing, and the Herd is pulling for you."

"Not the whole Herd," River said.

"Oh, who cares about Clayton and his minions? Skye and Scout can't beat you," April said.

"They've been training hard since the mud trap, too," River reminded her sister.

"Doesn't matter. You're a better Rider and Anjo is a better mare. And, sure, Skye has her little group of followers, but they'll all shut up once you and Anjo win today. Plus, can Skye really awaken a crystal?"

River shrugged. "Yeah, I think so. I've seen her do it a few times in class."

April scoffed. "A *few times*? In *class*? Please. You could awaken a crystal in your sleep. Even if something bizarre happens and Skye beats you in the Test, she must awaken a crystal so that the entire Mare Council can feel its properties—in front of the whole Herd. That's a lot of pressure, and Skye does not perform well under pressure. You do." She handed her sister a small mirror. "What do you think?"

River stared back at her reflection. April had braided her dark hair close to her scalp, weaving thin purple ribbons decorated with embroidered silver mane from Echo. Her braids fell all around her shoulders to almost reach her waist. Dressed with Magenti's purple, River looked fierce and ready for battle.

"I think you did a great job. Thank you," River said.

"I'm going to paint your face now, and as soon as your mare gets back I'll paint designs on her, and then we can braid the ribbons into her mane and tail and wrap her legs." Anjo snorted as she entered the tent, with April's newly bonded filly close behind. "There you are! And right on time." April smiled at Anjo, and then rubbed her filly's wide head.

"Hey there, Deinos. Thanks for getting up early with us." River stroked the filly's slick neck. "Her coat is really beautiful. We don't see many black-and-white paints in the Herd. I think she's going to grow into an exceptional mare."

"That means a lot coming from you." April smiled happily. "I'll look forward to which stallion you decide she's best bred to someday."

"I will, too," River said—taking a moment to relish the possibilities of the future. She would love nothing more than to lead Herd Magenti into another era of prosperity, peace, and strength—and part of that leadership would be choosing which mares are bred to which stallions and when.

"Hey, hold still and close your eyes. I know this is going to get all messed up as soon as you start sweating, but you and Anjo are going to look incredible until then."

River did as April commanded, relaxing under her sister's expert touch as she used lavender and white to highlight her dark eyes and then painted the wavy lines that symbolized a river—her namesake—on her cheeks. River was glad her sister was there, especially as her mother couldn't be. It was against Herd law for the Lead Mare Rider to show favoritism toward any of the Candidates who would take her place, and that included her daughter. Dawn and Echo would give the signal that would begin the first leg of the Test—a five-mile race to Bitter Creek, which is where the first of the Mare Test obstacles was set—and then the outgoing Lead Mare and Rider, along with the majority of the Herd Magenti, would cut across the prairie to be at the finish, where they would greet every pair. Dawn and Echo would wait with the rest of the Herd as the Mare Council tallied each pair's score. Then the Council would give Dawn a slip of purple ribbon on which would be embroidered the name of the new Lead Mare/Rider team. Dawn would then read the name of the team aloud to the entire Herd.

After that there was one more Test—perhaps the most important of them all, because if the Rider failed that Test she would never be allowed to be Lead Mare Rider. The Rider of the Lead Mare of Herd Magenti must be able to awaken a crystal before the Mare Council and the Herd—and be a strong enough Crystal Seer that the Council felt the crystal's awakening. If she could not do that, whoever the Council had placed second would be given the same opportunity—and so on until a Lead Mare Rider who was also a Crystal Seer was chosen.

The Mare Test was quite a bit different from the Stallion Run. For the stallions and their Riders the Run was a race—a test of strength and stamina. But a Lead Mare team needed more than strength and stamina—they needed wisdom, compassion, intuition, and courage, as well as being fast and strong. And then beyond all of that, the Rider of the Lead Mare must be a Crystal Seer.

The stallion who crossed the finish line first was always named Herd Stallion. Quite often the first mare team that crossed the finish line was not named Lead Mare and Rider.

"Hey, where did you go?" April asked.

"Huh? Oh, sorry. I was just thinking about the Test, and also about how difficult today must be for Mother."

"She's ready to step down. She's made that clear," said April as she opened the wooden chest that held her sister's most cherished possessions and lifted the amethyst necklace that used to belong to their grandmother. In the flickering candlelight it winked and twinkled magickally as April fastened it around River's neck, where it nestled against her bronze skin, spreading warmth and contentment throughout her body.

"Oh, I don't mean that. A decade is long enough to lead. Mother has earned the years of relaxation and respect that are waiting for her. I meant that it must be difficult for her to be forced to stay away from us while I get ready. I'll bet the only person more nervous than you and me is Mother." River's fingers brushed against the smooth purple stones, gathering the warmth from them and letting their comforting aspect soothe her.

"I'll be with Mother as soon as the Test begins. And don't forget—she has a lot of faith in Anjo and you. Speaking of your mare, I was asking if you want any symbol besides your two-wave river lines painted on her hips."

River's intuition spoke before she'd even processed the answer. "Yes. On one hip paint a dove in flight and paint two wavy lines on the other, as well as on her chest."

"What does the dove symbolize?"

The words came to River without her being conscious of thinking them. "Freedom and love."

"Huh. I didn't realize that's what doves symbolized," April said as she turned to Anjo and started painting her hip with thick purple dye.

"I'm not sure if doves symbolize that to everyone, but to me they definitely do." River bent to begin wrapping Anjo's legs as the image of a sweet, eyeless dove filled her mind.

April had been right. River decided she and Anjo did look incredible as they pranced through the camp, making their way to the starting line of the Mare Test. The entire Herd was already there, waiting and watching expectantly. A huge shout and cheer went up as a team took their position on the starting line. River was able to get a glimpse of who it was, and her stomach roiled when she realized it was Alani and her magnificent buckskin mare, Doe, they were cheering.

"I knew it. They're probably the strongest team here," River muttered, more to herself than aloud.

Walking beside her with her yearling, April whispered to her sister, "No, you and Anjo are the strongest team here, and you're from *our* Herd—not a stranger's."

River gave her sister a side look. "Herd Magenti East aren't strangers."

"Well, they also aren't *us*. You're the best of *us,* and the best of us is going to win today."

April is wise, Anjo's confident voice rang through River's mind.

"You're right. She is." River reached forward and stroked the side of her mare's neck affectionately.

"Who is what?" April asked.

"Anjo said you're wise, and I agreed." She smiled at her sister. "And you're right, too. I am the best of us, and I need to remember that part of being a Lead Mare Rider is confidence. I didn't lack it before today—and I'm not going to start lacking it now."

April's grin blazed. "There's the sister I know!"

Another cheer lifted from the starting line.

"Can you see who that is?" April asked.

"It's Skye and Scout."

April shook her head. "No wonder the cheer wasn't very loud. The only people who want her to win are Clayton and his friends."

River lifted her chin. "She's *not* going to win." She gazed at the crowd. There were more people there than River had expected. She saw a lot of

Riders from the other branches of Herd Magenti, as well as clusters of people and horses—mostly stallions—wearing the colors of other Herds.

River understood why, and she should have expected it. Only members of Herd Magenti could compete for Lead Mare and Rider, but any stud horse over the age of three could compete for Herd Stallion—he and his Rider didn't need to be from Herd Magenti. *Of course there are strangers and their stallions here. They want to see who will win, and whether they join the competition for Herd Stallion and Rider will depend on if they approve of the winner.*

They will approve of us. There will be many stallions competing on the last day of summer, Anjo said, sounding a little snobbish, though it made River smile. Then her mare added, *But Ghost could beat them all—and he should.*

River didn't respond. She agreed with her mare about Ghost. He was growing into an exceptional stallion.

But he didn't have a Rider, and River wasn't convinced allowing him to join the Stallion Run would be the best thing for Herd Magenti—even if the Mare Council agreed to allow her to ride him during the competition.

A flash of gold caught River's eye, and she saw Ghost standing on a little rise behind the bulk of the crowd. He tossed his head and reared.

Ghost sends us a mare's luck, Anjo said.

I'll take all the luck we can get.

The space before them opened to show the starting line. There were twelve teams entered in the Mare Test, and River quickly counted that eleven of them were there already. Some of the mares were prancing restlessly, but they were younger horses. Doe and the older mares waited calmly, with their ears pricked, saving their energy.

Dawn on her Echo had taken position in front of the starting line, facing the contestants. River knew the moment Echo spotted Anjo. The Lead Mare lifted her head, and neighed a welcome.

"Mother can't show favoritism, but Echo definitely can," River said.

Echo shows us great respect by welcoming us, Anjo said.

April touched her sister's leg. "I want you to look at the crowd. Everyone who is wearing an amethyst necklace is doing so in support of you. I would've told you before, but the Herd wanted to surprise you. Be smart. Be safe. And may a mare's luck be with you, Riv."

River squeezed her sister's hand. "Thank you. I love you."

"I love you right back. Now, go win this Test and take the place that is meant to be yours in our Herd."

"Anjo, let's show them that we're worthy of leading Herd Magenti."

Anjo's tail lifted and she trotted forward, picking her hooves up as if she were in the mud trap, arching her neck, and neighing an answering greeting to her Lead Mare. River sat deep in the trail saddle she'd chosen to use for the Test. It was lightweight—really not much more than a blanket pad with a horn and stirrups, with a saddle pack strapped behind it. The pad would make the daylong ride more comfortable for Anjo, and the stirrups would help River keep her seat if she had to ask Anjo to go up and down steep ridges, or over jumps.

As soon as the crowd caught sight of the silver mare prancing to the starting line, a great cheer sounded, startling River with its passion and intensity. Her eyes scanned the crowd of smiling, happy faces, and she was deeply moved by how much amethyst she saw winking at her from around the necks of her Herd.

They support us! Anjo didn't sound as surprised as River felt, but equally pleased.

Then let's show them we appreciate their support! River silently communicated with her mare.

Yes! Let's!

River knew her mare well enough to grip her with her thighs, which was a good thing because Anjo reared, pawing the air cheekily as River waved to the cheering crowd.

Then Anjo pranced into the only open position left and River met her mother's gaze. She knew she would never forget the unspoken emotions that passed between them in that moment. She saw her mother's love—and beyond that River saw her pride and her confidence. And she hoped that her mother could see just as clearly the love and gratitude within River's gaze.

Dawn raised one hand, and the Herd went silent.

"Today, on the last day of spring in this year that Echo and I step down as your Lead Mare-and-Rider team, I am gratified to see such a strong group of Candidates. Twelve teams! With representation from Herd Magenti East." Dawn paused as a cheer went up from Herd East visitors. "And Herd Magenti West." Another cheer. "As well as Herd Magenti South." Clapping and whoops drifted across the prairie. "Herd Magenti North." More clapping. "And our own *Herd Magenti Central!*" The Rendezvous Site exploded in whistles and cheers and applause. But one lifted hand from their Lead Mare Rider, and the exuberant crowd fell into a watching silence again.

"When Echo and I began the Test we ran against five other teams. The fact that there are *twelve* worthy pairs before me illustrates the prosperity and strength of *all* branches of Herd Magenti." The crowd roared their agreement. "I know whoever is named your Lead Mare-and-Rider team at the end of this day will continue to strengthen and grow our Herd, and will lead us into another era of prosperity." Dawn met River's gaze and smiled. "I feel nothing but excitement about our future."

After the crowd quieted, Dawn faced the line of Riders and mares. She had a purple flag in her hand that bore the standard of Herd Magenti, which was a cluster of crystals embroidered so that the threads glistened.

"Your first Test is a race. Bitter Creek is five miles from this spot. Unlike the rest of the course, here each team is free to find their own way to the creek."

River felt the jolt of surprise that went through Anjo. None of the Riders had known where the Test would begin until then, and relief flooded River.

We know the best way to get to Bitter Creek! Anjo communicated silently to her Rider, tossing her head with pleasure.

Good thing you like swimming! River had to work at not cheering and reminded herself to focus through her excitement on her mother's instructions.

"At Bitter Creek you will face your second Test, and from there you must follow the marked course. There will be decisions you must make today—as a team. My advice is to choose with wisdom and compassion—and to choose quickly. Finishing first will not assure your place as Lead Mare and Rider, but the Mare Council will seriously consider it as they tally the points you earn today during this amazing event we call our Mare Test.

"Stationed throughout the course will be members of the Mare Council. Some of them you will see, but many of them you will not. Just know that the Councilmembers will be judging each team.

"Do not forget that it is tradition that there is a two-mile sprint at the end of the course. There will be a black flag marking the beginning of the sprint, and another marking off the first mile. For that first mile it is expected that all Riders dismount and race *beside* their mares. The second black flag you see will mark the beginning of the second mile. You may remount then and race for the finish line, where I will be waiting to greet you.

"Riders, the year I won the Mare Test there was one fatality during the competition, and another mare was permanently lamed. The course is dangerous. Never forget that. Remember, you cannot be Lead Mare and Rider if you do not survive today.

"If you have not crossed the finish line before the sun sinks below the horizon, you will be disqualified from the Test. Are there any questions?"

River wanted to shout, *Yes! What can we expect? Should Anjo and I be conservative in our choices today? Should we be reckless and just get across the finish line first? Help! What should we do?*

We should be ourselves—wise, strong, and bold, came her mare's serene reply. *We are the best team for Herd Magenti. We will win.*

River stroked Anjo's neck. *You're right. We can do this—together.*

"When I drop this flag your Test begins. I wish blessings on each of you from the Great Mother Mare." Dawn's gaze found River again. "And may a mare's luck be with she who is to be our new leader."

Echo spun around so that her back was to the line of contestants. The beautiful mare had known almost twenty winters, but she moved like a filly. Her muscles rippled under her shining coat as she sprinted forward. Her white mane was dressed in purple ribbons that perfectly matched her Rider's—and that also was the same color as the huge amethyst crystal that hung from around Dawn's neck, silently showing support for her beloved daughter. Echo slid to a stop. Dawn raised her hand overhead and the purple flag whipped in the wind. Then, just as the sun broke above the horizon, the Lead Mare Rider dropped the flag—signaling the beginning of the Mare Test.

Anjo surged forward with the other eleven pairs. She and River had already decided how they were going to begin the race—not in the lead, but also not trotting away last. As expected, Alani and her buckskin mare raced to the lead, setting a pace that would be impossible to keep up for more than a quarter of a mile or so, but they had the crowd cheering in appreciation of the mare's speed.

River was surprised to see Luce and Blue keep pace with Alani and Doe, and behind them less than a mare's body length were Skye and Scout.

They waste energy to show off. None of them would be adequate Lead Mares or Riders, Anjo said smugly as she galloped in the middle of the rest of the contestants, lengthening her stride and breathing easily.

After about one mile the teams started to spread out. No matter how well conditioned, some mares would always be faster than others—and it only took the opening sprint to begin to weed out those who did not have speed from those who did.

Alani and Doe were still in the lead, though River had lost sight of them. She also didn't see Luce and Blue, but Skye and Scout had dropped back far enough that they were visible. There was one pair between them and Skye, a strong team from Herd Magenti West, Daisy and her eight-year-old mare, Strawberry, whose red roan coat was unmistakable.

Behind them the rest of the contestants spread out in a loose line. The closest were galloping easily like Anjo, but several of the other teams had dropped down to a canter, and when River glanced behind her she could just see that there were a few teams trotting in the rear.

"I don't blame them for saving their energy," River told Anjo.

They are not as well conditioned as I am, nor as fast, came her mare's arrogant, but true response.

Ahead of them River watched Skye and Scout veer sharply to the left, and then Daisy and Strawberry followed them.

"Straight on," River said.

I know. I like where we are going.

"Sometimes I think you're more fish than horse," River teased.

Anjo snorted. *Do those behind us follow or veer?*

River watched over her shoulder as Anjo continued her ground-eating gallop. "More than half of them veered. Most left, but some right."

Good.

"Left or right, they're going around the lake. That's going to put them behind us. Let's slow to a canter. Save your strength for the swim."

Anjo dropped to a canter and then a swift, but restful trot that ate up the remaining miles, which brought them to one of their favorite summer cooling-off spots, Willow Lake. For the past three summers River and Anjo had been enjoying the deep, spring-fed waters, which remained cool even when the prairie turned brown from unrelenting heat and rainless days.

"Straight across," River said.

Of course. We have no time for play today. Lift the saddlebags or my mash will be ruined.

"Oh, that's right. Thanks for reminding me." River turned and quickly pulled the tie that held the saddlebags and shifted them so that they rested up on Anjo's neck.

As the mare entered the water River kicked out of the stirrups, so that as soon as Anjo began swimming she slipped into the water beside her mare, careful to stay away from her pumping legs and hooves while she held on to her mane, swimming with her and keeping the saddlebags in place above the waterline.

Willow Lake was not huge, probably only a couple miles wide, but it was also not simply a pond—and it was deep. As the team moved out into the middle of the cool water, River spotted another team leaving the lake. Even wet, the grulla's distinctive coloring was impossible to miss.

"I see Luce and Blue in front of us, but not far."

Alani and Doe must be in front of them.

"Unless they chose to go around the lake."

They are too experienced for that—whether Doe likes to swim or not. Though I do not understand why she would not like to swim. It is quite nice.

"Water horse," River said affectionately. "But I agree with you. I like to swim, too."

Almost at the bank. You should mount.

River slid back into the saddle, holding the saddlebags up and dry. As soon as Anjo was on dry land she turned and hastily refastened the bags. "Ready!"

Anjo sped off, taking an easy curve to the right, which led to a steep climb up the side of a ridge. The mare didn't hesitate but attacked the ridge, moving fast, but holding her head low so that she could pick her way around rocks and holes. When they reached the summit they paused for an instant and could see that Luce and Blue had already made their way to the bottom and were approaching Bitter Creek.

River blinked sweat from her eyes so that she could be sure she was seeing correctly—and she was.

"Anjo, we don't get to swim the creek. They've built a bridge over it."

The mare snorted and tossed her head. *I do not like bridges.*

"You don't have to like it. You just have to cross it. Let's get down there. Luce and Blue are almost to it already."

River leaned back, balancing carefully and being sure she wasn't a hindrance to Anjo as the mare sat on her hocks, sliding most of the way down the steep ridge. They galloped abruptly to the right to arrive at the newly built bridge just as Luce was taking her shirt off Blue's head and remounting her mare on the other side. Luce turned her head to glance behind, and her eyes widened at the sight of River and Anjo. She cued her mare and the two sprinted away.

River kneed Anjo to the bridge. The creek wasn't wide—more of a stream really—and except for climbing up and down very steep banks, crossing it would have been nothing for Anjo. But during the past month the Mare Council had been secretly building the Mare Test course, and this bridge was brand-new. It was a suspension bridge, swaying gently in the wind. About the width of a horse, wood planks made the floor of it. The sides were completely open except for a single rope on either side at about the height of Anjo's chest.

Looks like it will fall.

"I can dismount and cover your head with my shirt like Luce did for Blue and lead you across."

Do you think it will fall? asked her mare. Anjo didn't feel frightened to River, just concerned.

"No," she said firmly. "I know it won't. The Mare Council wouldn't build the bridge if it could break and hurt one of us. That's not what this Test is about."

If you trust it—I trust it.

And just like that Anjo stepped out onto the bridge. She took her time crossing it, but the mare didn't falter. She didn't spook. She remained as true and steady as her trust in her Rider.

When they reached the other side River threw her arms around Anjo's neck. "You did great! You're perfect!"

Let us get away from here. I do not like bridges. Especially bridges that move.

"There! I see the purple ribbon on the tree. We need to take the trail to the left."

There is no trail to the left. Only another ridge with trees.

"I think that's the point. Let's go, but not too fast. We have to follow the ribbons because from here until the finish line the Council is taking us through the badlands, and that's not a territory any of us knows."

We will go forward carefully.

Anjo stepped into her ground-eating trot, a pace that was quicker than a walk, but one she could maintain easily without tiring herself—which was good after the exertion of crossing the lake, scaling the ridge, and conquering the suspension bridge.

They trotted on in companionable silence. Anjo kept a steady pace while River navigated, kneeing her mare to follow the marked path that really wasn't a path at all.

The trees thickened into clusterings of cross timber lines, which meant that they had to pass through sections of post oak, willows, and scrub—all choked with underbrush—and then there would be wide expanses of prairie, only to lead into another section of cross timbers. Within the cross timber line the purple ribbons were scarce—only rough markers at the beginning of the tree line, somewhere in the middle, and then again at the end, which meant that each team had to pick their own path through the rugged underbrush.

"Whoa, Anjo. Hold up," River said as they entered the second clump of cross timbers.

The mare stopped instantly, turning her ears to catch all of River's words.

"This section is filled with goathead brambles. They'll slice your legs. You can even get trapped in them. We need to slow down and choose our way carefully. I might need to walk in front of you to be sure none of the bramble vines catch your hooves. That's okay, because we can make up time sprinting between the timber sections."

As if she'd evoked trouble with her words, the squeal of a mare in pain echoed from somewhere in front of them, in the middle of the bramble thicket.

"Can you tell who that is?" River asked her mare.

Blue. She is caught. So is Luce.

"Okay, you stay here. I'm going to help them."

Anjo hesitated before replying, but finally her words rang through River's mind.

It is the right thing to do—the Lead Mare Rider thing to do. Help them, River.

Blue squealed again and River took the knife from her saddlebag, as well as some of the strips of clean cloth bandages she'd packed.

"I'll hurry."

Do what needs to be done. I will wait and watch for who passes us.

River jogged to the beginning of the next bramble thicket and then she slowed, picking her way carefully around clumps of sticky bushes. Goathead thistles were the worst kind of bramble in Wind Rider territory. Each thistle was small and covered with knife-sharp thorns. The goatheads dotted the viny branches of the brambles that whipped out, tentacle-like, with long, reaching arms that were sticky, like spiderwebs. Many of them rested against the ground, waiting to wrap around horse or human, and trap them.

Often packs of yoties, the ravenous little canine-like creatures who ran in huge packs, made their dens near goathead groves so they could feast on prey that became trapped or weakened from blood loss. Yoties were experts on using the natural world to catch prey for them, and as River picked her way through the bramble thicket she kept watch for clusters of small, beady eyes and sharp teeth.

Another shrill scream from the mare drew River to the right and up a little rise. From there she looked down on a pitiful scene.

Blue was on her knees. Long arms of goathead vines had wrapped around the mare's legs, holding her in place just as surely as if the vines had been knife-tipped wire. Bright splashes of scarlet ran down Blue's legs, painting the vines with blood. Luce was just a few yards away from Blue, struggling to disentangle herself from two vines—one wrapped around her arm and the other around her thigh. Blood flowed from both wounds and River could hear Luce speaking to Blue, trying to keep her calm and still.

"Luce! I'm coming! Hang on!" River shouted before she started down the little incline, careful to step over the vine traps that lay all around her.

As River reached her Luce looked ready to collapse with relief. "River! Oh, thank the Great Mother Mare! Blue and I were going too fast. We didn't see the goatheads until it was too late—then they were wrapped around Blue's legs so badly that she fell, throwing me into them. I–I've been trying to get free so that I could reach my saddlebag and my knife, but the goatheads kept cutting my hands and then the scent of so much of my blood spooked Blue, and she started to struggle because she was trying to help me." Luce broke off, crying as she held her mangled hands against her chest, causing blood to spread across her tunic.

"Hey, it's okay. It could've happened to Anjo and me, too. I have my knife. Hold still and I'll have you cut free in a second, and then we can work on Blue." River used her knife to slice two long, thin strips from one of the bandages she'd brought with her. "Let me wrap your hands first."

Luce offered River her hands. They were shaking badly. Blood ran freely from stab wounds in her fingers and palms. "I'm sorry. I know I'm causing you to fall behind."

"Don't be sorry. You'd do the same for me." River gently held Luce's wrists. "You need to calm down so that Blue calms, too."

"I know. I'm trying. I just—I just can't. It hurts so much, and I can feel Blue's pain, too," Luce sobbed.

River touched the center amethyst stone in her grandmother's necklace, feeling it warm instantly. She imagined a purple bubble surrounding her, as well as Luce. "Breathe in—one, two, three, four; and out—one, two, three, four."

"O-okay. I can try." The trembling of Luce's hands quieted as the crystal began to stabilize her.

"You're doing great. Now close your eyes and concentrate on breathing while I wrap your hands and cut you free." The purple crystals were all warm now, spreading that heat across River's chest. She imagined the healing properties of the stone filling Luce. The girl nodded—almost sleepily—closed her eyes, and began breathing in and out to a four count.

River wrapped her hands, and as she did she met the gaze of the agitated mare.

"It's going to be okay, Blue. Look, Luce is fine. You can feel that she's calming—you need to calm, too. That's how you can help her." While she spoke, River coaxed the image of the purple bubble of warmth to encompass the mare, too, and was relieved when Blue stopped struggling and rested on her knees, breathing hard with her muzzle on the ground as her blood pooled around her.

River cut the last of the vines away from Luce and pulled them from her ankle. "Okay, open your eyes."

Luce's eyelids fluttered open. She appeared unfocused and confused for a moment, as if she'd just awakened from a sweet dream—then she sucked in a huge breath and started to bolt to Blue, but River stepped in front of her, blocking her way.

"Hey, we have to be smart about this. Look down."

Luce did, spotting the entrapping vines where they lay against the earth, waiting to wrap around her feet again.

"River, I'm so sorry. I feel stupid."

"Don't. You're in a lot of pain and Blue has lost a lot of blood. Of course you're not yourself. Let's do this together. We'll get her free."

Carefully, River picked her way to the fallen mare as Luce walked in her footprints. When they reached Blue Luce went to her head. Even the mare's muzzle was lacerated and bloody, and Luce pressed her forehead to Blue's, sobbing and saying, "I'm so sorry—I'm so sorry" over and over.

"Luce, keep her still. I'll work around her, cutting these vines and unwrapping them. But she needs to hold still. The more she moves, the worse she's injuring herself."

Luce sniffled, wiping her nose with the back of the bloody bandage wrapped around her hand. "I can do that. Blue, sweet baby, just be still. I'm here. River is here. She's going to cut you free. River can do it—you know she can."

Blue nickered, sounding exhausted but a lot calmer, and River began working her way around the mare. First she'd cut a section of the vines, and then—in one motion—she'd pull it free from the mare's flesh.

"That's a good, brave girl, Blue," River said as she worked. "You're doing great."

"You hear her? You hear our River? She says you're doing great. We'll be just fine. It's okay sweet baby—it's okay . . ."

Luce continued to speak soothingly to her mare as River worked—

and all the while River cut and disentangled the knife-edged thorns from the mare's skin she also communed with her grandmother's stones, calling on them to blanket Luce and Blue in serenity.

Finally, River freed the last strand of the deadly vine from around Blue's rear hock and the mare got shakily to her feet, whinnying softly and nuzzling her Rider.

"There! Do you have any bandages in your saddlebag?" River asked Luce.

"No. I was too arrogant to believe Blue and I would need them, and that makes me feel like a complete fool now."

"That's okay. We can cut the rest of these up and bind the worst of her wounds." River started to put her knife to the remaining bandage strip when Luce's hand on her wrist stopped her.

"No, I can do that. You get back to Anjo and rejoin the Test. I'll finish bandaging Blue, and then we're going to walk slowly back to Bitter Creek and raise my white flag."

"You're quitting?"

Luce nodded. "We are. I realize now that Blue and I are not the best team. Remember what you said earlier? That I would've done this for you?"

River nodded slowly.

"Well, I'm not sure I would have. But I am sure of one thing. You are the right choice for Lead Mare Rider. Blue and I would follow you anywhere. Now get back to Anjo and win the Test. Your Herd needs you as much as Blue and I just did." And then Luce bowed to River, crossing her wrists over her heart in the traditional Herd salute to a Lead Mare and Rider.

River's heartbeat was pounding in her ears, but she returned Luce's salute by bowing her head in respectful acknowledgment of tribute paid by a member of her Herd, just as she'd watched her mother do for a decade.

"Make your way back slowly," River said. "You have a water skin, don't you?"

"We do," Luce said.

"Drink plenty of it, and share it with Blue. If you brought mash, give her some, too. Both of you have lost a lot of blood. Be safe."

"You be safe, too. Be strong—be wise—be fast, and I will see you after you cross the finish line—victorious," Luce said.

River didn't wait any longer. As quickly as possible she retraced her path back to Anjo. As she rejoined her mare, Anjo snorted and tossed her head.

You bleed!

River wiped her bloody hands on her pants. "Most of it isn't mine. Luce and Blue were in a bad way, but they're free now. They're quitting the Test."

Anjo snorted. *Hurry and mount!*

"Not while we're in the cross timbers. I think it'd be faster if I jogged ahead of you." River searched around them and quickly found a long, fallen branch. "I can move the vines out of your path with this. When we get to the clearing between the cross timbers I'll mount and we can sprint." River pointed into the goathead thicket, which looked deceptively like the quickest way through this section of cross timbers. "We're definitely not going that way." River started jogging in front of Anjo, the mare following close behind. "How many teams passed us?"

Many, but we will catch and pass them. We are stronger.

"Did none of them even pause to be sure you or I weren't hurt?"

Willow's Gontia asked me if we were well. I told her yes.

"Well, at least she asked. How many others passed us?"

I saw three other teams—Skye and Scout, Daisy and Strawberry, Keira and Gypsy. I heard at least two other teams pass, but could not see them.

"We have to catch up with them."

Do not fret—we will.

River's plan was a good one, and in the clearings between each of the cross timber patches they caught and passed a team—first Keira and her white mare, Gypsy, and then to River's surprise another team from her own Herd, Cali and her beautiful sorrel mare, Vixen. As she and Anjo sprinted past, River could see that Vixen was favoring a bloody left rear hock—probably another victim of trying to pass through the cross timbers too quickly.

Finally they were through the cross timber obstacle and the purple ribbons marked the trail to the left, which was a deceptively open stretch of prairie—so open that River could see purple ribbons beckoning them forward in the breeze.

"Finally! A chance to run and catch the rest of them!" River leaned in, cuing Anjo to take off, but the mare resisted. River immediately heeded her mare's intuition. "What is it?"

Many-colored grass that should be the same.

River stood in the stirrups, studying the flat prairie before them, and seeing what the mare noticed. The late spring grasses had reached a height of about Anjo's knees, and they should all have been a brilliant bluish-green, but in small clumps the grasses appeared shorter and were already turning summer brown.

"Gopher holes," River said darkly. Where the rodents built their dens into the fertile dirt of the prairie they also disrupted the grasses, dislodging roots and breaking their water supply, which caused them to wilt and discolor.

If I run through them I may break a leg.

"Not if we stick to the green patches," River said. "I'll guide you. You pick how fast we go."

Anjo snorted her agreement and then kicked into a slow lope—a gait that was easy for her to maintain as she changed directions according to River's leg pressure. They loped on and River had just noticed that the sun had gone past its midday zenith and was beginning to travel down the western sky. She cued Anjo to stop, and quickly fed the mare the energy-rich sweet mash packed in the saddlebags as well as herself the apples her sister had reminded her to eat. Not long after their short break Anjo's words echoed in her mind.

Rider and mare ahead—someone is with them.

"You look. I'm going to keep guiding you through these holes."

Anjo cantered past. River wanted to look—to stare—especially after

Anjo said, *It is Daisy and Strawberry—the mare is injured. There is a Councilmember with them.*

But River steeled herself and didn't so much as glance their way as Anjo cantered past.

"She has help. They don't need us," River said. "How badly is Strawberry hurt?"

Badly. They were racing through the holes.

Then Anjo wouldn't say more, and River knew that meant what had happened was too awful for the mare to share. River pushed away her sadness. There would be time for that later—after she and Anjo were safely across the finish line.

The course curved to the right as the land lifted, becoming rougher and rockier. They topped a rise to see a ravine before them. It split the earth like a giant had taken a hatchet to the prairie, slicing into it. To the right it met a thick cross timber line, and River could clearly see thickets of goathead thistles clustered in the underbrush.

To her left the gorge spread probably a mile or so, before it tapered back down to the grassy prairie.

"Is the ravine too steep?" she asked her mare.

I cannot tell from here.

"Okay, let's get down there and check it out."

Anjo galloped down the side of the hillock to where the prairie flattened and then broke open. She stopped at the lip of the ravine, studying it.

There are two teams down there. They attempt the ridge.

"If they can do it I know you can," River said.

But Anjo still didn't attack the ravine as River would have expected. Instead her nostrils flared as she tested the breeze lifting from within the slash in the earth.

I scent yoties.

"Ugh." River grimaced. "A whole pack?"

I scent their dens. That is not the safest way to go.

"Then we take the smart, safe way because you are fast enough to make up time. Let's go!"

Free of the gopher holes and goathead thickets, the powerful mare ran, stretching out her long stride and eating up the distance it took to go around the dangerous ravine.

River spotted the next purple flag, waving from halfway up the side of a rise in the prairie, and guided Anjo toward it as she nudged the mare into a slower gait.

I can run more.

"Save your strength. You're already sweating a lot. The sun is heading down, but I'm guessing we still have about ten miles left to go—and the very end is a race."

I can beat Doe.

"Not if you use up all your strength before we get to the race, you can't."

Anjo snorted, but slowed to a canter. The course curved sharply to the right and down to open up to a large patch of the prairie where the grasses had been shorn close to the ground. Throughout the area were obstacles situated in a circle, and a Councilmember was seated atop a gray-muzzled mare in the center. Leaving from the far end of the circle were Skye and Scout—and beyond them River could see a flash of buckskin amidst the dust Doe kicked up as she galloped away.

They are all that are still ahead of us.

"Then let's nail this course and catch them. You can outrun both of those mares."

Can you outrun Alani and Skye?

"Skye for sure. And Alani is a decade older; I can outrun her, too."

"Next team!" the Councilmember shouted.

Anjo galloped to the opening to the circular course. River looked at the old woman, waiting for her cue to begin.

"You are being judged on speed and confidence," the judge said. "Points will be deducted if you do not successfully complete an obstacle. When you step within the circle your time begins."

"Anjo, I see a water jump and a set of log jumps—not tall but close together. You'll have to pace yourself through them."

What is that wooden thing?

River followed her mare's gaze and saw a long, wide plank. One end of it was touching the ground. The other was lifted into the air—and there was a round log resting beneath it.

"You have to walk over it. Looks like the plank will move down after you get halfway."

I do not like it.

"It can't hurt you. No more than those branches hanging from those poles can."

Do we jump the deep ditch or go into it and climb out of it?

"I'm pretty sure they want us to do it the most difficult way, which would not be jumping it." River snorted, sounding like Anjo. "Do they really think you're going to balk at that patch of muddy water over there?"

I will not, but many mares would not walk into it. Could be snakes.

"Not on this course there won't be. Trust me."

Always.

"Then let's do this, and do it fast and clean."

Anjo's answer was to sprint into the obstacle course. The jumps were first—and she sailed over them easily, even the double log jump that was uncomfortably close together. Then she went over the tottering plank with her head lowered as she watched her footing. Without pausing River guided Anjo down into a deep, narrow ditch, and then up the backside of it. She balked at nothing—not even the muddy puddles or skeletal hanging branches meant to spook her. She picked her way through a series of logs that had been arranged against larger logs so that they were partially off the ground, partially grounded, in a crisscross pattern, making it impossible to jump them. The final obstacle was a jump that had a water-filled ditch on the far side of it. Anjo sailed over both easily.

At the end of the course River glanced back at the Councilmember, who nodded and signaled that she'd completed everything.

"Okay, let's catch those other two teams!" Anjo sprinted away.

The land kept lifting up and up, and Anjo attacked the ground, digging in and using her well-conditioned muscles to carry them forward with speed even Ghost would have envied.

They reached the top of the hill and looked down.

"I can see the finish flags!" River's voice trembled with excitement. "There, in the distance! I can just make them out." And then she glanced down to see the final obstacles before the sprint. The backside of the hill wasn't dangerously steep, but it was covered with rocks—large and small—which made it deadly if a horse attempted to run down it.

And there, halfway to the bottom, were Skye and Scout. Farther ahead, though not much, were Alani and Doe, but Alani had dismounted and was checking her mare's hoof.

Hold on. I'm going down this slope. Fast.

"Not *too* fast. Those rocks will bruise your hooves—they can even make you lame."

You know I am good at this. We have practiced.

River did as her mare said—she held on. Anjo was right. This was one of the obstacles they had prepared for, and it was also something her mare strangely enjoyed. Anjo liked picking her way down a rocky ridge. She'd told River once that it helped keep her mind sharp.

The mare attacked the rocky decline, moving nimbly around boulders, stepping lightly and carefully, and keeping her head low so that she could see her path. River had been concentrating so hard on the rocks that she didn't even notice that she and Anjo had pulled up beside Skye and Scout until the dapple gray mare squealed and kicked at Anjo.

Quick as a snake, Anjo struck out, biting Scout on her rump and causing the other mare to jump sideways and grunt in pain.

"Hey, get her off Scout!" Skye shouted.

"You know better than that," River said as she and Anjo passed the slower team. "A Lead Mare always disciplines the Herd—and Scout just got disciplined!"

They beat Skye and Scout to the bottom of the rocky ridge as Alani remounted Doe and galloped toward the final obstacle. A hundred yards or so from the bottom of the ridge the land opened again. This time it was a true gorge, with sides too impossibly steep to scale up *or* down.

"We have to jump the gorge," River said, suddenly feeling her heart lodge in her throat. "They've marked three crossing places." River used her hand to shade her eyes against the glare of the setting sun. "The closest is also the widest. Then a few hundred yards that way they've marked another, narrower crossing." River pointed to the left, where the gorge wrapped around, taking an opposite turn from the direction of the finish line. "And even farther that way I can see a third crossing. Look there—Alani is guiding Doe to the left. She's not going to attempt the widest jump."

I can make the widest jump.

River didn't question her mare. She felt Anjo's confidence and she trusted her completely.

"Then let's jump over it and beat Alani and Doe to the finish line!"

Anjo kicked into a canter and then lengthened her stride to a gallop. River leaned forward, gripping Anjo's sweaty sides and holding tightly to her mane as she readied herself to throw her heart over the gorge along with her mare.

They were just yards from the jump when Skye and Scout blew past them at a flat run, heading directly for the widest crossing point.

River knew what was going to happen before Scout balked. She saw the signs. Scout wasn't gathering herself. Her ears weren't pricked at the jump. And the mare looked spent, with white flecks of sweaty foam spraying from her shoulders and flanks. At the last moment Scout refused the jump, planting her hooves and digging into the earth.

With a sick stomach, River watched Skye fly over Scout's head and tumble over the edge of the gorge.

"Whoa! Whoa! Anjo!"

Anjo slid to a stop just feet from the yawning slash in the earth. River was off her back in an instant, sprinting to the edge.

"Skye!" River shouted as she ran.

Scout had been standing near the edge, legs splayed and head down, breathing in great gasps, but as River called for Skye the mare came back to herself. She lifted her head and, with the whites of her eyes showing, began neighing hysterically for her Rider.

River ran past the agitated mare, sliding to her stomach so she could peer over the lip of the gorge.

Skye was there! About five feet from the edge she'd managed to tangle her arms in a clump of vines and dig her toes into a small ledge. River could see that one of her arms was sticking out at an odd angle.

"Skye!"

She looked up—her eyes wide with terror. "River! Thank the Mare! Help me! My shoulder is dislocated and I'm barely hanging on!"

"Don't move! I'll get rope from my saddlebag."

But before River could scramble backwards and race for Anjo, Scout panicked. The mare ran to the edge of the gorge, whinnying pathetically.

River was turning to look up at Scout—to try to calm her—when the mare finally caught sight of her Rider and lunged to the side, stomping on River's right foot.

River screamed in agony and rolled to the side to avoid the mare's dangerous hooves.

"Scout! It's okay! I'm right here!" Skye tried to reassure Scout, but the mare was fully hysterical.

And then Anjo was there—standing between Scout and River. Anjo herded the agitated mare backwards, all the while nickering softly to her.

River got to her feet and limped over to Anjo. "Keep Scout back." She opened a saddlebag and pulled out her rope. "I'm going to drop this down to Skye and then we'll pull her up."

Your foot! You are in a lot of pain!

"I know, but Skye can't hold on much longer. Anjo, she can't survive that fall."

Save her. I will keep Scout as calm as possible.

Gritting her teeth against the pain, River hobbled back to the edge of the gorge. She shook out the loop in the hemp lasso and dropped to her belly again.

"Skye, you're going to have to put this rope around you, and then Anjo and I will pull you up."

Skye looked at her. Tears were streaming down her dirty, bruised cheeks. "I—I don't think I can. Only one of my arms works. If I let go I'm going to fall."

Thinking quickly, River said. "Okay, here's what you do—step into the loop. One foot at a time. Then shimmy it up around your waist. Can you do that?"

"I'll try."

"Good." River ignored the pulsing heat in her ankle, and spoke calm encouragement to Skye. "That's it. You've got it over one foot. You're doing great."

A gentle whinny came from beside River and Skye looked up, her eyes welling with tears again. "Scout! Oh honey! I'm so, so sorry I didn't listen to you when you said you were afraid to make the jump."

Anjo stepped between Scout and River, making sure the distressed mare didn't stomp on her Rider again.

Scout is better when she can see Skye. I will keep you safe from her hooves.

"Okay, it's around my waist," Skye said.

"Hang on. Just a few minutes more and we'll have you out of there." River managed to stand again, though she had to hop around, holding her injured foot off the ground. "Anjo, I'm going to wrap this rope around your butt. I'll anchor the end, and when I say go, start backing up—slowly."

River limped to Anjo, positioning the rope around her mare's hind end, then she moved to the side of the mare, finding a chair-sized rock. She wrapped the end of the rope low around the rock as an anchor.

"Okay, back, Anjo—back!"

Slowly the powerful mare dug her hooves in and backed, little by little pulling Skye up over the lip of the gorge, where she collapsed, sobbing in pain. Scout was there, nuzzling her Rider and nickering incessantly.

River hopped over to her, meaning to help her unwrap the rope from her waist and then tie her arm into a sling, but Skye had other plans. She looked up at River, and wiped tears and snot from her filthy face.

"Go! You saved me. One of the judges will get to me soon enough. Look—there's one."

River followed Skye's pointing finger to see that one of the judges was picking her way down the rocky slope, heading for them.

"Now go! Catch Alani and Doe; you still have time if Anjo can jump the gorge here—and I think she can. You *are* our Lead Mare Rider—*go claim your destiny!*"

River didn't hesitate. Anjo dropped to her knees and River threw herself on her mare's back. Once astride she gazed across the wide gorge. Skye was right. Alani and Doe had lost time choosing the narrower crossing and they were only just then returning to the path that led to the final sprint to the finish line.

River didn't need to ask Anjo if she could jump the gorge. That decision had already been made—not by River and arrogance, but by the mare herself. And River had complete confidence in Anjo.

Anjo whirled around and cantered back several yards. She paused there while River bent to put her injured foot in the stirrup. She gripped her mare with her thighs, grabbed two handfuls of mane, and leaned forward.

"I'm ready whenever you are!"

Then let us fly!

Anjo surged forward, heading toward the gorge in a fast, but controlled gallop. As the mare approached the jump, River could feel her powerful muscles gathering. Anjo's ears were pricked forward and she showed absolutely no hesitation.

Anjo leaped! River lifted up from the saddle, staying low against Anjo's neck and holding tightly to her mane. It seemed time suspended, because River was able to clearly see Skye waving at her and cheering as the open maw of the gorge passed beneath them. And then they were on the other side!

"Go! Go! Go! My brilliant, strong, beautiful girl!"

Anjo shot forward, eating up ground between them and the only other team in front of them.

Alani and Doe reached the black flag first. Alani was off Doe before the mare came to a stop, and began running at her side.

River steeled herself. Her foot was throbbing in time with her heartbeat, but she wasn't going to let that get in the way of destiny.

They reached the black flag. Anjo slid to a halt and River gingerly dismounted, unable to put any weight on the foot.

You cannot run!

"I can and I will. I have an idea." Moving quickly, River cut several long strips from the bottom of her shirt. Then she sat so that she could wrap them firmly around her broken ankle. Blood was oozing from inside her leather shoe, but River ignored it, and gritting her teeth against the pain she tied the bandage as tight as possible. Then she limped to Anjo's shoulder, putting her arm around her mare's neck. "Okay, let's go."

But you cannot run! Anjo was sniffing River's wrapped foot. *You bleed!*

"We're almost done. And, no, I can't run by myself, but I can if you help me. I'm going to lean on you. If you trot I'll keep up."

I will always help you.

The two started out onto the flat, two-mile course. Anjo trotted and River, holding tightly to her mare's neck, hobbled beside her. She tried not to keep staring at the backs of Alani and Doe as their lead lengthened.

I will catch them. Do not worry. Think only of your foot.

And that's what River did. She stopped looking ahead. She went inside herself, focusing on keeping pace with Anjo—and on the strength and stability her mare was sharing with her—lending her support and love—so, so much love.

I see the second black flag. We are almost there.

River didn't realize she was crying until she had to wipe her face to clear her vision. Her right leg was nothing but pain, and she couldn't even touch her foot to the ground, but within just a few strides Anjo had stopped and dropped to her knees. With the last of her strength, River threw her leg over Anjo. The instant she was astride, Anjo stood.

"Catch them, Anjo!"

The powerful mare needed no more encouragement. For the first time that day she was able to truly run. River leaned forward, staying close to Anjo's neck and balancing perfectly so that her mare would need only to concentrate on speed.

Anjo flew over the prairie. This time the tears that flowed from River's eyes were from the whipping of the wind. She'd run Anjo before, but the mare had never shown this kind of speed. As River peered ahead she could see the distance between them and the other team disappearing so that as they pounded toward the finish line and the roar of the watching Herd engulfed them, Anjo's muzzle was at Doe's flank.

Four more strides and Anjo's muzzle was at her competitor's shoulder.

Just a few more strides—that's all it would take and Anjo would pass Doe—but suddenly River saw her mother. Dawn was sitting tall and proud on Echo, with a huge purple flag raised over her head, and as they raced past her, Dawn threw down the flag, signaling that they'd reached the finish line—less than half a length behind Doe.

After that there was chaos. April was there, catching River as she began to fall out of the saddle—the pain in her ankle and foot finally having gone beyond bearable.

Anjo snorted and nuzzled River and she rested against her mare's side. Unlike Scout, Anjo didn't dissolve into panic or hysteria. Instead she flooded her Rider with comfort.

"Great Mother Mare, you look terrible! Where are you hurt?" April was running her hands over River, trying to find her wound.

"I'm fine. Gotta cool Anjo off."

River! The Herd will help me. The Healers must see to you.

River blinked sweat and tears from her eyes, just then noticing that she and Anjo were surrounded by familiar faces—Herd members, all wearing amethyst around their necks.

"Riv, let us help you," April said.

River nodded wearily. "It's my right foot. It's crushed. And I think my ankle is broken."

"I've got her," said a deep male voice.

River looked up to see Jasper, the Rider of the current Herd Stallion and father of Violet, River's youngest sister, standing in front of her. He was a little younger than her mother, with just a touch of gray beginning at his temples—and he was known for his kindness. His stallion, Blaze, the biggest bay stud in the Herd, was standing a little way off, obviously wanting to get closer to his Rider, but Ghost had planted himself firmly between the stallion and Anjo.

"If you allow, I'll carry you to the tent the Healers have set up not far from here."

"Can I see the finish line from there?" River asked.

"Absolutely."

"Then okay."

As if she weighed nothing, Jasper lifted her gently. She heard Ghost snort, and spoke quickly to her mare. "Anjo, tell Ghost to behave. Jasper is helping me."

Ghost is very worried.

"Hey, Anjo, everything is going to be okay," April said, stroking her sister's mare soothingly. "You and Ghost can come with me. I'll take your tack off, get you some water, wipe you down, and then you can come right back and be with River."

Slowly, Anjo let April lead her away as Jasper carried River to the Healers' tent, which was just beyond the finish line. From there she watched her mother drop the flag for two more teams—Cybill and Xanthos from their own branch of Herd Magenti, and then Magenti West's team of Lynette and her black mare Morgan.

As soon as they crossed the finish line, Echo galloped to the Healers' tent.

"River!" Dawn slid off her mare and rushed to her daughter.

"Mother, I'm okay. And I'm so, so sorry."

Dawn took her daughter's hand, grimacing as she gazed down at River's bloody foot. "Can you save it?" she asked the Healer.

River's stomach tensed as she waited for the Healer's response.

"It's not as bad as it could have been. Her ankle is broken, but the foot itself is mostly bruised and lacerated. Looks like a horse stomped it."

The Healer and Lead Mare Rider stared at River.

"Oh, no! Anjo didn't do that. Scout did. But not on purpose. She was in a panic." She gripped her mother's hand. "I'm so sorry, Mother," she repeated.

"My darling, I have no idea why you keep apologizing, but I must return to the finish line." She kissed River's sweaty forehead and gently touched her cheek. "I am proud of you and Anjo. Whatever happened out there, I know you did your best."

River bit her lip and nodded as her mother hurried back to the finish line, flagging in three more teams before the ancient Rider who was leader of the Mare Council made the announcement.

"The final team has crossed the finish line. All others have raised their white flags. The order of finish is thus: Alani and Doe in first. River and Anjo—second. Cybill and Xanthos—third. Lynette and Morgan—fourth. Willow and Gontia—fifth. Gillian and Gem—sixth."

The crowd spoke in hushed voices, wondering if any of the six missing teams had had fatal accidents, but they silenced the moment Dawn raised her hand.

"Now, following Herd tradition and law, the Mare Council will retreat to the tallying tent to confer," Dawn said. "And when they emerge it will be with the name of the victor of our Mare Test."

The Council disappeared into their tent and the Herd settled in to wait.

"Okay, I've splinted your ankle and cleaned your foot, but you're going to have to stay off of it for at least six weeks. And drink this. It'll help with the pain."

River brushed away the mug of tea that was heavily laced with something pungent that would definitely put her to sleep.

"Thanks. I'll be careful with my foot, but I can't drink the tea. Not yet." She didn't add, *because there is still a small chance I might be named the winner and then I'll have to awaken a crystal—which I can't do if I'm asleep,* but the Healer understood. She patted River's knee.

"I'll have the tea sent to your tent. Drink it tonight. The pain in your ankle must be terrible." She paused and then asked, "Did you really run a mile on it?"

"Yeah, but Anjo helped me." It was then that Anjo reappeared, snorting at the Healer and then nickering softly and nuzzling River.

"See, I told you I'd be fine. But you're going to have to carry me around for the next six weeks."

Always. I will always carry you.

"I know, my sweet, strong, wise girl. I know." River kissed her mare's nose.

"Well, she can start carrying you now. I have a place all ready for you," April said.

River smiled at her sister. "Thank you for cooling off Anjo. She looks great."

"A lot better than you. Hang on a second. Let me try to fix you." April dunked a clean bandage in a tub of fresh water and set about cleaning her sister's face. "How did you get all bruised? And what did you do to your hands?"

"It's a long story. And quit fussing. All the teams are going to look rough."

"Uh, yes. But not half dead. Hold still. I'm going to rebraid your hair. When they call your name you can't look so crazy that you frighten the Herd."

River snorted. "They already called my name. Anjo and I finished second."

"You know that means nothing until the Council stitches a name on a ribbon and hands it to Mother—and even then that Rider has to awaken a crystal," April said as she quickly braided River's long, dark hair.

"Alani's ten years older than me. I'm positive she can awaken a crystal," River said softly, staring down at her lap.

April tugged on her sister's newly plaited braid. "Hey, that won't matter if they call your name instead—and Alani is *twelve* years older than you. It took two Rendezvous until Doe came along and Chose her."

"That doesn't make me feel any better."

"Well, let's go out and wait for the Council. I'll bet your Herd will make you feel better."

Anjo knelt for River and April gently helped her sister mount. Then they made their way to a bench and table that April's filly and Ghost were standing beside.

"Thank you, clever girl. Good job keeping the table for us." April rubbed her filly's broad forehead.

Ghost says he is the reason no one took the table.

"Well, don't tell Deinos that," River whispered to her mare as she gingerly slid from her back. Then April supported her while she hobbled painfully to take a seat at the bench.

"What can I get you? I'll bet you're really thirsty," April said.

River had opened her mouth to say yes—and hungry, too—when the people started coming.

First came Cali. Her mare, Vixen, was not with her, and the young Rider looked pale. She placed a big wooden cup full of fresh spring water before River.

"I heard what happened out there. Luce told me. And I thought you might like some water," she said shyly.

"Thank you, that's nice of you, Cali. How is Vixen? I thought I saw that she'd injured one of her hocks."

"Yes, her hock is wounded. We had to raise the white flag, but she's resting in our tent."

"She'll be fine?" River asked.

"Yes. So will Luce and Blue—thanks to you." Cali bowed her head respectfully to River and added, "Do you mind if I wait here with you?"

"I don't mind at all," River said.

"Hey, what's this about Luce and Blue? I haven't heard anything—been too busy watching the finish line," April said.

"They got caught up in some goatheads. Anjo and I were there, so I helped."

"You did a lot more than that."

River looked up in surprise to see that Luce had joined their table. One of the Rider's arms was bandaged, as well as her thigh and both of her hands, but she was carrying a tray filled with spring berries.

"Luce! Put that tray down—that has to hurt your hands," River said. "How's Blue?"

"Because of you, she's going to recover. The Healer said had Blue struggled any more she would have sliced open a vein and bled out. You saved my mare's life—and mine as well, as I couldn't live without her."

"Oh, hey, anyone would have—"

"No! That is absolutely *not* true. Other riders passed us. You were the only one who stopped. Thank you. For what you did today you will forever have my loyalty."

River was so taken aback by Luce's words that she could only stutter, "Th-thank you."

"May I wait with you?" Luce asked.

"Sure!" River said.

Cali and Luce were only the beginning. As the evening stretched toward dusk, other Herd members paid tribute to River. Some just stopped for a quick word of congratulations, but many brought offerings—special tidbits of food, mulled wine—and as the wind increased, cooling the prairie, blankets were wrapped around her shoulders and pillows were put under her injured foot.

Anjo, too, was treated with care and respect. Sweet spring carrots—her favorite treat—were piled before her until the mare couldn't eat another.

Absent from the respectful tribute being paid to Anjo and River were Clayton and the group of young men who seemed to follow him everywhere. When River looked around for him she saw him sitting beside Alani, laughing at something the mare Rider had just said.

"Don't let him bother you," April whispered.

"Oh, he doesn't. He's only doing what comes natural to him—pandering to the Rider he thinks will benefit him the most."

"He needs to do a lot better if he thinks you'll ever be his friend again," April said.

"I'm pretty sure he's not interested in my friendship."

"His loss," April said, and turned her back on Clayton.

River and April were deep into a discussion about how Anjo crossed the suspension bridge when Skye's voice interrupted.

"River? How is your foot?"

"It'll be fine—and it's mostly my ankle." River nodded at Skye's arm, which was in a sling. "How's your shoulder."

"Sore, but it'll be well a lot faster than your ankle."

Beside Skye, Scout moved forward and reached her neck long so that she could nuzzle River.

"Scout says she's really sorry she hurt you." Skye spoke softly, obviously on the verge of tears.

River caressed the mare's nose, rubbing her forehead affectionately. "Oh, Scout, I know you didn't do it on purpose."

"Thank you, River. If you hadn't helped me I'm pretty sure I would have died, and Scout was so panicked she would have gone over the edge after me. Daisy's Strawberry died today. She broke her leg so badly in a gopher hole that she had to be sent to the Mother Mare. Daisy is missing—they believe she threw herself into the gorge. Th-that would have been Scout and me if you hadn't—" Skye had to stop and bite her lip to keep from sobbing.

"Oh, no! May the Great Mother Mare welcome Daisy and Strawberry joyously." River closed her eyes and prayed. When she opened them again tears were running freely down Skye's face. "Hey, you didn't die. Scout is well. Everything's okay." She and Skye hadn't been close since they were children, but she hated the guilt and despair she saw in the girl's eyes. "It isn't your fault I stopped. It was my choice, and I'd make the same choice again—I'd just be more careful with my feet," River added with a smile.

Skye returned River's smile. "May Scout and I wait with you?"

"Sure, if you can find room," River said.

The large crowd that surrounded River had begun to shift to make room for Skye and Scout when a rustle of excitement skittered through the Herd.

"Dawn and Echo come!"

"She holds the ribbon!"

"The Council has chosen!"

River clutched April's hand.

"Oh, Great Mother Mare—this is it," April said. She turned to face her sister. "I want you to know that no matter what name Mother reads, today you and Anjo acted like a Lead Mare-and-Rider team."

River couldn't speak. She could only nod and hold tight to her sister.

"The seven teams who finished the Mare Test—come forth!" Dawn called in a clear, calm voice.

Quickly, April helped her sister stand. Anjo knelt and River mounted. They joined the other six teams who faced Dawn on her Echo. River could see the wide purple ribbon folded in her mother's hand.

"I have in my hand the name of the team the Mare Council has chosen to be Lead Mare and Rider, but before I read it Morgana would like to speak."

River felt a jolt of surprise. Morgana was the leader of the Mare Council, and the oldest person she'd ever known—though she didn't know her well. Her mare, Ramoth, used to be a bright red sorrel, but now her coat was flecked with white. Herd lore had it that Ramoth was over sixty years old, but no one really knew for sure, and Morgana refused to say.

The old woman rode her mare with dignity, though. And though Ramoth was stiff with age, she carried her Rider with pride, holding her head high. They took their place beside Dawn and Echo, and then turned to face the curious Herd.

"Today one team has shown what it is to be a true leader—to put compassion over competition and selflessness over selfishness. Today one Rider stopped to rescue not one, but two teams. Both would surely have perished without her aid, and that would have been a terrible loss."

River listened—confused at first. *Someone else saved two teams? Was it Alani and Doe?*

She speaks of us. Anjo's voice was rich with satisfaction. *And she should. We did well today.*

River was about to say *But we didn't win* when Morgana nodded to her mother. Dawn raised her hand and let the ribbon unfurl as her voice, filled with joy and pride, rang through the Herd.

"The winner of the Mare Test is River and Anjo!"

The Herd erupted into uproarious cheers. River felt her body go hot and then icy cold as Anjo pranced forward. Eyes shining with happy tears, Dawn presented the purple ribbon to her daughter. Incredulous, River looked down at the letters that spelled out first her name, and then Anjo's.

"You have one more Test to pass, my darling girl," Dawn said. "But I believe in you and know you will have no problem doing so."

Then she moved aside so that Morgana could approach her.

"River, are you prepared to prove you are a Crystal Seer, and worthy to lead Herd Magenti?"

"I am." River was shocked that her voice didn't shake, as she had to ball her hands in Anjo's mane to keep them from trembling.

"Do you have the crystal you wish to awaken?"

For a moment River felt a terrible sense of panic. *How could I have forgotten the crystal?*

Anjo's strong voice steadied her. *You did not forget. You have the perfect crystal around your neck.*

"Yes!" River said quickly. "Yes, I do have my crystal."

Behind the old woman and her ancient mare the other eleven members of the Mare Council trotted up, forming a circle around River and Anjo.

"And what crystal will you awaken?" Morgana asked.

River reached up and touched the center stone in her grandmother's necklace. "Amethyst."

Morgana nodded her head in approval. "Then you must simply awaken your crystal so that the Council feels the properties of amethyst. Whenever you are ready, mare Rider, you may begin."

River closed her eyes, and her hand fisted around the crystal that rested a little above her heart.

Amethyst is a stone with many properties. It can balance the mind, the emotions, and the bodies of people in need. It clears auras and bestows stability, strength, and great peace. It helps in meditation and focus and can even enhance cooperation and unity. But one of its greatest properties is the ability to bring a great sense of contentment if wielded by a powerful Seer.

Show them how powerful you are. Show all of them, Anjo said.

Smiling at the trust and belief that filled her mare's words, River drew a deep breath and called the stone to awaken. It instantly heated. She cupped both hands around it as she concentrated, finding her way into the crystal, and then with a powerful mental *push* River flung her arms wide, imagining that she was washing her Herd in that unique, spectacular contentment her grandmother's stone possessed.

River heard the Council gasp—and that sound was followed by the susurrus of the Herd, as contentment filled not only the twelve members of the Mare Council, but *every member of Herd Magenti.*

You did it! We did it! Anjo's happiness filled River's mind, and she opened her eyes to see every member of the Council of Mares smiling at her.

"Herd Magenti Central—behold your new Lead Mare and Rider, River and her Anjo!"

And while dusk settled over the Plains of the Wind Riders, a great cheer went up from the Herd as they greeted their new leader. Tears of joy blinded River, so that she didn't see Clayton and several of his friends leave the celebration—as did Skye, hanging her head in shame as she backed slowly away from the group of merrymakers to follow after Clayton.

CHAPTER 20

As dusk settled over the Umbria River, Death consumed the first Saleesh village. It took them five full days to reach the Bonn Dam, and in that time they lost one of the Tribe's repaired boats and three rafts—though the God didn't appear upset at all about the loss. Not of human and canine life, nor of the boats. Instead He mysteriously kept saying that there would be plenty to take the place of those lost.

And that wasn't all that was mysterious about Death's behavior since they'd entered the Umbria River. The God had taken to sitting on the driftwood throne that had been moved to His raft, ordering His Attendants to leave Him be, and then speaking to the empty air around Him as if it were filled with people.

Ralina observed these bizarre one-sided conversations many times. Death spoke softly, assuring invisible hordes that He was coming and that He would set them free. Ralina hadn't asked Him to whom He was speaking or what He was saying. There was something about Death's tone, which was almost fatherly, that sent chills of trepidation over her skin. She suspected the God's answer would be life-altering and, most likely, terrifying—and after His immolation of the Tribe Ralina wasn't sure she could survive many more terrors, or at least survive them with her mind intact.

There was something about the Umbria River that made her blood feel cold and her heart empty, as if despair fell like spring rain over the entire area. At night she was glad that she had to pretend Renard was her lover. The God watched them, often—not so much with an eye looking for subterfuge, but more in a disturbing camaraderie, as her taking a young lover was a sign of strength to the God. And though she and Renard were not lovers, the time they spent together was pleasant, because they were definitely allies against Death, and slowly becoming friends as well.

The day had been clear and warm, and the setting sun washed the darkening sky in orange and pink and yellow when they docked their flotilla at a well-tended beach filled with beautiful boats of different sizes and shapes just before the ruins of the dam turned the Umbria into a white-water nightmare.

"Storyteller!" Death roared from His raft.

"My Lord, I am here," Ralina said as Renard and Daniel paddled their little boat beside the God's spacious raft.

"Ah, excellent. Storyteller, I would that you remain close beside me, as what will happen here will be an important chapter in my tale, but I also would not have you injured."

His words made Ralina feel ill with foreboding. "Are you expecting that the Saleesh will attack us, my Lord?"

"They might *try,*" came Thaddeus's snide response. He'd joined Death on His raft earlier that evening. The two of them had been speaking for hours, but Ralina had not been invited to listen and record their conversation, which was as disturbing as it was odd.

"Yes, and in their trying I do not want my Storyteller injured," Death said. "Thaddeus, I had thought to allow you to lead my Reapers into the village, but perhaps I will task Iron Fist with that job and instead you will remain by the Storyteller's side so that I can be sure she will come through the day unharmed."

"I will do as you command, my Lord." Thaddeus spoke the words and bowed subserviently, but the look he shot Ralina was venomous.

Ralina's heart was pounding so hard she was amazed the God didn't hear it. And then Renard spoke up.

"My Lord, I ask that you grant me that honor. Kong and I would die protecting Ralina, and I am sure Thaddeus would serve you better at the head of the Warriors." The young Warrior bowed deeply to Death. On his ballast, Kong did the same.

"Your lover has an excellent idea. Who better to protect you, Story-teller? I accept your offer, but know, young Renard, if my Ralina is injured today I will repay you tenfold," Death said darkly.

Renard bowed lower. "I understand, my Lord."

"Good!" Death clapped His hands happily. "And now let us go to shore. Thaddeus, as we discussed, you will lead the way. Warriors—stay close to him. My original Reapers—remain beside me and Iron Fist. The rest of you run the boats aground near this fascinating group of crafts that are already beached, and remain in the shadows until you are needed."

Then Death's oarsmen, along with the rest of the flotilla, beached their army of boats as several half-naked, tattooed men jogged down a steep path toward them. The men looked confused and surprised, but they were not armed.

Thaddeus strode to meet them, his Warriors spreading out behind him with their canines. Farther behind, Death waited in the shadows, His massive body was swathed in a cloak, and a large hood was pulled up and draped over His antlers. Ralina and Bear, along with Renard and his Kong, were in position not far behind the God, surrounded by His elite Reapers—who also were covered in cloaks and shadows.

"We did not expect travelers today," said a young man, nodding a greeting to Thaddeus. "I called for our leader, who shall be here momentarily to speak with you."

Thaddeus nodded in return. Ralina saw him smile, and her stomach tightened. Thaddeus only smiled when something horrible was going to happen.

They waited in silence while the Saleesh looked more and more uncomfortable. Soon a tall, thin figure hurried down the same path as the others had come by. His hair was long and dark, an unusual mixture of gray and dark blue running through it. He was wearing a long robe with large belled sleeves. Behind him Ralina counted a dozen or more men following him. They were younger and they carried lances barbed so that they looked like big fishhooks. The old priest stopped in front of Thaddeus and bowed his head slightly in greeting.

"I am Father John, priest and leader of this Saleesh village. May peace be with you." The priest paused, as if expecting a response from Thaddeus.

"I am Thaddeus, and I speak for the leader of the People. We require river passage."

The priest frowned, and Ralina could see that he was staring at the Shepherds who stood beside their Companions. "I must ask—are you allied with a group called the Pack? Their leaders are two young females who call themselves Moon Women."

Thaddeus's lip curled. "We know one Moon Woman. We are enemies of her people. Why do you ask?"

"They passed this way more than two weeks ago. They were uncommonly rude."

Thaddeus's laugh was humorless. "That bitch is always rude."

Father John's eyes narrowed. "Where is your Lynx guide?"

"We have none. We were hoping to hire one of your people to guide us the rest of the way to Lost Lake, and then across the lake to the base of the Rock Mountains."

Father John's smile was patronizing. "Oh, no. My people are not guides for hire, and they never leave our river. And, I mean no disrespect, but without a guide you will never make it past the ruins between our villages. Even if by some miracle you did, it would be suicide for you to attempt a Lost Lake crossing without someone who has experience leading people through there."

"And yet we *are* going to continue our trip. So, what will it cost to hire one of your people?"

"I am sorry, but you do not seem to understand. My people are not for hire. They do not leave their river or their homes. Ever. Now, we will grant you passage through our villages *after* you leave an appropriate offering—but we cannot move your boats tonight." The priest paused to give a disdainful look at their ragtag group of patched boats and hastily constructed rafts. "It is simply too late. There is a camp within easy walking distance that should suit you for tonight. In the morning, perhaps you will decide to call a Lynx guide. If so, we will allow you to remain at the camp for the days it will take for him to answer."

"So, let me be sure I understand perfectly," Thaddeus said. "You will not agree to let us hire one of your people. You will not allow us passage tonight. And you expect us to *pay you something*?"

Ralina's body went cold at the syrupy sweetness of his voice. By the priest's lack of alarm she knew that no Lynx guide had reached the village yet to warn the Saleesh about a group traveling without a guide. She took Renard's hand, squeezing it so that he looked at her. She mouthed: *Be ready—something bad is going to happen.*

The priest chuckled. "No, you misunderstand. We never hire out our people—it simply is not done. We are not refusing to give you passage tonight. We cannot, because the sun has set and the ruins of the dam are too dangerous, even for us, to cross in the dark. And we would never ask you to *pay* us for passage. We do require an offering for our Goddess, the Mother. So, if you will call forth your leader and have him follow me through our village, you may place your offering on the altar at the feet of the Mother, and then I will have you guided to the campsite where you can await your boats tomorrow and, should you decide, call for a Lynx guide."

Death moved forward then. In one motion He pulled off His concealing cloak. The priest stumbled back and had to be kept upright by the younger men standing behind him.

"There are several problems with your list of requirements." Death spoke in a voice that filled the beach. "Foremost is the fact that my people do not make offerings to *any* God but me."

Father John's dark eyes were huge with shock as he took in Death's mutated form. "I–I do not understand. Who are you?"

"I am the God of the Reapers—the God of the Tribe—I am the God of Death. I command you take me to this altar of which you speak. I would meet your Goddess."

"This is highly uncommon!" the priest sputtered.

"And yet I insist. Take me to the altar."

The priest scrambled back. "I will do so, but only because then you will see the beauty and power of the Mother and her people." Father John turned to one of the younger men in robes and whispered something to him. The man sprinted up the path, robes flapping ridiculously behind him. "Now, please follow me. And, as I mentioned before, bring your offering and whatever supplies you need for the night."

Death said nothing. He stood in magnificent silence until the priest made a motion for Him to follow. Then everyone headed back up the path.

Death turned his massive head and nodded to the Reapers waiting beside the boats. Like a deadly swarm, they left the beached craft and followed their God.

Ralina noted that the only supplies any of them carried were their sharp-tipped tridents.

The beauty of the resting Saleesh village made Ralina's heart hurt. She didn't know what Death had planned, but whatever it was she knew it would change this peaceful, prosperous people forevermore.

Incense drifted through the night air, along with the musical chimes of glass wind ornaments hanging from the roofs of neatly kept houses. Torches and campfires lit the village. Women, swathed in fabric from their heads to their toes, sat on porches and around the campfires, stirring big pots whose aromas mingled with the cozy sights and sounds.

Ralina wanted to scream at them to run—hide—*Do something, anything, but do not welcome Death into your village!* The women did nothing. They only stared at Death as He strode after their old priest.

Renard bumped her shoulder. When she looked at him he cut his eyes to the side. She followed his gaze to see that several dozen more young men—all in robes like the other young priests—had begun to appear. They were all armed with the fishhook lances.

Father John had stopped before a beautiful altar. The centerpiece was a larger-than-life statue of a woman. She was covered in a white dress and over that she wore a blue wrap, which concealed her hair and some of her lovely, downturned face. All around her were candles and other offerings—food and drink, and delicate jewelry and trinkets. Her back was to the river far below.

"Behold our Mother!" Father John announced, sweeping his arms out and bowing low to the idol.

Death moved closer and closer to the statue, so that finally His cloven hooves ground against the stone slab on which she stood, knocking over the candles and overturning the offerings.

"You must not—" the priest began, but Death rounded on him.

"Silence!" The word was deafening, and spittle flew from the God's mouth into Father John's face.

The priest paled and wiped his face with a trembling hand. The young men holding lances drew closer.

Death turned His back on the priest and continued to study the idol. Within a few breaths He threw back His head and laughed. Then He faced the priest.

"This is no Goddess. She is an empty statue who serves only as an extension of your ego. She is not the Mother, the Great Earth Goddess of Life. You are a fraud, Father John, and your people are fools."

"Brothers! Attack!" Father John shouted.

The dozen men who had accompanied the priest to the beach were closest to the God. They raised their lances and began moving forward, obviously attempting to herd Death and His people away from the altar.

"Stop them," Death commanded in a voice so calm—so quiet—that it was almost lost to the night.

Almost.

But Thaddeus heard. "Take them out!" he told the Warriors, and with smooth, practiced movements the Warriors drew crossbows from within their cloaks and fired—killing each of the young men.

Father John screamed and tried to run, but the long arm of Death caught him by his cloak and yanked him off his feet so that the priest crumbled to the ground.

"Behold what a real God can do!"

Death faced the river and threw his arms wide. In a voice impossibly loud He called out into the darkness of the listening night.

"Spirits of the dead, hear the call of your God! Come forth and do my bidding!" Then Death whirled around and pointed at the still bleeding bodies of the fallen Saleesh. From behind Him there was a great keening sound. Then up from the river poured a freezing mist. Within that mist Ralina could see shapes of all kinds of men—young, old, short, tall—all of them wearing odd clothing that hung from their bodies like they were living skeletons. The first of the specters rushed to the bodies, hurling themselves into the mouths of the newly dead.

Absolutely frozen with dread, Ralina watched those bodies twitch, moan, and then stagger to their feet, their open eyes milky orbs focused on the God of Death and the spirits that surrounded Him.

The other men in robes were frozen in fear. They halted just feet away from Thaddeus and the Warriors, staring at the reanimated men in dread.

Death smiled down on Father John and then lifted the huge statue and threw her down to break on the rocky shore so many feet below. "Do you see the power of a real God?"

"What are you doing? Why are you here?"

"When will you learn Gods do not suffer being questioned by mortals?" And then the God reached for Father John—lifted the shrieking, kicking man over His head—and threw him to his death beside his shattered idol.

Then the God turned his attention to the frozen Saleesh men.

"I will ask this once. Which of you would like to guide us up the river and across Lost Lake?" Death inquired in a pleasant voice.

One young man stumbled forward. "I-I can guide you."

Thaddeus grabbed him by the collar of his robe and pushed him to his knees before Death.

"A volunteer. How fortunate for you. What is your name, young man?"

"B-B-Brother Joseph," he stuttered. His body was trembling so hard that Ralina was surprised he was able to speak at all.

"Ah, Brother Joseph. You are an expert on the river?"

"I-I am. B-before I chose to enter the priesthood I was a River Driver."

"And you also know how to cross Lost Lake?"

"I have n-not c-crossed it, though I d-do k-know its d-dangers and how long it w-will t-take to cross. B-but n-none of our people have traveled over Lost Lake. W-we do not leave our river."

"Then what good is he?" Thaddeus sneered, kicking Brother Joseph in the side.

Death raised His hand. "Do not abuse my new guide! Can *you* guide us past all of the ruins between here and Lost Lake? Can *you* tell us intimate details about each of the Saleesh villages we will be conquering on our way there?"

Thaddeus blew out a long breath. "No, my Lord."

"Well, then, Brother Joseph shall join us. Now, please stand over there, beside my Storyteller, where you will be safe."

Brother Joseph tried to stand, but his legs didn't seem to work, so he crawled between the bodies of the reanimated dead—who were still staring with milky eyes at their God—to come to a whimpering halt at Ralina's feet. There he curled within himself, clutching his knees to his chest.

"Very good. Now that our guide problem is settled, let us make short work of the rest of this so that we may rest and relax." Death raised His voice, looking out at the silent, stunned village. "All of you who wish to join me, put down your weapons and go to your knees."

The God waited. A few of the men closest to their reanimated brothers dropped their lances and went to their knees, but the others were being joined by men running from all over the village—some robed, some bare-chested River Drivers. They held lances. They formed a half circle around the altar and began closing in, weapons held at the ready.

Death smiled his terrible smile. "I am so glad to see that you aren't all eunuchs like your priest. Warriors, Reapers—*kill them all!*"

Ralina swallowed her fear. "My Lord, what of the women and children?"

Death's head swiveled so that he could meet her gaze. "Thank you for reminding me, Storyteller."

"The women and children are spoils of war. Use them as you would, my People!" Death shouted. "But have care with the food cooking over the campfires. Battle makes me ravenous."

And then Death spread His arms wide again, touching the spirits that hovered around Him like wisps of noxious smoke.

"Spirits of the dead—you may claim any body you wish and be free to join my army!"

With the battle roar of a stag in rut, Death strode forward, lifting men and snapping their spines. The moment they slumped lifeless to the ground, spirits claimed them, reanimating the bodies with otherworldly moans—and then they joined their God as Death consumed the village.

Thus began a chapter in Ralina's life so horrible that at times she believed she would lose her mind. Had it not been for the stabilizing influence of Bear, Renard, Kong, and Daniel, she would have given up and quietly slid over the side of her boat one night and let herself drown.

But she couldn't do that—*wouldn't* do that to Bear.

She could have escaped—though it would've been without any supplies—but she knew Death would come after her immediately, recapture her, and then she would lose the small amount of status and freedom the God currently allowed her. Renard and Daniel would be infected and made to join the Warriors, and who knew what terrible things He might do to her Bear should He become angry with her.

So Ralina kept moving forward—taking one day at a time. She was grateful that the Saleesh villages were several days apart—one slaughter right after another would have been too much for her. When they arrived at the second village Ralina asked the God to allow her to remain with the boats, guarded by Renard and Daniel. Thankfully, Death agreed, saying that as she had already witnessed the most dramatic of His Saleesh victories she should have enough material for this part of His tale.

But remaining with the boats did not shield Ralina from the screams of the dying men or the terrified, gut-wrenching wails of women being raped and mothers trying to save their children. When she walked through the second decimated village, she asked Bear to lead her, intending to keep her eyes focused on her canine, but then Ralina remembered herself and found her courage. She lifted her head, blinked her eyes clear of tears, *looked, and remembered.* Just as she'd forced herself to watch the burning of her Tribe, she would not turn away from the atrocities Death and His army of mutants and reanimated corpses committed.

Ralina would tell this story, and the world would never forget.

It took almost three weeks to make their way from the first Saleesh village to Day Dam and the mouth of Lost Lake. In those weeks Death's army grew from one hundred men to more that five hundred. Long gone were the ragtag boats and rafts they'd begun in. They were replaced with slick, easily maneuvered canoes and larger, luxurious boats the priests used to travel from village to village. And the newly acquired watercraft were loaded with supplies stolen from the Saleesh—blankets, robes, wraps, iron pots, pieces of glass, and so much food that they had to leave some behind to rot with the bodies of the women and children. It was macabre to see Death's minions swathing themselves in the delicately wrought jewelry the talented Saleesh had been so good at creating. The entire army took on a blue tint so that at first glance one might think beauty, and not death approached—but a closer look at the reanimated corpses that made up the bulk of the army and any thoughts of beauty or goodness quickly dissipated.

Ralina named the living corpses Milks, after the color of their eyes. They were like nothing she could have imagined possible. Their bodies had died. Ralina had witnessed the deaths of many of them. But at the first Saleesh village Death had summoned spirits—ghosts—and they had truly reanimated those dead bodies. Moving forward from that first village, the ghosts followed the army, hovering around Death's opulent boat like mist swirling from the ancient pines on a winter night—waiting for the next Saleesh village to be taken so that they could enter the newly dead and walk again.

The Milks were strange things. They were no longer dead, which was obvious because their reanimated bodies did not decay. They ate. They slept. They even talked, though they used odd words Ralina didn't understand, but when she came close, listening, to a group of them they quit speaking, so she couldn't figure out what they were saying. They also seemed confused about the state of the world around them. One night when they camped beside the river between Saleesh villages Ralina had asked Death what they were, and His answer chilled her to the bone.

"They are the specters who have haunted the Umbria gorge for hundreds of years—since the destruction of the ancient world."

"You mean they're the ghosts of the people who built the cities and the bridges?" she'd asked.

"Indeed," He'd said.

"But why are they haunting the gorge?"

Death had shaken His massive head, His antlers casting eerie shadows behind Him. "They do not know—though they do all have intense feelings of guilt and of incompletion." He'd shrugged and smiled His terrible smile. "It is fortuitous, is it not? Unfinished business caused them to haunt this place for centuries, making them susceptible to my call."

"So, you did call them to you?"

"Of course, Storyteller! I sensed their presence the moment we entered the Umbria, and I began communing with them. They are difficult to communicate with, but the one thing they have made clear to me is that they could not rest until they completed something."

"Something?"

He took a long drink of a huge wooden mug His Attendants kept filled with the rich red wine the Saleesh had stockpiled. "As I said, they are difficult to communicate with—even now that they live again."

"I've noticed they don't talk much," Ralina said carefully. Death had already proven to be highly protective of his Milks.

"It is one of the things I appreciate most about them. I like to believe that they all lost their faith in the gods when their world was destroyed. Perhaps their unfinished business is the need to follow the will of a true God. And my will commands them to come with us to the Plains of the Wind Riders. There they will defeat all who attempt to stand against me."

That was all Death would say about the Milks. Ralina suspected that was because He didn't know any more about them and the God didn't like to appear anything but omnipotent. But Ralina watched everything. She noticed everything.

The Milks had cliques. They congregated in the same groups and rarely mixed with outsiders. They were all men. Not one woman was reanimated—nor one child. And they had night terrors, so that their screams and cries of fear echoed across the river every single night as they continued to journey upriver.

Canines hated the Milks. That was the one happy outcome of the Milks' presence. They were always hovering around Death, which meant that after trying unsuccessfully to coax Bear to join her on the God's boat while He told her stories about the twisted, nightmarish utopia He imagined their future to be, Death announced that the canines were too skittish to be close to His new army—which relieved Ralina immensely, as she could then leave Bear with Renard, Daniel, and Kong whenever she had to attend to the God.

When they finally arrived at the last Saleesh village and the mouth of Lost Lake, Ralina already knew what was before them. She'd befriended Brother Joseph—though "befriend" was not an entirely accurate word, as the young Saleesh man had gone completely mad. He slept as much as Death would allow—all curled in on himself. He ate little and cried often. When he was in Death's presence he couldn't force himself to stand, so he knelt before the God, stuttering his answers between sobs and hysterical laughter.

As Brother Joseph was, indeed, an expert on the river and he guided them well, Death didn't seem to mind, but Ralina felt terribly sorry for the young man—who wasn't even as old as Renard. She'd asked Death to allow Brother Joseph to remain with her outside the villages while Death and His army consumed them, and the God had readily agreed, thanking Ralina for thinking of it and saying that it would be a waste of time if Brother Joseph was accidentally killed and He had to choose a new guide. So, as Ralina, Renard, Daniel, and Brother Joseph waited with the boats during the destruction of the final Saleesh village, the young Brother had explained what was to come on the Lost Lake crossing.

"There are devil creatures that dwell around the islands and the ruins of the dead cities—Mouths and Monkeys. They work together, so you must avoid those things," Brother Joseph said.

And after he explained exactly what Mouths and Monkeys could do, Ralina completely agreed with him.

"But how long will it really take for us to cross Lost Lake?" Renard had asked him.

Along with stuttering when he was afraid, Brother Joseph had developed a tic that tended to become worse whenever he talked with Death, and now his head jerked spasmodically to the side, betraying how disturbed just the idea of the lake crossing made him.

"Months," the Brother said, his neck and head twitching to the left. "Some—sometimes you will go days w-without s-s-seeing land. And th-th-the islands are not a respite. M-M-Mouths and Monkeys are there."

"But you've never crossed the lake?" Renard asked.

"N-no. I-I-I've never b-been away from my r-r-river." Brother Joseph worried the edge of the left sleeve of his robe, which was already frayed from his anxious fingers.

"Hey, try thinking about the lake as nothing more than an extension of your river, which is the truth. Lost Lake was made when Day Dam broke, so a good part of the water did come from the Umbria."

"B-but our s-stories s-say the earth o-opened and w-water spewed forth. Th-the M-Mother saved us." Brother Joseph's gaze turned downcast and he chewed his lip. "B-but S-S-She must not l-love us now. S-She did not s-s-s-ave us from Death."

Ralina opened her mouth to speak platitudes, but found she could not. Brother Joseph was right. The Mother hadn't saved them. She hadn't saved any of them.

The next day when the armada entered Lost Lake, the sky was clear and deceptively beautiful, as if it didn't know that Death was spreading across the world below.

That night—the first night they spent on the lake—Brother Joseph tied one of the ancient cast-iron cauldrons Death had taken from the Saleesh to his ankles and then quietly slipped overboard and put an end to his misery. Ralina knew what he was doing. She'd watched him. Silently he'd filled the big pot with water before he took off his robe, folded it neatly, kissed it, and then met her gaze just before he and the water-filled iron pot dropped soundlessly overboard.

She'd started to sit up—to stop him—but he'd folded his hands as if praying to her and shook his head mouthing the words *Please let me go.* And she had. Ralina understood. It was not her right to take the peace from him that he sought to rediscover in the dark depths. She'd nodded and mouthed back, *I will tell your story.*

Then Brother Joseph had smiled. It was the first and only time Ralina had seen his expression free of fear, and she was struck anew by how young he was.

He was still smiling when the water closed over his upturned face.

Death hadn't been in the least bit upset by Brother Joseph's absence. Instead all the God had said was "Ah, the Brother found his happy ending. A good outcome for a task well done."

They didn't need the Brother for the lake crossing. He'd already told Death everything he knew about the lake and its dangers. Navigation was really rather simple—they were to keep heading southeast until they saw the Golden Man Ruins, then turn directly into the sunrise and row to the entrance of the Rock Mountains.

She had no idea what the Golden Man was, nor what ruins he topped, but neither had Brother Joseph. He'd only repeated what he'd heard the Lynx guides say. No one in their armada of death knew, and as one day merged into another, the Storyteller found it was best to focus on each moment rather than to speculate about the future—speculation led to hopelessness, and hopelessness led to the same watery grave Brother Joseph had chosen. Instead, she took one day at a time, focusing on her connection with her Companion and her growing appreciation for Renard and his father. They hadn't been family before they'd left the Tribe, but now they were the only sanity each other had. The three humans and their two canines clung to one another, and every day after Ralina returned from spending hours with Death, listening to Him prattle on and on about His magnificent plan to subjugate the world and awaken His Consort—the Great Goddess of Life—Daniel prepared untainted food for her, Bear curled beside her, sharing his strength, and Renard held her, whispering that she had survived one more day . . . one more day.

Ralina grew to despise Lost Lake, and it wasn't simply because it seemed never-ending. Nor was it because of the horrid Mouths and Monkeys—who claimed four entire boats filled with Milks on their first encounter. Ralina hated Lost Lake because she felt the presence of the uncounted thousands of dead beneath them. At night, when the armada tied up together and the cries of the dreaming Milks drifted across the lake, Ralina swore that she heard answering shrieks coming from far, far under the water, chilling her soul.

The unending days blurred together, one after another, dread and the dead weaving a nightmare tapestry that became the fabric of Ralina's inescapable life.

LOST LAKE—THE PACK

As the days stretched to weeks, and then the weeks to a new month, time seemed to Mari to begin to blur, weaving a dreamy tapestry that fashioned her new life.

She'd didn't hate Lost Lake—and after spending several weeks on it the Pack had settled into a rhythm that was surprisingly pleasant. When they neared islands or ruins, the entire Pack went on alert. The Mouths and Monkeys were almost always present, and they never became less disgusting, but after a couple run-ins the Pack learned how to spot both quickly. It was morbid and horrible, but they also learned that the easiest way to get by them was to kill a Monkey in the water. That was usually distraction enough to allow them to slip past any Mouths lurking below.

But often they went several days without seeing anything but water, and during those days the Pack relaxed and found time to practice the things that made life worth living.

Early on, Nik and Mari had been concerned about exercising the canines. Almost two months of rarely seeing land—and even a longer time not touching it—wouldn't keep the canines conditioned enough for the trek through the mountains ahead of them.

It'd been Mari's idea to have the Shepherds and Terriers swim alongside the boats.

"But there are *things* under the water," Sora said, shuddering in disgust as she glared down into the silent depths.

"Well, sure there are, but unless we can see ruins Antreas says there's nothing that can hurt us," Mari had countered.

"She's right," Antreas had said as he and Danita paddled around them in their little boat, Bast perched between them. "I'm going to agree about the need to exercise our Companions—and ourselves."

"I'm getting plenty of exercise," Sora said, showing off a flexed bicep. "My arms and back have never been so strong."

"What about your legs?" Mari asked.

"They're lovely. Thank you for asking," Sora quipped.

"Lovely legs aside," Antreas said, "staying conditioned will only help get us through the mountains faster. So, if any of you want to swim beside the boats, I say that is an excellent idea."

"But whether they want to or not, our canines need the exercise," Nik said.

"And our feline," Danita said.

Bast hissed and laid her ears flat against her head as she stared down at the water.

Antreas chuckled at his Lynx. "Yeah, I know you don't like it, but I'd hate to see the *dogs* show you up."

Bast's ears lifted, but her eyes narrowed at her Companion. She sighed, coughed, and began grooming herself.

"That's a yes. If a canine goes in the water, so will she," Danita said.

"I think I got that, too," Sora said. She picked up Chloe, who was almost too big now to fit into her swaddle. "Do we really have to swim?"

The pup licked her nose and wagged her tail so hard her rear end wriggled.

"I think that's another yes," Danita said.

"Sadly, I think you're right," Nik said. He shared a glance with Laru, who laid his ears back and looked as unenthused at the prospect as his Companion.

"Oh, come on! It'll be fun, especially on the really hot days," Mari said.

"Moon Woman?" Dove's sweet voice traveled across the water easily.

"Yes, Dove," Mari answered.

"Lily and I do not know how to swim."

"Would you like to learn?" Sora asked.

"We would!" Dove said enthusiastically. Beside her Lily nodded, though she looked a lot less excited.

"Okay, then, who's our best swimmer?" Antreas asked.

As one, every Companion turned to look at Wilkes.

Wilkes sighed. "I can swim. Well."

"Wilkes, would you teach Lily and me to swim?" Dove asked, turning her smiling face in the direction of his voice.

Wilkes sighed again. "Yes. I will teach you."

So began a series of lessons that proved to be highly amusing. Mari was amazed at how brave Dove was. She could see nothing, but was utterly free in the water, swimming almost daily and always going to the end of her safety tether. Lily learned to swim, too, but it was obvious she enjoyed it about as much as Nik—who looked like he'd rather have battled a herd of Monkeys than submerge himself in the lake.

The Pack was careful. They kept ropes looped around the waists of the canines—as well as anyone swimming with them. Even Bast, looking utterly disgruntled, was coaxed to swim with Danita—who Mari thought might be half fish because of how gracefully the girl moved through the water.

Mari loved those long, hot days and the cool lake water. She decided not to dwell on the fact that beneath them a whole society had drowned.

Instead she thought about the water washing away that which needed cleansing so that something new, something better, could take its place.

She wasn't delusional. Mari didn't believe that her little Pack would change the world, and it didn't have to. All it had to do was change *their* world, and that it already had done.

As they drew closer and closer to the Rock Mountains, the Pack grew stronger. Companions and Earth Walkers no longer segregated themselves from each other. They shared boats and supplies as easily as they shared fishing tips. When taking breaks from paddling, the Earth Walkers taught the Companions how to weave—and the Companions talked openly about how they created their City in the Trees, about the intricacies of pulley systems, and about how to build nests in trees so that the home grew *with* the tree, rather than strangling and killing it.

Mari thought often what a pleasure it was to watch good friends being made—and lovers being wooed. Danita slept every night in Antreas's arms—and somewhere about midway through their crossing her night terrors completely stopped.

Davis and Claudia were as inseparable as Cammy and the very obviously pregnant Mariah. Mari and Nik often chuckled about how little Cammyman seemed to grow more and more proud as the Shepherd's belly grew more and more round. She tried not to worry about Mariah giving birth on the lake, especially as Claudia and Davis didn't seem overly concerned, but every Third Night when she and Sora drew down the moon to Wash their Pack, Mari added a prayer to the Great Goddess asking for a healthy delivery for the sweet Shepherd, especially as the mountains, which had once seemed impossibly far away, began showing their snowy tips against the horizon.

Mariah went into labor the day the light of the rising sun suddenly reflected off something in the distance that sparkled and shone so much that it hurt Mari's eyes to stare at it.

"What is that?" Danita asked.

"The Golden Man Ruins!" Antreas shouted, sounding pleased. "We made it!"

"What? Are we almost off this Goddess-forsaken lake?" Nik said.

"Yes, we are," Antreas said. "We need to paddle for that golden statue. Once we pass it we take a sharp turn to the left and in one more day we meet dry land—for good."

"Thank the Sun!" Nik cheered.

"Oh, blessed Goddess! That is so exciting!" Dove said from the boat she shared with Davis, Claudia, Rose, Lily, and a large selection of canines.

"It is exciting," Antreas said. "But we need to circle up so I can let you know what we're facing." He cupped his hands around his mouth and yelled, "Pack! Circle up!"

"That doesn't sound good," Nik muttered.

"Why doesn't he tell us about this bad stuff *before* we're looking right at it?" Mari said.

"Probably because we'd all fret and make it worse than it actually is," said Sora as she and her boat, which held Sheena and her Captain, as well as O'Bryan, drew beside them.

"It's gonna be fine," O'Bryan said. "This is our last obstacle on the lake, and then we'll be free of it forever. Good news, right, Nik?"

"*Great* news," Nik said.

When they were circled around him, Antreas spoke quickly, explaining efficiently to the attentive Pack.

"This is the last ruin we face on Lost Lake. Tomorrow midday we reach land and the entrance to the Rock Mountain passage." He had to pause as the Pack cheered and whooped before continuing. "The Golden Man Ruins are as deadly as they are strange, and they also mark where we need to change direction to make land quickly."

"Well, we know they're right up there." Wilkes pointed at the winking spot of gold ahead of them. "Can't we just veer to the left now and avoid them completely."

"No. I stopped you here because of what happens as we draw closer to this part of the lake. The water changes for a wide area around these ruins. For some reason this particular sunken city created whirlpools and sections of deadly currents that can capsize boats much bigger than ours. Unless we want to add a week to our lake crossing, we must follow the path through the ruins rather than circumvent them and chance the water traps."

"Okay, we follow you just as we've been doing," Sora said. "We've gotten pretty good at it."

"You have," Antreas said—his expression grim. "You've also gotten good at getting safely past the Mouths and Monkeys. You'll need all those skills here. These ruins are odd for many reasons—the strangest might be that they're a major breeding ground for Mouths and Monkeys. We do not know why, but there are more of those creatures here than anywhere else on the lake."

"What kind of ruins are they?" Davis asked.

"We have no true idea. It seems to be one enormous building and has the look of a temple. It was built in a huge rectangle. There are six pointed towers that protrude above the water, as well as what looks like a roof that adjoins them and a good part of the building itself. It's from the highest of the towers that the Golden Man stands."

"Is he a god?" Mari asked.

"Not a god." Dove suddenly spoke. "But someone who proclaimed that their god was present—though he was not. The monument they built to him was filled with secrecy, not divinity. The Mouths and Monkeys began here—it was from somewhere very close to this temple that they escaped their old world and made a new one, more likeable to them. That is why they guard this ruin so jealously."

A chill shuddered through Mari. "How do you know that, Dove?

Dove shook her head. "The words simply come to me. I hope they are sent by the Great Mother Goddess."

"I believe the Goddess speaks through Dove," Davis said. "I feel it deep within me."

Sora nodded. "I believe so, too."

Mari's gaze sifted through her Pack. She saw her people nodding in agreement.

"I do not doubt Dove's vision," Antreas said. "It explains a lot—but it doesn't change the danger."

"Well, Nik's gotten really good at shooting Monkeys," Mari said. "He can do it one more time."

"Nik, you need to be ready to shoot more than one," Antreas said.

"We'll all be ready," Wilkes said.

"Okay, be sure everything is tied down securely and your ballasts are all even. Remain behind me—go double file, but do not stray or straggle. And when I tell you to go, *paddle fast.*"

It didn't take the Pack long to batten down their supplies and be sure the canines—and one Lynx—were secure as well. When all was ready, they set out in a double file behind Antreas and Danita.

"Nik, I'd like you to paddle beside us," Davis called. "We have Rose and the puppies with us, and also Mariah is moving really slow—particularly today—and she doesn't want to leave the nest she's made on her ballast."

"Yes, Nik," Claudia said, sending her very pregnant Shepherd a worried look. "I'd feel better if your crossbow was close by us. Mariah is feeling restless and out of sorts today."

"No problem. We'll stay near," Nik said as he and Mari paddled their little craft beside Davis and Claudia. Also in their much larger boat, along with Rose and the growing puppies, were Dove and Lily. "Lily, if you transfer over to our boat you can paddle with Mari so that I can focus on aiming this crossbow."

"I'm a stronger paddler than Lily." Dove spoke up immediately. "I would be happy to come to your boat and help out."

Nik shrugged and then nodded. "Sounds good. Let's do this fast, but safely."

By now they were all experts on the water, and moving Dove was easy. She settled in at Nik's place in the front of the canoe and Nik moved to the center, leaving Mari to steer—with Laru on one ballast and Rigel balancing the opposite side.

"All ready?" Antreas called back down the line.

"Ready!" the Pack responded.

They began paddling at a normal speed, but as the ruins drew closer Antreas shouted, "We'll keep this pace, but when I yell '*NOW*' I'm going to speed up and get us out of that Monkey-and-Mouth mess as fast as possible. Keep up with me. Let's go, Pack!"

The Pack bent their backs to their task, moving forward together as one. Mari was so proud of them. They had truly formed a family unit. Every few strokes Danita would call out a cadence, which Isabel repeated and then Spencer took up as well, so that it seemed as if the boats were shadow-dancing together.

As they drew closer and closer to the massive ruin, Mari felt a terrible crawling over her skin. The current became erratic. Sucking whirlpools suddenly appeared for as far as she could see around them. The temple was of a size like no building she'd ever seen, and it was filled with Monkeys. The ruin itself had cattails and maidenhair ferns covering it—and from the huge roof area grew a forest of willow trees. Among everything—hanging from all over the temple—were Monkeys.

The Golden Man was standing on a boulder-sized ball which rested on top of a pointed spire. Bizarrely, he looked to be in perfect condition. Mari could just make out that he was holding some kind of long flute to his lips. Monkeys perched on the ball and the ledge below it—all of them were staring in the direction of the boats.

"We'll be speeding up soon," Antreas shouted. "Get ready. Do *not* get off track. And don't stop. Stay with me and keep going no matter what."

"Davis!" Claudia's voice was tinged with fear. "It's Mariah!"

"What? Is she okay?" Davis called back.

Their boat was to Mari's right, and she was closest to the ballast on which Mariah had made a comfortable nest of woven mats and pelts. Cammy was usually beside her, but for the trip past the ruins he'd joined Rose and the puppies in the boat, and they'd balanced the other ballast with supplies. Just then he had his front paws up on the side of the boat, staring at Mariah and whining softly.

One look at the Shepherd and Mari knew what was happening before Claudia spoke again.

"She's fine. But she's in labor!" Claudia said.

"I'm steering closer to the ballast Mariah's on," Mari said.

"I will keep paddling," Dove said, bending to the task.

"And I'll focus on the water around her," said Nik.

They moved closer to Mariah's ballast just in time for Mari to see the Shepherd strain, and then in a liquid rush a puppy was born.

"The first pup is here!" Claudia shouted, wiping tears from her eyes. "Oh, good girl, Mariah! Sweet, strong girl!" Claudia looked around frantically. "Can't we stop? I need to get out there with her."

"Okay, everyone—time to paddle like you never have before! Now!" Antreas shouted.

"We can't stop!" Nik said. "Claudia, tell Mariah to hang on. Comfort her. Reassure her. We'll get her through this and you can join her as soon as possible."

Tears streaming down her cheeks, Claudia nodded, and then began talking to her Companion in a calm, soothing voice as she wiped her cheeks with her sleeve.

"Good girl, Mariah. Brave girl. You're doing wonderfully!"

There was a little coughing sound, and then the beautiful mewing whines of a newborn pup drifted across the water while Cammy barked joyfully.

"What's happening back there?" Sora shouted from her boat just ahead of them.

"Puppies!" Mari yelled. "Puppies are being born!"

"Oh, bloody beetle balls!" O'Bryan said, picking up his crossbow and loading it. "Mouths—to the left. I just saw a tentacle."

Drawn by the liquid scents of birth, Monkeys started dropping into the water. Some barked, sounding exactly like Cammy, and others whined and mewed, making a mockery of newborn puppy noises.

From farther up in the double line of boats, Wilkes fired two arrows in quick succession, killing two Monkeys. As their blood began to stain the water, it also started to froth and tentacles reached up, dragging the twitching creatures under the surface.

"Monkeys closing in! To our right!" Davis shouted.

"Got 'em!" Nik fired and skewered two of them with the same arrow. They screamed and convulsed and the water around them began to ripple—much too close to the boat that was carrying Mariah.

Something flashed in Mari's periphery vision, and she turned her head in time to see a thick white tentacle snake up from below the surface and reach for Mariah's ballast, wrapping around the Shepherd's tail, which was extending out over the water.

Mariah's piercing yelp of agony exploded across the lake.

"Nik! Help!" Mari shouted at the same moment Cammy began barking ferociously. The little Terrier leaped up and ran the length of the arm of the ballast. Still barking and snarling, he launched himself from the boat, hurling himself at the tentacle. Catching it in his jaws, he shook his head mightily, severing the thick, snakelike thing as easily as he could break a rabbit's back, forcing the Mouth to release Mariah's tail.

"Cammy! Get back to the boat!" Davis screamed.

"Keep paddling! I've got this!" Nik yelled.

But Nik didn't have it. He couldn't. Cammy still had the tentacle in his mouth and he was half swimming, half standing on top of the huge fish's head.

"Cammy! Move! I can't get a shot with you there!"

The brave Terrier instantly let loose the tentacle and jumped from the fish's back to paddle to the boat, but the Mouth was now focused on him—and two uninjured tentacles slithered around Cammy's rear legs, pulling him back toward the ravenous maw that opened like a cave just under the surface.

"Cammy!" Davis cried, dropping his paddle and leaning out of the boat, trying to grab the little Terrier. But he wasn't close enough. He'd never reach his Companion in time.

With a ferocious growl, Rigel leaped from his ballast and began swimming for the Mouth. From the ballast on the other side of their boat, Laru stood, barking frantically as their canoe dipped and tilted, trying to find its balance.

"Nik!" Mari shrieked.

"Laru, do not get in that water—you can't help! Rigel, get back! I can't get a clear shot!"

When tentacles wrapped around Rigel's neck, Mari didn't stop to think—she acted. She stood, gathering sunfire to herself, and lifted her hand to throw it like a ball at the fish—but Rigel was now at the Mouth's head, joining Cammy, who was being pulled into the beast's enormous, hook-toothed maw.

"No, you cannot have my Rigel or Cammyman!" Mari shouted as she grabbed a flint-tipped arrow from Nik's stash and then, moving swiftly, crawled on her hands and knees out on the ballast arm until the Mouth was directly below her.

"Mari! What are you—"

Mari let loose of the ballast arm, dropping to land on top of the gigantic fish. She straddled it like it was a slippery log. The fish bucked and began sinking, pulling Cammy and Rigel under with it. Like it was a spear, Mari raised the arrow and then with all of her strength plunged it down into the water and began stabbing the beast directly in its saucer-like black eye, over and over again.

The creature bucked and writhed in pain as the water was filled with blood and gore. It knocked Mari off its back at the same time it released Cammy and Rigel.

"Move! Move!" Nik shouted.

Mari, thanking the Goddess that they'd all practiced swimming, stroked quickly to the boat, with Rigel and Cammy beside her.

"Monkeys coming with more Mouths!" Davis yelled, pointing.

"Get in the boat! Get in the boat!" Claudia screamed.

Mari gripped the side of her boat. "Dove! Lean to your left!"

Dove did so, and Mari was able to pull against the boat and lift first herself in, and then she helped Rigel scramble aboard before reaching down and hefting a soggy, bleeding Cammyman into the boat as well.

"Rigel! Are you hurt?" Mari yelled at her Shepherd as she grabbed the paddle and rushed to her seat while the boat tilted and tipped precariously.

Rigel's answer was to lick her face in reassurance.

Mari kissed his nose and then told him, "Get back on your ballast before we capsize!" Rigel barked and then raced back along the ballast arm, and the little boat righted itself.

Thwack! Thwack! Thwack! Nik's arrows sang as they picked off two

Monkeys and one more big-eyed Mouth whose tentacles were reaching for Mariah again.

The water frothed scarlet, drawing every Mouth and Monkey nearby.

"We need to get out of here!" Mari shouted.

While the Mouths and Monkeys devoured their own, Nik took the paddle from Dove and Davis sat as well, taking over for a sweating Rose.

"Stroke! Stroke! Stroke!" Mari called cadence, and the two boats shot forward together, catching the rest of the Pack.

"Are you okay?" Sora called over her shoulder.

"Okay enough! Go! Get out of here!"

The boats ahead of them had some idea of what was happening, because Wilkes and Sheena began firing at a group of Monkeys who were chattering and shrieking as they dangled from the ruin. The creatures fell into the water, creating more of a distraction so that as the boats sped past the temple, its sides were stained red and the water around it was filled with blood and grasping tentacles as Mouths feasted on Monkeys and Monkeys feasted on Mouths—ignoring the Pack.

It seemed a terribly long time before Antreas called for them to circle up. Sweat ran down Mari's face and dripped from her arms, which shook with effort. Dove was sitting in the bottom of the canoe, cradling Cammy as she held pressure bandages on his two rear legs, which had been lacerated by the Mouth's barbed teeth. The last six inches or so of his tail had been completely desleeved. The moment Antreas called a halt, Mari went to Cammy.

"His rear legs and his tail are injured!" Davis said. "I'm coming over there!"

"Hang on, Davis. Stay where you are until I see how bad it is," Mari said. Then she called to Claudia. "How's Mariah?"

The Companion was crawling along the ballast arm toward her Shepherd. "The second pup is coming. Mariah is fine, but she's worried about Cammy."

"Hey there, little guy. Let me check you out." Mari gently unwrapped the makeshift bandages from his legs, grimacing at the lacerations—but they were only bleeding slightly. His tail looked terrible, showing bare cartilage and bloody ooze. She knew immediately that she was going to have to amputate it down to an uninjured nub, but neither his legs nor tail had suffered life-threatening injuries. "I have some healing to do, but he's going to be just fine!" she called to Davis, who sat so heavily Mari thought he was close to fainting. "Good job keeping the pressure on those wounds," Mari told Dove before pulling one of her medical satchels out from where it had been stowed under her seat and searching through it for salve and proper bandages.

"Oh, I was so worried for him," Dove said, feeling for Cammy's head and stroking it gently.

Cammy was panting with pain and whined as Mari applied the salve, causing Davis to stand again. "Cammy?"

"It's okay. I've just put some numbing salve on his wounds. Dove almost has the bleeding stopped. I'll sew the lacerations as soon as I've cleaned the wounds." She looked up, finding Sora's boat just a few feet away. "I'm going to need the surgical knife."

"Getting it!" Sora stood and hurried to the medical storage baskets stowed under the seats.

"Light that mini-brazier you rigged, too. I'm going to need to cauterize his tail," Mari said.

"What? His tail?" Davis was looking very pale, and sounding worse than Cammy.

"It's okay. It's not a serious injury—just painful. His tail is going to be shorter, but that's just a battle scar." Mari stroked the Terrier's head. "Right, brave boy?"

Cammy tried to wag his tail, but whined painfully instead.

"Good boy, Cammyman!" Davis said, tears in his voice. "You're so strong and brave. You saved Mariah and the puppies!"

"Nik, would you hand me a dry tunic?" Mari asked. Nik quickly tossed her a shirt, which she put into Dove's hands, saying, "Dove, could you carefully dry Cammy and then wrap this around him like a blanket? He's going into shock, which is dangerous, and being wet does not help. We need to keep him dry and warm."

"Of course! And I'll be very careful." Dove felt along the Terrier's body, drying him gently as she murmured encouragement to him.

Sheena and O'Bryan paddled Sora close enough to Mari's boat for her to pass Nik the surgical knife. Sora then began stoking the little brazier she'd used during the very long overwater trip to brew tea and render tinctures. She placed one of Leda's valuable cauterizing irons in it, waiting for it to heat.

"Another pup!" Claudia said.

"Goddess! I feel like I'm going to pass out." Davis sat again as all the remaining color drained from his face.

"All will be well." Lily moved closer and patted his back with a tentative but comforting hand. "Mari and the Goddess will heal your Cammy—and the Goddess has already protected sweet Mariah and her puppies."

Mari glanced up at Davis. "Put your head between your legs. If you pass out it's going to agitate Cammy, and I'm going to need him to stay still."

"Okay—okay. Cammy, everything is fine. I'm just worried about you, that's all. But be a brave boy and hold still for Mari so she can fix you," Davis called to his Companion before he put his head between his legs, breathing heavily.

Cammy panted and whined, but laid his head on Dove's thigh, allowing her to dry and comfort him.

By this time the boats were circled around them and the Pack was watching anxiously. Antreas guided his canoe over to them. He looked from one boat to the other, shaking his head.

"You scared me. Badly," he said. "Is anyone hurt?"

"My Cammyman is," Davis said.

"He's also a hero," said Claudia, smiling through tears at the little Terrier. "He saved Mariah and all of her puppies."

"And Rigel and Mari saved him!" Davis said.

"Will Cammy make it?" Antreas asked.

Mari lifted her head and tossed back her hair. "He will. We all will. We're bound, all of us, by strength and devotion and love. Nothing is going to tear us apart—especially not a watery death. Don't worry about brave Cammyman. Tonight I will draw down the moon and be sure he heals quickly and completely."

While the Pack cheered, Dove's hand sought and found Mari's. For her ears alone she said, "But He will find us eventually."

"Not today. Death is definitely *not* catching us *today*. Now, help me by holding Cammy still." Mari placed Dove's hands in the proper positions, and then she bent to the task of sewing his lacerations while the numbing salve soaked in so that she could amputate his mangled tail.

CHAPTER 21

ROCK MOUNTAINS—THE PACK

They made land mid-morning the next day, beaching the boats for the last time. Mari stared up at the mountains that seemed to touch the sky above them. They were covered with huge old pines, making her suddenly and terribly homesick.

"Beautiful, isn't it?" Nik put his arm around her.

"It is—and not just because it's dry land," said Mari. "Makes me miss home," she added softly.

"After we cross them we will be home. Forever," said Nik, kissing her gently.

"Kissing later—working now," Antreas said, striding past them and dragging his canoe behind him. "Be sure to pull all the boats well up past this waterline." He pointed. "I've allowed for three days to tear apart the ballasts and convert them into litters to carry our supplies." Antreas paused and smiled as Davis waded to shore, cradling Cammyman in his arms. Behind him Mariah was making her way to dry land beside Claudia, who was carrying a basket filled with all eleven of her newborn pups. "And they'll also carry our little hero, his mate, and a litter of puppies."

The Pack safely beached the boats and then gathered around Cammy, Mariah, and the pups, oohing and aahing over the newborns and praising Cammyman, who huffed in pleasure.

"How are they?" Mari asked, peering into the basket at the sleeping mound of pups.

"They're as perfect as their mother and father," said Claudia happily as she leaned into Davis and he slipped an arm around her.

"And Mariah is just fine?" asked Adira hesitantly. "Giving birth out there must have been difficult."

Claudia smiled at the older woman. "Mariah is completely well. And thanks to your weaving skills, she was very comfortable on the ballast. All those blankets you made for her were perfect."

"I was happy to do it. I have found that I like puppies."

"Who wouldn't? Look at them!" Jenna said, peeking around her at the pups.

"Their colors are really interesting," Nik said, bending to get a closer look at the litter. "I see a lot of Cammy's blond, but also sable, like Mariah."

"I wonder who they'll look more like," Sora said.

"I wonder how big they'll be," said Wilkes, looking over Nik's shoulder. "They seem to be several different sizes."

"Why are their eyes closed? Is something wrong?" asked Mason.

"Nothing is wrong," Claudia said. "Puppies are born with their eyes closed."

"That tiny blond one is so, so sweet." Jenna reached out to touch the pup, but she hesitated and turned to Mariah, who was sitting beside the basket watching everything. "May I touch your puppy?"

Mariah's tail wagged and she licked Jenna's face. Giggling, Jenna turned to Claudia. "I guess that's a yes?"

"It's definitely a yes, and Mariah thanks you for being considerate enough to ask first."

"Puppies are a blessing, but we should establish some rules, especially as so many of our Pack don't know much about puppies," Rose said.

"What we do know your puppies have taught us," Sora said, kissing Chloe on the nose before unwrapping her from her swaddle and letting her sniff around the beach and explore with her rapidly growing brood of brothers and sisters.

"And you all have done so well learning." Rose grinned at Sora.

"Mine was a crash course," said Sora. "And I've loved every minute of it."

"Rose is right, though." Mari spoke up. "Earth Walkers don't know anything about newborn puppies. What are the rules?"

Rose looked at Claudia, who nodded encouragement. "Go ahead. Isn't this Fala's second litter?"

"It is," Rose said. "And I'd be happy to explain." She faced the gathered Pack, who were all listening raptly. "It's simple if you use common sense. Their eyes are closed for from one to two weeks. During that time they need to be close to their mother." She paused to smile at Mariah and her Fala, who was peering into the basket while her tail wagged and wagged and wagged. "They shouldn't be handled too much during the first couple of weeks. They need sleep and milk. But once their eyes are open and they begin waddling around our whole Tribe used to mother them, especially when the weaning process begins at four weeks old—though they aren't fully weaned until they're about eight weeks old. But you've watched Fala wean her pups, and you have all been wonderful with them. Just do the same for Mariah's babies, and know if you have any questions please do ask me or anyone who used to belong to the Tribe."

"I have a question. I don't mean to get ahead of myself because they're just born, and I understand I might never get as lucky as my brother and no canine may ever pick me." Mason paused, glancing at Jaxom, who was petting his Fortina as they crowded in to get a glimpse of the pups. "But Chloe Chose Sora really early, right?"

"Right," Rose said. "I've never known of a pup to Choose a Companion so early. Have you, Wilkes?"

Wilkes shook his head. "No, never."

"My Chloe is spectacular," said Sora.

"Well, yeah, of course she is," said Mason. "But when do pups usually start to Choose their Companions?"

"Anytime after they're weaned," Rose said.

"But I've never known a pup to go past six months before they Choose.

Well, I'll take that back. I know of *one* pup who waited really late to Choose his Companion, but that was because his Companion wasn't part of the Tribe," Nik said, grinning at Mari.

"My Rigel is spectacular, too," Mari mimicked Sora.

Cammy barked and Davis said quickly, "My Cammyman is *very* spectacular!" Which caused the Pack to laugh as the little Terrier wagged the bandaged stub of his tail.

"In honor of our spectacular canines I would very much like someone to hunt something for dinner that does *not* live under the water. I've saved the last of the spices from my Saleesh trade to season a victory stew—and I do not want it to be a fish stew," said Sora.

There was a flurry of activity as several people agreed to hunt, Rose included, as Fala was currently the only Terrier able to be a Hunter. She went to her boat and unloaded her crossbow and a quiver of arrows, and was calling for Fala to join her when Mari, whose boat was beached beside Rose's, noticed that the little mama Terrier seemed agitated when she ran to her Companion. Rose knelt and communed with her canine, and then her face split into a brilliant smile. Rose stood, cupped her hands around her mouth, and shouted for the Pack to hear.

"A puppy is Choosing!"

Mari felt a jolt of happy shock and her gaze instantly found Nik's, who was smiling in delight. He cupped his hands around his mouth, too, and shouted joyfully, "A puppy is Choosing!"

Wilkes took up the cry, and Claudia echoed it.

Mari was looking around the beach, trying to tell which of the fat little Terrier pups was Choosing, when Jenna hurried up to Claudia and Mariah, carrying a folded hemp blanket.

"I thought Mariah might need a fresh blanket for tonight, and I wove an extra one on the lake. I'll wash the others and hang them out and then . . ." She paused, almost tripping over one of Fala's puppies. "Oh, I didn't see you there, little one. I'm sorry, I—" Jenna's words broke off abruptly and she froze, half bent to pet the pup, who was sitting on his haunches staring up at her, whining pitifully.

Jenna went to her knees, dropping the blanket. She pulled the pup into her arms. "Oh, Khan! Oh, sweet boy! Of course I want you! Of course I love you! You are absolutely perfect!"

Fala's muzzle went skyward and she howled her delight, and every canine on the beach followed her lead, even Khan's siblings.

Nik took Mari's hand and together they went to Jenna. She looked up at them, her eyes swimming with happy tears.

"His name is Khan. H-he Chose me!"

"Jenna, do you accept this pup and vow to love and care for him until fate parts you by death?" Nik asked formally.

"Oh, yes! Yes, I do!"

"Then may the Sun bless your union with Khan," Nik said, smiling joyfully.

"And also may the Great Earth Mother bless you and your new Companion," added Mari. She bent to hug Jenna and Khan together, whispering, "I'm so, so happy for you!"

"Oh, Mari! I didn't know I could feel like this!" Jenna wiped tears from her eyes as she stared at her Companion.

"And it only gets better from here." Mari ruffled the fur on the top of Rigel's head as he licked Khan and Jenna.

"Khan has Chosen!" Nik shouted while Laru wagged and barked beside him and the Pack erupted into cheers.

Mari slid her arm around Nik and the two of them, followed by their Companions, stepped back to allow the rest of the Pack to congratulate Jenna. Mari was wiping her eyes, too, when Sora joined them.

"Jenna will be free of Moon Fever now," Sora said. "It is absolutely wonderful."

"She's been lonely since her father died," Mari said softly, watching her happy friend. "Jenna wouldn't admit it, but I know her too well. And now she'll never be lonely again."

"That does it!" Nik said. "Laru, Rigel, let's get to hunting. Today calls for a magnificent celebration."

Rigel looked up at Mari and whined.

"Yes, you can go with Nik and Laru," she told her Companion. Then added, "Nik, if you find signs of rabbit don't kill them. Mark the area so that we can set out the live traps. The warren needs replenishing."

"Will do!" Nik grabbed his crossbow, arrows, and a travel pack and jogged away, with the two Shepherds at his side.

Lily led Dove to Mari and Sora. "This is a blessed beginning of our land journey," she said. "The births and the Choosing—they are signs the Great Mother is pleased with us."

"Not worried about death catching us anymore?" Mari asked, only half kidding.

Dove turned her face to Mari. "Death will catch us all someday."

"Well, yeah, none of us are immortal," Sora said.

"When I mentioned Him yesterday I was not speaking of the inevitability of death. I was speaking of the God."

Mari felt a horrible chill in her blood. "He's following us?"

"I know only the words the Goddess whispers through me, and yesterday She whispered of Death."

"Well, let us know if She whispers of Him anymore," said Sora.

"Oh, I will. Lily, would you lead me to the new puppies? I would like to ask Mariah's permission to see them through my fingers."

The two young women joined the happy group around the puppy basket, and Mari faced Sora.

"I don't like the way that sounds," Mari said.

"You don't believe Dove?"

"No. The problem is I *do* believe her."

"But all we can do is move forward," Sora said.

"I know. I just hope that we're not leading Death to the Wind Riders," said Mari.

"He's not our fault," Sora said firmly. "We cannot be held responsible for what a God does."

"Maybe not, but we can take Dove with us when we go to the Wind Riders. They'll need to be warned."

Sora sighed. "Not a great hello. I can see it now—*Hey, hi, we want to live here in your territory, but one little thing. Death might be stalking us.* I can't imagine they'll be very welcoming after that."

"But more welcoming than they'd be if Death showed up and we hadn't said anything," Mari countered. "Plus, it's the right thing to do."

"I know, but right doesn't mean easy."

Mari grinned at her friend. "Sometimes it seems right *never* means easy. Come on. I'll help you unpack that cauldron and get the campfire started. We have a celebrating Pack to feed."

Mari helped Sora, all the while chatting about puppies and the coming trek through the mountains. Never once did she mention the terrible image that haunted her: the God of Death standing on the ridge overlooking the doomed Tribe of the Trees, and staring directly at her.

It took three full days to deconstruct the boats and then rework them into litters that could be dragged or carried through the mountains. Each day made Mari more impressed with her Pack. They worked as one harmoniously. Because there were no settlements nearby, rabbits were thick in the forest just off the beach. And early on day two Rose and Fala brought down a huge stag, which Sora immediately set to smoking in long strips of jerky while Adira worked with Davis to expertly render the hide for tanning.

It was the morning of the fourth day when they were finally ready to enter the Rock Mountains.

"You've done so well!" Antreas congratulated the Pack that morning as they lined up, litters ready and supplies tucked away in every possible place—including packed to the backs of humans and canines. Even Bast carried a skinful of water and a sleeping pelt strapped across her back. "You know I was worried about our timing when we began this journey."

The Pack nodded and held their breath, waiting to hear the rest of Antreas's speech.

"But I'm not worried anymore. We've made better time than I thought possible. Do you think you can keep it up?"

"Yes!" the Pack shouted as one.

"Then by my predictions we will exit the Rock Mountains and enter the Plains of the Wind Riders right around the last day of summer. That'll give us enough time to build a temporary camp that will withstand the winter and petition the Wind Riders for the right to make it permanent."

"But what if they reject us? Will they make us go back through the mountains?" Adira's voice lifted from the middle of the Pack.

"If they reject us they will force us to leave their territory, but they are not inhumane. I have never known them to cast people out into the winter who have caused them no harm," said Antreas.

"They won't reject us," Mari said firmly. "Being allied with our Pack is an asset. We have valuable skills, and we are looking for nothing more than a peaceful place to settle."

"Yes, and it won't hurt if you weave that gift cloak we've talked about," said Antreas.

"The one for the—what did you call her?" Adira asked.

"The Lead Mare Rider," Antreas said. "Like the Pack, Wind Riders are led by women, and those women all are Riders of the Lead Mare for each Herd."

"We will weave her something she'll never forget," said Adira.

"I have no doubt about that," said Antreas. "Now, just a reminder." He backed up a few feet and then stood on a fallen log that made him several inches taller. "What I'm standing on is the beginning of what we call the Rail Trail. We are going to follow these iron rails all the way across these mountains. We'll lose them in several spots, but you don't need to be concerned about that. I've made this trip many times. I know how to follow the Rail Trail, even when it temporarily disappears."

"There aren't any people who live here?" Jenna asked. With Sora's help she'd made a sling for Khan, much like the one Chloe was outgrowing, but Sora, Rose, and Jenna had agreed that the pups would need to be carried frequently, especially in the beginning of the journey through the mountains. Khan was securely tucked close against Jenna's chest, his bright black eyes peeking out and taking in everything as he sniffed the air with youthful curiosity.

"Well, there are several Lynx Chains that make their dens in the Rock Mountains, but I doubt if we'll meet any of them; this time of year is busy for guides. There are also small groups of mountain people, those who, for whatever reason, would rather live secluded lives in the mountains, though they're always in the lower elevations. I've only run into a few of the mountain people. They're a strange lot who spend the vast majority of their time stockpiling food stores. Once it starts to snow they're trapped until the spring thaw."

"Sounds like a lonely way to live," said Jenna.

"Lonely, but peaceful," said Antreas.

"And the worst predator we're going to run into are the wolverines?" asked Jaxom.

"Yes, but predators don't get much worse than wolverines. Remember that even though they're only a little bigger than a Terrier, they have claws and teeth to rival Bast's." The big Lynx coughed, and Antreas added, "Though their sight is not as good as Bast's—nor is their hearing."

The Pack chuckled.

"They're solitary, which is good for us, as I can't imagine trying to fight off more than one of them. What isn't good for us is their ability to scent us from quite a distance. Expect that a wolverine is following us at all times. They will rarely attack if we stay together, but wander off alone and you will probably not return."

"No one goes anywhere alone," Mari said.

"Not even Hunters," Antreas added. "The only reason you were able to hunt alone here is because wolverines don't leave the mountains. Once we enter this pass we stay together. And when we reach the creeping juniper line we must be vigilant, especially at night. Wolverines prefer to hunt at night, and make their dens at the snow line near juniper groves."

"Anything else frightening up there?" Spencer asked, giving the mountains a wary look.

"Until we get to the snow line, beware of snakes. If their heads are shaped like a triangle they are poisonous. But once it gets cold you don't have to worry about them anymore."

"Doesn't sound as bad as the damned Mouths and Monkeys," Davis said.

The Pack murmured in agreement, breaking the tension and nervousness that had begun to build.

"Antreas, we're ready!" Mari called.

"More than ready," Sora agreed. "Let's go to our new home!"

With a cheer, the Pack entered the Rock Mountains as the sun began to climb their eastern edge.

Mari glanced over her shoulder one time at the neat grouping of abandoned, stripped boats that had carried them so faithfully.

"I hope someone who can make use of them finds the boats," said Nik, following her gaze as he walked beside her.

"Me, too," Mari said, silently adding, *I hope whoever finds them isn't looking for us.*

CHAPTER 22

T he Mare Council has come to a unanimous vote," said Morgana, the ancient leader of the Council, motioning for Dawn to approach her.

River's mother sent her daughter a quick, reassuring smile before hurrying from her side to face the Mare Council. Her boots clicked against the rock floor of the cave, which had been smoothed by generations of horses and their Riders. Dawn bowed low to Morgana, her wrists crossed over her heart. Then the old woman handed her a slim sheet of paper. Dawn read it, nodded, and then turned to face her daughter.

"River, Lead Mare Rider of Herd Magenti Central, the Mare Council has unanimously voted that the decision about whether Ghost be allowed to join the Stallion Run with you as his Rider is best left up to you."

River felt a jolt of shock. April, who was standing beside her, as River had formally named her sister as her Second just that day, grabbed her hand and squeezed it quickly before releasing it.

Dawn smiled. "I agree with the Council's ruling. I have spent these past months transitioning my leadership of our Herd to you, and though I was confident in your ability to Lead before you won the Mare Test, I am pleased to announce to the Council and to our Herd that you have exceeded even my expectations. River, I have no doubt that you will make a wise, considered choice—and beyond all, I know that the choice you make will be what you believe is best for Herd Magenti."

River crossed her wrists over her heart and bowed to her mother respectfully. "Thank you, Mother."

"Young River, have you decided where your Herd will spend the rest of the summer?" Morgana's strong voice carried across the cavernous room, which had been fitted with comfortable pelt chairs and padded with straw for the ancient mares resting beside their Riders.

"I have," River said. Though she had been Lead Mare Rider of her Herd for the past months, it was Herd tradition for the outgoing Lead Mare Rider to help in the transition of leadership, most especially in deciding which mares were bred to which stallions—and River had been grateful for her mother's experience and wisdom that summer. But when it came to decisions like when the Herd was to move and to which camp, the new Lead Mare Rider had the final word—no matter how inexperienced she was. River cleared her throat and continued confidently. She'd made a wise choice—April had agreed, and so had her mother. "Herd Magenti is going to remain here, at the Rendezvous Site for the remainder of the summer and into fall."

Morgana nodded, but asked, "And what is your rationale for remaining here and not heading to one of Herd Magenti's usual summer campsites?"

"I decided we should remain here because of the Stallion Run. This is a traditional site for it, and so I thought it best if my Herd rest here while the stallions prepare for their Run. It's a comfortable site, and close enough to the Rock Mountains that it doesn't get too hot during the height of the summer. I'll watch the leaves on the mountains, and when enough of them have turned we'll move to our winter campsite in the Valley of Vapors."

"That is a sound decision," said Morgana. "And now you have stallion Riders to speak with. I know they are anxious to hear the decisions made today." The old woman paused and added, "I am not anxious to hear your decision on the Stallion Run. Like your mother, I have been impressed by you and your ability to put the needs of your Herd first—as you did so beautifully during the Mare Test."

"Thank you, Morgana," said River.

"So, I am *not* anxious about your decision—but I am curious. I look forward to hearing what you decide." The old woman stood and pronounced, "I call this meeting of the Mare Council closed!"

"It has been said!" echoed the other eleven members of the Council.

Bowing respectfully, River, April, and their mother left the side room of the cave and made their way through the huge entryway, waving as Herdmembers called their greetings.

"Where are the stallion Riders gathered?" April asked.

"I told them to wait at the Choosing Theater," River said.

"Good idea," said her mother. "They'll be holding mock races and running the flags. It gives them something constructive to do while they wait for word about Ghost." Dawn gave her a sideways glance. "You have made your decision, haven't you?"

"I have, but I'm going to use this as I announce the decision to the stallion Riders." River reached into the pocket of her tunic and brought out a brilliant blue stone that nestled in her palm, catching the light of the midday sun and shining with all the colors of the clear summer sky above them.

Dawn smiled. "Blue tourmaline! That is an excellent choice. It provides insight during difficult times and helps with clarity and focus."

"*And* it's a masculine stone," added April. "So it'll resonate with the energy of the stallions and their Riders, automatically calming them."

"My girls have become such wise women," said Dawn, putting an arm around each of them and holding them close.

"We had a perfect role model," said River.

"Tell that to your younger sisters. Violet wants to cut off her hair. All of it. And Amber will be petitioning you soon to change the Candidate age from sixteen to fourteen."

River snorted. "I wouldn't do that if I could—and I can't. That's a Mare Council decision."

"Exactly what I told her, but I'm just the *old* Lead Mare Rider. What do I know?"

"Mostly everything," muttered April.

"And I don't care whether Violet cuts her hair." River gave her mother a perplexed look. "That's something she goes to you about."

"Yes, and she already has. I told her no. She announced that she was taking the question to you."

"Great. Well, I have that to look forward to *after* I make some of the stallion Riders mad."

"You don't think they'll agree with your decision?" Dawn asked.

"Oh, I'm sure many of them will, but as you know it's impossible to please everyone, and with something this important emotions are running high."

"You'll do the right thing—and I will support you," Dawn said. "So will Jasper. He's already told me that as the outgoing Herd Stallion Rider he believes it is his responsibility to transfer his loyalty from me to you."

"I appreciate that. He and Blaze have been a great team these past eight years," River said.

"They have, but like me they are ready to enjoy the retirement they've earned." Echo trotted up, nickering a greeting, Anjo and April's Deinos following close behind. Dawn greeted her mare by rubbing her wide forehead affectionately. "And now Echo and I will leave you to address the stallion Riders. Keep an eye on Clayton. He's definitely leader of a group of young Riders. They follow him around like foals."

River sighed. "Yeah, I've noticed. I don't think they have any idea how brainless they look."

"I don't mind them as much as I do Skye and her clique," April said.

Dawn shook her head and grimaced. "I will never understand why some young women lose themselves in men. It's as if they would rather forfeit their wills than spend one night alone in their tents."

"And River saved Skye's life during the Mare Test!" April exclaimed. "The way she's acted since makes me think she's foolish or stupid."

"Skye isn't foolish or stupid. She's weak," River said. "That's why she's with Clayton. Clayton needs a woman who is too weak to think for herself. That's also why she's not Lead Mare Rider."

"Exactly!" said April.

"Each Lead Mare Rider has to face disagreeing factions within her Herd. My biggest test was right after I took over leadership. The outgoing Mare Rider was ill and unable to give me much guidance, and the Herd Stallion Rider disagreed with *every* breeding decision I made. Every single one. It was tiresome, and it did test my leadership skills, but Echo and I prevailed—and so will you, River. I believe in you."

"I believe in you, too. And so does the majority of our Herd," said April.

"Go give the Riders your decision. Stay strong. Stand proud. Do not waver. They're like yoties—they can smell fear." Dawn kissed each of her daughters. Just before she mounted Echo and trotted away she said, "Don't ever forget. A Lead Mare and Rider must always . . ." And then she mounted Echo and trotted away.

"Be one step ahead of the herd!" River and April recited together.

"You will do well . . ." Dawn's parting words drifted back to her daughters.

Anjo butted her gently with her head. *I am ready to face the stallions. And I believe in you, too.* Her sweet voice filled River with confidence.

"Let's mount and give the stallions a little show," said River mischievously.

"Oooh! Good idea. I'll join you on the field," said April.

Anjo knelt and River mounted her. She took a moment to neaten the purple ribbons that dressed her mare's mane, and then she smoothed her own wild curls, which were similarly decorated in purple.

"Take me to the Choosing Theater! Fast! Let's remind them that if I hadn't broken my ankle Alani and Doe would've never beaten us in any race."

Hold on!

Anjo leaped forward into a gallop, weaving around tents and people without breaking her stride. River moved with her as if they were the same being—purple ribbons streaming behind them. Someone had closed the gate that opened to the outdoor arena where all of the stallions of the Herd and their Riders were congregated, running sprint match races while weaving between long poles, practicing their maneuverability. At the sound of Anjo's powerful hooves pounding against the dirt, as one the Riders and stallions looked her way.

"Gate's down!" River told Anjo.

I know. That is why I told you to hold on.

Anjo gathered herself and gracefully jumped over the gate, clearing it easily. When she landed, she didn't slow. Instead she stretched out into a flat run, sprinting through the group of stallions so that they had to scramble to clear the way for her. When Anjo got to the poles she barely slowed, but wove through each one before turning to prance back to the stallions, head and tail high, ears pricked, confidence, strength, and beauty radiating from her.

Led by Jasper, the Riders clapped and cheered as their Lead Mare and Rider approached, and the stallions trumpeted greetings—the loudest of all being Ghost, who was present, but held himself off from the group of stallions and Riders.

Anjo halted in front of the group, and River raised her hand so that they quieted.

"Thank you for that greeting. Anjo appreciates the enthusiasm of her stallions." The horses tossed their heads and looked pleased. "And I come with news for my stallion Riders. The Mare Council has made their decision about Ghost."

Jasper stepped forward, with Blaze by his side. He bowed respectfully to River. "Your stallion Riders are eager to hear their decision."

"Good! The Mare Council decided that it should be my choice whether Ghost joins the Run or not—but if he does, they agree that I must be his Rider."

There was a brief smattering of whispers that rustled through the Riders, but as soon as Jasper spoke again they stilled.

"And what is your decision, Mare Rider?"

"Before I tell you that, I want to announce a change. I have listened to talk among our Herd, and I am going to hold to most of our traditions, because those traditions have brought us peace and prosperity for so, so many years, but I also believe there is room for new traditions. The stallion Riders should have more of a voice in decisions that pertain to breeding. I propose that beginning at the end of this summer, after the Stallion Run, each stallion Rider will get to vote on my choice of which mares should be bred to which stallions. Those votes will be tallied and then presented to me. I will weigh the majority vote carefully, along with the recommendations of the new Herd Stallion Rider, before announcing my final decisions."

"So it will be like the new Herd Stallion Rider gets one vote, and then the rest of the Riders also get one—with the majority being that vote?" Jasper asked.

"Exactly."

Clayton stepped up beside Jasper, causing River to frown at him. He was not Herd Stallion Rider—yet. He had no right to step out of the Herd with Jasper. But before River could admonish him, Anjo's serene voice advised otherwise.

That is stallion business—and it is Jasper's place to hold the young Riders in check.

River gritted her teeth, but she agreed with her mare. The fact that Jasper allowed such a breach in behavior was evidence of the obvious— that it was time he and Blaze stepped aside.

"And what if you decide to ride Ghost and he wins?" Clayton asked in a voice that boomed across the field.

"Then Ghost will be Herd Stallion," River said.

"Yes, we understand that," Clayton said. "But how will that affect the vote? Doesn't that give you two votes and the stallion Riders one?"

"Well, yes, it would. Though the stallion Riders don't even have one vote right now. But if I choose to ride Ghost, and if we win, I will not be his Rider. He and I are not bonded. So, the stallion vote will serve in the place of the Herd Stallion Rider vote."

"So, you'll still get one vote?" Clayton asked.

"Yes, Clayton. I will still get only one vote—the *deciding* vote. The same vote I have whether Ghost runs and wins or not." River met and held Clayton's gaze until the Rider eventually looked away. She noticed then that Clayton was looking exceptionally thin, and it suddenly struck her why. He was anticipating her decision, and believed she would ride Ghost in the Run—and River weighed much less than any of the stallion Riders. Her weight could give Ghost an advantage, especially over fifty miles of racing.

Clayton starves himself so that he can beat you and Ghost. He wastes his time, Anjo scoffed.

"And what is your decision, Mare Rider?" Jasper repeated the question.

River lifted the fist-sized blue gemstone so that all of the Riders could see it. "I am going to call on tourmaline for clarity before I speak my decision."

Jasper nodded. "Very wise, Mare Rider."

"Tourmaline is a masculine stone," River explained quickly. "It is also a clarifying crystal. Seers called it a Teller Stone for the insight it can provide during difficult decisions. What I ask of my stallion Riders is for each of you to simply be genuine. Think of your true feelings about Ghost and me competing in the Run. The stone and I will do the rest. Are you ready?"

As one, the stallion Riders nodded.

Still astride Anjo, River lifted the gemstone again, holding it up in front of her face in the palm of her right hand. She focused on her breathing, making sure it was deep and even, and then passed her left hand over the stone as she whispered to it.

"Awaken."

Instantly, the stone warmed in her hand. River stared into its faceted surface. Concentrating with all of her will, River spoke to the blue tourmaline, with Anjo echoing.

"Mighty Teller Stone, I ask for your clarification."

Mighty Teller Stone, my Rider is in need.

"Help me to focus."

Help her focus.

"Help me to understand my stallion Riders."

Speak to her with the voice of stallions.

"Help me to be wise."

My Rider is wise.

"And always, always, help me to know what is best for my Herd."

"The Herd first and always!"

Within the stone, images swirled in a sea of cerulean crystal. First she saw Jasper, his kind, open face nodding at her in agreement. Many of the Riders behind him were also nodding in agreement, though had River glanced up from the Teller Stone she would have seen that not one of them had actually moved.

The image swirled within the crystal again, and when it cleared it showed Clayton. In the stone he was no longer standing beside Jasper, but he'd pushed the older man out of the way and had taken his place. He was staring to his right with a look of rage. The crystal followed his gaze to show Ghost before it refocused on Clayton. Under the influence of the crystal, the image that was reflected showed Clayton's rage, but as River kept studying him she realized she was seeing more than anger. Clayton was afraid.

With a jolt River understood exactly what her childhood friend feared. Clayton believed Ghost would win if he entered the Run. If he didn't believe that, Clayton wouldn't be bothered at all by Ghost's rivalry. And as River continued to commune with the stone, she understood more and more.

If Ghost and I win, Clayton is going to try to split the Herd!

River knew she was right. She could feel it through the stone, and she also knew Clayton well enough that she didn't doubt for an instant that he was capable of leading a revolt within the Herd.

And if Ghost does not compete and Clayton wins? River silently asked the Teller Stone.

The scene within the stone shifted again to show Clayton shouting and red-faced as she stood up to him. And then another scene swam into focus. Riders were behind Clayton—young men and Skye, along with the small clique of girls that followed her almost everywhere. And everyone with Clayton had expressions filled with anger and hate as they glowered at the rest of the Herd where they stood behind River and Anjo—holding steady and true.

He and his followers are not good for our Herd.

Anjo's voice drifted through the stone just before it went blank.

River blinked, and her focus returned to the here and now. She closed her fist around the Teller Stone and bowed her forehead to press against it, publicly showing her appreciation and respect for the power it had shared with her. Holding it in her lap, she met Jasper's gaze and announced:

"What I saw in the Teller Stone solidified the decision I'd already made. In one month, on the last day of summer, Ghost will be competing in the Stallion Run, and I will ride him!"

"Yes! I'm so glad!" April's voice came from somewhere behind River, and as she clapped and cheered, Jasper joined her—nodding his head and smiling. The rest of the stallion Riders applauded, too, some more enthusiastically than others.

Except for Clayton. He did not move. And he only took his narrowed gaze from River when Ghost reared and neighed triumphantly.

River ignored Clayton and smiled at the Riders. "You only have about a month until the last day of summer, so practice up, Riders. You're going to have to compete against a prime stallion's brawn and the brains of a Lead Mare Rider."

She turned Anjo with slight pressure from the inside of her calf and the mare galloped from the field, with Ghost at their heels. They didn't need to jump over the gate again, as April had left it open when she joined her sister. As soon as they were out of view of the stallion Riders, River stopped Anjo and slid quickly from her back, walking toward Ghost, who trotted to her, his ears pricked and attentive.

"Anjo, ask Ghost if he really wants to win the Stallion Run."

Before her mare could relay his answer, Ghost snorted and tossed his head. River smiled. "I think that's a yes."

It is. Ghost wants to win the Run.

"Ask him why he wants to be Lead Stallion."

Ghost rested his muzzle on her shoulder as Anjo responded for him.

He says the Herd will need a champion, and he believes he is strong enough to be that champion. He wants to protect the Herd—always.

"Good. Then let's win this. Starting right now. Anjo, I'm going to mount Ghost, and I need him to do as I say."

Of course! Ghost is honored that you will be his Rider, if only temporarily.

As the golden stallion knelt gracefully so that River could mount him for the very first time, she spoke hastily to her mare, who relayed everything to the stallion . . .

Later, April told River that just before she and Ghost thundered back to the Choosing Theater, Clayton had been making a lot of noise, saying that no one even knew if she *could* ride Ghost in the Run. Had anyone seen River ride the stallion? Even once? Anyone?

When no one spoke, Clayton had continued railing against Ghost, saying he was, after all, nothing but a rogue stallion who should probably be put down before he became dangerous.

But the field went silent when Ghost thundered back with River confidently astride. The stallion slid to a stop, snorting and prancing in place.

"I almost forgot to wish my Riders luck." She grinned at them. Even that short sprint had her head reeling with Ghost's speed. River was positive no stallion in Herd Magenti—in all of the Herds—had his power and speed. *And he's been letting Anjo win races against him—clever boy!* "So, best of luck to all of the stallion Riders racing against Ghost and me, but you'll understand if I don't wish you a mare's luck—I think it only proper that I keep *that* particular luck for myself."

She cued Ghost, and like she'd been riding him for years instead of mere minutes, the stallion whirled around and sprinted from the field, throwing dirt and grass behind him and all over the other Riders.

"I'm not sure that was necessary," River told him as they rejoined Anjo and she slid from his back, petting his smooth neck affectionately.

Not necessary, but fun? her mare asked.

River looked up at the golden stallion and her beautiful silver mare. "It definitely was fun. Anjo, we're going to beat every one of them."

Anjo's response was tinged with humor. *Of course you are! The only horse who can beat Ghost is me—and then only when he lets me.*

"You know he lets you win?"

Ghost's snort sounded a lot like laughter, and Anjo nipped him playfully on the neck before her typically confident answer sounded in River's mind.

I am Lead Mare. I know everything.

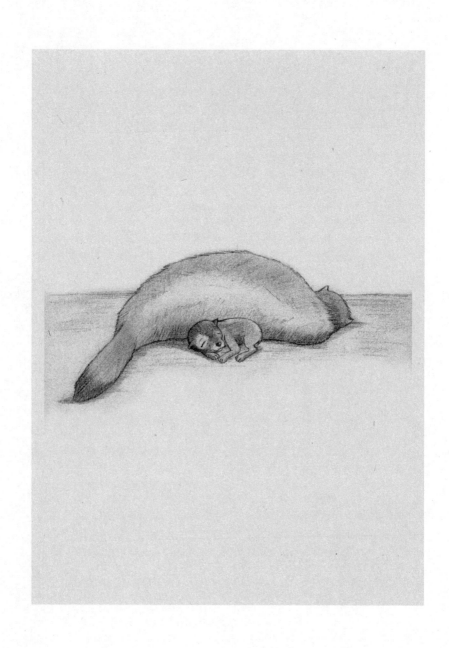

CHAPTER 23

I t took two weeks for the Pack to acclimate to the constant climb that was their path through the Rock Mountains. Mari decided it really wouldn't have been that difficult had they not had a whole world of supplies with them, and because of that it took a while for new blisters and then calluses to form on shoulders and hips from where they'd rigged the straps for carrying the litters. Thankfully, every Pack member's hands had been toughened from months of using paddles or oars, so getting used to their new method of travel wasn't too hard. And everyone—even Danita and Dove, who had come to love the water—was happy to be on dry land.

At the two-week mark they reached the snow line, which meant they were able to camp every night safely on the ground, instead of climbing into the boughs of the giant pines and strapping themselves there in the travel cloaks the Tribe had called cocoons. But when they came to the snow line, Antreas had explained that the swarm and other predatory insects, like wolf spiders, would not bother them, as they could not tolerate the cold. Even at that altitude there was still plenty of green in the forest around them and the days weren't terribly cold. The nights got frigid, but the Pack soon learned to circle around a large campfire—everyone close together for warmth. Antreas taught them to build temporary lean-tos using those same travel cloaks the Earth Walkers had been busily weaving all during the trip. They blocked much of the cutting night wind, and made the frosty darkness a lot easier to bear. It was strange for every member of the Pack except Antreas to sleep in a forest and *not* be either fifty plus feet above the ground or snug in a burrow below.

The morning that began their third week in the mountains, there was a dusting of snow on the lean-tos, though the sky was clear and the sun they greeted painted the sky with watercolors of mauve and daffodil.

"We're crossing a treacherous part of the pass today," Antreas told the Pack after they'd greeted the sun, broken their fast, and repacked the litters. "The rail runs along the side of a steep cliff, and then we have to cross a bridge."

"A rail bridge? How is that still standing and safe?" Nik asked.

"It's not the original bridge the rails were on—none of those are still standing. Lynx guides built a suspension bridge where the rail ends and anchored it to the other side of the gorge where it begins again. It's just wide enough to accommodate the litters, but we'll have to cross in single file. I'm really proud of you. We've made better time than I expected. If we keep going at this pace we'll be leaving the mountains in just two more weeks, at the end of summer—giving us enough warm days left to build shelters for the winter, just as we planned."

The Pack cheered themselves and then set out. Today Mari and Nik were walking beside a litter carrying Mariah's eleven pups—as well as their father, Cammyman, after Mari decided that, though his lacerated legs and amputated tail were healing well, he'd walked long enough. Mariah was completely recovered from giving birth, and generally the only time the well-conditioned Shepherd rode on the litter was when she needed to nurse her pups.

"They're starting to open their eyes!" Mari picked up one of the blond puppies and kissed its nose as it blinked, molelike, at her. Beside her, Rigel whined, and Mari bent so that he could sniff and lick the pup before she put her back on the litter. "That puppy smell—I'll never get over how much I love it."

"Apparently, neither will Rigel," Nik said, grinning at the young Shepherd.

"My Rigel is going to make a wonderful father someday," Mari said.

Beside him, Laru grumbled, making Nik laugh. "Oh, don't be so grumpy. Everyone knows you are already an excellent father."

"Puppy smell is intoxicating, isn't it?" Claudia called over her shoulder. She and Davis had rigged their litter so that they could share pulling it between them.

"I believe it is how they survive," said Dove, who was walking on the other side of the litter. One hand rested on its rail. The other held a long stick that she kept sweeping out in front of her so that she knew when to step over forest debris in the path. "They are terribly helpless when they're little."

"Oh, I don't know. I think they are so beautiful that we would love and care for them even if they were stinky," said Lily shyly. Though Dove was becoming more and more independent, Lily chose to remain close to her ex-mistress. The two young women chatted easily and were obviously good friends.

"They're definitely cute," said Mari. "I can't wait to see what this litter is going to look like full grown."

"Don't you mean who?" Davis said, chuckling softly. "Cammy or Mariah?

From his spot on the litter, snuggled against eleven pups, Cammy barked in agreement.

Mari laughed. "I think we can already guess which ones will take after their father." She touched the soft heads of the pups as she spoke. "This one, this one, this one, and this one are all blond, and smaller than the others. I'll bet they'll look just like their brave father."

"I hope they take after him, too!" said Claudia, smiling over her shoulder at Cammyman.

Walking beside her Companion, Mariah huffed happily.

"Oh, good! There you are, Lily!" Rose hurried up with one of Fala's pups in her arms. "Would you watch this little boy for me? His two sisters are sound asleep, but this one won't settle. He always has been the most curious of the litter, and for some reason today he's being extra precocious. Fala and I want to hunt ahead, and he's just not big enough to come with us yet."

"Of course!" Lily held out her arms and a harried-looking Rose handed the pup to her. The bright-eyed Terrier looked up at Lily, licked her face, and wriggled his whole rear end happily.

"If he's too whiny you can let him walk beside you for a while. He shouldn't wander—he knows better." Rose gave the pup a hard look and scratched him under his chin, where there was a grayish-white patch of hair growing like an old man's beard.

The pup yapped in excitement and wriggled some more.

"Okay, I'll let you walk, but you have to stay with me, and when you get tired you can curl up with Cammy and the other puppies," Lily said.

"Whether he agrees or not, that sounds like an excellent idea. I'll get him when I come back," Rose said.

"No hurry. I like watching him," said Lily.

"Hey, you're not hunting alone, are you?" Mari asked.

"Absolutely not! Sheena and Captain are joining me. Oh, and Antreas said he found wolverine scat. Would you pass that down the line so everyone knows?"

"Sure," Mari said as Rose jogged away to join Fala, Sheena, and her Captain. Mari turned to look behind her at Sora, who was walking on one side of O'Bryan, with Jenna, carrying her Companion, Khan, on his other side. O'Bryan pulled one of the smaller litters, and the two young women took turns spelling him when he got tired. "Did you hear that?"

"Sure did. Chloe and I will go back and tell the rest of the Pack, and I'll also tell them to tighten up the line. With wolverines around, we don't want anyone to be straggling." She took Chloe out of her sling. The pup touched noses with the little male Rose had dropped off with Lily.

"Khan and I will come with you. He needs the exercise. I think he's getting fat." Jenna lifted her pup from her sling and studied his round belly. "What do you think, O'Bryan?"

"I think he's as well fed as he is well loved."

"Which means he needs the exercise," said Sora. "Just like Chloe. Be back in a little while, and then I'll take the litter for the next few miles."

"No rush. I'm not tired at all, and Antreas says the bridge we have to cross is pretty close. We'll all get a short break then while we line up to go across," said O'Bryan.

"Okay, well, don't wear yourself out." Sora nodded to Jenna, and they started down the line of the Pack, passing the news about wolverine sign and making sure everyone remained close and safe, with their pups trotting behind them, chubby butts wriggling in perfect time together.

Mari watched them for a little while before turning to Nik. "Is it normal that I'm missing Rigel's puppy days? He's big and magnificent, but I do miss his gangly legs and floppy ears." She petted the top of her Companion's head, which was now as tall as his father's.

"It's completely normal. Puppies are magickal." Nik lowered his voice and whispered: "But adult canines are much less trouble."

"I heard that!" Claudia said.

"Yeah, so did I," said Davis. "We know we're in for trouble times eleven."

They were all laughing when the rail path emerged from the forest and took a sharp turn to the left, snaking along a sheer cliff that ended in an abrupt drop to a white-water gorge far below, with the iron rails reaching out to connect to nothing. Beside the broken rails was a suspension bridge that was swaying gently in the cold midday breeze.

"I do not like how that looks," said Lily as she crouched to pet the little male pup who was batting around a pinecone at her feet.

"Okay." Antreas spoke in a booming voice as he walked up and down the paused line. "We'll cross single file—one small group at a time. Give the group in front of you a few yards before you begin. That should keep the bridge from bowing down or up too much. It's normal that it sways. And we need to double up on the litters. Don't drag them over the bridge. They'll get hung up on the wooden slats and may even pull some free, which is not a good thing."

"You're sure it's safe?" Sora asked.

"It's perfectly safe—as long as you don't fall off," said Antreas.

"Antreas, Bast, and I will cross with our litter first," said Danita.

Bast coughed and chirped from her place in line, which was always close to Danita.

"That's right. Like Bast says, we'll show you how easy it is," said Antreas. "It really does look a lot worse than it is."

Mari stared over the edge of the cliff at the rapids below. "It's a long way down, that's for sure."

"It is—so don't fall. Keep any free hands you have on the ropes that serve as railings," said Antreas. "Okay, Danita and I will cross. I think it'd be a good idea for Mariah and the pups to cross behind us."

Cammy barked and tried to get off the litter, but Davis caught him. "Hang on, big guy. The pups are going to need you up there with them to keep them calm during the crossing. You're a lot lighter than Mariah."

Cammy huffed but settled again, and the eleven pups quit whining and curled up against him. Mariah came to sniff her family, and Cammy licked her.

"We're all set," said Davis. "If the Pack would make way we'll move up and be ready to start across as soon as Antreas lets us know we should."

"Shall I cross with them?" Dove asked.

"Yes. How about you let Fala's pup ride with Cammy and the babies so that Lily can help you across?" said Mari.

"That's a good idea," said Lily, picking up the restless pup and plopping him down beside Cammy. The pup instantly flopped over on his side and started batting at Cammy's long blond beard.

Mari swore she heard the adult Terrier sigh in annoyance, but he continued to tolerate the playful pup.

"You're a good boy, Cammyman," Mari said, sending him an image of the extra helping of cooked rabbit that she was planning to add to his dinner.

Cammy's nub of a tail began wagging, and he gave her an open-mouthed canine grin.

"You're spoiling him," Davis said without turning around.

"I can't help it," Mari said. "He's adorable."

"You won't say that if he gets fat and you have to take a turn dragging his litter," Davis said.

Cammyman huffed and sneezed, making Nik chuckle.

"Let's cross with Dove and Lily. That way we can be on the other side to encourage those who are frightened by heights," said Mari.

Nik nodded. "Good idea." They moved into position behind Davis and Claudia as they made their way to the front of the line and the suspension bridge.

Antreas entered the bridge first, moving at an unhurried, but confident pace. Lifting the rear of the litter that held their supplies, Danita crossed right behind, and Bast padded along after them.

When Antreas was several yards out on the swaying bridge, he called back.

"Okay, Davis and Claudia, you can cross with the litter. Mari and Nik, give them a few yards and then cross with Lily and Dove."

"Will do!" Nik shouted.

Mari glanced behind them. Spencer and Jaxom were sharing litter duty. Jaxom looked worried, but Spencer just seemed curious.

"Are you two ready to go next?"

"No!"

"Yes!"

They'd answered together, and Spencer pushed Jaxom's shoulder. "Hey, don't worry about it. I'll take the front of the litter."

Fortina, who was always at Jaxom's side, barked encouragement. "Okay, then Fortina and I will follow you."

"Everyone ready to follow Jaxom and Spencer?" Mari asked.

The Pack nodded, though Mari saw several pale faces among her people. O'Bryan, Sora, and Jenna were in line behind Jaxom and Spencer. O'Bryan nodded enthusiastically. "I'm ready to cross! This is lots better than battling Mouths and Monkeys," he shouted down the line, eliciting nervous smiles and nods of agreement.

"The bridge is really just a larger, longer version of the walkways that connected our nests and platforms," Nik said.

"It sure is," said O'Bryan. He looked at the Earth Walkers around him, grinning easily. "This will be easy. Those bridges are sturdy *because* they have the ability to sway. So, don't be afraid."

"Oh, I guess that does make sense," said an obviously nervous-looking Sora, who had returned with Jenna and their pups to stand beside O'Bryan.

"We'll cross together," said O'Bryan. "I'll show you how."

"Thank you!" Sora's voice was filled with relief as she and Jenna tucked their pups back into their slinglike carriers.

"If any of you are feeling too nervous, pair with someone from the Tribe," called Mari.

"Yeah, I'll be happy to come back and help you over," said Nik.

"As will I," said O'Bryan.

From farther down the line Lydia, Sarah, and Wilkes echoed their words.

Rose and Sheena jogged up. Their hunting satchels were bulging with newly killed game.

"Lily, are you okay to cross with the pup?" Rose called out to her.

"He's already crossing," Lily responded. "He's on the litter with Cammy and the pups."

"That's perfect!" Rose said. "I'll carry the other two across if Sora and Jenna are fine going together."

"We'll be fine crossing with O'Bryan," said Sora, still looking pale and shooting nervous glances at the swaying bridge.

"Okay, let's go," Mari said. "Nik, would you please lead. Then Lily can follow you. Dove will follow her—holding on to the back of her tunic—and I'll come after Dove, keeping a hand on her in case she gets unbalanced."

"Thank you, Moon Woman," Dove said, smiling and turning her face to Mari. "My balance is usually excellent, but I've never crossed a swaying bridge before."

"Well, I did very briefly at the Tribe of the Trees, and it wasn't entirely unpleasant," Mari said.

"I wish I could see it," said Dove as they stepped out on the wooden slats of the moving bridge.

"No you don't," said Lily firmly.

The crossing went surprisingly well. Mari simply didn't look down. Not once. She stared at the other side of the bridge, where Danita was calling encouragement. Halfway across Lily stumbled, catching the toe of her shoe on an uneven slat of wood. As she tripped Dove's grip on her tightened, so that in a turnabout of the norm, it was she who righted Lily, and not the other way around.

"Oh, thank you!" Lily said, running a hand across her damp brow.

"You are most wel—" Dove began, but panicked yips and whines from the litter in front of them interrupted her.

Mari looked over Nik's shoulder to see the little gray bearded pup Lily had so recently been babysitting standing up at the edge of the litter, staring back at Lily, obviously upset.

"He's worried about Lily," called Claudia. "Say something to him so he knows you're okay."

"Oh! Yes, of course," Lily said. "Little boy, all is well. I simply tripped, but Dove saved me."

"Well, you were not *really* in danger," said Dove.

"You wouldn't say that if you could see where we are," Lily whispered before raising her voice again and calling to the pup. "Almost to the other side. I promise I will give you an extra-big cuddle soon."

The pup sat his fat butt down, but continued to whine pitifully.

"Precious baby," Lily cooed from the bridge. "It's okay."

Suddenly Mari saw Lily's back stiffen. At first she thought the girl had tripped again—until Lily spoke.

"Oh! Oh, my! Your name is Dash! Oh, precious one! I'm coming!"

Nik looked over his shoulder at Lily, and his face broke into a radiant smile.

"The pup has Chosen!" he shouted.

Behind them, O'Bryan took up the call. "The pup has Chosen!"

Lily gasped. "Me? He Chose me?"

Dash stood again and wagged his whole body, yipping excitedly.

"Oh, he did! Dash Chose *me*!" Lily exclaimed. "I'm coming, my precious one! I'm coming!"

Her voice filled with happiness, Dove was the first to congratulate her friend. "Lily, that is wonderful! I am so, so happy for you!"

"May the Sun bless your union!" Nik said.

"Thank you! Thank you so much!" Lily said.

As soon as the litter had crossed over, Dash jumped from it and started to run toward Lily, who was just a few yards from the end of the bridge.

"Danita, grab him! He could easily slide off the bridge," Mari called, worry spiking through her as the pup barreled toward the swaying length of rope and wood.

Jenna nodded and reached for the pup, who lunged to the side, trying to avoid being caught.

But Dash had misjudged. He'd moved too far too fast, and his paws slipped on the loose rock. He was going too fast to right himself, and with a scream of terror, the little Terrier slid over the edge of the cliff.

"No!" Lily cried.

Fala's howl of agony sounded from behind them, echoed by Rose's grief-stricken shriek.

"Oh, Goddess!" Mari said. "Hurry, Nik!"

They surged from the bridge. Lily was sobbing as she raced to the cliff's edge. "No! Oh, no no no! Dash! Dash!"

Mari pulled her back. "There's nothing you can do," she said as she wiped a tear from Lily's cheek. "He's gone."

"No! He can't be! I will not let him be!" Lily sobbed. "Dash! Come back to me! Dash!"

From below them came a miserable whine. "It's him! It's my Dash!" Lily dropped to her belly, and Mari could think of nothing to do but sit on her legs, trying to anchor her.

"There he is! I see him! He's on a ledge below us!" Lily cried.

"Tell him to stay calm. We'll go down and get him," said Nik.

"Dash! Dash! Listen to me! We're going to come down to you. Just stay really still," said Lily.

The pup yipped pitifully.

"He understands, but he's afraid!" Lily said. "And he's hurt!"

Mari focused on connecting with the pup. Unlike the other Companions, she had the ability to communicate with all the canines. She could even talk with Bast, though the feline's mind felt decidedly different from a Terrier's or Shepherd's. Mari didn't like to use her special ability, as she felt it was an intrusion, but as she connected with the distraught pup she silently thanked the Goddess for her gift.

It's okay, little Dash. We're coming for you. While she spoke to the pup Mari painted a picture of him being very still as hands reached out to lift him to safety.

Dash whined and yipped again.

Where do you hurt? she asked him.

He sent her an image of his right front leg. Mari was trying to decide whether it was broken or not when the pup relayed another picture to her that had Mari's breath stopping.

"Nik!"

He hurried to her as he tied a noose into a long length of rope. "I'm hurrying," he said.

"The pup's hurt, but I don't think badly. It's his right front leg." Then she lowered her voice and whispered to Nik, "And he isn't alone down there."

His eyes widened. *Danger?* he mouthed.

Mari nodded.

The pup whimpered and whined.

"It's okay, my precious one!" Lily soothed. "We're coming to save you!"

O'Bryan rushed over to them. "Set up the anchor. I'm better at rappelling than you are. I'm going over the edge."

"Agreed," Nik said. Then Mari watched him whisper to his cousin.

O'Bryan nodded grimly and unsheathed the long knife he wore on his belt. "Sora, I need that sling you carry Chloe in."

"Of course!" Sora unwound the sling and then rushed to O'Bryan, rewrapping it around him. "Just stuff the pup in the front here. He'll stay."

"Perfect. Thank you."

Sora touched his arm gently. "Please don't fall."

"I'll do my best," he said.

Nik worked quickly, with Antreas helping him. First they looped rope around Lily's legs, securing it to a scrub tree that grew by the bridge. Then they used a boulder as an anchor for O'Bryan's rappelling line, wrapping the thick length of braided hemp around it.

Wilkes and Sheena hurried off the bridge. Immediately they helped with the anchor. Rose rushed to Lily's side, dropping to her stomach to peer over the edge as she took Lily's hand in hers. Davis tied another rope around Rose's legs, securing her to another immovable rock.

"It's okay. O'Bryan will save you—just like he did during the forest fire," Rose called down to Dash. Fala, pressed against her Companion, barked encouragement down to her puppy.

Behind them, Mari could hear Dove praying to the Goddess to keep Dash and O'Bryan safe.

O'Bryan stepped into the makeshift harness Nik had created with an intricate series of knots. He nodded to Nik, who moved back, following the rope. Most of the Pack had crossed, and when Nik called, "I need the strongest of you! Wrap your hands and take hold of this rope. We anchor O'Bryan and drop him over the side *slowly*," Wilkes, Jaxom, Mason, Davis, Antreas, and Sheena didn't hesitate in joining Nik on the rope.

"Okay, I'm ready," O'Bryan said.

"Start rappelling. We've got you," said Nik.

"I don't doubt you for a second, Cuz." O'Bryan flashed a smile at Nik and patted the handle of his wickedly sharp knife. "And I'm ready for whatever I find down there." Then he disappeared over the edge.

The rope went taut.

"Steady!" Nik said. "We release him slowly."

Mari moved off Lily's legs and someone anchored her legs as she lay on her belly beside the distraught newly Chosen Companion, watching O'Bryan rappel smoothly down the impossibly steep cliff.

"Almost to the ledge!" O'Bryan called.

"About three more feet," Mari told Nik.

"Got it—let him down gently—three feet," Nik said.

"He's on the ledge!" Mari said.

"Hey there, little Dash. I've got you!" O'Bryan said, squatting to pick up the pup. Dash cried sharply. "Oh, I see! Come here. That hurts, doesn't it? Okay, I'll be careful, but let me wrap you in this sling." As he gently put the pup in the sling, O'Bryan looked up and shouted, "Looks like he might have broken his leg, but other than that he seems scared, but fine." Then his gaze slid to the far side of the ledge, which was covered in shadow. "Give me a foot or so. I have to check out—" O'Bryan began. His words cut off, and Mari tried to see what he was looking at, but she could only make out something that looked like a pile of forest debris.

"Be careful, O'Bryan. You have the pup. Let's get you two up here," said Mari.

"I'm coming. I just—" O'Bryan stopped abruptly and then he crouched, staring at the pile of debris and poking it with his long knife. Mari saw him jump in surprise. "Bloody beetle balls! I don't believe it!"

"What is it?" she asked.

He reached into the shadowy pile and pulled out something white that wriggled and cried. "Bloody beetle balls!" he repeated, staring up, up, up above Mari and the rest of them to the cliff that protruded over them, before stuffing the white thing in the sling with Dash.

O'Bryan stood, put away his knife, and went to the cliffside, reaching up to find two secure handholds. "Okay, I'm ready! Pull me back up. I'll do what I can to help."

It took a lot longer to pull him up than it'd taken to drop him down, but O'Bryan was finally within reach, and Mari, Lily, and Rose grabbed onto him, helping him the final few feet.

He spilled out onto the path with a grunt, landing on his back to protect the pup wrapped against his chest.

Dash immediately began whining pitifully, and Lily went to her knees beside O'Bryan, reaching for her pup.

O'Bryan sat and carefully pulled Dash from the sling, handing him to Lily. "It's his right front leg. Don't worry. Mari's fixed far worse."

"Oh, precious one! My boy! Oh, Dash, let me look at you!" Lily cooed as the pup buried his head against her neck. He was still whining and in obvious pain, but his little tail was wagging.

"Hold him close for a little while to calm him, and once he understands he's safe I'll take a look at that leg," said Mari. Then she turned to O'Bryan, who was peering down into the sling. "What else was down there?"

"Well, I think it was a dead wolverine," said O'Bryan.

Antreas pushed through the crowd that had formed around them. "Long brown fur with some white—usually framing the face and sometimes on the body? Huge paws—as big as Bast's—with long, visible claws?"

"Yeah, that's what it looked like," O'Bryan said as he reached back into the sling. "And this was pressed against its belly."

He lifted the little creature from the sling. It was perfectly white and about the size of the smallest of Mariah's pups, though this baby was obviously much younger—maybe even newborn. Its eyes were tightly closed and it was hardly moving and mewing weakly.

"Great Stormshaker! That's a wolverine kit! I've never seen one before—only heard about them from another guide who found a mother and two kits dead after a bad flood one spring. But that's exactly what he described."

"It looks really young," said Rose. She held out her hands. "May I?"

O'Bryan nodded and handed the baby to Rose. She studied it, turning the kit and looking for injuries.

"It looks uninjured, but this is a newborn. There's no telling how long it's been down there."

"The mother was rigid. She'd been dead a while," O'Bryan said.

"This baby is close to death as well," Rose said sadly, handing it back to O'Bryan.

"But, we can save it, right?" Mari asked, reaching out to stroke the baby gently with one finger.

"It needs milk," said O'Bryan, his gaze searching the Pack until he found Claudia. "Excuse me," he said as he started pushing his way through the crowd to her.

Mari and Nik followed. She understood what O'Bryan intended—and she hoped it would work.

Once he reached Claudia he wasted no time. "This is a newborn wolverine kit—that's what Antreas says to call a baby wolverine. Its mother is dead on the ledge." O'Bryan pointed up. "From down there I could see that there's an opening to a den on the face of the cliff above us. The mother must have somehow fallen, and the pup came with her. Her neck was twisted at a weird angle, so I'm thinking she died instantly, but she must have broken the fall for her kit. May I show it to you?"

Claudia was already looking with obvious curiosity at the mewing baby in his hands, and she nodded. "Of course!"

He opened his hands, and Claudia gasped. "It looks so much like a puppy!"

Davis moved up beside her and touched the kit hesitantly. "It really does."

"It's going to die without help. Claudia, I would like to ask that you allow Mariah to feed the kit. Please. It would mean a lot to me."

"Before you answer, I just want to add some common sense," said Antreas. "I have never known of a wolverine to tolerate the presence of a human, a canine, or a feline. They are ferocious and solitary. I am not saying we should let this young one die. I only want you to understand you might be saving a creature that will turn on you, on a pup, on any of us."

Danita slid her hand into Antreas's and spoke in a clear voice that carried through the watching, waiting Pack.

"Didn't you tell me Lynxes are solitary as well—always?"

"Yes, that's true," said Antreas.

"But you and Bast were not happy with that life. You wanted—*needed* our Pack. So, just because people see wolverines one way, like people see Lynxes, that doesn't hold true for *every* Lynx." Beside her, Bast chirped in agreement.

Antreas looked at Mari. "What do you think, Moon Woman?"

Mari answered without hesitation. "I think that's a newborn who needs our help, and I wouldn't want to withhold that help because we're judging the baby by the mother. Sora?"

"I am in complete agreement with you," said the other Moon Woman.

"We are not heartless. Nor are we cruel. And we would have to be one or both to allow a newborn to die."

"Claudia?" O'Bryan asked.

"I agree with our Moon Women. That's a baby—not an enemy. And maybe if we take it in and love and nurture it, the baby won't grow up to be an enemy. But I cannot answer for my Companion. It is Mariah's decision, and I will abide by that."

"I agree, with one additional thought," Davis said. "I hope very, very much that Mariah agrees."

Mari saw that the Pack was nodding in response to Davis's comment, and it made her heart soar to see their compassion.

"Let's ask her," said Claudia, leading the way to their litter.

Cammy was curled up beside Mariah, who was nursing her puppies and looking utterly content. As they approached, Cammy and Mariah pricked their ears, sniffing the air curiously.

"Go ahead, show her. And then ask her. I'll let you know if she has any questions," said Claudia.

O'Bryan went to Mariah. He still had the kit in his hands, cradling it against his chest, trying to keep the baby warm.

"Mariah, I need to ask a large favor. I found this newborn wolverine kit by its dead mother. It's going to die, too—soon, if it doesn't nurse and stay warm. Would you please allow it to nurse with your litter?"

Mariah looked from O'Bryan to her Companion.

"She would like to sniff it," explained Claudia.

"Oh, sure." O'Bryan sat on the side of the litter and held the kit so the female Shepherd could inspect it.

As Mariah sniffed the baby, Cammy limped to join her, his stub wagging in welcome. Then Mariah nuzzled the kit and licked it—tentatively at first. Then, as it wriggled and cried pathetically, she whined and licked it some more.

"Oh, that's my kind, wise girl!" Claudia's eyes were shining with tears when she told O'Bryan, in a voice that carried throughout the Pack, "Mariah will mother the kit!"

"Oh, thank the Sun!" O'Bryan said. "Now?"

"Yes! Yes! That baby needs milk and comfort right away!" said Claudia.

O'Bryan quickly guided the kit to an empty nipple in the middle of the pile of Mariah's fat, sleepy puppies—who mewed and complained and then fell immediately back to sleep.

The kit sniffed at the nipple, and it looked for a moment like it was going to refuse. Then Mariah took over. She pushed O'Bryan's hands away and nuzzled the kit, licking it and whining softly to the baby. The kit responded quickly and began rooting around her stomach until *finally* it latched on and began suckling with enthusiasm and kneading Mariah's soft belly fur. The mother sighed and lay back as Cammy huffed and wagged.

"He does understand that's not his kit, right?" Nik asked Davis.

"Oh, make no mistake, Cammy has claimed the baby just as surely as O'Bryan and Mariah," said Davis. Then he added in a reverent voice, "Thank you, Great Earth Mother! Thank you for this small, special life and the heroes who are saving it."

O'Bryan petted Mariah. "Thank you! What a good, good girl you are. Thank you so much." Then he stood and faced Mari and Sora—and the rest of the Pack. "And I give my word that I will take full responsibility for this kit. If he, or she—I'm not even sure which it is."

"He," Claudia spoke up. "Mariah says it is a little boy."

"Well, he then! If *he* causes problems, it will be me who solves those problems, even if it means bringing him back to these mountains and releasing him."

Dove pushed through the crowd with Lily. She was still cradling Dash, but the little Terrier had gone silent. His eyes were closed and his head was tucked against Lily's neck.

Dove stopped beside O'Bryan and reached out to touch his face. She smiled radiantly, and Mari thought—not for the first time—how delicately beautiful she was.

"You will not have to release him. He will be the second greatest love of

your life." Dove spoke with the singsong tone that signified her words came from the Goddess. *"You will be greatly blessed for this act of kindness—we all will be."*

O'Bryan put his hand over hers. "Thank you, Dove."

She shook her head, still smiling kindly. "Do not thank me, O'Bryan. Thank our benevolent Goddess."

"But I worship the Sun God," said O'Bryan.

"Is there not room in your heart to love more than one God?" Dove asked.

O'Bryan blinked in surprise. "I've never thought of it like that before. Yes! Yes, my heart is big enough to love more than one God."

"When we stop for the night I was planning on leaving an offering for the Great Earth Mother to thank her for putting this little life in our path. You may join me if you'd like," said Davis.

"I would. I would like that very much," said O'Bryan.

As the Pack crowded around Mariah's unusual family, Mari set and wrapped Dash's leg, and then, after conferring with Rose, she made a tincture of horsetail for healing and a quick broth from deer jerky and a healthy dose of dried devil's claw to control his pain.

"That should hold him until we camp and I draw down the moon," said Mari, caressing Dash's silky fur as the pup slept soundly in Lily's arms.

"Lily, you and Dash can ride on our litter," said Antreas. "It's not far to our campsite."

"Yeah, and you and little Dash don't weigh much," added Danita, touching the pup gently. "And congratulations, Companion."

Lily turned her happy, tearstained face up to smile her relief to Antreas and Danita. "Oh, thank you so much. I would like to ride. I'm feeling a little odd."

"That's normal," Antreas said. "When our Companions are hurt or stressed, it affects us. But on the positive side, it also affects us when they're happy, which they usually are." He reached down and ruffled Bast's scruff as the big feline purred.

Just before the Pack moved out, Laru padded ahead and barked sharply, calling to attention every canine in the group. Nik nodded to Laru and then went to Lily where she was resting comfortably on Antreas and Danita's litter, her sleeping puppy in her arms.

"Lily, do you accept and vow to love and care for Dash until fate parts you by death?" Nik asked her formally.

"Oh, yes! Yes I do!"

"May the Sun bless your union with Dash." Nik spoke ceremonially, his voice deep and filled with joy.

Lily's smile was radiant. "Thank you, Sun Priest."

Then Laru raised his muzzle and howled, the traditional greeting for a newly made Companion bond, and every canine in the Pack—even Mariah's young litter, minus the kit, who was still nursing, with increasing strength—raised their muzzles and joined their Alpha in welcoming Lily and her precious Companion, Dash.

That night they camped beside an icy waterfall, where everyone replenished their water stores and Sora made a delectable rabbit stew seasoned with truffles Fala's sharp nose had discovered. The night was cold, so many of the flaps on the lean-tos of those who had later watches were closed against the biting wind.

Antreas ducked under the closed flap of the shelter he shared with Danita and Bast. He grinned at Danita's sleepy look as she scooted over, causing Bast to complain, as she had to roll onto a cold spot amongst their pelts.

"How is the little kit doing?" Danita asked around a yawn.

"According to O'Bryan and Mariah, he is perfect. Apparently Mariah says he has lost almost all of his wolverine smell, and currently smells like a canine—which pleases Mariah immensely."

"I'm really glad O'Bryan saved that baby. I'll be interested to see what he grows up to be."

"I will, too."

As Antreas lay beside her, Danita lifted herself up on her elbow so that she could study him. "Do you really think the kit's going to turn into a monster?"

Antreas shrugged. "I have no idea—though I do respect Dove's ability to channel whatever she channels from the Goddess."

"Are you being grumpy?"

Antreas blinked in surprise. "No! I'm being pragmatic." Then he smiled. "But I do think that kit is very interesting."

"It's amazing how much he looks like a puppy."

"He won't stay that way. He's going to grow faster than a pup, and his body and coloring will change dramatically. I just hope his personality remains puppy-like."

"I don't," Danita said firmly. "I hope he stays a wolverine—but he's our Pack's wolverine. Like Bast. She's not like other Lynxes, because she doesn't like to be alone, but isn't she still very Lynx-like?"

"Bast is totally Lynx-like, except for that one thing," agreed Antreas.

"Then that's what I wish for O'Bryan's kit, too. He'll be *our* wolverine—and if he needs to be ferocious, it will be in protection of our Pack."

Antreas smoothed her hair back. "I like the way you think."

"That's good, because I'm not very fond of change."

Antreas barked a laugh. "Not fond of change? You're changing your entire life by going on this journey and falling in love with Bast and me."

"That's different. Where I'm going and who I'm with changed, but I didn't. At least not much." She chewed her lip, and Antreas could see she was thinking about the attack that had, indeed, caused parts of her personality to change.

He took her hand. "When you put it like that I understand. And know I love you exactly as you are."

Danita pulled herself out of her dark thoughts and grinned cheekily. "I do know! And that's one of the things I love best about you." She leaned into Antreas and kissed him.

Antreas relaxed, loving the feel and the taste of her. He kept his arms loosely draped around her—understanding after the months they'd been together that he had to be careful not to make Danita feel trapped in any way.

He expected her to stop kissing him as she always did, which was fine. Of course he would rather have continued to touch her—to make love to her—but he did love Danita and it had only been a few months since she had been attacked. It would take patience and love, but that didn't deter Antreas. Danita was worth it. And he would wait as long as she needed to heal.

But she didn't stop kissing him. Instead her arms slid around his shoulders and she sighed in contentment as their kiss deepened. Then, tentatively at first, Danita's hands found his chest, which she explored with sweet, soft caresses. When her lips moved down his neck to follow the path of her hands, he moaned in pleasure.

"That feels good?" she asked.

"Better than good," he said breathlessly.

She grinned. "That means I'm doing it right!"

"Hey, you couldn't do it wrong. It's just us. You can touch me wherever—however you want."

Her grin widened. "You make this fun."

"That's my plan!"

She kissed his neck again, tasting him with her tongue and nipping his earlobe playfully.

He laughed and shifted her so that she was on her back and he was over her. She reached up, pulling his lips down to hers, and Antreas kissed her passionately, his arms tightening around her.

Danita froze, and her breath caught in her throat.

Instantly, Antreas lifted himself off her—touching her hair and face gently as he soothed, "It's okay—it's okay. It's just me. You're safe. You're always safe with me."

Danita sat up and with a trembling hand wiped tears from her cheeks. This was usually when she became defeated and quiet, though she'd eventually fall asleep and return to herself by morning. But this night it was different—*she* was different.

"I have an idea," she said.

"Okay . . ."

"I like kissing you. I like it a lot," Danita said.

"I like kissing you, too. A lot."

"But when you're on top of me I get scared," she said.

"Yep. I'm sorry about that. I didn't mean to—"

She pressed her fingers against his lips. "No, don't apologize. I want to be in your arms. That's all you were doing—pulling me into your arms. But what if I did all the pulling?"

His lips twitched up at the corners. "'Pulling'?"

"Yeah, like this." He was on his back, half propped up against the pelts behind him. Danita leaned into him, putting her arms firmly around him and pulling herself *to him,* and then kissing him thoroughly. When she sat up she asked, "How was that?"

Antreas sounded like he'd been sprinting, but his answer was swift. "Wonderful."

"Oh, good. Let me practice. But would you please keep your arms by your side and let me do everything?"

"It would be my great pleasure to let you do *anything* to me," he said.

And Danita did. She kissed him and explored his body. She even pulled off his shirt, but hesitated when she got to the waist of his pants.

"I—I don't think I can go there."

Antreas opened his mouth to respond, but again Danita shushed, this time by pressing her lips to his and whispering, *"Yet."*

Finally, when the night grew long and they both became sleepy, Danita curled up on Antreas's chest. Her arms wrapped firmly around him, she fell asleep with her lips lifted into a smile and Bast purring loudly, pressed against her back.

Antreas's heartbeat slowed. Moving carefully, he draped his arms around her—in sleep able to hold her without causing her to panic. He kissed her forehead, breathing in her scent and loving the way she melted into him, proving nightly that she truly trusted him—truly loved him.

Just before Antreas drifted off to a contented sleep, he realized that never in his life had he been so thoroughly happy.

CHAPTER 24

THE ENTRANCE TO THE ROCK MOUNTAIN
PASS—DEATH'S ARMY

Ralina longed for contentment. She didn't long for happiness. She couldn't imagine her way to happiness anymore. But contentment—that Ralina could still imagine, though just barely.

Death's army had finally beached at the base of the Rock Mountains as the sun rose into a clear summer sky. Ralina was one of the first to leave the boats, as Death expected her to be near Him for anything He might consider monumental, so she saw the familiar little group of stripped boats that had been beached before them.

"These are ours!" Thaddeus growled, kicking one of the canoes.

Death chuckled cruelly. "Do you not mean they *were* yours?"

Thaddeus's mean little eyes glared at Death, but as usual, the Hunter held his anger against the God, choosing to spew poison instead.

"That means the bitch was here with the traitor, Nik, and those other cowards who followed him. They stole these boats that night they escaped the Tribe."

Death looked at his Blade, Iron Fist, who nodded and said, "These do appear to be the craft I followed."

"Wait, you *followed* those fucking traitors and didn't do anything about them? Didn't say anything about them? We could have gone after Nik and that bitch—and I'll bet that's where O'Bryan and Davis, as well as Wilkes and Claudia, disappeared to. What the hell is wrong with you?" Thaddeus shouted at Iron Fist.

Ralina bit the side of her cheek to keep herself from speaking the truth—that Thaddeus was the traitor, not Nik and not the lucky Tribe members who had the good sense to follow him. But she didn't have to say anything. Nor did she have to wait for Thaddeus to be reprimanded.

"Thaddeus, my Blade was following my orders. Do you presume to question my command?" Death spoke in a deceptively calm voice that Ralina recognized all too well as the precursor to terrible violence.

Thaddeus recognized it, too, because he paled and bowed quickly to the God. "Of course not, my Lord. I was just surprised. I assumed you would have shared information about the traitors with me."

"Why?"

"Because they are traitors to my people!"

"Your people are now my people," Death said. "And I have a very special way I like to deal with traitors. We will catch them, and I just might let you observe how I admonish them."

"They are traveling to the Plains of the Wind Riders, too?" Thaddeus asked.

Death glanced at Iron Fist and nodded.

The Reaper answered Thaddeus. "They are. They plan to begin anew there by forming something they call a Pack."

"That's a lucky coincidence—but not for them," Thaddeus said cruelly before he walked from the neatly beached group of boats to stand at Death's side. "My Lord, should the Hunters and I go into the mountains and try to track and hire another Lynx guide?"

Death laughed. "No, my eager Hunter. That will not be necessary."

"But we are going to travel through the mountains, aren't we?"

"We are, indeed," Death said.

Thaddeus sighed in exasperation. "Then we'll need a guide. I'm not going into those Sun-be-damned mountains near the end of summer without one."

Death rounded on him, using one massive hand at Thaddeus's throat to lift him off his feet.

"Then do not enter the mountains!" the God roared, raining spittle onto Thaddeus's face. "Remain behind, like the Saleesh women and children, good only for temporary amusement, but not strong enough to complete the journey!"

Thaddeus tried to speak, but all he could manage was a squeak.

Ralina tried not to enjoy Thaddeus's humiliation too much. Sadly, she was sure Death wouldn't kill the Hunter—he was too valuable as long as they journeyed. He led his Hunters and Warriors in daily hunts, being sure there was always fresh fish or game, which was a good thing as the Reapers were terrible at hunting. And the Milks? So far they were only good for killing and dying.

And they had died—by the boatloads in the lake crossing, most especially as they'd traveled past the last ruin of the Golden Man.

Ralina shuddered at the memory. She didn't think she would ever get rid of the vision of Mouths and Monkeys swarming capsized boats and pulling the shrieking Milks under the water.

They'd lost almost half of Death's army during the lake crossing—and still there were hundreds of them crowded onto boats, their white eyes staring at the horizon as they murmured strange, fragmented things to one another.

Thaddeus's Hunters and Warriors had only lost one small boat, though, and that was early in the journey. Thaddeus was a cowardly monster, but he was sly. After the first disastrous ruin crossing he'd taken to following in the wake of Death's boat when they passed any ruin.

Death's Reapers, too, had survived the water crossing with only a few losses, as they never strayed too far from their God's side.

Death dropped Thaddeus, and the Hunter gasped for air, fishlike.

"Now, ask me why a Lynx guide is not necessary," Death said, sounding reasonable, even fatherly.

Ralina had decided one of the most frightening things about the God was His ability to *appear* compassionate. The truth was, Death was utterly amoral. The only reason He ever showed compassion was because it either amused or benefited Him.

"W-why don't you need a guide?" Thaddeus rasped on cue.

"Ah! Good of you to ask and not assume!" Death said as if He had not just almost choked the life from Thaddeus. "I do not need a guide because I already have one."

Thaddeus frowned and glanced behind Death at the armada filled with Milks. The Tribesmen had already beached their craft, followed by Death's Reapers, but the Milks waited, always gazing at Death, watching for Him to give them a command.

Death followed Thaddeus's gaze, threw back His enormous head, and laughed. "Not the Milks, though you are partially right."

It had only taken Death's hearing Ralina refer to the awakened dead as "Milks" for him to adopt the name. Ralina had been surprised. She'd expected Him to chastise her, as they were His army, and completely loyal to Him, but the God had found the nickname amusing. He'd laughed and commended Ralina's imagination. Since then they had officially become "the Milks."

Death turned to his Blade. "Iron Fist, while I conjure our guide, call the Milks to shore. Have them abandon their boats close enough to the beach that they can carry the supplies to dry land without soaking them, and then command that they swim back and break holes in the bellies of the craft. Sink them all. Then, after the Reapers unload our supplies"—Death nodded in the direction of the Reaper craft, as well as the beached boats that had carried Thaddeus and his Hunters and Warriors—"fire the boats."

"Yes, my Lord. Your craft as well?"

Death's boat, the largest and most opulent of the armada, had run aground several yards before the others. Currently the Reapers were carrying Death's harem of Attendants from the craft, as well as the piles of supplies He and His army had stolen from the Saleesh after consuming them, swarmlike.

"Mine as well. All of the boats! Including these." Death gestured to the little group of craft Nik and his people had carefully left behind so that others could make use of them. "No one runs from Death. I will have no one using any of these boats to try to flee me."

"Yes, my Lord!" Iron Fist said, and rushed back to the waterline to begin shouting Death's commands.

"Thaddeus, I would that you come with me and observe." Death found and met Ralina's gaze. "You, too, little Storyteller. You will not want to miss this. But bring your young lover. I have come to understand that at times you have rather delicate sensibilities. You may need the bolstering presence of your plaything." Death turned His back to them and strode toward the opening of the mountain path.

Thinking quickly, Ralina whispered to Daniel, "Hide our boat. Pretend like you're dragging it over to the group Nik left behind, but use the bushes up there to camouflage it."

"I will do my best," said the older man.

Death glanced over His shoulder and frowned at Thaddeus, who was still on the ground, rubbing his throat. "Get up! You aren't badly wounded. There are times I wish your little canine was still with you—he was a lot stronger. Come! And come now, Storyteller. I am anxious to begin the last leg of our journey." Death turned and paced away as Ralina nodded to Daniel and then slid her hand within Renard's. The two of them hastily followed Death, with Bear and Kong pressed against their sides, as her lover's father, ignored by Reapers and Tribesmen alike, dragged their little boat up the beach.

As she passed Thaddeus, she got a glimpse of the Hunter's unfiltered expression. He was staring at the God's back with raw hatred—and Ralina felt a small tickle of hope. Thaddeus would never be her ally, but maybe he could serve as a distraction when she figured out how to defeat the God.

"Come! Hurry! I would begin our trek through the mountains immediately," Death bellowed back at them.

Thaddeus pushed past Ralina and Renard, bumping Renard purposefully with his shoulder. "Watch out, plaything."

Renard's hand tightened within Ralina's, and his big Shepherd, Kong, bristled, growling low in his throat.

"Ssh, Kong," Renard whispered to his Companion. "Not today—but someday Thaddeus will get what he deserves."

"Yes, he will," Ralina agreed, squeezing Renard's hand.

The irony was that in a fair fight Thaddeus wouldn't stand a chance against the younger, stronger Warrior. But Ralina, Renard, *and* Thaddeus—especially Thaddeus—knew Death would not tolerate an attack on His pet Hunter, not even by Ralina's lover.

Someday I will take Thaddeus down, and Renard will be there to witness it, Ralina promised herself silently. At her side, Bear looked up at her, whining in eager agreement. *Oh, yes, my brave Bear. You will be there to witness it, too.*

They climbed and climbed, following the steep rise in the path, and finally caught up to Death after they took a sharp turn to the left and were looking out over the first valley the pass traversed before taking another, sharper, climb up into the mountains.

"Ah, there you are! Thaddeus, do you have a knife with you?" Death asked.

"I do."

Death extended His hand, and Thaddeus pulled a sharp-edged knife from the sheath at his waist, giving it to him.

"Now, observe well, Storyteller. I would that you create a ballad for this part of my tale. I would like to hear this sung for ages."

"Yes, my Lord," Ralina said automatically, though internally she flinched. The Storyteller had realized months before that the God had no understanding that true heroes did not dictate that ballads, poems, and stories be told in their honor. True heroes were celebrated by others *more* than they celebrated themselves.

Death faced the valley. He cupped His hands around His mouth and bellowed. This call was one Ralina had not heard from Him before. Unlike the bestial roars the God usually sounded, this one seemed gentler, and it rose and fell, reminding Ralina in a strange way of a barking canine. He kept calling and calling, over and over again, until at the very edge of the valley there was movement.

"Ah, she comes!" Death said. He cupped His hands around His mouth again and strode out into the valley.

Thaddeus followed him. Ralina and Renard went to the rise in the path from which Death had made the call, and waited there with a clear view of the valley below.

"It's a doe," Ralina said.

Renard nodded. "And it's coming to Him."

"I know I can't, but I want to shout or scream and warn her off," Ralina said, more to herself than Renard.

"I understand completely. Every night I want to sneak away from this terrible nightmare journey," he said.

"You should," Ralina said, though even the thought of not having the comfort of Renard's arms and the kindness of his father to count on to balance the cruelty of Death and His minions made her feel sick and light-headed with despair. "If I could force Bear to go with you I would send him away to safety."

Renard turned the Storyteller so that she looked into his eyes. "I would not leave you to face Death alone any more than your Bear would."

"You should," Ralina repeated. "Especially now that we're in the mountains. You, Kong, and your father could slip away at dusk one night. I would cover for you so you could put hours between you and the Hunters that might come after you. I'd tell Death that we quarreled and that I became tired of you. He may not send anyone after you at all. You and Daniel would be free. You could—"

"No," Renard stopped her words. "We will not leave you. *I* will not leave you."

"But we're heading into a war, and I may never find a way to defeat Death," Ralina said miserably.

"Then I will stay with you to the end. But I believe in you. You're closer than anyone to that God. You'll find His weakness and use it to send Him back to wherever He slept for centuries."

Ralina stepped into his strong arms, letting Renard comfort her.

"*Storyteller!*" the God shouted.

Ralina moved out of Renard's arms instantly.

"You must get closer," Death commanded from the valley below.

"I hate this. I hate it so much," said Ralina as they hurried down the path to join Death and Thaddeus in the valley.

"Think of it as information—that's all," Renard said. "The more you learn about Death, the more you learn about how to defeat Him. So, whatever new horror He shows you today, do not dwell on the horror itself, but what it teaches you about the God."

"It's just information," Ralina said firmly.

"It's just information," Renard repeated like a prayer.

They joined Death and Thaddeus in the middle of the valley as the animal the God had summoned trotted fearlessly up to Him. She was an exquisite doe. Her body was covered with thick, brownish gray fur that lightened as it reached her delicate cloven hooves. Her tail and underbelly were shockingly white. Her eyes were huge and brown, and fixed in a glassy stare as she stretched out her black muzzle to sniff the God, as if He'd cast a spell over her.

"You are quite a beauty," Death murmured softly to the doe, stroking her forehead gently. "Thank you for coming when I called. I shall not forget your noble sacrifice to your God. When I awaken my Goddess we shall erect a shrine to you and I will command candles to always burn at your feet."

The doe rubbed her head against the God and He laughed like a child—a sound that had Ralina trembling with fearful anticipation.

Renard held tightly to her hand.

It's just information . . . It's just information . . . It's just information . . .

"Come, sweet one. Give yourself to me," said the God.

With gentle, guileless eyes fixed and staring at the God, the doe stretched out her neck.

In a movement so swift that Ralina didn't even have time to startle, Death drew the blade of the knife across the doe's throat, slicing her from ear to ear. The doe staggered and then fell to her knees. The God dropped to His knees with her, cradling her head in His lap as her blood bathed Him in scarlet. He held her like that until the light began to flicker from her sightless eyes, and as life was extinguished from the doe, the God of Death bent and kissed the doe's forehead.

"Now, come to me. I command it!"

A white mist immediately swirled from the gaping wound on the doe's neck. As the river of blood slowed, the mist increased.

Death stood, holding out His arms as if He welcomed a lover.

"I BID YOU COME TO ME!" Death said.

The white mist lifted with the God, and as it coalesced it formed the shape of the doe—only this doe's eyes weren't brown and gentle and glassy from the God's spell. They were empty of any emotion at all, oddly reminding Ralina of the Milks.

"You will guide me through these mountains," Death commanded the spirit of the sacrificed doe. "You will not let me out of your sight until we reach the plains beyond the mountains and I free you. Then, and only then, shall I allow you to join my Goddess and be reborn."

Ralina did see an expression in the doe's eyes then. Just before the doe bowed to Death, her spirit met Ralina's gaze, and the Storyteller saw despair—utter despair. Then the deer dropped her head and touched her muzzle to the bloody ground at the God's feet, and Ralina had a jolt of understanding.

Not even Death's call could keep the doe from showing sadness at being kept from the Goddess. That is something I must remember—something I might be able to use.

Death stretched His arms above His head, sighing dramatically.

"It is so very good to be on dry land again!" He tossed Thaddeus's bloody knife back to him.

"It is!" Thaddeus said, speaking to Death as if the two of them were equals—friends even. "That was really something you just did. So, this spirit is going to guide us through the mountains?"

Death slowly turned His massive head to stare at Thaddeus. "Did I not just command the doe to do just that?"

"Well, yes."

"Then do not waste my time with idle questions. Dress the doe. The scent of her blood has made me hungry for venison steaks." Death glanced around them at the lovely valley. "We will camp here tonight while the Milks repack our supplies. We begin our trek through the mountains tomorrow at first light."

Ralina turned with Renard to go back to the beach, but Death's voice stopped her.

"Storyteller, do you realize what day tomorrow is?"

Ralina considered before answering, but each day had bled into another to make weeks that multiplied into months in the unending misery that had become her life, until she had lost all track of time.

"No, my Lord. I'm sorry, but I do not."

"No matter! I will educate you. Tomorrow the dawn brings the last day of summer. Quite auspicious, don't you think?"

Only in that this trip has taken too long because of your self-indulgence and your belief that you are indestructible, Ralina thought, but aloud she said, "Yes, my Lord. Very auspicious. I will be sure to note it in your tale."

"Excellent! And do not leave me, Storyteller. I would that you build a fire while your lover returns to the beach and relays my orders to Iron Fist and then gathers my Attendants. Boy," he addressed Renard. "Bring my women here quickly. I find that I am ravenous for more than venison."

"Yes, my Lord," Renard said. He squeezed Ralina's hand one more time before jogging back up the trail.

"I hear a stream close by. I will find it and bathe. My Attendants are energetic young women, but they have an odd aversion to blood. Be sure the fire is built by the time I return. I will need to warm myself! And prepare yourself. Tonight while I feast on sweet doe flesh I wish to hear your 'Tale of Endings and Beginnings' once more. It has become one of my favorites."

"Yes, my Lord," Ralina said, dread filling her. The God had completely ruined that beautiful story with His obsession of hearing her retell it over and over. He particularly liked the parts describing how the world of the ancients destroyed itself.

Death headed across the valley, leaving behind the spirit of the slain doe. She remained motionless by her corpse, her head lowered and her eyes filled with despair as she stared after Death while Thaddeus began dressing her body—spilling guts onto the already blood-soaked ground and then ripping flesh from hide.

Thaddeus ignored the spirit of the doe and Ralina, turning his back on them both. Moving silently, Ralina went to stand in front of the spirit. The ethereal doe lifted her head and looked at the Storyteller.

"I am so sorry," Ralina whispered to the spirit.

The doe closed her eyes as transparent tears trekked down her misty face, and then, with a jolt, the spirit of the doe staggered after Death before the God left her sight, and Ralina turned and began collecting firewood—all while the Storyteller altered her silent mantra.

It is more than just information and I will use it to stop Him . . . It is more than just information and I will use it to stop Him . . . It is more than just information and I will use it to stop Him . . .

CHAPTER 25

River woke before everyone else the morning of the Stallion Run. Anjo's eyes began to flutter open, and the mare lifted her head from her spot beside River's pallet.

"Ssh," whispered River. "Sleep. I'll wake you and Ghost when it's time."

With a contented sigh, Anjo put her head down. She lay beside Ghost, who was still sleeping soundly. The stallion did not usually spend nights inside River's tent, but she'd been unwilling to let him out of her sight with the Run looming. Though Anjo assured her he wasn't nervous at all, Ghost had willingly slept beside Anjo and River.

Not sure what had awakened her, River rearranged her pillows, intending to try to sleep. The lack of any sounds from outside the tent told her that it was before dawn—and the lack of April bursting in and insisting they were going to be late told her it was *well* before dawn.

"*River!*"

River sat up in bed, listening intently.

"*River!*"

Quietly, River tiptoed to the door flap of her tent and peered out into the darkness—and almost accidentally smacked Skye in the face with the flap.

"What are you doing out here?"

"May I come in?" Skye whispered, looking around as if she expected to be followed.

"Well, sure. But keep it down. Anjo and Ghost are sleeping." River stepped out of the way and Skye followed her quickly inside the tent.

"This will only take a second, and I'm sorry to bother you before the Run, but there's some things you need to know," said Skye.

"Then tell me." River was careful to keep her voice and expression neutral. Since the Mare Test, Skye had stopped the haughty, antagonistic behaviors she'd shown before, but the young woman was still followed around by a cliquish group of girls—most of them April's age and new Riders. And, of course, she was rarely away from Clayton. River had decided the best way to deal with Skye and Clayton was not to give them the attention they so obviously craved—but the Lead Mare Rider couldn't help but feel annoyed that Skye, whose life she and Anjo had saved, hadn't seemed to mature or grow, and was instead still catering to a selfish man and a group of immature girls.

Skye fidgeted nervously. "Do you mind if we sit?"

"I do." River spoke honestly. "I probably won't be able to sleep more, but if I'm going to be awake I might as well begin combing out Ghost's mane and braiding the ribbons into it. So, what is it you need to tell me?"

"I could help you," Skye said.

River stifled a sigh. Maybe Skye was reaching out to her in friendship—maybe she wanted to change, wanted to be a better mare Rider. River understood it was her responsibility to encourage Skye, even if she'd chosen an inconvenient time.

"Okay, sure. Just wait here while I let Ghost know you're coming in."

River went to the far side of the tent, which smelled of horse and the straw bedding that was changed daily. Anjo raised her head, instantly sighting Skye.

Why is she here?

She has to tell me something. Would you wake Ghost and let him know we aren't alone? Tell him Skye and I are going to begin dressing his mane. Tell him he doesn't have to stand—yet.

I will. It will be good for Ghost to rest as long as he can before the race.

I know, silly. Do not worry. Ghost and I will be fine.

Anjo snorted, and then Ghost's eyes fluttered open. He raised his head and looked from River to Skye, before he rested it along Anjo's back and closed his eyes again.

"Okay, he knows you're here. He's going to keep resting while we braid his mane." River spoke as she went to her chest and gathered wooden currycombs and purple ribbons, as well as the wide, soft-bristled brush she'd use to groom his golden coat to a lustrous shine. "Here's an extra comb. Want to start on his tail while I work his mane?"

"Yes. I can do that." Skye approached the stallion cautiously. "He's really big this close—bigger even than Bard."

"Yeah, he's well over sixteen hands. He's grown like crazy this past year, and filled out, too." River sat behind the stallion's neck while Skye moved to his tail.

"Do you talk to him?" Skye asked.

"Well, yeah. All the time."

"Does he answer you?"

"You mean with words like Anjo does?" River took a section of Ghost's silver-white mane and began working the comb gently through the tangles.

"You can hear words from Anjo?"

"Yep. Can't you hear them from Scout?"

Skye shook her head as she sectioned off part of Ghost's long, thick tail. "No, she only sends me images."

"There's nothing wrong with that. That's the way most horses communicate with their Riders. It's easier for them to share pictures than it is to share language."

"Is that what Ghost does with you?" Skye asked.

"No. He listens to me, but we mostly communicate through Anjo. Why do you ask?"

"I wondered if he ever told you why he saved me from that snake last winter," Skye asked softly.

"He didn't have to tell me. I know why he saved you. It's who he is—a stallion made to protect his Herd," River said.

"Would you thank him for me sometime?"

River met Skye's gaze. "I think he'd appreciate it if you thanked him yourself."

Skye reached out hesitantly and rested her hand on Ghost's back. She cleared her throat and then said, "Ghost, thank you for killing that snake. I'm sorry it's taken me so long to thank you. I do appreciate what you did, though, very much."

The golden stallion lifted his head and nickered softly to Skye before closing his eyes again and resting against Anjo.

"He really is beautiful," Skye said.

"Yes, he really is," River agreed.

They worked on Ghost's mane and tail for a time in easy silence. Though River had only been Lead Mare Rider for three months, she had already mastered the skill of patiently listening. It was one of her mother's greatest strengths. River had grown up watching Dawn wait quietly for others to get their thoughts, and sometimes their courage, in order before speaking. So, River was utterly relaxed and enjoying the silence when Skye finally did speak.

"I wanted to warn you about Clayton."

Skye's words didn't surprise River. She'd known Clayton a long time, and in that time she'd watched him change from a confident, friendly child into an arrogant, sullen young man.

The first two tenet laws of the Herd were: Never harm a horse, and Never harm a Rider. The penalty for breaking either law was to be banished from the Herd—but first a Rider had to be caught breaking the law and, unlike during the Mare Test, there would be no judges' eyes watching and recording the happenings during the fifty long miles they would race that day.

It would be a prime opportunity for Clayton to attack Ghost or River—or both.

"You're going to have to explain what you mean by that." River kept her voice calm. She'd expected Clayton to cause trouble during the Run—the only thing she hadn't expected was Skye to warn her about it.

The girl nodded and drew in a deep breath, letting it out slowly before she spoke, and when she did, River heard tears in Skye's voice.

"He says Ghost is his only real competition and he doesn't think it's fair that he's running."

"What Clayton thinks or doesn't think about Ghost isn't relevant," River said, working hard to control the anger Skye's words had begun to build within her. "The Mare Council decided it was up to me whether he competes or not. They support my choice to allow it."

"I know that. Everyone does, even Clayton and the Riders who follow him—but they don't agree with it. I heard them talking. Clayton told them he's going to do whatever it takes to beat Ghost—even if that means hurting him."

River's hands stilled. "Then it's not just Clayton. It's those Riders, too."

Skye nodded and wiped at her tears. "Most of the stallion Riders support you, except . . ." Her voice trailed off as if she couldn't force herself to speak the terrible words.

So, River spoke them for her. "Except for the arrogant little group who worship Clayton. Does he have a specific plan? Do you know what he intends to do to Ghost?"

Skye sniffled and moved her shoulders restlessly. "The only thing I know for sure is that he's going to try to make it look like an accident."

"But that's ridiculous. I'll know it's not an accident—and so will Ghost."

When Skye didn't say anything, River understood the awful truth.

"Clayton is going to be sure Ghost and I don't survive the Run."

"I—I don't know."

"Yes you do. You just don't want to admit it." River's voice went hard. "What else do you *not* know? Even something small could help me."

"He never talks with me about hurting Ghost and you. Everyone quiets when I'm near, but he's been spending a lot of time out on the Plains—tracing every possible course the Run could follow."

"So that he can plan several ways to get rid of us."

Skye nodded. Then she continued. "What Clayton does talk about around me is what he intends to do if he and Bard aren't able to get past Ghost."

"By fairly beating him or killing him," River added.

"Yes." Skye wiped her tearstained face with her sleeve. "If he doesn't win he has decided he is going to splinter the Herd." Skye's voice broke on the last word.

River nodded and continued to braid Ghost's mane. "Thank you for letting me know. I appreciate it."

"You don't seem surprised," Skye said.

"Oh, I'm not. Skye, I spent my childhood with Clayton. We were as close as if he'd been my brother. I've always known he is capable of great good—and also of great selfishness, even cruelty. So, no, I'm not surprised that he's willing to harm a stallion and cause his Lead Mare Rider to be killed. It is more proof of what I've come to believe over the past several years—that Clayton is unfit to serve this Herd in any capacity, but especially not as Herd Stallion Rider."

"Then why haven't you spoken against him?"

"For what? For acting like a petulant child? No, Skye, that would only give him the attention he so desperately craves. It would also fragment the Herd even more than he has already attempted to do. Until today I had no evidence that Clayton intended to break any of our laws."

Skye's gaze shot to River, the girl's eyes wide with panic. "You're not going to ban him from the Run, are you?"

"No, Skye, I am not. What I'm going to do is beat him. Soundly. In front of the entire Herd."

"But then he'll leave!"

"Yes. Exactly."

"No, River!"

"Skye, why did you come to me? Why did you warn me and tell me what Clayton was planning?"

Skye bowed her head as she gently stroked the stallion's silky coat. "Because I owe you and Ghost a debt. I'm not strong like you, but I couldn't live with myself if something happened to you and I hadn't warned you."

"But you expect me to, what? Allow Clayton, who is clearly a terrible choice for Herd Stallion Rider, to beat Ghost?" River asked incredulously.

"I—I don't know," Skye said.

"Listen to me, Skye. I will *never* allow Clayton to be Lead Stallion Rider of this Herd. Ever. And it *is* best if he and those who are of like mind with him leave our Herd. Actually, once the Run is over I'm going to insist on it."

"You'll allow them to form another branch of Herd Magenti?" Skye's voice was suddenly lighter and filled with hope.

"No. Clayton will not be rewarded for the dissension he's caused. If he does not willingly leave after he loses the Stallion Run, I will banish him. He will *not* be allowed to claim the name Magenti or wear the purple ever again."

"It will break his heart," Skye said.

"With his words he has already broken our most sacred tenets, and that means he surrenders the right to be part of Herd Magenti. He and his followers are free to begin their own Herd. Where they'll find mares to follow them, I do not know. Let alone a Lead Mare Rider."

When Skye said nothing, River studied her, and saw the girl's unspoken response.

"You're going with him," River said.

"Yes."

"Why? You don't want to leave Herd Magenti. What will your mother say? And your sisters? How can you leave them? What does Scout say about this?"

"She keeps showing me terrible pictures. She doesn't want us to go, and I don't want to leave our Herd and my family. Oh, River, I wouldn't have to if you would just grant Clayton the right to begin another branch of Magenti."

River stopped braiding Ghost's mane and took Skye's cold hands in hers. She looked into the girl's eyes and spoke slowly and clearly.

"I will never allow Clayton to carry our Herd's name. And if he causes any kind of trouble I will hand him over to the Mare Council and tell them everything. I will tell them how he's purposefully, spitefully sown discontent for years. I will tell them that he planned to fragment our Herd. *I will tell them he was willing to kill a stallion and a Lead Mare Rider.*"

Skye paled—she knew what that meant. The Mare Council was fair and merciful. They were also, every one of them, women who had served as Lead Mare Riders to their Herds, and when they learned a stallion Rider had been willing to murder one of their own, their retribution would be swift and brutal. Clayton would not live to see another sunrise.

"So, you need to be wise," River continued. "Clayton will pay the consequences of his poor choices and, sadly, so will his stallion. I hope that your coming to me means that you will make a wiser choice."

Skye pulled her hands from River's. "You don't understand, because you don't love anyone."

"That's a lie. I love many people and horses. I love my Anjo, Ghost, Echo, April's Deinos, and others. I love my mother, my sisters, my friends. Most important, I love my Herd. Do not believe for one instant that just because I have never fallen in love I do not understand love."

"Then you should understand why I'll be leaving with Clayton. I love him."

"That's not love, Skye. That's need or obsession or even manipulation. Love doesn't require you to betray your ideals. You said you're not strong, but you could be—one step at a time. You took the first one coming to warn me tonight. Take the next by not following Clayton."

Skye stood. "I need to leave. I've done what I had to do. You've been warned. My debt to you and to Ghost has been paid. If you repeat anything I told you, even if it's to the Mare Council, I'll deny it." Then Skye hurried from River's tent.

Anjo and Ghost lifted their heads the moment she was gone.

It seems she forgot we were here, too. Anjo's voice was tinged with sarcasm. *The Mare Council will always believe a Lead Mare and her Rider.*

"Skye knows how idle her threats are. She just sees me through her own weakness. I don't think she believes that I'll survive the Run, and if I do she can't imagine me standing against Clayton."

Skye is very wrong.

Ghost snorted in disgust, then River moved aside so that both horses could stand. The stallion turned to her and rested his head against her chest.

Ghost will not let you down. He will be Herd Stallion by the end of today.

"I know he will, and he won't have to cheat to win," said River.

Never! said her mare.

"Never," repeated River.

Ghost lifted his head and neighed a challenge.

"That probably woke up the entire herd," said River as she smiled and stroked Ghost's golden neck.

It is a stallion's job to alert his Herd to coming danger.

"Yes, it is," River said as she gazed into his intelligent eyes. "And it's the Lead Mare Rider's job to listen and heed his warning. That is exactly what I'm going to do today."

⁂

"Are you sure you want to carry that extra weight?" April asked one last time before they left the tent to join the line of stallions and Riders waiting for sunrise and the signal for the Run to begin.

"I weigh half of what some of those other Riders weigh. And Anjo says Ghost isn't bothered by the saddle pack at all," River said, tying the last loop of the pack onto the back of Ghost's saddle pad. "Also, I have no idea what Clayton is planning, so I need to be ready." She patted the saddlebag that she'd filled with a water skin, dried fruit for her, and grain for Ghost—as well as an assortment of survival tools, like a knife, bandages, a leather throwing strap, and several light spears that were the perfect size to fit inside the pack, and a light blanket that rolled neatly and was easily strapped to the pack, along with everything she might need to make a fire. Lastly, she wrapped a lasso rope loosely around the wooden part of the saddle they called a horn.

"I still think you should call Clayton out before the Run. Tell Jasper. He's still Herd Stallion Rider until sunset. It's his job to keep our Herd safe, and that means especially our Lead Mare Rider. He could take him into custody until the Mare Council can decide what to do about his treachery." April spoke in sentences clipped with anger.

"No. I'm handling it my way. I'm going to face him and beat him—and then, *beaten,* he will leave our Herd. His followers will all know he is not good enough to be our Herd Stallion Rider. Maybe that will wake some of them up. Maybe not. But either way Clayton needs to be defeated—publicly."

"Anjo's okay with this?" April asked, stroking the silver mare's neck.

"Anjo and Ghost are in complete agreement with me. Clayton needs to be taught a lesson, and then he needs to leave Magenti forever." River pulled her sister into her arms and hugged her tightly. "Trust me. Trust Ghost."

"I do!" April clung to her. "I'm just scared."

River let her go and grinned at her. "I'm not."

Anjo stomped and Ghost snorted, tossing his head.

"Neither are they," April said. She drew a deep breath and nodded. "Okay, Lead Mare Rider. But if something bad happens, know that Anjo and I will go to the Mare Council and tell them everything Skye said."

"It won't come to that, but thank you."

"Anything for my big sister. Now, go get 'em!"

River turned to her mare and wrapped her arms around Anjo's neck. "I love you. Watch the Herd while I'm gone."

Be safe, my Rider. Bring home our Herd Stallion.

"I will!"

Then River went to Ghost. She stood at his side with her hand resting on his shoulder as she gazed up into his dark eye.

"I want you to know that I am very proud to be your Rider, even if it is only for one day."

Ghost bent his head and nuzzled her, lipping her cheek gently and causing River to laugh. She kissed his muzzle affectionately before the stallion knelt so that she could mount. Once astride, River paused Ghost with pressure from her heels and pressed her hand over the center crystal of her grandmother's amethyst necklace. The crystal warmed instantly, sending its soothing energy washing through River and Ghost.

She felt the big stallion draw a deep, calming breath and let it out slowly, in perfect time with her.

Then April held aside the tent flap and River clucked to him. The stallion moved forward. The instant he was outside the tent his demeanor changed. Gone was the affable, sleepy stallion who had waited so patiently while his mane and tail were dressed with ribbons.

Ghost's head lifted and his golden neck arched. At their side, Anjo did the same. River could only imagine how they must look to the Herd—a magnificent silver mare, dressed in purple ribbons, beside an equally spectacular golden stallion, also wearing Magenti purple and carrying the Lead Mare Rider of their Herd.

There was a large group waiting just outside River's tent, and as she, Ghost, and Anjo appeared a cheer lifted from them.

"Ghost and River! Ghost and River!"

River's heart swelled with pride and pleasure. She nodded and smiled at her people, appreciating the fact that again they all wore necklaces of amethyst to show their support for her. Then she squeezed slightly with her thighs. Ghost reacted on cue by surging into a gallop, which Anjo matched, stride for stride.

They wove their way through the purple tents. All along the path to the Choosing Theater Herd Magenti cheered them, leaving their tents to run after as they chanted, "Ghost and River! Ghost and River!"

Closer to the Choosing Theater the color of the tents changed. River easily counted at least one tent from each of the other four Herds: Virides, Cinnabar, Indigo, and Jonquil. Unlike the Mare Test, stallions from any of the Herds were welcome to join the Run, and though many of the tents were filled with spectators from other Herds curious to watch the only Stallion Run wherein a horse ridden by a Lead Mare Rider competed, many stallions from other Herds had entered the Run as well.

Wow, that's a lot of Riders, River thought as they galloped to the Choosing Theater and she got her first glimpse of the racers, who were all lined up at the start. The predominant color worn was purple, but there was also at least one stallion from each of the other Herds, creating a symphony of color and beauty.

They honor us. Many wish to be our Herd Stallion. They will learn respect for our Ghost when he defeats every one of them. Go make me proud, my beloved Rider.

"Count on it!" River told Anjo. Then she cued Ghost.

Ghost's neck arched even more. His tail went up and he lifted his legs like he was plowing through the mud trap. Moving with incredible grace and strength, the stallion entered the Choosing Theater, sounding a neigh that declared to every Herdmember present his intent to win the Run. An answering roar went up from the spectators. River didn't know if that greeting was for her, or for the novelty of a horse labeled a rogue stallion being ridden in the Run.

The reason does not matter, her mare's wise voice lifted through her mind from where Anjo had taken position beside April and Deinos in the viewing stands. *They will all cheer both of you when you return victorious.*

Ghost snorted and tossed his head in agreement, and River bared her teeth in a fierce smile.

Before them, two stallions made room for Ghost in the middle of the line. River had time to gaze down the long line of stallion-Rider teams. She counted quickly, though she already knew a record-breaking twenty-five horses raced that day.

The first team that caught her eye was Clayton and Bard. They were only four teams to her right—and flanked by his toadies on lesser stallions. River ignored the wannabes and focused on Clayton and Bard. The jolt of shock River felt at how thin Clayton looked made her realize that this was the closest she'd been to her childhood friend since the day she'd announced she and Ghost would compete. Unlike his Rider, Bard was in peak shape, prancing in place and blowing through his nose. Against the black of his shining coat, the purple Herd Magenti ribbons looked beautiful.

I hope Bard enjoys them. Because of his Rider's choices it will be the last time he'll be allowed to wear the purple, River thought—and the warmth that filled her from her watching mare echoed that thought.

Clayton tried to catch River's gaze, but she looked away, her lip lifted in a dismissive sneer. She kept scanning the line, looking for the other stallion teams she knew would be her toughest competition.

Several teams to the right of Clayton and Bard, River spotted Jonathan and his big sorrel stallion, Red. Jonathan tipped his head respectfully to her, and River returned the gesture. Red was a powerful contender, and a well-respected Herd Magenti stallion; they would be tough to beat if Red's stamina held over the fifty miles of the race.

Another strong team from Herd Magenti was Kaleb and his stallion, Pharaoh. She spotted them near the edge of the line of stallions, easy to identify because of Pharaoh's distinctive buckskin markings. The stallion looked great—in perfect flesh. He was well known as one of the toughest horses in the Herd—and was especially good at being able to speed up and over hills and ridges.

But so is Ghost, River thought. *And Pharaoh hadn't had to survive on his own in those hills for a winter by himself.*

Green ribbons caught River's gaze. From Virides, the Herd well known for the fastest horses on the Plains of the Wind Riders, River recognized Regis and his blond stallion, Hobbs. Hobbs was pawing the earth restlessly and blowing through his nose.

Good. He'll wear himself out. River dismissed him. A stallion's reputation—or their Herd's reputation—didn't matter during the Run, especially if a fast stallion wore himself out before the fifty miles even began.

Then everyone's attention shifted as Echo galloped into the Choosing Theater carrying Dawn. The aging mare looked spectacular, dressed in purple ribbons embroidered with her silver-white mane. River was filled with pride as her mother sat her mare, straight and strong, looking every bit like the magnificent Lead Mare Rider she had been for a decade. She carried their purple standard, which waved gracefully in the gentle summer breeze.

The cheer that greeted her was deafening, and River joined in enthusiastically. Then every stallion in the theater neighed a greeting—showing the ultimate respect to a beloved Mare Rider.

Smiling, Dawn raised her hand as Echo faced the line of stallions and their Riders.

"Greetings, guests, Riders, and their stallions!"

The crowd cheered again, but quieted quickly.

"As you all know, today's Run is unusual, which is why I am addressing you and opening the race instead of the Lead Mare Rider of our Herd Magenti. For the first time in Herd history a Lead Mare Rider will race with the stallions on an unbonded horse." Dawn paused for the smattering of applause and murmuring from the viewing stands. "So, my daughter River, Herd Magenti's current Lead Mare Rider, asked me to open the race for her, which I am proud to do."

River took a good grip of Ghost's mane. Her mother would give the signal to begin soon, and she knew exactly what Ghost had decided to do. The stallion was determined to take the lead early to show everyone in the huge crowd that he was strong enough to win the Run—from beginning to end.

"You know the rules. Follow the fifty-mile course, which is marked clearly. Riders and their stallions will have several choices to make today. The most conservative choice is always marked by the purple flags. When you see a black flag it will mark a shortcut, but those trails are always more difficult. So, choose wisely, Riders. When you see the shortcut marked by double black flags, that will signify the last one. When the shortcut course joins the main track again it will lead into the valley and the five-mile stretch that is the conclusion of the Run. The finish will be at the base of the Rock Mountains at the end of Foal Valley. The first team to pass beneath the Magenti standard before dusk wins.

"I am pleased to see so many strong teams competing. It honors my daughter and her mare, as well as Herd Magenti. Race safely and"— Dawn paused long enough to catch River's gaze—"may a mare's luck be with you!"

Echo whirled around and trotted several yards to the middle of the Choosing Theater. Dawn raised the purple flag, and then with a sharp motion she waved it back and forth above her head, signaling the beginning of the Stallion Run.

Ghost surged forward. River leaned low against his neck, lifting a little in her stirrups so that she remained still on his back—doing her best to balance perfectly.

Within six strides Ghost had pulled ahead of every stallion except Bard and Hobbs. The three stallions were running neck and neck.

"Faster!" River shouted, and Ghost's stride stretched out so that within ten strides he had taken the lead, and as they thundered from the Choosing Theater out onto the grassy plain surrounding it, Ghost was leading Hobbs and Bard by two lengths—then three—then four.

River was breathless at Ghost's speed—and it seemed to be never-ending. He didn't slow, even when they were out of view of the crowd. He didn't slow, even after she tapped his neck, alerting him to the first of the purple flags that marked a turn to the left.

River gave Ghost his head. She trusted the stallion completely to know himself—to judge how long he could maintain his top speed. If Ghost was wrong, if he ran out of stamina and lost the race, that meant she had misjudged his ability to lead the Herd, and then he *should* be beaten.

Though not by Clayton and Bard. Never by them.

Ghost didn't slow until River cued him that she'd spotted a black flag, signaling their first shortcut, and their first decision as a team. The stallion slowed to a gallop, then a smooth canter—and finally a trot.

River lifted in her stirrups, looking behind them. This section of the prairie was flat, and she could easily see that about one hundred yards behind them Hobbs was running second, his green ribbons streaming against his body. And behind Hobbs by only a few lengths was Bard. Spread out in a staggered line were half a dozen more stallions, led by Jonathan's big sorrel stallion, Red.

She turned quickly, not wasting more time looking behind, to assess the shortcut. As with all of the teams competing from Herd Magenti, River and Ghost had an advantage over the Riders from outside Herds. This was their territory, and especially this close to the Rendezvous Site, they knew it well.

"I see what they're doing here. The shortcut will take us through the cross timber line at the widest part of Weanling Creek, which means we'll have to go down a steep bank, swim the creek, and climb another bank," River reasoned aloud. Even though, unlike her Anjo, Ghost didn't understand all of her words, she knew he caught some of what she said, and he for sure felt her emotions. "That's nothing for you! We're taking the shortcut!" River cued him with her knee, and without hesitation Ghost followed the black flags, entering the cross timber line shortly to begin the climb up to the steep, northernmost bank of Weanling Creek.

River had Ghost pause at the top of the bank long enough for her to look behind them. Between the trees she caught a flash of black and white.

"Bard took the shortcut. Don't see Hobbs, though. Not surprising. He doesn't know this territory well. Go!"

Ghost plunged down the steep bank as River leaned back, balancing him. She didn't take the time to untie her saddle or hold the bags over her head—whatever got wet would just have to stay wet. The Stallion Run was a race. They would not be stopping.

She did kick out of the saddle to make swimming easier for Ghost, as the current was swift where the creek was this deep, then River easily slid astride before the stallion surged out of the creek and attacked the next bank. After the creek the course joined the purple-marked path again. The next time River looked back she saw Bard and Hobbs, with Red and Kaleb's Pharaoh trailing them by several lengths in fourth and fifth place.

"It's Bard in second and Hobbs in third," River told the stallion. Ghost didn't hesitate. He kicked into a ground-eating gallop, pulling well ahead of Bard and Hobbs again—slowing to a canter and then a trot only after he'd increased his lead by several more lengths.

That set the pattern for the very long day. Ghost never lost his lead. Bard and Hobbs changed positions frequently—as did Red and Pharaoh—until sometime after midday, when they topped a ridge and River could gaze out over the plains behind them. She could not see Pharaoh at all, though Red had pulled within just a few lengths of Bard and Hobbs.

Ghost snorted and began to move down the ridge, but River cued him to stop. Quickly, she slid from his back and opened the saddlebags, taking out the water skin and an apple for herself, and several handfuls of the sticky molasses and grain mixture that would help maintain the stallion's energy reserves.

"Here—you've pulled far enough ahead that you can eat this." Ghost lipped the grain from her hands, and then drank his fill of water as she cupped that for him as well. River gulped some water and bit the apple, holding it with her teeth as she remounted so that she could eat as the stallion rested by falling into a steady trot—a pace he could maintain for miles and miles.

River marveled at Ghost's strength. She'd grown up listening to stories of the greatest stallions in Herd history. Names like Eclipse, Admiral, Dancer, and Ruffian were as familiar to her as their tales of bravery, speed, and strength, but by the time the sun was halfway down its westerly trek to the horizon River was convinced that none of those legendary stallions had been any braver, stronger, or faster than Ghost.

That didn't mean the Run was easy for the stallion. His golden coat was frothed with white, and her saddle pad was drenched with his sweat and hers by the time she spotted the double black flags that marked the last shortcut.

"This is it! The sprint to the finish will be just after this shortcut meets the main course again!"

Ghost snorted wearily and automatically turned to take the shortcut—as they had chosen to take each one before then—but River pressed her heels into his flank to stop him.

"We can't take this one! I recognize this place. This section of the cross timbers is filled with goathead thistle groves. It's shorter, but I don't know the way through it—Anjo and I have always avoided these groves. Unless you've been this way before it'll slow us down—maybe even trap us like it did Luce and Blue during the Mare Test."

Ghost hesitated, looking behind them, but the trees were too thick and it was impossible to see who was trailing them or how close they were. The stallion tossed his head fretfully.

"We have the lead. We can afford to take the longer way—but we can't afford hesitation."

Her words must have made sense to the stallion, because Ghost turned from the black flags to continue cantering on the original course. River stroked his sweat-soaked neck and murmured encouragement, and as soon as the trail climbed a rise she stood in her stirrups and looked behind them.

"Bard's second. He's almost at the shortcut. Hobbs is several lengths behind him, neck and neck with Red. Oh, I can see Pharaoh again, but he's moving slow—only trotting—and Kaleb is running beside him. He must be injured." She was just going to say that she was sorry Pharaoh was out of the competition when Bard disappeared between the black flags of the shortcut. "Ghost! Bard's taking the shortcut!"

Her words worked like a goad on the stallion. He broke from his restful trot into a gallop, though he quickly seemed to think better of it and slowed to a more easily maintained canter. River leaned forward, riding low on his neck, as the mighty stallion's hooves beat against the dirt track, pounding out a staccato rhythm.

It seemed to River to take forever for them to circle around the goathead grove, but finally she caught sight of the two black flags heralding the end of the shortcut—and the two purple flags that signified the main course of the race.

There was no sign of Bard and Clayton.

"Did they get that far ahead of us?" River stood in her stirrups, trying to see ahead of them, but they were at the edge of the cross timbers, and hadn't reached the entrance to Foal Valley yet, so the path was still curving around trees and visibility was limited. "I can't believe Clayton would've taken that shortcut if he didn't already know the way through the goatheads. We have to catch him."

Ghost didn't need more encouragement. He lengthened his stride to a gallop and they wove expertly through the trees and scrub.

River was so utterly focused on guiding Ghost through the cross timbers that she didn't notice Clayton and Bard until it was almost too late.

It was Ghost who noticed. His ears flattened against his head and he squealed a warning. Completely caught off guard, River glanced behind in time to see Bard leap from a hiding place behind a pile of scrub and thunder toward them. In Clayton's hand was a noosed rope that he was twirling over his head. River could see that Clayton was aiming for Ghost's rear hock—not surprising, as that was how he'd tripped him up so long ago—but there was something strange about the rope. It looked heavier, thicker than normal. However, there was no time for her to figure out what it was, or why—there was only time for her to act.

She yanked her lasso from around the horn of her sweat-soaked saddle and shook it out. Then she leaned close to Ghost's neck, speaking into his flattened ears—hoping beyond hope the stallion would understand.

"Slow. Let them get closer. I'm going to cue you when to stop and turn." River held her breath until Ghost began to slow. *He must understand me—he must!*

She glanced back once more. Bard was gaining on them—less than three lengths behind—now two lengths—now Clayton was leaning forward, his eyes glinting with intensity as he took aim at Ghost's hock.

"Now!" River shouted into Ghost's ear as she cued him to stop and turn to his left—away from Clayton and Bard.

The stallion performed perfectly. Ghost dug his back hooves into the ground and whirled to the left. It happened too fast for Clayton to correct Bard, and as they blazed past River threw her lasso. It settled around the unusually fat noose Clayton was still twirling over his head. River yanked and with a shout of surprise she pulled the rope out of Clayton's hands.

River reeled in her lasso, gasping in shock as the rope Clayton had been twirling—had been aiming at Ghost's vulnerable rear hock—reached her hand.

Clayton had wrapped the noose of his lasso in goathead thistle strands. Had he captured Ghost's hock with it, one swift jerk of the rope would have been enough to sever the stallion's tendon—laming him for life—and at the speed they'd been going there was little doubt that River would have been thrown or even been trapped beneath the massive horse. Either way, both Ghost and River might very well have been mortally wounded, and it would have appeared to whoever eventually found them that they'd taken the shortcut and tried to travel too quickly through the goathead grove.

"What happened to you? You used to have honor. You used to be decent!" River shouted at Clayton as her heart broke for the boy she'd once loved as a brother. He and Bard were only yards away from them. The two stallions were facing each other—both covered with white foam and breathing hard.

Instead of answering, Clayton dug his heels into Bard and shouted, "Go! Go! Go!"

The big black stallion sprinted ahead.

Ghost pranced in place, aching to chase them, but River held him still as she yanked open a saddlebag and pulled out the neatly rolled up blanket. She flipped it open, quickly and carefully wrapping it around the razor-tipped goathead noose, and shoved it back in the bag—and as she did so Hobbs and Red thundered past them just a few yards to their right.

"Got it! Now let's win this race!"

Ghost squealed a challenge as he flew forward, tearing the earth as he pounded after the three stallions, weaving through the trees with such speed that River could only duck her head against low-hanging branches and hold on.

The cross timber line gave way to the mouth of the wide, lush Foal Valley bordering the Rock Mountains. As they entered the valley River could see, far in the distance, the colorful crowd that waited at the finish with purple flags streaming in a line clearly marking the end.

Bard was at least seven lengths ahead, with Hobbs and Red running together three or four lengths behind and gaining on him.

Ghost attacked the ground, stretching his stride to a seemingly impossible length. The wind whipped past River's face, causing tears to cascade from her eyes, but she leaned low, calling encouragement to the stallion.

Hobbs pulled away from Red and caught Bard first. There was a pause, and then Hobbs passed the laboring black stallion. River saw Clayton startle—he sat straight up, causing Bard's stride to falter. Then Clayton reached up under his tunic, pulling a thick length of stick from his waistbelt, which he raised and began cruelly striking Bard across the rump.

River didn't need to be bonded with Ghost to understand his reaction. The magnificent stallion bellowed with rage and he miraculously increased his speed, easily passing Red.

Then they were gaining on Bard. Clayton was still whipping the stallion, and the brave black was trying valiantly to increase his speed, but River could see that he was at the point of exhaustion, and as they drew alongside Bard, River kneed Ghost closer to Clayton.

Clayton looked at her then. His face was red with anger; his teeth were bared in a feral grimace.

For just an instant River met his gaze. Then, *"Go, Ghost! Go!"* she shouted, and the mighty stallion somehow found a reserve of strength and blazed ahead of Bard—and as he did River spat back at Clayton, hitting him in his scarlet face.

Then she turned her back on Clayton—and closed her mind to him forever as well.

She could hear the shouts of the watching crowd as she leaned low against Ghost's neck, grasping his silver mane in both hands, urging him forward with faith and love and joy.

They caught Hobbs so quickly that she only had a moment to see Regis's startled expression as Ghost blew past him—and then there was nothing before them except wide, flat valley and the cheers of their Herd.

Ghost didn't slow. He found more strength—more speed—as if the cheers of *his* Herd had restored his exhausted body, and by the time he and River thundered across the finish line his lead had grown to thirty-one lengths.

River sat up, lifting her arms in victory while the Herd cheered. She cued Ghost to slow gently, guiding him into a wide circle that looped them past the entrance to the main Rock Mountain passage.

She didn't notice the strangers at first; she was too busy stroking Ghost's neck and telling the stallion how completely magnificent he was. River didn't even understand something was wrong when Ghost staggered to a stop and lifted his head, blowing hard and scenting the air.

She felt his entire body tense just before he trumpeted a call that was filled with joy—complete joy.

River laughed and leaned forward to hug his sweat-drenched neck.

"That's right! You won! You are Lead Stallion!"

But instead of turning to trot back to the celebrating Herd, Ghost leaped forward into a gallop, shocking River so completely that she had to scramble not to slide off his back.

"Hey, you're done. Everything's fine," she tried to soothe the stallion, cuing him with her heels to stop.

He completely ignored her.

Strangers!

Anjo's voice was inside her head and had River looking behind her for her mare, who was racing for her, with April clinging to her back. Her sister was shouting and pointing at the mountains.

At first River didn't understand. She peered at the mountains, which Ghost was galloping toward, squinting against the sun that was just setting behind them, and then her eyes caught movement and she saw that a group of several people, perhaps thirty or forty, were pouring from the pass—and Ghost was heading directly for them.

🐎🐎🐎

Mari was filled with equal measures of joy and exhaustion as the Pack staggered down the last steps of the Rock Mountain pass. The steep path opened to greet a valley, green as their forest they'd left so, so far behind. Just the sight of the flat, verdant land gave the Pack the injection of energy they needed, and they gathered around Antreas excitedly.

"Is this really it? Really the Plains of the Wind Riders?" Danita asked.

Antreas slid his arm around her. "It really is."

"Oh, Dove, I wish you could see it," Lily gushed. She and Dove were at the front of the Pack, because since Dash had Chosen her, Lily had taken to walking beside Sora and Mari; she liked to talk puppy with Sora and healing with Mari. Currently, Dove and Lily were standing next to Mari. She had just rechecked the splint on Dash's leg, declaring to Lily's delight that he would probably only need to wear it for two more weeks.

"I'm sure it is quite lovely." The irritated tone of Dove's answer caught Mari by surprise. Over the course of their long journey Dove had proven herself to be extremely kind. Mari had never heard her speak to Lily in anger, but when Mari studied the blind girl's face she saw that it was un-usually pale. She looked obviously tense—upset even.

"Bloody beetle balls, are those Wind Riders?" O'Bryan pointed toward one end of the valley.

"Yes! Those are definitely horses!" Antreas said.

A cheer lifted from the valley, drawing Mari's gaze to their right. "Do you know what they're doing?" she asked Antreas. "There's a whole group of people over there."

"It looks like some kind of race. Well, I guess we won't have time to prepare to meet the Wind Riders after all," he said.

"We've had plenty of time," Danita said. "For months we've been—"

"I have to get down there," Dove interrupted. "Now. Lily, guide me. Quickly—quickly!"

Lily stared at her friend in confusion. "But, why do you—"

Instead of arguing with her, Dove reached out, searching with her hand, calling, "Mari! Moon Woman! I need you."

"I'm here, Dove." Mari took her hand.

"Help me. Please. I have to go to the valley."

"Can you tell me why?" Mari asked.

"I—I do not know. I only know I must go there. Now."

"Dove, we're all going there." Antreas spoke gently, clearly as con-cerned as Mari by Dove's sudden mood change.

"Not fast enough! It has to be now! Faster than the Pack will travel. Please, Moon Woman—I beseech you!"

Mari looked at Sora, and the other Moon Woman shrugged.

"Okay, Dove. I'll take you. Here, hold on to my arm. The path is still steep in some places—and there are roots you can trip over."

"I have my stick. Do not think you need to slow because of me."

"All right. Let's go then."

"I'm coming with you," Nik said. "And so are Rigel and Laru."

"Sounds good to me," Mari said.

"Most Wind Riders have never seen a canine, but they know of them. I don't like it that you're rushing down there with them," said Antreas.

"So, I'm coming with you." He looked over his shoulder at the rest of the Pack.

"We can make it down there just fine," Sora assured him. "Go with them!"

Mari could feel the tension that gripped Dove's slight body as she pulled the Moon Woman forward with her, forcing her to half slide, half jog down the widening path.

They'd reached the floor of the valley when one of the horses—the golden one Mari had watched race ahead of the other three—stopped, faced the mountains, and trumpeted a cry that seemed to fill the air around them.

Dove's body jerked at the sound, and her grip tightened on Mari's arm so desperately that they would leave fingerprint bruises the next day.

"Take me to him!" Dove cried.

"But, he's a horse. And there's someone on him," Mari said—utterly confused.

"Doesn't look like that matters. He's heading our way," Nik said.

"Nik, Mari, be sure you keep Rigel and Laru close," Antreas warned.

Mari had just projected a picture to both Shepherds of them remaining close by when the creature stormed up to them, followed by a white horse with dusky mane and tail being ridden by a dark-skinned girl who didn't look any older than Dove. They were coming fast, trying to catch the golden horse—and behind them, farther back, came a whole group of horses, all carrying riders.

Then another girl, perhaps slightly older than the one on the white horse, who also had dark, beautiful skin and a mane of black curls dressed with the same purple ribbons so many of the horses wore, dropped from the golden horse's back.

This close, Mari could see that the golden horse was covered in sweat. His sides were heaving and he was breathing hard. The girl had her hand on his shoulder, and was speaking earnestly to him, but the massive creature paid no attention to her. Instead he sprinted forward—directly at Mari and Dove.

"Don't move!" Antreas said.

"Ghost!" the girl cried, running after him, but as the white horse caught up with her the girl suddenly stopped—her eyes widening in a look of compete shock.

To Mari, time seemed to move very slowly. She was able to see the younger girl slide off the white horse's back, and the horse immediately drop to her knees so that the older girl could mount her. And then she watched as they chased after the golden horse—who was staggering to a halt right in front of Dove.

No one moved. No one spoke. The only sounds were the golden horse's labored breathing and the approaching hooves of the white horse.

She reached them quickly. Mari had managed to tear her gaze from the golden horse, and she was looking at the girl as she and her mount joined the frozen group.

The girl dismounted before her white horse had come to a stop. She hurried to the golden horse's head.

It was then that she saw Dove—really *saw* Dove—and Mari watched a myriad of emotions cross the girl's expressive face: shock, disbelief . . . and then, quickly, both were overshadowed by joy—pure joy.

"I am River," she said, speaking directly to Dove. "May I ask your name?"

Dove dropped Mari's arm and turned her face toward River's voice. "I am Dove."

River staggered then—as if Dove had punched her—but when she looked up her smile was beatific.

"Where is he? Where is my Tulpar?" Dove asked, stretching out her hands blindly before her.

The huge golden horse made a noise then, low in his great chest—and Mari didn't need to understand horses to recognize the love that resonated in that sound.

"I can hear you! I can hear you!" Dove said, searching with her hands.

"Here. He's right here." River stepped forward, gently guiding Dove's hands to the horse's head.

At her first touch, Dove's hands shook—but as soon as she spoke Mari realized she wasn't shaking from fear, but from excitement.

"You're wet! And hot! And you're breathing so hard," Dove murmured to the horse.

"Use your hands to find his nostrils." River spoke in a calm, steady voice, though Mari could see that tears were cascading down her cheeks. "When you reach a nostril, blow in it and he will be yours forever."

Dove didn't hesitate. She moved closer to the horse, following her hands, until she pressed her lips to the horse's muzzle and blew into his nostril.

The massive animal sighed then, with a great, wavelike sound, as if he was releasing a lifetime of loneliness.

"Never! You will never be alone again!" Dove said as she rushed forward, throwing her arms around the trembling horse. "It's okay! It's okay," she soothed as the horse bent his head and nuzzled her, nickering softly over and over. Dove ran her hands up his neck, and then laughed with glee. "Oh! You're so big!"

"He's a stallion. Actually, he just won a race that makes him the most important stallion of our Herd," said River as she wiped the tears from her eyes.

"Of course he is," Dove said. "He's too magnificent to be anything but a leader." She smiled radiantly, speaking to the stallion again. "No, my Tulpar, I am not afraid of you. How could I be?" Dove turned her head then, searching, as she said, "He wants me to ride him. River, would you help me?"

"Yes. Yes, I will."

River moved to the side of the stallion as he dropped to his knees, and then she helped Dove swing one leg over his wide back as she fitted herself into the wet blanket strapped to him.

"Yes, I am ready!" Dove said. Gently, slowly, the stallion stood.

Then Dove's smile shifted—changed—to an expression of pure shock.

"I—I can see! I see! Through my magnificent Tulpar's eyes, I can see!"

Mari staggered in shock against Nik, whose arm went around her. Behind them she heard Antreas gasp as well.

"Mari! Look at you!" Dove's eyeless face was pointed straight at Mari—but it was Tulpar's eye the Moon Woman smiled through her tears into.

"Rigel! And Laru! Oh, look how beautiful you are! Nik! Antreas! You are all so beautiful!"

"I don't understand what's happening, but it is beyond wonderful," Mari said.

"Yes, it absolutely is," said River, smiling up at Dove. "River!" Dove said as Tulpar's gaze shifted. "Thank you! Thank you! Tulpar was so, so lonely. You helped him—you loved him—while he was waiting for me. I owe you a debt I can *never* repay."

River's honest face flushed. "You owe no debt at all. Ghost—I'm sorry—I mean *Tulpar* is family."

"I hope that means I am now family, too. And that's Anjo! Tulpar, she is spectacular!"

Anjo nickered softly.

There was a sound from the mountain pass behind them as the Pack poured out onto the valley. Tulpar's head turned in their direction.

"Oh, Tulpar! That is my Pack—those are my people. They will be your people, too! We just traveled so far. Over water and finally through those mountains and—"

The change came over Dove the moment Tulpar's gaze lifted from the Pack to the mountains. The joy slid from her face like tallow from a candle and was replaced by a look of absolute terror. Tears cascaded down her suddenly pale cheeks, and when she spoke her voice had taken on a familiar singsong tone that had Mari's blood turning cold with fear.

> "I see it now—they who follow
>> Blue like a wave—dark as the grave
> We must fight Him—we must fight Him—with our last breath
>> He brings destruction and blight
>>> He is Death!"

THE END . . . for now.